Music in My Heart

My Journey with Melody

by Erin Falligant
with Denise Lewis Patrick

★ AmericanGirl®

Published by American Girl Publishing

16 17 18 19 20 21 LEO 10 9 8 7 6 5 4 3 2 1

All American Girl marks, BeForever™, Melody™,
and Melody Ellison™ are trademarks of American Girl.

This book is a work of fiction. Any similarity to real persons, living or dead,
is coincidental and not intended by American Girl. References to real events,
people, or places are used fictitiously. Other names, characters, places, and
incidents are the products of imagination.

Grateful acknowledgment is made to the Rosa and Raymond Parks Institute
for Self Development for permission to reference Mrs. Parks.

Cover image by Michael Dwornik and Juliana Kolesova
Erin Falligant photo by Reverie Photography
Denise Lewis Patrick photo by Fran Baltzer Photo

Cataloging-in-Publication Data available from the Library of Congress
© 2016 American Girl. All rights reserved. Todos los derechos reservados. Tous droits réservés. All American Girl marks are trademarks of American Girl. Marcas registradas utilizadas bajo licencia. American Girl ainsi que les marques et designs y afférents appartiennent à American Girl. **MADE IN CHINA. HECHO EN CHINA. FABRIQUÉ EN CHINE.** Retain this address for future reference: American Girl, 8400 Fairway Place, Middleton, WI 53562, U.S.A. **Importado y distribuido por** A.G. México Retail, S. de R.L. de C.V., Miguel de Cervantes Saavedra No. 193 Pisos 10 y 11, Col. Granada, Delegación Miguel Hidalgo, C.P. 11520 México, D.F. Conserver ces informations pour s'y référer en cas de besoin. American Girl Canada, 8400 Fairway Place, Middleton, WI 53562, U.S.A. **Manufactured for and imported into the EU by:** Mattel Europa B.V., Gondel 1, 1186 MJ Amstelveen, Nederland.

*For Mark, who understands
the power of music*

Beforever™

The adventurous characters you'll meet in
the BeForever books will spark your curiosity
about the past, inspire you to find your voice
in the present, and excite you about your future.
You'll make friends with these girls as you share
their fun and their challenges. Like you, they are
bright and brave, imaginative and energetic,
creative and kind. Just as you are, they are
discovering what really matters: Helping others.
Being a true friend. Protecting the earth.
Standing up for what's right. Read their stories,
explore their worlds, join their adventures.
Your friendship with them will BeForever.

A Journey Begins

This book is about Melody, but it's also about a girl like you who travels back in time to Melody's world of 1964. You, the reader, get to decide what happens in the story. The choices you make will lead to different journeys and new discoveries.

When you reach a page in this book that asks you to make a decision, choose carefully. The decisions you make will lead to different endings. (Hint: Use a pencil to check off your choices. That way, you'll never read the same story twice.)

Want to try another ending? Go back to a choice point and find out what happens when you make different choices.

Before your journey ends, take a peek into the past, on page 166, to discover more about Melody's time.

When Melody's story takes place, the terms "Negro," "colored," and "black" were all used to describe Americans of African descent. You'll see all of those words used in this book.

Today, "Negro" and "colored" can be offensive because they are associated with racial inequality. "African American" is a more contemporary term, but it wasn't commonly used until the late 1980s.

1

It's funny how one song can change *everything*.

I'm sitting at the piano on Saturday afternoon, playing my recital piece again. The *tick, tick, tick* of the metronome keeps my fingers moving, but my mind wanders. *One more piano recital*, I remind myself. *Then on to guitar!* Our fifth-grade class will learn guitar at school this fall. I can picture it now . . . my best friend, Anika, and me jamming together. Bye-bye, classical music. Hello, pop!

The metronome grows louder. Then I realize that the sound is actually my piano teacher, clapping her hands to get my attention. "Stop, stop, stop . . ." Ms. Stricker scolds. She's frowning. Anika and I don't call her "Ms. Strict" for nothing!

My hands drop to my lap. "Did I make a mistake?"

"No," she says. "You're playing the notes perfectly. But there's no *passion* in the piece—your heart's not in it."

She sounds like my dad, who is always telling me to "find my passion." He's a politician, so he's really passionate about helping people and making a difference in our community. *But what's my passion?* I wonder. I'm not so sure it's piano. Sometimes when

2

I read music, it flows straight from my eyes to my fingertips. It must skip my brain, because I can think about something else while I'm playing. *Maybe it skips my heart, too*, I think sadly.

"Sorry," I say to Ms. Stricker, trying not to stare at the mole above her left eyebrow. If I blur my eyes, it looks like a quarter note without the stem.

Ms. Stricker sighs. She checks the clock on top of the piano. "I think," she says, "it's time for a different song."

A different song? The recital is only two weeks away! As Ms. Stricker rummages around in her cabinet, I hum the melody of my new favorite song, "Lemonade Days." I can't hit the high notes like Zoey Gatz does in her music video, but Anika can. I wish Ms. Stricker would let me play *that* song!

Instead, she hands me an old, stained piece of music with dog-eared corners. The title is "Lift Every Voice and Sing." "Try this one," she says.

As my fingers find the notes, the music takes shape. It sounds like the gospel songs my grandma and I used to sing at her church. As I play the slow, soulful song, I feel a pang of sadness. Grammy died a

3

few months ago. I can almost hear her singing the first line: *"Lift every voice and sing, till earth and heaven ring."*

When I reach the second verse, something happens. That single voice in my head swells, joined by other voices. I glance up from the keys, expecting to see a room full of people. There's no one there.

I can't hear the metronome anymore. I don't hear the phone ring either. When Ms. Stricker says she'll be right back—that she has to take a call—I keep playing. It's as if I can't stop.

"Let us march on till victory is won," the imaginary choir sings. And my fingers march on, too, across the keys. My heart speeds up, urging me toward the end of the song.

As I play the final note, I feel a breeze. The sheet music flutters, and the room darkens, as if someone pulled a curtain. I see nothing except the blue numbers on the digital clock, blinking 1:26, 1:26, 1:26. Then it all fades away.

Turn to page 4.

4

I rub my eyes. The sheet music is still in front of me, but everything else has changed. There's a clock on the piano, but it's round and squat, with two bells on top. And this isn't Ms. Stricker's piano at all! Hers is made of shiny mahogany, almost red. This piano is lighter and covered with a fine layer of dust.

There's a bulletin board hanging above the piano. My eyes are drawn to a familiar face—a black man—staring out from a poster. "Walk to Freedom with Dr. Martin Luther King Jr.," the poster reads. I squint to read the print at the bottom: "Detroit, Michigan. Sunday, June 23, 1963."

"Wow!" says a girl's voice from behind me.

I whirl around. She's standing in the doorway: a girl about my age wearing a sleeveless green-and-blue-checked dress that pops against her golden brown skin. The dress is short and flares out at the hem. It reminds me of the dress my grandma is wearing in a photo of her as a teenager.

"That was *amazing*," the girl says.

What is she talking about? I wonder, turning back to the poster. "The, um, Walk to Freedom, you mean?" I stammer.

5

She laughs. "No, silly—your piano playing!" she says. "But the Walk to Freedom here in Detroit last summer was pretty amazing, too. My family and I marched in it."

Last summer? The poster says that the Walk to Freedom happened in June of 1963. I do the math. That was more than fifty years ago.

Then I notice the room around me. It's filled with fold-up tables and chairs, like a meeting hall. On the table closest to me, I see an old typewriter. My mom has one in her office, but just for decoration. It's too hard to press down on those raised keys. There's a black telephone on the table, too, with a long, twisted cord. My grandma had one like that in her apartment.

Everything in this room seems old-fashioned, like a scene from a black-and-white movie. A question swirls through my mind. *Is this my craziest daydream ever, or did I just play my way back in time?*

Turn to page 6.

6

"I'm Melody," says the girl in the doorway, "and I *love* the song you just played. So does my grandma. She's here at church, upstairs. If I go get her, will you play it again?"

Her brown eyes smile at me from beneath her turquoise headband. She's real. This can't be a daydream!

"Please?" she asks.

When I nod, the girl spins on her heel. I hear her footsteps clattering up a set of stairs.

I try to remember the last time anyone seemed so happy to hear me play piano. Definitely not Ms. Strict at lessons this afternoon! But there *is* something special about the song I just finished. My fingers stroke the keys again, softly at first. But after the first verse, I barely need to read the music. I sail through it, hearing the voices rise up around me.

> *Sing a song full of the faith*
>   *that the dark past has taught us,*
> *Sing a song full of the hope*
>   *that the present has brought us.*

I close my eyes and let the music fill me up. As the

7

last notes fade away, I hear a *tick, tick, tick*. I open my eyes and see the silver bar of Ms. Stricker's metronome. It swings from side to side, as if gesturing toward the clock on the piano—the clock with blue numbers that still read 1:26.

When Ms. Stricker steps into the room, I jump. Then I see the expression on her face. She's actually smiling.

"That was beautiful," she says—for the first time ever. I've heard her say "perfect," but never "beautiful."

Pride swells in my chest, followed by excitement. I did it again! I played this magical song and somehow traveled through time. Then I think of Melody, that mysterious girl I left behind. My fingers itch to play the song again and get back to her in that basement room.

"Your mom will be here in a couple of minutes," Ms. Stricker says. "Take the music home with you, my dear. Polish it up and make it yours."

I place the music carefully in my book bag. This song already feels like mine, more than anything else I've ever played. *Wait for me, Melody,* I think, trying to send a message across time. *I'll be back soon!*

Turn to page 8.

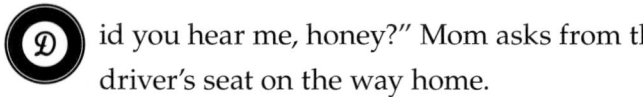

"**D**id you hear me, honey?" Mom asks from the driver's seat on the way home.

"Huh?"

"Wow, you're really in la-la land," she says, patting my knee.

More like Melody land, I want to say.

"I said I have some bad news," Mom says, growing serious. "Budgets are tight this year, and that's going to mean changes at school this fall."

Mom is the principal of my school, which has its pluses and minuses. Some kids think I get special treatment. But mostly, I just get to hear news about the school before other kids do.

"The music program may have to scale back," Mom says slowly.

That gets my attention. "What do you mean?" I ask, sitting up. My seat belt squeezes against my chest.

Mom sighs. "There aren't enough instruments for all the students, and there's no money to buy more. So there may not be any guitars this year, sweetie."

She might as well have socked me in the stomach. I can't breathe.

"I'm still working on it," she says, "but . . ."

9

"But it's already August!" I blurt. "School starts in less than a month!"

"I know, honey," says Mom. "It doesn't look good."

We drive on in silence, and then she says, "Dad is campaigning this afternoon, so it's just you and me."

Again? I think. Dad has been working hard to get reelected to Congress. He stays up late writing speeches, and he's gone a lot at night and on the weekends. *Dad has plenty of passion for his job,* I think. *Ms. Strict would approve.*

"Want to join me in my office for a while?" Mom asks as we turn into our driveway.

She has a special corner in her home office with a purple beanbag chair and fuzzy blanket. I curl up there sometimes and read while Mom is working. But today, I want to go straight to my room. I'm bummed about the guitars, but I know what will make me feel better: I have to find my way back to Melody. Will she still be there?

"I . . . um . . . want to practice more," I say, holding up my folder with piano music inside.

"Really?" says Mom, raising her eyebrows.

I can't blame her. I'm usually not much for

10

practicing. "I have a new song," I quickly explain. "For the recital in two weeks."

I burst through the front door ahead of Mom and try my hardest not to run across the living room. If I race to practice the piano, Mom will *really* know something's up! Instead, I walk slowly down the hall, running my fingertips along the spines of the books on the shelves.

My family must own every book ever printed, and we all love to read. My mom reminds me of how lucky we are. She says lots of kids don't have books of their own—even the ones they need to do their schoolwork.

I would grab a book right now, but there's something else I need to do. I close my bedroom door behind me and hurry to the keyboard beneath my window. Anika's photo, in a heart-shaped frame on the window ledge, catches my eye. Her knowing eyes bore into me from beneath her black bangs, as if to say, "I know you have a new secret. Tell me. Please!"

I tell Anika *everything,* even the stuff that's kind of impossible to believe, like meeting Melody. I fish my phone out of my pocket and send her a quick text: *You won't believe what happened today.*

11

Then I lean toward the window, straining to see if Anika's mom is working in the flower beds two houses down. Anika's yard is empty, but the new girl is playing in the yard next door. She's throwing a Frisbee to her little brother, calling something to him in Spanish.

When she glances my way, I duck, almost hitting my chin on my keyboard. Did she see me? I don't want her to think I'm spying on her.

I settle back in front of my keyboard and turn it on. Do I need to play a piano to get back to Melody or will this work? I start to pull the sheet music out of my bag, but I stop mid-reach. I don't need the music anymore— I know I don't. I feel as if I've been playing this song my whole life.

I take a deep breath, close my eyes, and begin again.

♪ Turn to page 12.

12

"We're back!"

Melody's voice sends a joyful tingle down my spine. I'm at the piano in the church basement again. *It worked!* I think. *As long as I play "Lift Every Voice and Sing," I can get to Melody and back home again.*

When I turn to smile at Melody, I see an older woman standing in the doorway with her. She's not much taller than Melody, and she's flicking a paper fan in front of her face.

"This is Big Momma—oops, I mean Mrs. Porter," Melody says. "She's my grandma."

"Mmm, mmm," Mrs. Porter says, shaking her head. "I don't know what's warming me up more—this August heat, or that glorious song you just played, child."

She liked my playing! Her smile warms me up, too, from the inside out. "Thank you, ma'am . . . um, Mrs. Porter."

"Where'd you learn to play like that?" Melody asks, skipping over to the piano bench. She smells like fresh air and flowers.

"Piano lessons," I admit. "Lots of lessons." *Too many*, I used to think. But right now, I'm proud of what I've

learned to do. My cheeks are burning.

"You're really good," says Melody. "Are you part of the traveling youth choir that's visiting our church?"

"Mercy me," says Mrs. Porter, overhearing. "I think that choir bus is leaving soon. Did you get lost in the music, baby? We'd better get you upstairs." She waves me toward the door.

Melody sees me hesitate. She tilts her head and asks, "Or are you here for the Student Walk to Freedom Club? My big sister, Yvonne, is leading that. We drove her here. She'll be down any minute."

> ♪ *To follow Mrs. Porter upstairs,*
> *turn to page 17.*

> ♪ *To wait here and meet Melody's sister,*
> *turn to page 14.*

14

I don't want Mrs. Porter to put me on a bus. I just got here! And if Melody's sister Yvonne is anything like Melody, I want to meet her.

Clearing my throat, I say, "I'm not with the choir. I'd, um, like to stay for the meeting."

"The Student Walk to Freedom Club?" Melody repeats. "Good. Maybe I can stay, too." She looks at her grandma with pleading eyes.

"That's all right by me," says Mrs. Porter. "But you girls will have to walk home after."

Melody nods. "Thanks, Big Momma."

After she leaves, teenagers begin to file into the room. Melody keeps her eye on the door. Finally, she points. "There's Yvonne!" A pretty young woman rushes in wearing an orange blouse and a patterned scarf over her head. There's a cast on her left wrist.

"Hey, Dee-Dee," she says to Melody. "I didn't expect you here." Then she gets pulled away by another young woman who is gesturing toward the clock.

Yvonne steps to the front of the room. "Thank you for joining us this week," she says. "Thank you for coming from other churches and towns to help the Student Walk to Freedom Club. Some of us are just

15

back from the Mississippi Summer Project, and we've got a lot to tell you. Together, we're making a *difference* for black people all over the country!"

As people whistle and cheer, I scoot closer to Melody. "What's the Mississippi Summer Project?" I whisper.

She leans over and says, "A bunch of college students—black and white—went to Mississippi. They helped black people register to vote, and they set up Freedom Schools for black kids. Yvonne says voting is really important."

I nod. "My dad says that, too," I whisper. "He's a politician, and he's always saying how important it is to get out and vote."

"Wow," says Melody. "Your dad is a politician?"

The way she looks at me makes me feel proud. I hope she doesn't ask what my dad does, though, because I'm not exactly sure. He's gone a lot. He travels to Washington, D.C., but I don't really know what he does there. I don't ever ask him, because politics seems like grown-up stuff.

I have trouble paying attention to Yvonne's speech, because I'm busy looking around the room. It's full

16

of young people. Most of them are older than me and Melody, but they're still younger than the people who show up for my dad's speeches.

All of a sudden Yvonne looks right at me and Melody and says, "There's plenty we can do to help black people right here in Detroit. And that's where *you* come in."

Me? I think, slinking down in my seat. *What can girls like Melody and me do?*

I glance at Melody. She's leaning forward, like she's ready to get started *now*.

Turn to page 20.

17

"m, I did get a little lost in the music," I admit, because it's true.

Mrs. Porter clucks her tongue, but her eyes are smiling. "Well then, girls," she says. "Follow me."

As we cross the room, Melody sings softly. *"Lift every voice and sing, till earth and heaven ring."* Her voice is pure and sweet, like Anika's.

"You're a really good singer!" I say.

Melody flashes a smile. "Thanks. We sang that song for Youth Day last fall." She lowers her voice shyly and adds, "I had a solo."

I'm not surprised to hear that. If I had a voice like Melody's, I'd be brave enough to sing all by myself. But I could never sing alone in front of a crowd.

Mrs. Porter waves us along. When she puts her hand on my shoulder, I smell flowers again. Big Momma smells like roses.

When we reach the bend in the stairs, we run into a woman wearing a tidy suit and high heels. "Miss Dorothy!" says Melody. "This is our choir director," she explains to me.

"Just the woman we're looking for," Mrs. Porter says. "Is the youth choir getting ready to leave?

We found one of its members playing her sweet heart out downstairs."

Miss Dorothy stares at me through little round glasses. "Oh, dear," she says. "That bus left fifteen minutes ago."

Melody sucks in her breath.

"The choir is heading north for a few shows before coming back for their Tuesday night performance," Miss Dorothy says. "I wonder if someone can drive her to catch the bus . . ." She checks her watch.

"It's all right," I say quickly. "I can get myself back home." I don't want to catch that bus, not knowing where it's going. And besides, why would I want to leave Melody and Mrs. Porter right now, when I'm just getting to know them?

Melody's eyes sparkle like fireworks. "If the traveling choir is coming back Tuesday," she says thoughtfully, "maybe someone from the congregation could let her stay with them till then. Maybe *you* could take her in, Big Momma. Couldn't you?"

Mrs. Porter hesitates, and then her face eases into a smile. "Don't fret, Melody," she says. "We wouldn't turn this little chick away now, would we?"

19

I smile right back—I can't help it. There's something so comforting about Melody's grandma. When Melody wraps her arms around her, I want to hug her, too.

Melody grabs my hand. "Oh, we're gonna have so much fun!"

I can already feel it—that tingle running from my fingertips to my toes, telling me that I'm about to set off on an amazing adventure.

"Now, I suspect your suitcase is riding on that bus you missed," says Mrs. Porter.

Suitcase? I didn't think about that. I glance down at what I'm wearing. This is all I have with me!

"That's okay," says Melody brightly. "You can borrow some clothes from me. We're about the same size." She seems pretty happy that I'm staying, and I am, too.

As I follow her out of the church and into the sunshine, I remind myself that I can go home anytime I want. I just have to play that song and I'll be back in my bedroom—as if no time has passed at all.

I smile, skipping down the steps after Melody.

Turn to page 22.

20

Yvonne tells us exactly what we can do to help: stuff envelopes, make posters, and help cook food for volunteers. Those all sound like things I can do—except for maybe the cooking part.

Then Yvonne picks up a clipboard. "Let's talk about where you'll be staying this week," she says. "Those of you from out of town have been paired up with host families from our church." She taps the clipboard. "Has anyone not met their family yet?"

Uh-oh. I'm not on that list! Where will I stay?

Melody is way ahead of me. "You can stay with me," she says. "Or . . . do you have another place?"

I shake my head. "I didn't plan on staying. I just wanted to hear what the meeting was all about, but . . . I'd like to stay—at least for a couple of days."

Melody smiles, her eyes bright. "I'll call Mommy," she says. She uses the black telephone on the card table, lifting the phone to her ear and using her finger to spin a round wheel on the base of the phone.

When she hangs up, I can tell by the grin on her face that her mom said yes. "Do you have to call home, too?" she asks.

I hesitate. Back home, Mom is still working in her

21

office. She isn't missing me. And even if she were, I can't call her from an old phone in 1964. Mom wasn't even born back then!

Turn to page 25.

22

"Have you been to Detroit before?" Mrs. Porter asks. She's looking at me in her rearview mirror as we drive away from the church.

"What? No, never, ma'am," I say. I'm only half listening, because I just realized there are no seat belts in the back of the car! Melody isn't even searching for one. So I settle back in my seat, too, and try not to worry.

Luckily, Mrs. Porter is a careful driver. As she pulls up to a stoplight, the nose of her car stretches out long in front of us. *All* of the cars around us are long, low, and narrow. I'm used to being up higher when I ride in my mom's SUV.

"You'll be seeing all kinds of new places with the traveling choir, won't you?" Mrs. Porter continues. "You know, it seems like a hundred years ago now, but I was once in a traveling singing group, too."

"With Miss Dorothy," Melody pipes up. "They had their own gospel group."

Mrs. Porter winks at me in the mirror. "In fact," she says, "Miss Dorothy and I are going to go hear some gospel music downtown after dinner. It's a special show—the owners of the performance hall are friends of mine from way, way back."

"Do you mean Auntie Josephine and Uncle Al?" asks Melody. "Oh, I wish we could go, too."

Mrs. Porter has a twinkle in her eye when she says, "Well, maybe you can—if your momma says it's all right." When the light in front of us turns green, she eases the car forward.

"You'll love the performance hall," Melody says to me in a breathy voice. "There's a big stage and a piano. They have lots of parties there, and recitals. My youth choir was even onstage once! And they have concerts with *amazing* gospel music. I'm not sure what's more fun—singing there or listening to someone else perform."

"It sounds awesome," I say. I've only heard gospel music at church, and on my grandma's old records. I'm excited to go to a concert with Melody, but somehow, sadness creeps into my chest again as I think about Grammy.

As soon as we reach Mrs. Porter's, though, I feel better. The first thing I see in her living room is an old upright piano. It's taller than Ms. Stricker's, and there are flowers carved into the music stand. It's beautiful! My fingers itch to play. Would Mrs. Porter mind?

She's already nudging me with her hand. "Go on," she says with a chuckle. "Play me something pretty while I work in the kitchen."

Turn to page 27.

"t's okay," I tell Melody. "My parents want me to get involved in things like this."

It's true. My dad would be excited to know that I'm learning about helping people vote. And Mom is all about kids getting a good education. Maybe I can ask her if she knows about the Mississippi Summer Project when I get home.

After the meeting, Melody and I walk to her house. It's a sticky August afternoon, but the walk gives us time to talk.

As we pass a pretty park, Melody pauses by the fence. "My friends and I just fixed this up," she says. "We started a Junior Block Club this spring, and we painted those benches and planted all these flowers. We're even growing vegetables."

"Really?" I say. "You and your friends did all that by yourselves?" Anika and I tried to build a tree house in our neighborhood once, but we gave up after half a day. It seemed like too much work for kids.

"Well, we had help from Miss Esther, who lives across the street," she says, nodding toward a yellow house. "And my grandpa helped us plant that vegetable garden."

A garden, too? Wow. Maybe that's why Melody didn't seem scared listening to Yvonne talk about how we could make a difference. Melody's already doing it!

Melody pushes open the gate, and I follow on her heels. We both hop on one foot down the hopscotch board painted on the sidewalk. And soon we're hanging upside down on the jungle gym.

As Melody sits up, she asks, "What grade are you going into this year?"

"Fifth," I say, feeling a bit dizzy as I sit up, too.

"I knew it!" she says. "So am I." She flashes me a smile.

And I already know something else, I think with a grin. *We're going to be great friends.*

When Melody leaps off the jungle gym and lands in the soft dirt below, I follow her, shrieking with laughter.

Turn to page 30.

While Melody settles onto the sofa, I play a few scales. The piano keys are more yellow than white, but the sound is pure and rich—more *real* than the "tinny" sound of my electric keyboard.

"Play a song," says Melody.

My mind goes blank. I can't play "Lift Every Voice and Sing." That'll take me home! I start to play my recital piece, but Ms. Stricker was right—it sounds flat. So I play the song in the open music book in front of me: "We Shall Not Be Moved."

Mrs. Porter pops her head through the swinging door. "You know that one, too, baby?" she asks, wiping her hands on her apron.

"No," I admit. "This is my first time playing it."

Melody scoots to the edge of the couch. "You've *never* played it before?" she asks, sounding surprised. "You're really good at reading music."

Mrs. Porter shakes her head. "Have mercy," she says. "Go on and sing with her, Melody. The two of you have more talent between you than most congregations put together."

As I start to play again, Melody's voice blends with the rich notes of the piano.

28

We shall not,
We shall not be moved.
We shall not,
We shall not be moved.
Just like a tree that's standing by the water,
We shall not be—

Just then, the front door opens, and a tall teenager bursts into the room.

"Aha!" he says. "I thought I heard the voice of my favorite sister, the extraordinary Melody Ellison."

She laughs and runs to hug him. "What're you doing here, Dwayne?"

"And did you forget how to knock?" scolds Mrs. Porter.

"Big Momma, I knocked," says Dwayne. "You just didn't hear me over the choir." He winks at Melody and then notices me. "Don't stop playing on my account," he says. "I'll join you."

As he sits down beside me on the bench, I suddenly feel shy. I have to wipe my sweaty palms on my pants. When Melody stands beside me, though, I feel better—especially when she starts to sing.

Then Dwayne taps out the rhythm with his hand on the side of the piano. And Mrs. Porter begins clapping her hands on the offbeat. Pretty soon, I hear her deep voice layered beneath Melody's sweet, high voice.

Dwayne sings softly, too. *"We're fighting for our freedom, we shall not be moved,"* he croons.

The music fills me up and spills over, like a wave of happiness. *Is this what Ms. Stricker meant by playing with passion?* I wonder. I don't want the song to ever end.

Then, as I play the last few notes, something happens: Melody keeps singing. Is there another verse?

I turn the page, but that's it—it's the end of the song. What should I do? I don't want to mess up!

Turn to page 31.

When we get to Melody's house, no one's home—except for her dog, Bo. I scratch the black-and-white terrier behind the ears, and he wags his tail.

"C'mon," says Melody, racing toward the stairs with the dog at her heels. "I'll show you my bedroom."

Her room is small, but it holds three beds. "I share this with my sister Lila," says Melody. "Vonnie moved across the hall to Dwayne's old room, so you can sleep in her old bed."

"You have another sister?" I ask, trying to imagine three girls fitting in here with all their stuff.

"Yeah," says Melody. She sits down on a bed with a bright orange bedspread. "Lila's fourteen and she'll be starting at a private school this fall. She and my mom are out buying her textbooks right now. My brother, Dwayne, calls Lila 'Miss Bookworm' because she's *always* reading."

Melody has a brother, too? She's got such a big family! I can't wait to meet them all. Then I notice a stack of books by her bed. There's one by Langston Hughes and a worn copy of *The Secret Garden*.

Turn to page 34.

elody keeps singing, even though I've stopped playing. Her grandmother and brother do, too.

"Just like a tree . . ." Mrs. Porter sings, swaying her shoulders as she claps.

"Ooh, ooh, ooh," adds Dwayne.

So I put my hands on the keys and repeat the last few bars of the song. I don't know what else to do! It seems to work, the notes and the voices around me blending into one.

Then somehow, magically, we all stop at the exact same moment. The hairs stand up on my arms. For a few seconds, there's pure silence.

"Whoo!" says Dwayne. "That was some jam."

I laugh with relief. "I thought I was going to mess up," I admit.

"Really?" says Melody. "You were so good!"

"And remember," says Mrs. Porter. "There's no messing up with improvisation."

"That's right. Lots of Motown artists improvise," Dwayne adds. "They make up their own words or melodies while they play."

"Motown?" I ask, wanting to understand.

Dwayne's jaw drops open. "Girl, have you been

32

living under a rock?" he asks. "Motown is Mr. Berry Gordy's record label here in Detroit. He puts out music by The Temptations, The Supremes, Little Stevie Wonder . . ."

I recognize that last name, sort of. I nod with relief.

"It's not just musicians who improvise," Mrs. Porter says. "Preachers do, too. Our own Dr. Martin Luther King didn't just read the words of his 'I Have a Dream' speech. Every time he gave the speech he changed it a little bit, depending on the event and the audience. He let his heart find the words as he spoke."

Mrs. Porter talks about Martin Luther King as if she knows him. Then I remember that Melody and her family heard him speak at the Detroit Walk to Freedom last summer. I get chills, imagining what that must have been like.

"You know," says Melody, "my brother's a Motown star, too. His group, The Three Ravens, just recorded a song!"

"Really?" I say. Suddenly, I can't look at Dwayne. He's a real star—like Zoey Gatz.

"But that's not the whole story, Dee-Dee," he says. "Are you gonna tell your friend that you're officially

a recording artist now, too?"

A slow smile spreads across Melody's face, and I can tell she's excited. "I recorded with Dwayne at the studio," she says. "Just singing backup, though."

My jaw drops. I can't believe I just jammed with not one Motown star, but two!

Turn to page 37.

read that," I say, pointing toward *The Secret Garden*.

Melody follows my gaze. "It's one of my all-time favorite books," she says. "I *love* gardens. My grandpa says I got my green thumb from him. Poppa grew up on a farm in Alabama. We actually took a trip to see it last month."

"Was it fun?" I ask, sitting down on the bed. I used to love taking trips with my grammy.

Melody nods. "So much happened! We stayed with my mom's Aunt Beck, and we got to see lots of cousins on the Fourth of July. We talked about how great it is that President Johnson signed the Civil Rights Act. Now it's the law that black people have to be treated equally. My mom says it's what we've been protesting and marching for all this time." A shadow passes over her face as she adds, "But not everyone is happy about the new law. Some scary things happened, too."

"Like what?" I ask, scooting closer.

Melody pulls her knees to her chest. "Everyone was talking about the three civil rights workers who disappeared in June." She shivers. "They were part of the Mississippi Summer Project, like Yvonne, trying

to help black people register to vote. But white people complained and the police arrested them. They just vanished, and they're still missing." Melody's lip trembles. "While we were still in Alabama, we found out . . ." Melody takes a shaky breath. "We found out Yvonne was arrested, too."

I suck in my breath. "She went to *jail*?"

Melody nods. "That's how she broke her wrist. She tripped while the police were arresting her. Mommy and Poppa had to go get her out of jail the next day."

I don't even know what to say. Melody must have been afraid that her sister would disappear, too. I can't understand why anyone would try to keep black people from having equal rights.

I want to tell Melody that things are better now—in my time—but a memory tickles the back of my mind. My family had gone out to eat with Mr. Chapman, Dad's campaign manager, who is black. When Mr. Chapman stepped outside, a white man handed him his car keys.

I tell Melody that story.

"Why'd he do that—with the keys?" she asks.

"Because he thought Mr. Chapman was a *valet*,

someone who parks cars for customers eating at the restaurant. He thought that because Mr. Chapman was black, he must be working there, not out to dinner. Dad says things like that still happen a lot."

Melody shakes her head. "It's not fair," she says. "It's discrimination to treat someone differently just because of the color of their skin."

Bo whines from his spot on the rug, as if agreeing with her.

Then Melody hops up and says, "That's why Yvonne says we gotta *do* something. We have to make it better, even here in Detroit."

I smile. I like that Melody wants to help other people—that she's not afraid to try, even though she's young like me. And that makes me want to make things better, too.

Turn to page 39.

"Speaking of Motown, I've gotta run," says Dwayne, standing up and stretching his long legs. "We have a rehearsal at the studio tonight, and I've gotta take care of some things before then."

As he kisses Mrs. Porter's cheek, I try to think of something to say. Should I get his autograph? My mouth goes dry.

Before I can say anything, Dwayne is on his way out the door. But all of a sudden, he stops and turns around. "Hey, Dee-Dee, do you and your friend want to hang out at the studio tonight and watch the rehearsal?"

Yes! I think.

"Yes!" says Melody. "Wait, no—we're going to listen to gospel music with Big Momma tonight."

Melody looks just as torn about that as I feel. Going to the studio would be so cool! But we already told Mrs. Porter we'd go to the performance hall with her, and that'll be fun, too.

Mrs. Porter says, "Don't you chicks fret. You go on down to the studio if that's what you want to do." Her warm smile says she means it, but somehow, that doesn't make our decision any easier.

Melody looks at me with a question in her eyes: *What do we do?*

> *To go hear gospel music with Mrs. Porter, turn to page 43.*

> *To visit Dwayne at the studio, turn to page 46.*

I get to see Yvonne again at dinner that night, along with Melody's sister Lila and their parents.

Melody's parents are kind of like mine. Her mom is a teacher, like Mom used to be before she became a principal. And Melody's dad, who works at a car factory, is gone a lot, just like mine.

But everything else about Melody's big family is way different. When she and her sisters start talking, the whole room fills with their voices and laughter. It's never *this* noisy at my house!

After dinner, I'm watching Lila braid Melody's hair in their bedroom. Yvonne, with a towel wrapped around her wet head, is curled up on the bed giving instructions.

Music pipes out of the radio on the headboard—"Motown music," Melody calls it. Her foot taps along to the beat.

"Melody, sit still!" Yvonne says, laughing. "You're making it hard for Lila."

"She sure is," says Lila, pushing her glasses up on her nose. "I'm getting better at it, though."

"You're still not quite as good as Yvonne is," says

Melody. "When is that wrist gonna heal again?"

Yvonne sighs. "Not soon enough."

I'm dying to ask her about her broken wrist—about how it happened and what it was like to be arrested. But that wouldn't be polite. Instead, I ask, "Does it hurt much?"

Yvonne shakes her head. "Not too much. And when it does? I just remind myself how it happened, and that makes me mad enough to forget the pain." She smiles, but I know she's being serious.

"You're so brave, Vonnie," says Melody. "I wish I were as brave as you."

Yvonne reaches out to grab her sister's toes. "You are, Dee-Dee. And anyway, I wish I were as good a *singer* as you."

Melody laughs and yanks her foot away.

"Sit still, Dee-Dee!" says Lila with an exasperated sigh. Then, after a moment of silence, she asks, "So don't either of you wish you were as *smart* as me?"

That cracks me up. Melody laughs, too, which Lila doesn't seem to appreciate. "You're smart all right, Lila," she says, patting her sister's arm. "Big Momma says we've all got our own lights to shine."

At that, Melody catches Yvonne's eye. And then the sisters erupt into song. *"This little light of mine,"* sings Melody. *"I'm gonna let it shine."*

Hey, I know this song!

Yvonne sings into a hairbrush, as if it were a microphone. *"This little light of mine, I'm gonna let it shine."*

Lila finally gives up and lets go of Melody's hair. *"This little light of mine, I'm gonna let it shine,"* she adds in her high soprano voice.

And even I jump in for the last line: *"Let it shine, let it shine, let it shine."*

"Let's do it in rounds!" says Melody, standing up. When Bo jumps up on her legs, she takes his front paws and dances with him around the room.

"This little light of mine," she sings. And Bo adds two barks, right on beat.

We sing, laugh, and bark our way through a whole round, until someone raps loudly on the door. "What on earth is going on in here?" Melody's mom asks, poking her head into the room.

"Sorry, Mommy," says Melody, laughing. "Just doing our sister-thing." She looks at me. "That's what Dwayne calls it, anyway."

This sister-thing is so fun! I wish these girls were my sisters, too. Maybe I'm even a little like them. I like to read books, like Lila. I love music, like Melody. And I hope someday I'll be just as brave as Yvonne.

Later, I'm lying in Yvonne's old bed in Melody and Lila's room. I feel a pang of homesickness, like I always do at sleepovers. But then I hear Melody's daddy snoring down the hall. And is that Yvonne talking on the phone downstairs? I strain my ears. Then Bo starts scratching at his collar at the foot of Melody's bed: *jingle, jingle, jingle.*

The sounds blend together like music. *It was music that brought me here to meet Melody,* I remember. So it's no wonder that her house is so full of joyful sound.

This little light of mine, I hum, remembering the sister-thing. And then I'm not homesick anymore.

Turn to page 45.

43

"I think we should go listen to gospel music," I say. Maybe it's because Mrs. Porter reminds me of my grandma. There's no one I'd rather spend the evening with than my grandma—not even Zoey Gatz. I miss Grammy so much!

Melody nods. "Me, too," she says. "Sorry, Dwayne."

"Some other time," he says with an easy grin. Then he ducks out the door and is gone.

"Good, that's settled," Mrs. Porter says, her cheeks dimpling. "Now why don't you two come and have a snack while I make supper."

"Okay," says Melody, racing toward the kitchen. "C'mon!"

As we push through the swinging door, I glance around the tidy kitchen. The first thing I notice is the refrigerator. It's white and rounded, with one door instead of two. Doesn't it have a freezer?

As Mrs. Porter opens the door to get a pitcher of lemonade, I see the freezer—it has its own inside door. She opens it, slides out an ice cube tray, and pops a couple of cubes into each glass on the counter.

"Thank you, Mrs. Porter," I say as she places a glass in front of me.

44

She touches my cheek with the back of her hand and says, "Go ahead and call me 'Big Momma,' baby.
"It's okay."

My heart melts like an ice cube on a hot August day. I want to hug her and never let go.

Turn to page 49.

Sunday morning, I go to church with Melody's family. Mrs. Porter pats the bench, inviting me to slide in next to her. As we sing the first hymn, I remember the song that brought me here: "Lift Every Voice and Sing." Will I still be able to play the music when it's time to go home? My fingers begin to tap out the notes on my lap. *Yes*, I think, smiling. *How could I ever forget?*

After the service, Melody and I go down to the community room for another Student Walk to Freedom Club meeting. It's time to choose a project. "Some of us will stay here and make signs," Yvonne says. "We're picketing the Windwood grocery store this week because they won't hire black people."

A low murmur ripples through the room.

"If enough people show up, Windwood *has* to listen," Yvonne continues. "So we'll need plenty of signs for picketing."

"Making signs could be kind of fun," Melody says.

It *does* sound fun. But then Yvonne reminds us there's another choice.

Turn to page 51.

46

my legs want to follow Dwayne right out that door. I can still feel the tingle from that jam session, and I want to know more about this Motown music.

Mrs. Porter puts her hand on her hip. "I know that look," she says, smiling. "That's a girl who's feeling like a trip to Motown."

I grin, relieved that she's not upset.

"Okay, then," says Melody. "We're coming with you, Dwayne." She seems happy about the decision, too.

"All right," says Dwayne. "Your chariot will be back to pick you up after dinner." He gives an exaggerated bow and then trots down the steps toward his car, a long brown sedan with more than a few dents and scratches on it.

The car starts up with a choke and a cough. "Some chariot!" says Melody. "Dwayne's new car is a little scary. But you're going to *love* the studio." Then she checks the clock and says, "Oh, my TV show's on!" She races across the living room.

The television is big and brown, with buttons running down one side of the screen like a microwave. It has two long metal rods coming out of the top, like the

antennae on my dad's old radio.

Melody turns a knob on the front of the TV. At first, there's nothing to see. It takes a while for the picture to appear on the screen, and when it does, it's in black and white. Melody turns another knob and flips past a few channels before she stops. "Here it is," she says, plopping down on the floor and patting the rug. "Sit by me."

A man is playing the piano and singing. The show is kind of spotty and hard to see, as if I were watching it through a snowstorm. But the music sounds really good.

The show reminds me of the ones I watch at home, where singers and musicians compete to be the next big star. Anika and I watch them and dream of the day when we'll both make it big. *She has a better chance than I do,* I think, wishing I had Anika's voice.

As three glamorous black women file onstage, Melody sits up. "The Supremes!" she says. "Oh, I hope they play my song. Please, please, please." She clasps her hands as if she's begging for a treat.

One of the women stands in front of the other two and starts to sing.

As the other women join in, Melody squeals and jumps to her feet. "Yes!" she says. "I love this song. Don't you?"

The song sounds familiar, but I don't know what it is. Melody sure does. She sings with her hand by her chin, as if she were holding a microphone. "C'mon, sing with me," she says, waving me to my feet.

"But I don't know the words," I say, panicking.

"That's okay," Melody says. "Just *ooh* and dance." She points to the TV. Two of the singers are swaying from side to side as they sing. Then they circle their arms overhead.

Even if I just *ooh*, I don't want Melody to hear my voice. What if she thinks it's terrible?

Turn to page 52.

The sun hangs low in the sky as we step into Big Momma's backyard after dinner.

"Taste this," says Melody's grandpa, whom she calls "Poppa." He plucks a cherry tomato off the vine for me.

I'm so full from Big Momma's chicken dinner that I can barely eat another bite. When the tomato bursts in my mouth, though, its juice tastes so sweet! "Yum," I say, forgetting not to talk with my mouth full.

"You should taste the ones Melody grows at her house," says Poppa, stroking his silver beard. "She's got dirt under her fingernails, just like I do."

I glance at Melody's fingernails, but they're clean.

She laughs. "He just means I love to garden," she says. "Poppa owns a flower shop, and he helped me and my Junior Block Club plant flowers and a vegetable garden at a park in our neighborhood. It's been a lot of work, but it sure looks great."

"I'd like to see it," I say. I can tell that gardening is one of Melody's "passions," as my dad would say. And I wonder again, *What's mine?*

As Melody bites down on a tomato, juice squirts out. "Oops!" She clamps a hand over her mouth.

"You girls better not mess up your clothes out

there," calls Big Momma from the back door. "Miss Dorothy will be here any minute to pick us up."

Melody and I smother giggles as she wipes the juice off her chin. Then we hear the doorbell ring.

"She's here," says Melody, running up the steps.

"No good-bye hug, Little One?" calls Poppa in his booming voice.

Melody stops mid-step and turns around. "Oh, sorry, Poppa," she says, racing back and wrapping her arms around his middle. "I wish you were coming with us."

"Oh, I'm much too tired," he says. "I'll just sing to myself out here in the garden." He winks at me as I wave good-bye.

Turn to page 54.

51

"We also need volunteers to stuff envelopes," Yvonne says. "We'll join some other youth groups at a meeting hall downtown. We want to get the word out to vote for Conyers."

Conyers? I don't know who that is. But I've stuffed plenty of envelopes for my dad's campaign. It's easy, and it would leave Melody and me time to talk. *But so would making posters,* I remind myself.

"Either one sounds like fun," Melody says. "You choose."

> *To make posters,
> turn to page 66.*

> *To stuff envelopes,
> turn to page 56.*

52

Oooh quietly and sway along to the music.

Luckily, the TV is loud. And Melody's beautiful voice drowns mine out. Suddenly, she darts toward the dining room. When she comes back, she's holding two bananas from the fruit bowl—one like a microphone in her hand, and another one for me.

Every time I sing into that banana, it cracks me up. By the time the song ends, we're both out of breath and laughing.

"That was really fun," Melody says. "I love The Supremes. Did you know that Dwayne actually *knows* Diana Ross, the lead singer?"

"No way!" I say. I've heard that name before, which means Diana Ross must be a big star. She does seem really elegant and has an amazing voice.

"Well," says Melody, "they're not like best friends or anything. But we saw Miss Ross at Hudson's department store in February, and she waved at Dwayne!"

"Gosh," I say, "I've imagined meeting Zoey Gatz lots of times. But I don't think it'll ever happen."

"Zoey Gatz?" asks Melody, her forehead creasing.

Oops! Of course Melody doesn't know Zoey Gatz. But if she lived in my time, she would. Zoey is *always*

on the cover of magazines. "She's . . . pretty new," I say. "My mom doesn't think she's all that great, but I like her."

"Why doesn't your mom like her?" asks Melody, cocking her head.

"She's kind of rude to reporters," I say. "She sometimes gets into trouble. Mom says she 'makes bad choices.'" I do my best impersonation of Mom when I say those words.

As Melody laughs, I wonder, *Will Zoey Gatz be famous for a long time, just like Diana Ross?* I'm not so sure.

When Mrs. Porter pushes through the kitchen door carrying a stack of plates, she says, "Speaking of choices, are you girls going to eat those bananas, or just sing the life out of 'em?"

I whirl around to face Melody. *Did Mrs. Porter see us dancing and singing like that? How embarrassing!*

Melody and I start laughing again. Then she shrugs and delivers our bananas back to the fruit bowl.

Turn to page 59.

54

Miss Dorothy's car doesn't have seat belts either.
I try not to think about that as we cruise down 12th Street toward the performance hall.

"There's Poppa's flower shop," Melody says, pointing. The words "Frank's Flowers" stand out against the darkened windows of the shop.

A few minutes later, we slow down in front of an old brick building. The hall doesn't look fancy from the outside, but as soon as we step inside, I feel a shiver of excitement. The walls of the entryway are lined with photographs of performers, and some of them look really glamorous and professional. Other photos show groups of kids onstage.

"Are you in one of these pictures?" I ask Melody, remembering that her choir sang here once.

"Maybe!" she says, her eyes scanning the wall. But as musicians begin tuning their instruments from the stage at the back of the room, Miss Dorothy and Big Momma wave us on to find a seat.

When we're about halfway down the row of chairs, a woman calls out, "Dorothy! Geneva!" The woman steps off the stage and hurries over. She's tall and slender, with black hair piled high atop her head. "I'm so

glad you're here," she says, wrapping them in a hug.

"Ah, Josephine," says Miss Dorothy. "It's been too long."

Then Josephine smiles warmly at Melody and me. "I'm so glad you brought a friend," she says to Melody.

"Me, too," Melody says, squeezing my hand before introducing me to Josephine.

"Where's that husband of yours?" Big Momma asks Josephine.

"He's around here somewhere," says Josephine. "And he's *thrilled* that you could make it tonight." She gestures toward the stage. "Come with me. We have front-row seats for you."

I follow Melody. The stage is so close! If I reached out my hand, I could almost touch it. There's a saxophone player warming up onstage, plus a guitar player, a drummer, and a man seated at a huge piano.

By the time the lights dim even more, the tables around us have filled with people. Big Momma raises a finger to her lips. The show's about to start!

Turn to page 62.

56

Yvonne drives Melody and me to a meeting hall downtown. When we get there, I'm surprised by how many volunteers—young and old—are already in the room. Signs on the walls read "Elect John Conyers Jr. for Congress."

"Congress? My dad was elected to Congress!" I say under my breath.

But Melody hears me. "That's really cool!" she says. "What does your dad do?"

Oh, man, I think, because I don't really know what to say. I mumble something about him trying to create more jobs and "make sure people get paid enough."

Melody nods. "That's important," she says. "If people don't earn enough money, they have to work twice as hard—double shifts sometimes. Daddy has to work those at the auto factory, so he's gone a lot."

Her words linger in my head as we take seats at a long table. I never thought about it that way—that what my dad does matters for families like Melody's.

We tag-team to stuff the envelopes. I fold the flyers, and Melody slides them into envelopes. The work is kind of boring, until Yvonne whispers, "Don't look now. You'll never believe who's here!"

"Ouch!" Yvonne's announcement surprises me right into a paper cut. As I suck my finger, I do exactly what Yvonne told me not to do. I turn around and look. There's an older woman with glasses sitting nearby, a polka-dot umbrella hanging from the back of her chair.

"It's Mrs. Rosa Parks," Yvonne whispers.

Rosa Parks! Anika wrote a report about her for history class last year. Rosa Parks is the black woman who refused to give up her seat on a bus to a white person. Anika said people call her "the mother of the civil rights movement."

"Is she really stuffing envelopes, just like us?" asks Melody.

"Sure she is," says Yvonne. "She lives here in Detroit now. Did you think she was still sitting on a bus somewhere? She's out here all the time, working with young people and for politicians, getting things done behind the scenes."

I can't believe Rosa Parks is here. Our work just got a whole lot more interesting—and feels more important, too.

"Should we talk to her?" asks Melody after a few minutes of watching.

Should we? I wonder. The thought of talking to Rosa Parks makes my heart race. But I wait too long to decide. Suddenly, Mrs. Parks pushes away from the table and stands up. Is she leaving?

Sure enough, Mrs. Parks says a few good-byes and heads for the door.

As soon as she's gone, Melody slumps down in her chair. "I can't believe we didn't say a single word to her," she says.

"I know, but what would we have said? My tongue would have been tied in knots," I admit.

Melody sighs. "Mine, too."

That's when I see the umbrella still hanging from Mrs. Parks's chair. "Melody, look," I say, pointing.

"Her umbrella!" she says. "Should we go after her?"

"Go after who?" asks Yvonne, sliding into the empty seat next to me.

> *To run after Mrs. Parks,
> turn to page 65.*

> *To tell Yvonne about the umbrella,
> turn to page 61.*

After dinner, we hear Dwayne's car chug to a stop out front. Before he can even ring the doorbell, Melody and I are halfway out the door.

As we slide into the backseat, Melody says, "I wonder if we'll see anybody famous at the studio. Maybe The Temptations . . ." she says, her eyes hopeful.

"Or The Supremes?" I add, happy that I finally know some of the Motown stars.

"Or The Three Ravens?" asks Dwayne, winking at us in his rearview mirror.

Melody giggles. At first, I don't get the joke. Then I remember that Dwayne's band is called The Three Ravens.

When the car backfires, Melody says, "What I *really* wonder is whether we're even going to make it to the studio in this car. Are we leaving a trail of smoke?" As she turns to look out the back window, Melody catches my eye and grins.

Dwayne chuckles. "She's old, all right," he says. "But as soon as my album starts selling, I'll buy something newer. Maybe a Ford Mustang like those rich producers down at the studio drive."

"Ooh," says Melody. "A Mustang!" She must know

her cars, because her eyes light up.

"That's right," says Dwayne, puffing out his chest proudly. Then the car backfires again, and he smacks the steering wheel and sinks back down in his seat, laughing with us.

Turn to page 68.

melody isn't exactly leaping out of her chair to get the umbrella, and I hang back, too. What would we say to Rosa Parks even if we caught up with her? Instead, we tell Yvonne about the umbrella.

"Ah," she says. "I'll make sure it finds its way back to her."

But as Melody and I go back to stuffing envelopes, I keep thinking: *Did we just miss out on something big?* Our work isn't nearly as exciting anymore. So when Yvonne tells us it's time to do something else, we're ready.

"You two can help me with voter registration," she says as we get into the car. "We'll go door to door, making sure people know how to sign up to vote."

Door to door? Like we're selling cookies or magazines? I was never very good at that.

"Like you did in Mississippi?" Melody asks. She looks nervous. Is she afraid we'll get arrested the way Yvonne did? My stomach lurches at the thought.

Turn to page 71.

62

Four women come out onto the stage. As one of them steps to the microphone, silence falls over the audience. Then the piano player begins.

"Why should I feel discouraged?" the woman sings in a deep, soulful voice. *"No, no, no . . ."* She shakes her finger at us. *"Why should the shadows come?"*

A couple of people in the audience start to clap. Melody and I turn to face each other. We know the song, too! My grandma taught it to me. My fingers tap out the notes on my lap as the refrain begins.

> *I sing because I'm happy,*
> *I sing because I'm free,*
> *For His eye is on the sparrow,*
> *And I know He watches me.*

The other women onstage are singing now, too, standing behind the lead singer.

> *Watches over me,*
> *I'm so glad that He,*
> *Watches over me,*
> *I'm so glad that He . . .*

All around the room, the crowd sways in time to the music, like one great congregation. When we first got here, I was afraid that listening to this kind of music without Grammy would make me feel sad. But it actually makes me feel like she's right here beside me.

When the song ends, Big Momma and Miss Dorothy stand up and applaud, so Melody and I jump up, too. I lean close to Melody. "That was beautiful," I whisper. She smiles at me and claps louder.

The lead singer laughs and bows her head, sweat glistening on her forehead. Then she nods to the guitar player, and they begin again.

Every song is just as incredible as the last. I don't know them all, but I sure want to. After about five or six songs, a man steps onstage, and the crowd cheers. Is he another musician?

"There's Al," whispers Miss Dorothy, nudging Big Momma.

Al must be Josephine's husband, the owner of the performance hall. He raises his hands to quiet the crowd. "Thank you for coming out for this very special performance," he says in a deep, friendly voice.

He clears his throat and then continues. "As most

of you know, this will be our last performance here. On Monday, the city will start turning this old building into your newest paved parking lot."

What? Melody whirls around to face me.

Turn to page 76.

"We'll be right back!" I say, jumping up. I grab the umbrella, and Melody races after me out the front door.

At the base of the steps, we look both ways. The sidewalk is empty. "She's gone," I say, my stomach sinking. Then I see her—about to turn the corner. "This way!" I cry.

We sprint down the sidewalk. But as we get closer to Mrs. Parks, I wonder again: *What will we say to her? How do you talk to your hero?*

At the sound of our footsteps, Mrs. Parks turns around. "Oh, my umbrella! Thank you, girls. You're so kind."

She's not much taller than we are, but I feel like I'm looking up to her. The sun over her shoulders is blinding.

Say something! says the voice in my head. My palms are sweating, but my mouth is bone dry.

Turn to page 74.

melody and I decide to stay at the church and make posters. We sit at a card table, stenciling big letters onto poster board.

"How's this?" asks Melody, holding up her sign. It reads "DOWN WITH DISCRIMINATION."

"That's really good!" I say, noticing how evenly spaced her letters are. "Have you done this before?"

Melody reaches for a pot of paint. "I made signs for the Walk to Freedom last year," she says. "And I made signs when we picketed at Fieldston's Clothing Store this year. The people who work there weren't very nice to black people." Her face hardens. "The manager accused my brother and me of shoplifting and told us to leave."

For a moment, I'm speechless. "They kicked you out?" I finally say. "That's so unfair. Did the picketing do any good?"

Melody nods and begins to paint in the letters on her poster. "It took a while. We started in February. We handed out leaflets explaining how Fieldston's treated black customers. People stopped shopping there, and Fieldston's lost money." Melody smiles. "The store's manager has finally agreed to change things."

"Wow," I say, amazed. "So picketing the store made things better?"

"It didn't happen right away," says Melody, "but what we did made things better." Then she looks at my poster board and says, "Your sign is really good, too."

I stenciled "JUSTICE NOW" on my sign, because I saw another girl do that. My letters aren't as perfect as Melody's, but after I fill them in with paint, they look a lot nicer.

Then Melody and I add our own touches to the signs. She adds arrows pointing downward to go with the slogan "DOWN WITH DISCRIMINATION." I underline the "NOW!" on my sign with a rainbow of stripes.

We make more signs, too. By the time we're done, my hands are smudged with paint.

"Nice work, you two," says Yvonne. "Now can I ask a favor? I've got to get these signs to a friend's shop a few blocks away. Can you help me carry them?"

Melody and I agree to help. That's before we find out how heavy the signs are—and how *hot* it is outside. We can hardly wait to get to the shop!

Turn to page 79.

I expected the record studio to be in a big office building. Instead, the Motown studio looks like a small house with two front doors and a big picture window between them. A sign over the window reads "Hitsville U.S.A." Excitement ripples through my body. *Will we hear some hits tonight?* I wonder.

As Melody and I follow Dwayne through one of the doors, a teenage guy greets us. "Well, well," he says, "if it isn't Miss Melody Ellison herself. Long time no see, lil sis."

Melody grins. "Hey, Artie," she says. "Artie's one of The Three Ravens," she tells me. "And Phil is the other one."

I meet Phil, too, after Artie leads us through a maze of rooms and hallways into the rehearsal room. I'm surprised to see a drummer and a piano player warming up beside Phil. "Wait, I thought there were only three Ravens," I whisper to Melody.

"Those two musicians are part of Motown's house band, the Funk Brothers," she explains. "They play during recordings and rehearsals. They're really good—those guys can play *anything*."

I watch the man at the piano. He does seem super

talented. I try to imagine recording a song with the musicians here at Hitsville. My stomach flip-flops at the thought, knowing that the recorded song would be heard by millions of people . . .

Dwayne snaps his fingers, breaking my daydream. "Okay, let's do it," he says to his bandmates. "Show's in three days."

The Three Ravens line up in a row. As the drummer finds a beat, Dwayne steps forward and begins to croon in his high voice. Behind him, Artie and Phil dance, moving like mirror images of each other.

"Give it a chance, girl," sings Dwayne. *"Just one chance."*

Artie and Phil each lift their pointer fingers like the number one. Then they spin in a circle and sing, *"Just one . . . just one . . ."*

Melody sings and sways along from her chair beside me. I'm not the only one who notices, because after The Three Ravens finish, Artie says, "I think we could use a couple more backup singers." He strokes his chin.

"That's right," says Dwayne, catching on. "The Temptations usually have five singers. How come we

only have three? What do you say, Melody?"

She's instantly up and standing beside Artie and Phil, but my bottom is glued to the chair. As they all stare at me, my face starts to burn.

"C'mon," says Melody. "It'll be fun. It's your chance to sing at an actual recording studio!"

Dwayne starts singing to me, *"Give it a chance, girl. Just one chance."*

My cheek twitches, and I smile nervously. It would be pretty cool, but I'm not a very good singer.

Then Artie, Phil, and Melody add, *"Just one."*

I laugh, but my stomach is still flip-flopping like a fish. I finally stand up, mostly so that they'll all stop singing to me! *Just sing softly,* I think as I take my place in line. *Like you did at Mrs. Porter's when The Supremes were on TV.*

So I do, whispering the words. And soon I get lost in the swirl of voices around me. But as the song comes to an end, I realize what I'm actually doing. *I'm singing with Motown stars at Hitsville U.S.A.—a real recording studio!* And now I'm grinning like crazy.

Turn to page 83.

71

"I'm not sure about this voter-registration thing," Melody whispers. "I wish Yvonne had given us a choice to do something else."

Yvonne overhears from the driver's seat. She purses her lips and then says, "You mean, you didn't get to vote on something that mattered to you, Melody? How'd that feel?"

Melody hangs her head, as if she just got caught talking in class. "Not good."

"Right. So you see what I'm saying?" says Yvonne. "We have to make sure people can vote. Remember, Daddy always says that voting is like having a voice. Everyone should have a voice about things that matter to them."

"But, Yvonne," Melody says softly. "Your wrist . . ."

Understanding spreads across Yvonne's face. "Oh, I see," she says. "Are you girls scared?"

Melody nods. "Why aren't you?" she asks.

Yvonne straightens up in her seat. "Because when I was sitting in that jail, I told myself that I wasn't going to let fear hold me back. I don't want you to either, Dee-Dee. No matter where we are, we can't let fear keep us from doing what's right. Do you understand?"

Melody nods and sits a little taller.

Through the window beside her, I see a tall concrete wall built along the road. It seems to stretch on for miles. "What's that?" I ask Yvonne.

She glances out the window. "That was built by developers who wanted to keep white neighborhoods separate from black neighborhoods. It's six feet high and about a foot thick."

"They built an actual *wall*?" I say.

"A big, ugly concrete wall," Melody says. "It looks like it's crumbling in parts, though."

Yvonne shakes her head. "It's still much too strong. There are still lines drawn between white neighborhoods and black neighborhoods, even if there aren't actual walls built between all of them."

"Like my cousin Val's neighborhood," Melody tells me. "It's mostly white, and it was hard for her family to buy their house. Some of the neighbors didn't want them there. But they finally found someone to sell to them."

Yvonne glances in the rearview mirror. "Did you help Val plant flowers at her new place yet, Dee-Dee?"

"Yes!" she says. Then she turns to me. "You should

see them. Wait, maybe you can. Maybe Mommy will let us go to Val's tomorrow."

"That sounds fun," I say. And we could use some fun right now, after hearing about how badly Melody's cousin and other black families are being treated.

Turn to page 86.

efore I lose my nerve, I say, "Mrs. Parks, you're my role model."

She smiles warmly. "Thank you. I hope you have *many* role models, as I do," she says. "Even people who are much younger than I am. You know, I'm learning all the time from the young people in my neighborhood block club."

"I started a block club, too!" Melody says excitedly. "Well, a Junior Block Club. We fixed up a playground and planted a vegetable garden. I really like to garden."

"Is that right?" says Mrs. Parks. "Starting a block club is a lot like gardening: planting a seed and watching it grow. My brother is a gardener, too, and I enjoy helping him harvest and can those fresh vegetables."

Beside me, Melody is about bursting with pride now.

"Thank you for this," says Mrs. Parks again, raising her umbrella. "Not that I'll be needing it on what turned into such a beautiful day." Before she walks away, she says, "You're never too young to be a role model—remember that, girls. Anyone can be a leader. We're all leaders of *something*. Start leading, and others will follow." Then she turns the corner . . . and is gone.

We're all leaders of something. Mrs. Parks's words bounce around in my head as Melody and I walk back to the meeting hall.

"You should be proud," I say to Melody. "You're already a leader, with your Junior Block Club and your gardening." But then I think, *What am I a leader of? Can I be a role model, too?*

🎵 **Turn to page 81.**

13 ig Momma and Miss Dorothy don't seem surprised by Al's news—they must have known already.

"It's part of Detroit's 'urban renewal' project," Big Momma explains while the band takes a break. "Sometimes when the city's leaders decide to build new freeways or parking lots, they tear down the old businesses that we love. And homes, too. Al and Josephine live in the apartment upstairs," she says, pointing upward. "Urban renewal seems to hit colored folks' homes and businesses the hardest."

Melody sighs. "We talked about urban renewal at our last Junior Block Club meeting. When homes are torn down, sometimes beautiful gardens are ruined, too." She slumps in her seat.

Big Momma pats Melody's hand. "What's important to you and me isn't always what's important to others, baby," she says. "Like music. Remember what I told you about the part of Detroit called Paradise Valley? Some of the finest musicians performed there. But the city built a freeway, and they bulldozed Paradise Valley to make room for it."

Miss Dorothy shakes her head sadly. "I remember

seeing Ella Fitzgerald perform at the Forest Club. Or was it the Horseshoe Lounge? There were so many clubs, and restaurants and hotels, too—almost all owned by colored people. It was like we had our own city within a city. Oh, there was such energy there!" She shivers, as if she can still feel it.

"I saw Billie Holiday in Paradise Valley. That woman could *sing*," says Big Momma. "But after the I-75 freeway came on through, it was all gone. The businesses. The music. The magic. All of it."

A knot forms in my stomach. The last time I felt this way was when Mom said we wouldn't have guitars for music class. *Why don't people care about music?* I want to holler. *Or gardens? Or people's businesses?* I wish I could *do* something.

"Why the long faces?" asks Josephine, pulling up a chair. "Are you all worrying about Al and me? Don't you be doing that, now."

Big Momma forces a smile. "You two are going to land on your feet," she says encouragingly. "But you're losing your home, aren't you, Jo? Where will you go?"

"We're moving in with our daughter, at least for a while," says Josephine. "We'll spend some time with

our grandbabies." Then a shadow passes over her face, and she says, "You know, I think it's our old piano that Al is going to miss the most."

"Aren't you taking it with you?" I ask shyly. It's hard to imagine leaving a piano behind.

"It's not worth the money to move it," Josephine explains. "Those old keys are as sticky as molasses. But it's the first time we'll be without a piano—at least until we can afford a new one." She shakes her head, as if shaking off the bad feeling. "We'll start over," she says. "We always do."

I can tell that her heart hurts. Suddenly, I wish I could talk to Dad. As a politician, he makes decisions about things that affect my hometown, and people listen to him. He'd be able to help Al and Josephine save the performance hall, wouldn't he?

Then I remind myself where I am: Detroit. 1964. *Dad isn't here,* I realize sadly. But is there something that *I* can do?

Turn to page 90.

79

s soon as we drop off the signs, Melody says, "I'm hot, Vonnie. And *really* thirsty."

Yvonne glances down the street. There's a sign for Sam's Soda Shop on the corner. "How about there?" she asks. "I'll buy you girls a soda for your help today."

Melody looks tempted but then shakes her head. "Not there," she says.

Why not? I want to ask. I can taste the ice-cold soda already.

"Mommy won't go there," Melody explains. "She was treated badly by a white waitress once."

Yvonne stops walking. "Is that so?" she says, arching an eyebrow. "Mom never mentioned that to me."

Melody's mouth clamps shut. "Well . . ." she begins, "that's probably because she knew you'd go in there and make a scene. You're not going to, are you, Vonnie?"

Yvonne stares at Melody, as if trying to figure out what to do. "Do you want a soda or not?" she finally asks. "Because if you do, Dee-Dee, we should go in. It's important to take a stand on things like this. Someone has to fight for what's right."

Then Yvonne turns to me and asks, "What do you

think? Should we try to make a difference here? Or would you rather keep walking?"

Help! I catch Melody's eye, but she looks just as unsure as I feel.

> 🎵 *To keep walking,
> turn to page 104.*

> 🎵 *To go into the shop,
> turn to page 93.*

That night, Melody and I stay up way too late talking about Rosa Parks. I can't stop thinking about what Mrs. Parks said about role models and leaders, and about how my dad's always encouraging me to get involved in the things I care about. I don't think I'll ever fall asleep, but suddenly, it's Monday morning.

"Wake up," says Melody, nudging me. "It's time to go meet the bookmobile."

"The what?" I ask, yawning.

"It's like a library on wheels," says Melody. "Lila and I just found out about it this summer. We go meet it every Monday morning." She grabs a book bag out of her closet.

After I'm dressed, we hurry downstairs, where Lila is just finishing her cereal.

"Bookmobile time?" asks Melody's mom, sipping her coffee. "Take the dog, too, please. He could use some fresh air."

When we get outside, Bo takes the lead, sniffing every bush along the sidewalk.

Lila's behind us with an open book. "Slow down, Melody," she scolds.

"Stop reading," Melody retorts. "Then you'll be able to keep up. And anyway, haven't you read that book a thousand times already?"

Lila shrugs. "Yvonne says we should read more books by black authors," she says. "And this is the only one that the bookmobile has."

I see the author's name on the cover: Langston Hughes. "Hey, I know about him," I say. "My mom gave me a book of his poems."

"I have one of his books, too," says Melody. "He signed it at Hudson's downtown."

"No way!" I would *love* to meet a real author. Then I realize what Lila said a minute ago. "Wait . . . the bookmobile has only one book by a black author?"

Lila nods, and Melody doesn't look at all surprised.

I own lots of books written by black authors—Mom even helped me write a letter to one of them once. But would Lila recognize any of those authors' names? Were their books even around in 1964?

I don't know, so I keep my mouth shut.

Turn to page 88.

The Three Ravens are halfway through their third song when a woman pokes her head into the room. "Are you ready to head across the street?" she asks.

Dwayne checks the clock and says, "Yeah, we'd better wrap it up here."

"What's across the street?" I ask Melody.

"Artist Development," she says. "It's like a school where musicians learn about everything *besides* music—like how to dress, how to dance, how to act, how to talk to reporters . . ."

"Really?" I say. "They learn all that?"

Melody nods. "Motown stars do. That's why they look so polished. Remember The Supremes on TV?"

I do. Maybe that's why Diana Ross looked so elegant and graceful. She'd taken lessons!

My mind flashes to a poster of Zoey Gatz on my bedroom wall. She's sticking out her tongue, which I always thought was kind of funny. But she sure doesn't look very "polished."

A few minutes later, Melody and I are watching a man with a gray beard teach The Three Ravens *choreography*, a fancy word for "dancing." Artie and Phil

are practicing their footwork, crossing one foot over the other and spinning in a low circle. When Artie wobbles, I expect him to laugh at himself. But he doesn't. He's working really hard.

I turn to say so to Melody, but she's gone. She's standing in the doorway, watching something across the hall. When I join her, I can see into the other room, too. A woman with a friendly face is coaching a teenage girl on how to walk gracefully.

"Do you know that girl?" I ask, wondering if she's famous.

"Not yet," says Melody. "But maybe we will *someday.*"

I try to memorize the girl's face. When I get home, I'll look up Motown stars online. Will I find her there?

"Stand taller," the woman says. "Show that you respect yourself. Then other people will respect you, too."

"Wow," I whisper. "That's what my grammy used to say."

Just then, Dwayne steps into the hall and says, "I've got to run an errand for one of the producers. Wanna join me? We'll be cruisin' in a brand-new Mustang."

He holds up a set of shiny keys.

Melody's eyes light up. "I've never ridden in a Mustang before," she says. Then she glances back at the girl taking lessons on how to be a superstar. "But we're having fun here, too."

She turns to me. "What should we do?"

> 🎵 *To stay at the studio,
> turn to page 101.*

> 🎵 *To go with Dwayne,
> turn to page 95.*

On Monday morning, as Melody's mother turns the car into Val's neighborhood, I press my face up against the window. Tall trees shade the street, and lawns stretch out long and green in front of the houses. "It looks so different from the neighborhood we visited yesterday with Yvonne," I say.

Registering voters took us through a black neighborhood where kids played outside on the steps and sidewalks. There's much more space to play here, in Val's new neighborhood, but I don't see as many kids.

"Has Val made any friends yet?" I ask, craning my neck to watch a boy coast down his driveway on a blue bike.

Melody shakes her head. "I don't think so, and she and her parents moved in a few months ago."

As we turn into Val's driveway, the front door of the house bursts open. A tall girl a little older than me hurries down the steps. "You're here!" she says, hugging Melody.

She introduces herself to me and then gestures toward the backyard. "Daddy just put up a swing set," she says. "Want to come see?"

"Go ahead, girls," says Melody's mom. "I'm going

to go inside and visit with Cousin Tish."

We follow Val along the fenceline toward the backyard. When a blonde woman with a sun hat pops up on the other side of the fence, Melody takes a quick step backward in surprise.

"Oh, hello!" she says to the woman, who is wearing gardening gloves. But the woman must not have heard her because she bends back down without saying anything.

There's a girl sitting on the porch behind the woman. She's blonde, too, with a high ponytail. I wave at the girl, but she immediately looks away.

"My mom says our neighbors aren't used to having black families on their block," Val says quietly.

Val's neighbors won't even talk to her? I wonder. *That's so wrong!*

When I glance back at the blonde girl, she's looking at me again, too. She may not be talking to us, but she sure seems curious.

Turn to page 99.

The bookmobile looks like a long white ice cream truck, with a short line of kids waiting to get in. When we reach the entrance, Melody and I stay outside with Bo while Lila steps inside.

When it's our turn to board the bookmobile, I'm amazed: I feel like I'm in a real library, standing between two shelves of books! While Melody searches one shelf, I step toward the other one.

"Can I help you find something?" asks the librarian, who is white.

I'm about to say "No, thanks." But then I decide to speak up. "Do you have any books by black authors?" I ask.

"We do have one that was just returned," she says. "Poetry by Mr. Langston Hughes. Have you heard of him?"

My hopes sink. I've heard of him, all right. But that book can't be the *only* one. "Do you have any others?" I ask.

The librarian shakes her head sadly. "Publishers don't put out enough books by Negro authors." She smiles and adds, "It does my heart good to see you asking for them, though. If enough people asked,

publishers would have to listen, wouldn't they?"

"You mean like if we all signed a petition?" I ask.

She cocks her head. "Well, yes. If I had more children like you asking for books by Negro authors, I'd start a petition myself."

When she turns away to help another kid, my mind starts racing.

Turn to page 97.

When we get back to her house, Big Momma makes a bed for me on her couch and another one on the rug for Melody. My new friend and I are having a Saturday night sleepover. But as Big Momma turns out the lights, Melody seems sad and far away.

"I wish we could help Auntie Josephine and Uncle Al save the performance hall," she whispers into the darkness. She loves music as much as I do.

I have weird dreams all night. I dream that I'm performing onstage at the hall with my brand-new guitar, and I don't feel the slightest bit nervous! But then the front door opens and cars start zooming into the room—as if a freeway were running right through it. And after the last car passes by, I glance down and realize that my guitar is gone.

When I finally open my eyes to the morning light, Melody is awake, too.

"I didn't get much sleep last night," she says, fighting a huge yawn.

"Me, neither," I confess. "I'm so worried about the performance hall."

Melody nods sadly. "I think we should talk to my sister Yvonne. She'll know what to do."

Just then, Big Momma bursts through the kitchen door with a towel draped over her shoulder. "Good morning, my chicks," she sings. "Come and have some breakfast before church."

Melody nods as another yawn sneaks up on her.

"Are you feeling okay, baby?" asks Big Momma. She leans over to put a hand against Melody's forehead.

"We just didn't sleep well," says Melody. "We were worrying about Uncle Al and Auntie Josephine."

Big Momma straightens back up. "I'm worrying about them, too. But I have an idea that might make you feel better. After church, your cousin Val and her parents are driving to Windsor for the Emancipation Celebration. How would you girls like to go, too?"

"Mancipation?" I ask.

"*E*-mancipation," Big Momma corrects me. "It means 'freedom'—of the slaves in our country and in other parts of the world. The Emancipation Celebration is a celebration of our freedom."

"It's in Canada, just across the Detroit River," says Melody. "Because that's where the Underground Railroad ended and slaves from the South found freedom, right, Big Momma?"

"That's right," says Big Momma.

"There's this giant parade," says Melody, spreading her hands. "Plus a pet show, a beauty contest, and lots of music."

"Four choirs performing, in fact," Big Momma adds.

"And don't forget the barbecued spareribs!" says Poppa, coming down the stairs.

Melody laughs. "You like barbecue as much as Daddy does—and that's a *lot*."

Poppa holds his palms up. "Guilty as charged," he booms good-naturedly.

"So is that a yes?" asks Big Momma.

Melody turns to me and says, "It'd be great if you could meet my cousin, Val." Then the spark fades from her eyes. "But if we go, we won't have time to figure out how to help Uncle Al and Auntie Josephine."

"I know," I whisper sadly.

To try to help Al and Josephine, turn to page 98.

To go to the celebration, go online to **beforever.com/endings**

I think about Dad's campaign manager, Mr. Chapman, who was mistaken for a valet just because of the color of his skin. I think of Melody and her brother, who were asked to leave Fieldston's because they were black. Then I think about how hurt Melody looked when she talked about that.

I know in my head—and heart—what to do. I take a deep breath. "I think we should go in," I say, hoping Melody isn't mad at me.

She doesn't look mad—only a little scared, maybe. But she nods and says, "I think we should, too."

Yvonne puts a hand on my shoulder. "Good for you, girls," she tells us. "That's a brave decision."

I don't feel brave, though, as I follow her into the shop. The bell above the door jingles, and my mind starts racing. *Will the waitresses be mean to us? Will they make us leave?*

Melody stands close to me just inside the door. The waitress at the cash register glances up but then quickly looks away. The letters on her name tag read "SUE."

Yvonne clears her throat, but Sue turns her back on us. Without a word, the waitress grabs a pitcher of water and starts working her way down a row of tables.

"What do we do now?" whispers Melody. "I don't think she's coming back!"

Yvonne's mouth is set in a determined line. "We wait," she says.

♪ Turn to page 108.

"It smells so *new*," I say, climbing into the back of the Mustang. Everything in the car is red, from the leather seats to the steering wheel.

"That's because it *is* new," says Melody. "A 1964 Ford Mustang! Daddy says it's the most popular car of the year. Dwayne, turn on the radio."

"You got it," he says. He starts the engine and reaches for the radio.

As soon as the music flows through the speakers, Melody recognizes the song. "The Temptations!" she says. "Turn it up louder."

Dwayne does. Then he adjusts his mirrors and rolls down his window halfway. "Pretty soon, Dee-Dee," he says as he eases away from the curb, "you're going to be hearing a lot more of me when you turn on the radio." He looks proud as a peacock sitting up there.

"I know," says Melody. "And then people will be running errands for *you*."

"They'll treat you like a king," I add. The pop stars I know are even more famous than kings and queens. The last time I saw Zoey Gatz on TV, she was walking down a royal red carpet at an awards show.

Dwayne chuckles. "Right," he says. "All except for

that 'king' part. I don't care if you're The Temptations or Smokey Robinson himself. No black musician is treated like a king on the road, especially in the South."

Melody nods solemnly. Then she tells me, "Dwayne went on tour down South, and he said the black musicians couldn't stay in the same hotels as white people. They couldn't use the front doors of clubs, either, because those were for white people. They had to go in the back."

"Really?" I say, trying to understand. Zoey Gatz is black, but I can't imagine a hotel ever turning her away.

Suddenly, a siren swells behind us, and red and blue flashing lights pour through the back window.

Turn to page 113.

After Melody chooses her books, we step back outside. The line of kids has grown now, snaking around the corner.

"Ready to go?" asks Lila.

Melody nods, but my feet are frozen to the sidewalk. Most of the kids waiting in this line are black. *Don't they want to read books by black authors?* I wonder.

"We have to do something," I say.

"What do you mean?" asks Melody, confused.

"The librarian said that more kids have to ask for books by black authors," I explain. "Then she'll start a petition to send to the publishers. We have to get kids to ask for those books." *But how?* I think about the ways my dad spreads the word when he's campaigning. He uses the Internet: making videos, posting on blogs, and e-mailing people. But I can't do any of that in Melody's time. There's no Internet. There aren't even any computers.

Suddenly, Bo barks, as if to say, "Speak!"

"That's it!" I say. I don't need the Internet. I can spread the word using my own voice.

Turn to page 103.

When Melody and I decide to stay home, Big Momma pulls us both into a hug. "It's hard to celebrate when people we care about are hurting," she says. "But going to church will help our hearts, and so will having family over for Sunday dinner. Doesn't that sound good?"

Melody nods. "Yvonne will come to dinner, too, right? I want to talk to her about the performance hall."

"Both your sisters will be coming," says Big Momma.

"Wait, *sisters*?" I say to Melody. "You have more than one?"

She nods. "There's Lila, too. She's a little older than me—well, she'd say she's a *lot* older. She's kind of a know-it-all." Melody rolls her eyes. "But that's because she reads all the time."

Big Momma clucks her tongue. "That's enough now. The Good Book says to love thy sisters—*all* of them."

Melody laughs. "The Bible doesn't say that!"

But Big Momma is already back in the kitchen, chuckling to herself.

Turn to page 105.

Val's new swing set has a couple of yellow swings and a red glider. "You two swing first," she says, climbing onto the glider. "Wait until you see how high they go!"

Melody settles into the swing next to me and starts pumping her legs. "I can see the flowers we planted from up here," she says, her feet flying high overhead.

The only thing I can see from my swing is the girl next door. When her mom gathers her gardening tools and goes inside, the girl takes a step toward the fence.

"Do you want a turn?" I call to her.

She slowly nods. Then she walks toward the gate connecting the two lawns to each other. I wonder if it's ever been used.

I drag my feet on the grass to stop the swing, and then I hop off and hand it to the girl. "Thanks," she says shyly.

Val quickly introduces herself to the girl, who says her name is Cindy. "You can come swing anytime you want," Val says, grinning.

Cindy's face lights up. "I'd like that," she says. "Mom won't let me get a swing set of my own. She'd have to tear out some of her flowers to make room!"

Melody laughs and then challenges Cindy to a who-can-swing-higher contest. So I climb on the other side of Val's glider, and pretty soon we're seesawing back and forth, too.

"Girls!" calls a woman from the back of Val's house. It must be Cousin Tish. "Do you want some lemonade and—"

She stops talking when she catches sight of Cindy on the swing. Then Cousin Tish smiles thoughtfully and adds, "Lemonade and cookies?"

"Yes, please!" shouts Val.

Before Cousin Tish can go back inside, the blonde woman comes out of the house next door. She hurries toward the fence, her mouth open as if to call Cindy back home.

Uh-oh, I think. *This means trouble . . .*

Turn to page 109.

"Can we stay?" I ask Melody. It's my first time at a Motown studio, and I'm pretty sure it will be my last.

Melody doesn't seem disappointed. She may like cars, but I think she likes music even more—like me.

Dwayne tosses the keys in the air and catches them as he strides down the long hallway toward the front door. But a moment later, he's back.

"What happened?" asks Melody.

"The producer found another errand boy so that I could hang back and look after you two," he says, his face long. I bet he was already picturing himself behind the wheel of that fancy car.

"Oh, sorry," says Melody, biting her lip.

"Don't worry about it," says Dwayne. "I wouldn't want to miss learning how to walk now, would I?" He grins, pointing at the women in the room. "Did you know that's Mr. Gordy's sister? She works for her brother, polishing up Motown stars till they shine."

"Really?" says Melody. Then she says playfully, "If you ever want to go into business with *me*, Dwayne, I'd be happy to teach you some manners."

Dwayne jokes right back. "That wouldn't be half

bad, little sis," he says. "Then I could be the boss of you—for real." His face grows serious, though, when he says, "There *is* something I could use your help with."

"What?" Melody asks, all ears.

Dwayne glances down the hall. "Later," he says. "I'll tell you later."

As he disappears into the rehearsal room, Melody says, "I wonder what *that* was all about."

I do, too. What's Dwayne's big secret?

Turn to page 120.

I step toward the first person in line, a boy about my age. "Ask the librarians if they have any books by black authors," I tell him. "If enough kids ask, they'll petition the publishers to print more. Pass it on."

The boy raises his eyebrows in surprise, but then he cups his hand and whispers to the girl behind him.

When Melody sees what I did, she starts talking with kids in the middle of the line. "Pass it on," she says.

Then we stand back and watch the kids whispering, each one turning toward the next. I feel huge relief—we actually did something!

Anyone can lead, Rosa Parks said to me. I'm not a politician like Dad. I'm just a girl. But like Melody and her gardening, I planted a seed, and now I'm watching it grow.

The End

To read this story another way and see how different choices lead to a different ending, turn back to page 58.

I've never had a waitress be mean to me before. So I tell Melody and Yvonne the truth. "I don't really want to go into Sam's Soda Shop."

"Me either," Melody adds. "Can we go to the soda fountain at Barthwell's?" she asks Yvonne. "You always say we should give our business to shops that are owned by black people."

Yvonne sighs. "Yes. We want to support them. But, Dee-Dee, think about it: If we only shopped at those places, nothing would ever change. Businesses like this one would keep treating black people poorly. That's not okay, is it?"

Melody's shoulders sag. She shakes her head.

"Let's just go home," says Yvonne. "Mom is making food for the volunteers, and we can help her."

Melody and I are quiet on the walk back to the church. Did we disappoint Yvonne by not going into the soda shop? Maybe. *At least we can make food with Melody's mom*, I remind myself. *At least we can still help.*

🎵 *Turn to page 117.*

An hour later, I'm sitting beside Melody in church, but all I can think about is Al and Josephine. While Pastor Daniels talks about helping others, I wonder, *How can Melody and I save the performance hall? We're just two girls. Two girls can't go up against a whole city!*

I can't wait for Sunday dinner—mostly because I want to meet Melody's big sister, Yvonne. Melody says Yvonne will know what to do. I hope, hope, hope she's right.

I decide I like *all* of Melody's siblings when we're back at Big Momma's house a couple of hours later. Lila is quiet but nice. And Melody was right—she does read all the time. She sneaks a book to read under the table before dinner starts. I've done that before! I catch her eye and grin.

As Dwayne taps out a rhythm on the table with his spoon, he winks at me. I still feel shy around him, knowing that he's sort of famous.

And then there's Yvonne. She rushed through the front door a minute ago, wearing a colorful scarf over her Afro. I noticed a cast on her wrist, but before I could ask Melody about it, Poppa started carrying

bowls of steaming food in from the kitchen. The delicious smell brought us all to the table.

Sitting down, surrounded by Melody's family, I suddenly feel homesick. I start thinking about my mom and dad—until I hear Melody telling Yvonne about Al and Josephine's place.

"They're going to start tearing it down tomorrow!" says Melody.

Yvonne furrows her brow. "We should stage a demonstration," she says. "I'll talk to my friends in the Student Walk to Freedom Club this afternoon. If enough of us show up and surround the building, they *can't* tear it down."

"Whoa, let's slow down," says Melody's dad from the other end of the table.

"That sounds dangerous," adds her mom.

"But Mommy," Melody says, "you let me march in the protest at Fieldston's Clothing Store."

"That was organized," her mom says. "We didn't just show up there without thinking it through."

"And there were no bulldozers at Fieldston's," Melody's dad adds.

"Just because we move quickly doesn't mean we're

not organized," Yvonne says to her mother.

As Big Momma sets a bowl of potatoes on the table, she says, "There are other ways to raise your voices." She sounds worried, too.

Out of the corner of my eye, I see Yvonne and Melody exchange a look. Yvonne's jaw is set with determination. "I can bring the girls with me," she says. "I'll look out for them. I think it could be a good experience for them, to stand up for something they believe in."

Melody's parents look doubtful. I have to admit, standing in the way of a construction crew *does* sound dangerous. *What would my own parents think about that?* I wonder. My stomach flutters with nerves and homesickness.

Melody gives me that look again, the one that says, What do you think we should do?

> *To go to the demonstration, turn to page 122.*

> *To raise your voices another way, turn to page 110.*

Just then, the door jingles behind us. A white woman and her teenage daughter step into the shop. When the girl smiles at us, I smile back, but my cheek is quivering.

Sue, the waitress, comes back to the cash register. She puts the water pitcher down, grabs a couple of menus, and motions for the woman and her daughter to follow her.

The teenage girl points at me, Melody, and Yvonne. "They were here first," she says kindly.

The sour look on Sue's face says that the last thing she wants to do is seat us. Finally, she waves her hand toward a table in the way, way back. "There's a booth back there," she says.

Yvonne smiles politely. "We'll take these open seats right here, please," she says, stepping toward the counter.

Melody follows Yvonne toward the stools, her chin set in the same determined way as her sister's. I hurry along behind them, hoping my wobbly legs don't give out.

Turn to page 115.

13 efore the woman can say anything, Cousin Tish steps forward. "It looks like our girls have made friends," she says warmly, extending her hand. "I'm Tish Porter. It's very nice to meet you."

Time stands still as we all watch and wait. The white woman stares at Tish's outstretched hand. Then, finally, she extends her own.

I slowly release my breath. *Did I just help break down one of those walls that Yvonne was talking about?* I wonder. I think maybe, just maybe, I did.

Then I remember another neighbor girl, the dark-haired girl who moved in between Anika's house and mine. The last time I saw her, I was staring at her through the window, not waving or going out to say hello. *Did that make her feel bad?* I wonder. *Like I don't want her in my neighborhood?*

As we drive back to Melody's house, I realize something: It's time to go home. There's something I really, *really* want to do when I get there.

Turn to page 124.

fter dinner, Melody and I sit on the front steps and make a plan.

"I'm kind of scared to go to the demonstration," I admit.

She looks relieved. "I am, too," she says. "But we *have* to help Auntie Josephine and Uncle Al. They're losing everything—even their piano. Can't we do something?"

I shrug. "Not unless we win a million dollars and can buy them a new piano."

Melody laughs. "Well, with a million dollars, we could buy them a whole new *building*."

"That's true," I say, propping my elbows on my knees. For some reason, an image of my dad pops into my mind. "That's it!" I say. "We can do a fund-raiser." I explain to Melody that my dad is a politician who raises money for his campaigns.

"Your dad is a politician?" she asks. She looks as starstruck as I was when I found out her brother is a Motown star.

"Yes," I say. "But the point is, we can fund-raise like he does. We can ask people to help Al and Josephine get a new piano."

Melody takes a deep breath and blows it out slowly. "That might not be so easy," she says. "My Junior Block Club wanted new swings at the playground. We wrote letters to the Parks Department, but it took a long time to get help." Melody shakes her head. "I don't know who to write to about a new piano for Uncle Al and Auntie Josephine."

"Hmm," I say, my hopes beginning to sink again. "If you want to raise money for a piano, you have to talk to people who care about music as much as we do."

That's when Melody gets a glint in her eye. "I know where to find people like that," she says. "My church."

"Yes!" I say. "Can we do a concert there or something?"

Melody chews her lip. "We can ask Miss Dorothy about it. Wait, there's already a concert on the church calendar. *Your* concert on Tuesday night."

Huh?

"The traveling youth choir, silly," she says.

Worry nibbles at my stomach. I'm not actually a part of that choir. "I'd much rather do a fund-raiser with *you*," I say.

Melody's face softens. "We could ask Miss Dorothy

if we can play something during the performance—like halfway through. Then we can talk to the congregation and ask them to donate money for the new piano."

I nod. "That could work!" Now my worry's gone and I'm feeling something else—pride. Melody and I put our heads together and came up with a good idea.

Dad would be proud of me, too, I think happily as I follow Melody inside.

Turn to page 126.

"Is it a fire truck?" I ask, spinning around. The flashing lights are blinding.

"I think it's the police!" says Melody, her eyes wide.

Dwayne immediately pulls the car to the side of the street. His eyes in the rearview mirror look scared, but his mouth is set in a straight, hard line.

Did he do something wrong? I wonder. *Was he speeding?*

A police officer taps on the window next to Dwayne. Another officer appears on my side of the car.

Dwayne rolls the window all the way down, and the officer glances into the backseat at me and Melody. My stomach tightens, and I look away.

"This your car?" asks the officer hovering over Dwayne's window.

The other officer says, "How does a boy like you drive a car like this?"

What does he mean, "a boy like you"? I wonder. *Does he think Dwayne is too young to drive?*

"Answer me, boy," says the first officer. "This your car? Don't lie to me, now."

Then it hits me. I can tell by his voice that he thinks Dwayne *stole* this car.

"No, sir," Dwayne says politely, staring straight ahead. "I'm just borrowing the car from a friend."

The officer doesn't seem to believe him. "This friend got a name?" he asks. "How about if we take you down to the station and you can tell us more about this 'friend'?"

Melody's hand finds mine. I can feel her trembling.

Dwayne's voice is steady as he says, "This car belongs to Mr. James Hartman down at Hitsville, sir. Mr. Hartman is a producer."

The officer stares hard at Dwayne for what feels like an eternity. Then he says, "I'm gonna need you to step out of the car."

I freeze—I can't even breathe. *Is Dwayne going to get arrested?*

Turn to page 131.

he stool is cold and hard. I hold on tight to the counter to steady myself.

As the teenage girl and her mom sit down beside us, Sue grabs a pad and the pencil from behind her ear. "What can I get you?" she asks the girl's mother.

"Coffee for me, please," says the woman. "And two slices of cherry pie."

Sue jots that down. She turns toward the coffee pot, fills a cup, and places it on a saucer in front of the woman. But even after she serves the pie, Sue doesn't ask Yvonne, Melody, or me for our orders.

When Sue steps to the cash register, Yvonne says, "I'd like a cup of coffee, too, and a couple of sodas, please."

Sue doesn't look up. "We're out of coffee," she says curtly.

I can see the nearly full pot simmering behind the counter. Melody sees it, too. "There's coffee right there," she says to me, pointing.

Sue stares at us. The air feels cold and still, like just before a thunderstorm. Part of me wants to get off my stool and run away, before something bad happens. But I don't.

I remember Yvonne's words: *It's important to take a stand on things like this. Someone has to fight for what's right.*

"There's, um, plenty of coffee, isn't there?" I hear myself saying to Sue. My voice isn't loud. It sounds very far away. But Yvonne raises an eyebrow, as if she's impressed.

The white woman smiles at me, too. "Yes, the pot is definitely full," she says.

By the time Sue pours that cup of coffee for Yvonne, my palms are sweating. Melody and I get our sodas, too, and I swear, ice-cold soda *never* tasted so good.

Finally, I feel like a regular kid in a soda shop again. But I've learned something: Even girls like Melody and me can make a difference.

I guess sometimes taking a stand means being brave enough to sit down—to sit on a stool and wait to be served, just like everyone else.

♪ The End ♪

To read this story another way and see how different choices lead to a different ending, turn back to page 51.

"**A**re you studying *already*?" Melody asks Lila. "School hasn't even started yet!"

We're standing at the kitchen counter at Melody's house, helping Yvonne and Melody's mom make bologna and cheese sandwiches. I'm adding lettuce and Melody is adding tomatoes. But Lila is hunched over the table in front of an open book.

"This happens to be my new American History book," says Lila. "And I'm not studying. I'm just *looking* at it."

"Focus on your own work, Melody," her mom scolds, handing her squares of wax paper. "Wrap those sandwiches tightly so that the tomato juice doesn't leak out."

Melody wipes her hands on a paper napkin. "The tomatoes are definitely juicy," she says, popping a slice into her mouth. "I grew them myself."

"Really?" I say.

"Sure," she says. "And the lettuce. My garden is out back."

"Those vegetables are going to feed a bunch of volunteers today, Dee-Dee," says Yvonne. "You should feel good about that." She doesn't sound upset about the soda shop anymore.

Melody nods proudly. Then she spots Lila sniffing the pages of her new book. "I think Lila wants to eat her *book* instead of a bologna sandwich," she jokes.

Lila laughs sheepishly. "I can't help it!" she says. "I love the smell of books."

I laugh, too. I know just how she feels.

"Volunteers could have used more books like that when they were teaching at Freedom Schools down in Mississippi this summer," says Yvonne. "They didn't have a lot of great materials to work with."

"Well, that's been true even here in Detroit," adds Melody's mom. "We're finally getting materials in my classroom that teach about black history—and that show the miseries of slavery instead of painting a pretty picture of it. But we've sure waited a long time for them."

As I wrap my last sandwich in wax paper, I try to imagine that. In fourth grade, we spent the whole month of February learning about black history. I got an A on my report about Frederick Douglass, who escaped from slavery and became a great writer and leader. What if I'd never learned about him? Or Harriet Tubman? Or the Underground Railroad? A whole

chunk of history would just be . . . *missing*.

A bark at the back door makes us all jump. It's Bo waiting to be let out.

"I'll take him," says Lila, reaching for the dog's leash.

I wash my hands and then take a seat at the table. While I wait for Melody to finish, I flip through Lila's new book. *What will it say about Frederick Douglass?* I wonder. I page to the index and slide my finger down the Ds. But Frederick Douglass isn't listed. *Huh.*

I search the Ts next for Harriet Tubman. Nothing. My cheeks start to burn.

When Lila comes back inside, I close the book—too quickly.

"What is it?" she asks. "What did you see?"

I don't know how to tell her that it's not what I saw. It's what I *didn't* see.

Turn to page 128.

𝓐s soon as we climb into Dwayne's old car to head home, Melody taps on the back of his seat. "Tell us, Dwayne!" she says. "What do you need my help with?"

Dwayne spins around and rests his arm on the seat. "Okay, check this out," he says. "I'm cutting another record—another single."

"Really?" says Melody. "Two records in one summer? Wow . . . The Three Ravens must be hitting it big!"

Dwayne cuts her off. "Not The Three Ravens," he says. "This one I'm doing on my own. I know this guy who owns a small studio, and he owes me a favor, so . . . I'm going to record some of my own stuff Monday night."

Melody's mouth hangs open. "You're leaving The Three Ravens?" she says.

"No," says Dwayne quickly. "It's nothing like that. I just want to try a solo song. But Artie and Phil don't know yet, so . . ."

Melody pinches her thumb and finger together and slides them across her lips, as if zipping her mouth closed.

Dwayne's face softens. "Thanks, Dee-Dee. Now are

you going to help your brother-man rehearse?"

She nods. "We both can," she says, grinning at me. "Tomorrow. At Big Momma's. Right?"

"Right," I say, remembering the last time we played music together there. I can't wait!

Turn to page 136.

By nighttime, Melody and I have made a big decision. We're going to the demonstration tomorrow, but I'm still nervous—especially when Melody tells me why Yvonne's wrist is in a cast. "She broke it when she got arrested," she explains.

"Arrested? When? Why?" I say, the questions tumbling out of my mouth.

"In Mississippi. She went down with other college students to help black people register to vote and to teach school to kids. Some people in the area—some white people—weren't too happy about that. Yvonne was just talking to some black folks and she got arrested for disturbing the peace. A police officer pulled her off their porch, and that's when she tripped and hurt herself."

I can't believe what I'm hearing. Yvonne seems even braver now, but I feel more scared than ever. *Will we get arrested tomorrow, too?* I want to ask. *Or hurt?* But I don't want to disappoint Melody, and I know that Al and Josephine need our help—no matter what.

Even though tomorrow is really important, there's something I have to admit to Melody. It's just too big to keep inside. "I'm kind of homesick," I tell her. "I think

I need to go home tomorrow. After the demonstration, I mean."

Melody looks surprised. "Don't you have to wait for the choir bus?" she asks.

I shake my head. "No, I can get home on my own," I say honestly. "I haven't left yet because it's been really fun to stay with you and your family. But now I want to see my own family."

Melody's face falls, but she squeezes my hand. I know she understands.

"I'm glad you'll be at the demonstration in the morning," she says. "I wouldn't want to be there without you."

Turn to page 139.

Saying good-bye to Melody is hard, but when I'm back in that church basement, I can't wait to sit at the piano and play my way home. I close my eyes, remembering the melody for "Lift Every Voice and Sing." *I found a new way to lift my voice today,* I realize, remembering the moment when I invited Val's neighbor to swing with us.

As soon as I'm back in my bedroom, I grab my phone. It *dings* in my hand—a text from Anika. I write back immediately: *Meet me outside.* Then I run to Mom's office.

"Can I go outside and play?" I ask.

Mom looks surprised. She nods but then asks, "What about practicing the piano?"

I grin. "There's something more important that I've got to do."

As I step outside, I hear voices. My new neighbor is still playing Frisbee with her brother. As I round the corner of the house, she smiles shyly.

I cross the grass to introduce myself, and I see Anika hurrying down her front steps toward us, too. Then this warm feeling spreads through me like a sip of hot cocoa. I just *know* that the three of us are going to

get along well, kind of like I knew that Melody and I would.

For a moment, I miss Melody. But in some ways, it feels like she's still with me, helping me break down walls and make a difference—right here at home.

🎵 *The End* 🎵

To read this story another way and see how different choices lead to a different ending, turn back to page 13.

On Monday, we call Miss Dorothy, who thinks the fund-raiser is a great idea. Now there's only one thing left to do: choose a song to play.

"We don't have a lot of time to practice," says Melody. "Maybe we should play a song we already know."

"Right," I say. "What do we both know?"

We're sitting on Big Momma's couch when it comes to us, just as it did on Saturday night. "'His Eye Is on the Sparrow,'" we say together.

"Yes!" says Melody, clapping her hands together.

"It's perfect," I say, "because we heard it first at the performance hall. Should we practice it now?"

We sit together at Big Momma's piano, and I'm thrilled to see that my fingers still remember the notes. Melody knows every word of the song, too, because her youth choir sang it.

We practice the song several times, polishing it until it's perfect. Melody brushes her hands together as we finish one last time. "This sounds *good*!"

That's when it strikes me: I'm not going to *look* all that good Tuesday night. I should dress up for the concert, but I don't have anything fancy to wear.

When I tell Melody, a huge grin spreads across her face. "I can help with that," she says. "C'mon."

🎵 *Turn to page 141.*

ow everyone's staring at me—not just Lila, but Melody, Yvonne, and their mom, too. "What's wrong?" Melody asks.

I feel the same pressure I did when we were standing outside Sam's Soda Shop. I'd chickened out then— I was too scared to go inside. *Are you going to chicken out again now?* I ask myself.

I swallow the lump in my throat and point toward the book. "There's, um, some really important stuff missing in here." I tell them that I can't find anything about Frederick Douglass or Harriet Tubman.

"Really?" says Yvonne, crossing the floor. As she flips through the book, I can tell she's getting angry.

"When was it printed?" asks Melody's mom.

Yvonne turns to the first few pages. "In 1959," she says. "Just five years ago. But I can't even find a picture of a black person in here." Despite her injured wrist, she flips through the pages so fast, I'm afraid she's going to rip one.

Lila puts her hand on Yvonne's and says, "Wait, I just saw one!" But when Yvonne turns back a page or two, Lila's face crumples. "Oh," she says. "It's a picture of a slave."

"So the only black people featured in this book are slaves," says Yvonne, shaking her head.

Lila's brow furrows. "No black scientists or inventors? What about George Washington Carver?" She checks the index again and then slumps back in her chair. "I thought I was going to a good school!"

Her mom squeezes her shoulders. "In a lot of ways, it *is* a good school. But it's a mostly white school, so some changes are going to be slower in coming."

Lila falls silent, but Melody stirs beside her. "You can change things, Lila," she says. "You can write letters to your school—like the Junior Block Club did when we wanted to make the playground better. Remember how we wrote to the Parks Department?"

Lila nods, and I can see her spark return.

"That's a good idea, Melody," Mrs. Ellison says.

"I'll help you write letters," Melody promises Lila. "We'll tell your school how books like this make us feel, and we'll ask them to buy new books."

"New books that teach about *all* the famous black scientists," adds Lila. "Like Carver, Charles Drew, Lewis Latimer . . . " She counts them off on her fingers.

"Can I help, too?" I ask. I want to help make things

better for Lila—and for all the students at her school.

Lila grins and hugs me and Melody at the same time.

"That's the spirit," says Yvonne, clapping her hands together.

Turn to page 133.

Dwayne opens the door and steps onto the sidewalk. That's when Melody tugs on my hand and darts out the door, too. "We'll go get Mr. Hartman!" she says to the officers. "We'll go get him right now."

I trip out of the car after her, our hands still connected.

"Melody, no!" says Dwayne. "You stay put."

But the officer holds Dwayne back. "Let 'em go," says the officer. "I want to hear what this Mr. Hartman has to say."

Melody takes off down the street and I race behind her, my eyes fixed on her bouncing braids. I don't look over my shoulder. I'm afraid I'll see the officers arresting Dwayne.

When we reach the studio, we burst through the front doors. Melody calls out the producer's name. "Mr. Hartman!"

Artie pokes his head out of a room. "Melody, what—?" he starts to say.

But a man in a suit comes down the hall from the other direction. "I'm Mr. Hartman," he says, his brow furrowed. "What's wrong?"

Melody tells him all in one breath. She finishes

with, "They're going to arrest Dwayne!"

Mr. Hartman's eyes widen, and he runs out the door ahead of us. Artie goes, too.

"But why?" I ask Melody as we take the steps two at a time. "Why do they think Dwayne stole the car?"

"Because," she says, her eyes welling up with tears. "Because he's black, and they don't think a black person could own a car like that." Then she sets her jaw and takes off down the street again.

We can't catch up with Artie and Mr. Hartman, but we try. *Will Dwayne still be there when we get to the car?* I wonder. *Or will he be on his way to jail?*

Turn to page 144.

On Monday afternoon, we're back at the church with the Student Walk to Freedom Club. The pile of envelopes on the table makes me proud.

"I sure hope this works," says Melody, licking the last envelope and sealing it shut.

"Me, too," I say.

Yvonne gives a big thank-you to the volunteers. "We did our part today to help black students get a good education," she says proudly. "They need to learn about leaders in black history. That's how they begin to believe that they can become leaders, too."

I let those words sink in. *I kind of already feel like a leader*, I realize. Dad would be proud of me for getting involved—for telling Melody's family what I found in that book instead of pretending I didn't see. Mom would be proud, too.

That's when it hits me how much I miss my parents. It's time to go home.

After everyone leaves the community room, I break the news to Melody. She's sad, but I think she feels just as good as I do about everything we did together. "Do you want me to wait here with you?" she asks sweetly. She thinks my parents are coming to pick me up.

"No," I tell her. "That'll just make me more sad." It's true. Leaving my new friend is hard. I have to make my good-bye quick—like ripping off a bandage.

So after she follows Yvonne up the stairs, I sit down at the piano. I hum the melody for "Lift Every Voice," and then I start to play.

This time, the voices that swell up around me belong to the people I've met on my journey: Melody's pure, sweet voice and Big Momma's low, powerful voice. If I listen hard, I can even hear Lila and Yvonne, doing their sister-thing.

I know I'm home when I hear the *ding* of my phone. It's probably Anika, but I don't have time to answer right now. Instead, I fling open my bedroom door and race down the hall.

I can't wait to see Mom again, to tell her that I'm proud of her. I'm proud that she's a principal and that she fights to make sure kids get a good education.

And when Dad gets home, maybe I'll ask him more about his job, too. Now that I know that girls like Melody and me can make a difference, it makes me wonder, *What can I do here in my own hometown?*

I laugh, imagining how excited my dad will be to

hear me ask that. He'll have plenty of ideas for me, but I know now that I'll have a few good ideas of my *own*, too.

♪ *The End* ♪

To read this story another way and see how different choices lead to a different ending, turn back to page 80.

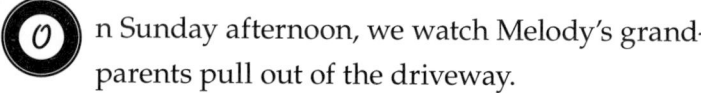

On Sunday afternoon, we watch Melody's grandparents pull out of the driveway.

"They're driving to Canada?" I ask, trying to figure out how they can drive to another *country* just for the day.

"The Emancipation Celebration festival is across the river in Windsor, Ontario," Melody explains. "It only takes a half hour or so to get there." She sighs as she shuts the door. "Part of me wishes we could have gone with them, but Dwayne needs our help."

She's right. When Dwayne arrives, he looks anxious. He shakes out his arms and legs. "I've got the jitters," he says.

"You?" says Melody. "You *never* get nervous!"

Dwayne shrugs. "What can I say?" he says. "Guess I got used to having Artie and Phil standing there beside me."

"Well, we'll be Artie and Phil today," Melody says. "I mean"—she makes her voice as deep as it'll go—"we'll be Artie and Phil today."

Dwayne laughs and pulls one of her pigtails. "Thanks, Dee-Dee. I'll take you up on that."

He sits at the piano and starts playing something

slow and sweet. When he hits a sour note, he shakes out his hands again. "I'm so jazzed right now, I can't even remember the notes. I'll be right back—I need my music."

He darts out the front door, and we hear a car door slam. Then he's back with a sheet of music in his hands. It's handwritten and messy, but when Dwayne sits back down at the piano, the music pours out of his fingertips.

Melody and I cheer like crazy when he's done. "I can't believe you wrote that!" I tell him.

"And you played it perfectly," adds Melody. "You're ready!"

Dwayne shakes his head. "Thanks," he says. "But I've gotta practice it away from the piano. The house band at the studio will play for me so I can focus on my voice." He clears his throat and sings a few bars.

"Wait," says Melody. "We can be your band. It'll feel more real that way."

She points me toward the piano, where Dwayne's handwritten music is still set up. I shrug. Why not? As long as I can read it, I should be able to play it.

As I sit at the piano, Melody disappears into the

kitchen—and comes back out with a pan and a wooden spoon. Dwayne laughs. "Just like the old days, eh, little sis?" he says. "You're the best saucepan drummer I know."

Melody turns the pan upside down, tapping the bottom with the wooden spoon. It *does* sound like a drum, especially when I play piano and Dwayne sings along.

When we finish, Dwayne doesn't seem so nervous anymore. "I've got my house band right here," he says. "What more does a guy need? Except maybe a microphone."

Melody and I look at each other and grin. She gets to the fruit bowl first and tosses Dwayne a banana.

He stares at the fruit and then laughs. "Looks like I'm gonna have to change the name of my band after today," he says. "Dwayne and the Banana Splits." Then he peels the banana and takes a big bite.

Turn to page 145.

onday morning comes way too quickly. Before I know it, Yvonne is standing in Big Momma's living room. Her eyes are lit up, like she's been awake for hours. Now that I know how Yvonne's wrist got hurt, I'm even more impressed with her courage. No wonder she doesn't seem nervous about today.

"Are you girls ready?" Yvonne asks.

"Ready," says Melody. "Except we have to tell Big Momma we're leaving—and I know she's going to worry." She calls upstairs, but there's no response.

Yvonne and I follow Melody into the kitchen, where we find a note on the counter. It reads:

Went to visit a friend. Help yourself to breakfast, and I'll be back soon.—Big Momma

"She's already gone!" says Melody with a loud sigh of relief. "Good. Now no one will be worried about us going to the demonstration."

Except me, I think. But there's no turning back now.

We set out for 12th Street, Yvonne in the lead. The distance feels farther on foot than it did in Miss Dorothy's car last night. And Yvonne is walking so fast, Melody and I can barely keep up.

"Slow down, Vonnie," Melody cries.

But Yvonne keeps going. "We don't want to be late," she calls over her shoulder.

And then it occurs to me: *What if the construction crew is already there? What if the demolition has started?*

My fast walk turns into a run.

🎵 ***Turn to page 148.***

It's Tuesday evening—"Matching Tuesday," Melody calls it. I'm sitting on a church bench wearing pink hair ribbons, and Melody is, too. Her dress has pink flowers on it, and the one that Lila loaned to me is solid pink. But the folds of my skirt are gathered with a bow at the waist, just like Melody's.

"My friend Sharon and I do Matching Mondays at school," she told me this afternoon when we were standing in front of her closet. "But you and I'll do a Matching Tuesday, okay?"

Definitely okay, I think. For the first time in my life, I feel like I have a sister. I wish I could take her home with me!

The youth choir is just finishing the first half of their performance. I told Melody I was too nervous about our song to sing with the choir, which is true. Butterflies flit through my chest.

"Thank you to the Second Baptist Youth Choir for visiting us here in Detroit," says Miss Dorothy, standing at the microphone. "Thank you for lifting your beautiful voices for us." She claps for the choir, and the congregation joins in.

Then she says, "Before the youth choir concludes

their performance, we have two more performers with a special request. Girls, are you ready?"

My knees wobble as I follow Melody to the front of the church. As I sit down on the piano bench, she steps to the microphone. Her voice shakes as she introduces us. But she doesn't let her nerves stop her from doing what's right.

"There's a performance hall on 12th Street that some of you might know," she says, describing Al and Josephine's place.

Most of the people in the congregation nod their heads, and several people even clap.

"Well, the city is supposed to start tearing it down this week," says Melody sadly.

Low murmurs ripple through the congregation.

"The owners of the hall, Al and Josephine Moore, lost everything—their home, their business, and even their piano. They have to start all over," says Melody. "My friend and I want to raise money to buy a new piano so that they can keep playing music. Will you help us?" Applause spreads like a wave across the congregation.

Melody grins at me. Then she says, "We're going

to play a song that reminds us all that we're not alone. Then we'll pass the collection plates, in case you want to donate money for the new piano. Thank you."

As Melody bows her head, there are more cheers and claps. And then it's time to begin.

♪ Turn to page 154.

"ook!" Melody pants. She points down the street at the red Mustang, still parked along the curb with the officers standing beside it. Dwayne must be inside the car. Phew!

Mr. Hartman is gesturing with his hands, talking to the officers. Artie stands off to the side, like he's afraid to get too close. Then Mr. Hartman ducks his head into the car and pops back out with an envelope.

"The registration is right here," he says, handing it to an officer. He pulls out his wallet and offers his driver's license, too.

The officers study the registration, as if they think it's fake. But they finally nod at Mr. Hartman and hand back the paperwork.

I wait until they're back in their police car and pulling away from the curb. Then I let out my breath. I feel sick to my stomach.

Melody's face is twisted with emotion. "Dwayne!" she calls, rushing to the door of the Mustang.

Turn to page 152.

On Monday night, Dwayne drives us to the recording studio, which is in the basement of a record shop. As soon as I step out of the car, I hear music.

"Where's that coming from?" asks Melody.

"The studio. That's a record being made," Dwayne says. "The sound gets piped out through speakers right onto the sidewalk. It's my voice you'll be hearing next." He smiles nervously.

We wait in the record shop for the recording to finish. Dwayne paces the aisles, but Melody and I flip through albums. I've never seen so many records—rows and rows of the flat, square covers. Grammy had a collection, but hers all fit into one little cupboard.

Then Melody races over to a section of small records tucked into paper sleeves. She searches through them and pulls out a shiny black disc with a bright blue label. I see the word "Motown" written across the top.

"Have you heard this one?" she asks with a smile.

I squint to read the label: *Move On Up. The Three Ravens.* "Is this Dwayne's record?" I squeal. "Is your voice on here, too, Melody?"

She nods, grinning.

I wish I could listen to the record right now. But when a few guys with instrument cases come up from the basement, Dwayne waves us toward the stairs. "Let's go, girls," he says. "We're up."

When we get downstairs, a man wearing headphones nods at Dwayne. Then he glances behind us. "Where's your band?" he asks.

"It's just me, Mac," says Dwayne. "It's a solo recording, remember?"

Mac says, "No, I mean your musicians."

"You don't have a house band?" Dwayne asks.

Mac snorts. "This ain't Motown, brother. We can't afford to keep musicians on the payroll."

Dwayne sighs. "I can play the piano, too," he says, shaking out his hands. "I've just been so focused on the vocals."

Mac frowns. "You want to do this another day, Dwayne? I mean, if you're not ready . . ."

Dwayne's shoulders sag. He looks at the clock, as if he can't stand to let another second go by before doing this thing.

"We can be your band," Melody pipes up. "Just like we practiced."

My stomach drops. Practicing in someone's living room is one thing. Playing in a studio for a recording that will be heard by thousands of people . . . that's totally different!

🎵 ***Turn to page 156.***

When we're a block away from the performance hall, we see a yellow crane and lots of men wearing white hard hats. "Oh, no," groans Melody. "Are we too late?"

"No," says Yvonne. "I don't think they've started yet. But let's hurry."

Then we see something else: a crowd of people, mostly teenagers, gathered in front of the building. Melody stops short, and I plow into the back of her, making her fall forward.

"Sorry," I say, reaching out to steady her. "What's wrong?"

She points. It's Josephine, standing tall and proud among the crowd. And next to her? Big Momma. She sees us at the same moment, and she opens her arms wide.

Big Momma has tears in her eyes when we reach her. "I couldn't stay away either, baby chicks," she says. "Some things are just worth fighting for."

I feel safe wrapped up in Big Momma's hug, until I hear sirens. A nervous energy runs through the crowd of protesters, and Big Momma pulls Melody and me even closer.

A construction crew manager jogs over to meet the police officers as they climb out of a squad car. They talk for a moment, and then the police officers walk toward us. Melody's hand slips into mine. I squeeze it tight.

Yvonne doesn't shrink back. She steps forward to meet the officers. "We're staging a peaceful protest," she says in a clear, brave voice.

Isn't she afraid she'll be arrested again? I wonder.

"Peaceful or not, miss," says the first officer, "you're standing in the way of city business. We need you to clear out—now."

When no one moves, the second officer strokes his mustache. "Go on home now," he says. "You're just a bunch of kids. This doesn't involve you."

He sounds like he's trying to be nice, but his words sting. *We may be kids*, I think, *but we **are** involved. We know what matters. This performance hall matters. Music matters.*

Yvonne reaches out her right hand to the boy next to her. Others clasp hands, too, until they form a wall between the police and the building behind them.

I reach for Melody's hand, and then Big Momma's.

None of the volunteers flinch or move out of the way, not even when the first officer starts talking about arresting us. "Anyone who refuses to leave will be taken downtown," he says.

I can tell that the officer with the mustache doesn't want that. "Let's all just go on home now," he tries again.

I look up at Big Momma. "Are they really going to arrest us all?" I whisper. She pulls me toward her. Melody's eyes widen, too.

"Don't be scared," Big Momma says. "You know what we're gonna do? We're gonna sing. Sing with love in our hearts and a good feeling in our souls." With that, Big Momma's low, powerful voice begins.

> *We shall not,*
> *We shall not be moved.*

Josephine joins in right away. Then Melody is singing, too, and her sweet, high voice is strong.

> *Just like a tree that's standing by the water,*
> *We shall not be moved.*

As the others around us begin to sing, something happens. It's like someone tipped a bucket of warm water inside me, and it fills me with such a good feeling that I can't help it. I start singing, too.

My voice isn't as deep and strong as Big Momma's. It's not as pure and sweet as Melody's. But it's all I've got, and I sing with everything I have in me.

We keep singing, and we sing for a long time. When one of the protesters starts a song I don't know, I hum along until the words are familiar. That warm-water feeling stays with me.

The construction crew stands and watches while their manager talks to the police. I'm still singing when a police van appears. All of a sudden, the officers lead a group of protesters toward the van. One of them is Yvonne!

Turn to page 157.

"re you sure you're okay?" Melody asks Dwayne.

"I'm fine, Dee-Dee," he says. "It's not the first time I've been stopped by the police, and it's probably not gonna be the last." He's in the passenger seat now next to Mr. Hartman, who is driving us back to the studio.

Artie sits between me and Melody. "They pull over black guys all the time," he says. "For no good reason."

Mr. Hartman sighs. "I think we need more black officers on the police force," he says. "If more of them looked like you and me, they wouldn't be looking at us as if we were criminals."

Dwayne's face is set in stone. He doesn't look scared anymore, but he doesn't look mad either. He's just staring straight ahead.

I can still hear the way he talked to that police officer, calling him "sir." But the police officer called *him* "boy." Grammy always told me that people who act with respect will be treated with respect. That sure didn't happen tonight.

"It's not fair," I say to Melody. Dwayne overhears.

"Lots of things aren't fair," he says. "That's how it's always been and how it's always gonna be." Suddenly,

Dwayne grins. "I'm just gonna keep playing my music. Someday, I'll make enough money to buy a Mustang of my own." He winks at Melody and adds, "With papers to prove it!"

I can't believe he's not angry anymore! *Dwayne may not be a famous singer yet*, I think to myself, *but he's kind of already a star. He treats himself and other people with respect.*

Those officers may not have respected him back, but I sure do. So maybe Grammy was right after all.

I think of Zoey Gatz, sticking out her tongue or strutting down the red carpet. Sure, she has lots of money, but she doesn't act like she respects herself—or anyone else. Somehow, she seems kind of silly to me now.

Maybe when I get home, I'll take down my Zoey Gatz posters and put up something new. There are plenty of talented people to choose from, now that I know where—and when—to look for them.

♪ The End ♪

To read this story another way and see how different choices lead to a different ending, turn back to page 13.

my heart races as I play those first few notes, almost as if I'm playing in front of judges at a piano recital. But something's different. *You're not alone,* I remind myself. *Melody is right here beside you.*

There's something else, too: My heart feels so full, it almost hurts. Tonight, I'm definitely playing with *passion,* as Ms. Stricker would say. How could I not? Melody and I are performing for something that matters, *really* matters.

Melody's voice rises up to meet the rafters. Wow! She sounds even better than she did at Big Momma's. And she doesn't look scared anymore.

> *I sing because I'm happy,*
> *I sing because I'm free*

People in the audience sing, too, raising their hands and their voices upward.

> *For His eye is on the sparrow,*
> *And I know He watches me.*

I feel like I'm right back at the performance hall in the midst of a crowd that is moved by the music.

As Melody sings the last few words, someone nudges me. It's Miss Dorothy, holding out a wooden collection plate. "Let's pass the plates while that gorgeous music is still ringing in their ears," she says, winking at me.

Melody takes a plate, too, and we stand on opposite ends of the benches, passing the plates back and forth along the rows of people. Every time the plate comes back to me, I try not to count how much money is in it. Even if there's not enough for a new piano, I hope there's enough to let Al and Josephine know that people care.

As we hand the full plates to Miss Dorothy at the back of the church, Melody and I lock eyes and smile.

"Psst . . ." says someone from the hallway. It's Big Momma. "C'mon, chicks," she says, waving us out into the hall. "I have a surprise for you."

Turn to page 160.

I feel frozen, like I did at Hitsville. Playing keyboard for Dwayne's recording feels even scarier, though. I can't *pretend* to play, like I pretended to sing. And I can't mess up!

Mac frowns at Melody and me like we're little kids.

"They can do it," Dwayne says. "They're good."

I stand taller then. *Dwayne believes in us,* I think. *He needs us.*

Dwayne hands me the sheet music, and for a moment, all those notes blur together. But when Melody picks up a tambourine from the instrument rack, the jingle clears my head.

Pretend there's no one else in the room, I tell myself. *It's just me, Dwayne, and Melody.* At Dwayne's cue, I start to play. And I do pretty well. We only have to record the song twice! It's like Dwayne and the Banana Splits have been playing together forever. And then, before I know it, it's over.

I follow Dwayne and Melody back upstairs into the record shop. There, we stop short. A crowd of people is gathered outside the front window. What's going on?

Turn to page 159.

onnie!" squeals Melody, lunging forward.

"She's okay, baby," Big Momma soothes. "She's going to be all right."

But Melody breaks free and races after her sister.

"Melody!" Big Momma cries, pushing through the crowd after her. "Melody Elizabeth Ellison!"

I try to follow, but there are too many people! Their hands are locked together, holding me back. When I finally break free, I see a police officer coming my way. Is he going to arrest me? I run the other way—toward the performance hall. Then I hear my name. I spin around wildly, trying to find Melody. Where is she?

She's across the street, with Big Momma by her side. Melody is waving me toward her, but I can't get there. The river of people is too wide to cross.

I stumble into someone. It's Josephine.

"It's okay, sweetie," she says soothingly. "We'll get you to Melody." She takes my hand and starts to push her way through the crowd. But there's only one place I want to go right now: *home.*

I tug back on Josephine's hand. "Can you do something for me?" I ask her.

"Anything, baby," she says, leaning close.

"Please tell Melody I had to go home," I say. "She knows"—my voice catches a little—"she knows I miss my family."

Josephine hesitates. "All right, but let me take you," she says. "I'll take you home."

I shake my head. "I can get there," I say. "It's close."

And it is, if I can just get to a piano. Then I remember the old piano inside the performance hall. Is it safe? I scan the crowd, looking for the construction crew. "Miss Josephine, look," I say, barely breathing.

She follows my gaze and sees the construction workers heading toward their trucks.

"Are they leaving?" I ask.

Josephine shakes her head. "They're just taking a coffee break, I think," she says. "They have to wait for the police to clear the crowd, which will take a while."

That's all I need to hear. I hug Josephine, and then as she makes her way across the crowded street, I go the other way—toward the door of the performance hall. When I'm sure no one is looking, I duck inside.

Turn to page 162.

"hat are they here for?" asks Melody, pointing toward the crowd of people outside.

The store clerk says, "They're waiting for more music. They're loving your sound."

Wow. The people out there liked our music. They want to hear more!

Melody bites her lip, trying not to smile too wide. But Dwayne steps into the middle of the crowd like a superstar, holding his head high.

As I follow him, I make a plan. When I get back home, I'll search online for his record. *Will I be able to find it?* I wonder. *And if I do, will I hear my own keyboard playing?*

I may never be a superstar myself, but now I'm thinking that's okay. As I walk beside Dwayne, I'm feeling pretty proud of what we just did. I guess you don't always have to be the star to shine.

♪ The End ♪

To read this story another way and see how different choices lead to a different ending, turn back to page 85.

I instantly recognize the couple standing next to Big Momma. It's Al and Josephine! Were they here all along?

"Girls, that was really something special," says Josephine, her eyes glistening. "Thank you from the bottom of my heart."

So they *did* hear the performance!

Al adds, "If we ever open another hall, I hope you'll consider performing. You could be the next big act."

"I like the sound of that," says Melody.

I do, too. I'm proud that I could use my talents to help Al and Josephine. And I've never had so much fun creating music as I've had these last few days with Melody. I don't want to say good-bye to her, but I know it's almost time.

After the youth choir finishes, I go to the restroom to change out of Lila's fancy dress and into my own clothes. Then I hurry back out to Melody and Big Momma.

"Your voice was so beautiful tonight," I tell Melody.

"Thanks," is the only word she can get out. She looks as if she's going to cry.

"Melody sang like an angel," Big Momma agrees,

rubbing Melody's back. Then she reaches for my hands and says, "But your hands are *your* strength, baby, your light. You know that, right? You have to let your own light shine."

Big Momma won't let go—not until I nod and show her that I understand. Then she says, "Good. Now you two chicks say your good-byes." As she steps away, I see that she's fighting tears, too.

I pull Melody into a hug. All I can say to her is, "Thank you. I'll never forget you." She still smells like roses, left over from one of Big Momma's embraces. I breathe in the scent, hoping I'll remember it always, and then I let go.

My throat is tight as I hurry downstairs toward the community room. A few of the youth choir members are leaving, carrying their black-and-white gowns on hangers.

When the room is empty, I sit down. Then I quietly, but quickly, play the song—the song that will take me home.

Turn to page 163.

It's so dark in here! As my eyes adjust, I see the shadowy stage and the hulking piano at the back of the room. I hurry down the aisle and crawl up onto the stage. There's no piano bench to sit on, but that's okay. I lean forward over the keys.

I start to play, but my hands are shaking. I fumble and start over.

I do better the second time, but halfway through, I hear the deep voice of a police officer. "Who's in here?" he calls. The glare of a flashlight streaks across the room.

Don't stop, I tell myself. *Keep playing!*

🎵 *Turn to page 164.*

Back in my bedroom, I soak up the silence. Then the *ding* of my phone jolts me into action. It's a text from Anika:

What happened???

She's responding to my text, the one I sent her a couple of minutes ago—minutes that feel like days.

I scroll up to my text: *You won't believe what happened today.*

Will she believe it? I don't know. So I just tell her the most important part:

Mom said there's no money for guitars in music class, but I came up with the BEST idea for a fund-raiser. We're going to have a concert!

I didn't even know I had the idea until it poured out of my fingertips into the text. But now, I can't wait to talk to Mom about it. Maybe Ms. Stricker can help, too. Maybe we can raise money at the piano recital!

I drop the phone on my bed and race out the bedroom door. "Mom!"

The End

To read this story another way and see how different choices lead to a different ending, turn back to page 38.

I don't stop. I play as if my life depended on it.

And when I reach the end of the song, something shines brightly into my eyes. The flashlight? No. It's afternoon sunlight pouring through my bedroom window. I'm home. I'm home!

I push away from my keyboard, wanting to run to my mom. But when I fling open my bedroom door, Mom's already there. I throw myself into her arms.

"Honey, what is it?" she asks, stroking my hair.

"I . . . just missed you," I say, pressing my face against her shoulder.

She squeezes me tight and says, "I heard you playing."

Uh-oh.

"That song . . ." she says. "You played with so much passion, so much feeling. Your grandma would have loved it."

"I know." I swallow hard and say, "I really miss Grammy."

Mom says, "Me, too. But when you play that song, I feel like Grammy's still here with us. I hope you'll keep playing music like that. Will you?"

"I will," I say, my voice cracking. I only wish Al and

Josephine could keep playing, too—that they could keep their business. Will Melody and her family keep fighting for it?

Then I remember something. "Mom?" I say. "About the guitars. I don't think we should give up so easily. Music is . . . well, it's worth fighting for."

Mom smiles. "I feel the same way. I'll keep pushing for the music program, sweetie."

"Me, too, Mom. I'll help," I promise her. I don't know how yet, but I do know one thing: I've found my passion.

Cool relief washes over me. And when Mom asks if I want to come read in her office now, I'm ready.

"Thank you, Melody," I whisper. I take one last look at my keyboard and then follow Mom down the hall.

♪ *The End* ♪

To read this story another way and see how different choices lead to a different ending, turn back to page 107.

ABOUT Melody's Time

When Melody was growing up in the 1960s, the civil rights movement had many well-known leaders. People like Dr. Martin Luther King Jr., Rosa Parks, Ella Baker, and John Lewis took action against segregation and discrimination. There were also thousands of ordinary citizens who fought for equality. Many of them were young adults, high school students, and children Melody's age and younger.

Six-year-old Ruby Bridges bravely attended an all-white school in Louisiana in 1960. She was the first black child to go to a white school in the South, and most of the white parents did not want her there. Crowds gathered in front of the building yelling insults and throwing things at her. One woman even threatened to poison Ruby! But Ruby didn't back down—and she didn't miss a single day of first grade. Her courage and strength helped pave the way for school integration so that children of all races could learn together.

This same kind of courage and strength filled the streets of Birmingham, Alabama, in May 1963. When Dr. King and other civil rights organizers planned to protest segregation, many of Birmingham's black citizens were afraid to participate. They worried that their white employers would fire them for joining the marches. Many couldn't afford to go without pay if they got arrested and missed work. So the children of Birmingham stepped in.

Audrey Faye Hendricks, a nine-year-old, was one of them. On the morning of May 2, Audrey left school and joined 800 other children from all over the city in a peaceful protest. She was arrested and spent seven days in jail. "I wasn't nervous or scared," Audrey said about marching. After a week in jail, she knew her courage and strength had made a difference. "I felt like I was helping to gain what we were trying to get, and that was freedom."

Many of the event's organizers were worried about letting kids participate. No one wanted children to get hurt. Despite their concerns, leaders let the kids march in what became known as "the Children's Crusade." The kids' spirits were high. They laughed and sang as they headed to City Hall, and crowds gathered to cheer on the young protesters.

The next day, more than 1,500 kids showed up to protest. But the positive mood quickly changed when the police blasted the marchers with fire hoses, knocking the children off their feet. Police then used dogs to attack the protesters. Images of the event were in the papers and on the news. The use of violence captured national headlines, and people were shocked.

The Children's Crusade was an important turning point in the civil rights movement. It made people pay attention to the inequalities black people faced. The extraordinary role young people played in the event inspired courage and strength in girls like Melody who went on to make a difference in their own communities.

Read more of MELODY'S stories,
available from booksellers and at *americangirl.com*

♪ *Classics* ♪
Melody's classic series, now in two volumes:

Volume 1:
No Ordinary Sound
Melody can't wait to sing her first solo at church. She spends the summer practicing the perfect song—and helping her brother become a Motown singer. When an unimaginable tragedy leaves her silent, Melody has to find her voice.

Volume 2:
Never Stop Singing
Now that her brother is singing for Motown, Melody gets to visit a real recording studio. She also starts a children's block club. Melody is determined to help her neighborhood bloom—and make her community stronger.

♪ *Journey in Time* ♪
Travel back in time—and spend a few days with Melody!

Music in My Heart
Step into Melody's world of the 1960s! Volunteer with a civil rights group, join a demonstration, or use your voice to sing backup for a Motown musician! Choose your own path through this multiple-ending story.

♪ A Sneak Peek at ♪

No Ordinary Sound

A Melody Classic

Volume 1

Melody's adventures continue in the
first volume of her classic stories.

Big Momma brought the roast in and everyone took their places around the table, with Poppa at one end and Daddy at the other. With Yvonne home from college, the family was truly all together, the way their Sundays used to be.

"Did you study all the time, Vonnie?" Melody asked. Mommy had gone to college at Tuskegee, and this year Dwayne had applied and been accepted. Melody knew that her parents hoped all their children would graduate from Tuskegee one day, too.

Yvonne shook her head so that her small earrings sparkled. "There's so much more to do at school besides studying," she said, reaching for more gravy.

"Like what?" Poppa asked, propping his elbows on the table. Melody held back a giggle when she saw Big Momma frown the same way Mommy had, but Poppa paid no attention.

"Well, last week before finals a bunch of us went out to help black people in the community register to vote," Yvonne said. "And do you know, a lady told me she was too afraid to sign up."

"Why was she afraid?" Melody interrupted.

"Because somebody threw a rock through her next-door neighbor's window after her neighbor voted," Yvonne explained, her eyes flashing with anger. "This is 1963! How can anybody get away with that?"

Melody looked from Yvonne to her father. "You always say not voting is like not being able to talk. Why wouldn't anybody want to talk?"

Daddy sighed. "It's not that she doesn't want to vote, Melody. There are a lot of unfair rules down South that keep our people from exercising their rights. Some white people will do anything, including scaring black people, to keep change from happening. They don't want to share jobs or neighborhoods or schools with us. Voting is like a man or woman's voice speaking out to change those laws and rules."

"And it's not just about voting," Mommy said. "Remember what Rosa Parks did in Montgomery? She stood up for her rights."

"You mean she *sat down* for her rights," Melody said. Melody knew all about Mrs. Parks, who got arrested for simply sitting down on a city bus. She had paid her fare like everybody else, but because she was a Negro the bus driver told her she had to give her seat to a white person! *But that happened eight years ago,* Melody realized. *Why haven't things changed?*

"Aren't we just as good as anybody else?" Melody asked as she looked around the table. "The laws should be fair everywhere, for everybody, right?"

"That's not always the way life works," Poppa said.

"Why not?" Lila asked.

Poppa sat back and rubbed his silvery mustache. That always meant he was about to tell a story.

"Back in Alabama, there was a white farmer who owned the land next to ours. Palmer was his name. Decent fellow. We went into town the same day to sell our peanut crops. It wasn't a good growing year, but I'd lucked out with twice as many sacks of peanuts as Palmer. Well, at the market they counted and weighed his sacks. Then they counted and weighed my sacks. Somehow Palmer got twice as much money as I got for selling half the crop I had. They never even checked the quality of what we had, either."

"What?" Lila blurted out.

"How?" Melody scooted to the edge of her chair.

"Wait, now." Poppa waved his grandchildren

quiet. "I asked the man to weigh it again, but he refused. I complained. Even Palmer spoke up for me. But that man turned to me and said, 'Boy—'"

"He called you *boy*?" Dwayne interrupted, putting his fork down.

"'Boy,'" Poppa continued, "'this is all you're gonna get. And if you keep up this trouble, you won't have any farm to go back to!'"

Melody's mouth fell open. "What was he talking about? You did have a farm," she said, glancing at Big Momma.

"He meant we were in danger of losing our farm—our home—because your grandfather spoke out to a white man," Big Momma explained. She shook her head slowly. "As hard as we'd worked to buy that land, as hard as it was for colored people to own anything in Alabama, we decided that day that we had to sell and move north."

Although Melody had heard many of her grandfather's stories about life in Alabama before, she'd never heard this one. And as she considered it, she realized that on their many trips down South, she'd never seen the old family farm. Maybe her

grandparents didn't want to go back.

Melody sighed. Maybe the lady Yvonne mentioned didn't want to risk losing *her* home if she "spoke out" by voting. But Yvonne was right—it was hard to understand how that could happen in the United States of America in 1963!

Poppa was shaking his head. "It's a shame that colored people today still have to be afraid of standing up or speaking out for themselves."

"Negroes," Mommy corrected him.

"Black people," Yvonne said firmly.

"Well, what *are* we supposed to call ourselves?" Lila asked.

Melody thought about how her grandparents usually said "colored." They were older and from the South, and Big Momma said that's what was proper when they were growing up. Mommy and Daddy mostly said "Negroes." But ever since she went to college, Yvonne was saying "black people." Melody noticed that Mommy and Daddy were saying it sometimes, too. She liked the way it went with "white people," like a matched set. But sometimes she wished they didn't need all these color words at all. Melody

spoke up. "What about 'Americans'?" she said.

Yvonne still seemed upset. "That's right, Dee-Dee. We're Americans. We have the same rights as white Americans. There shouldn't be any separate water fountains or waiting rooms or public bathrooms. Black Americans deserve equal treatment and equal pay. And sometimes we have to remind people."

"How do we remind them?" Lila asked. Melody was wondering the same thing.

"By not shopping at stores that won't hire black workers," Yvonne explained. "By picketing in front of a restaurant that won't serve black people. By marching."

"You won't catch me protesting or picketing or marching in any street," Dwayne interrupted, working on his third helping of potatoes. "I'm gonna be onstage or in the recording studio, making music and getting famous."

Mr. Ellison shook his head, and Melody knew there was going to be another argument, the way there always was when Dwayne talked about becoming a music star.

About the Author

ERIN FALLIGANT grew up in the seventies, ten years after Melody's stories take place. But like Melody, she loved singing into her hairbrush to music from Motown star Diana Ross. Erin had a passion for writing stories—and dreamed of becoming an author one day. Now she has written more than 25 books for children, including advice books, picture books, and contemporary fiction. Erin writes from her home in Madison, Wisconsin, and often takes breaks to cuddle with a cat or to turn up the music and dance.

About the Author

DENISE LEWIS PATRICK grew up in the town of Natchitoches, Louisiana. Lots of relatives lived nearby, so there was always someone watching out for her and always someone to play with. Every week, Denise and her brother went to the library, where she would read and dream in the children's room overlooking a wonderful river. She wrote and illustrated her first book when she was ten. Today, Denise lives in New Jersey, but she loves returning to her hometown and taking her four sons to all the places she enjoyed as a child.

Advisory Board

*American Girl extends its deepest appreciation
to the advisory board that authenticated Melody's stories.*

Julian Bond
Chairman Emeritus, NAACP Board of Directors, and founding
member of Student Nonviolent Coordinating Committee (SNCC)

Rebecca de Schweinitz
Associate Professor of History, Brigham Young University,
and author of *If We Could Change the World: Young People and
America's Long Struggle for Racial Equality* (Chapel Hill:
University of North Carolina Press, 2009)

Gloria House
Director and Professor Emerita, African and African American
Studies, University of Michigan–Dearborn, and SNCC Field
Secretary, Lowndes County, Alabama, 1963-1965

Juanita Moore
President and CEO of Charles H. Wright Museum of
African American History, Detroit, and founding executive director
of the National Civil Rights Museum, Memphis, Tennessee

Thomas J. Sugrue
Professor of History, New York University, and author of
*Sweet Land of Liberty: The Forgotten Struggle for Civil Rights
in the North* (Random House, 2008)

JoAnn Watson
Native of Detroit, ordained minister, and former
executive director of the Detroit NAACP

No Ordinary Sound

A Melody Classic
Volume 1

by Denise Lewis Patrick

★ AmericanGirl®

Published by American Girl Publishing

16 17 18 19 20 21 22 LEO 10 9 8 7 6 5 4 3

All American Girl marks, BeForever™, Melody™,
and Melody Ellison™ are trademarks of American Girl.

"Shop Around" composed by Smokey Robinson and Berry Gordy.
"Please Mr. Postman" composed by Georgia Dobbins, William Garrett, Freddie
Gorman, Brian Holland, and Robert Batemen.

This book is a work of fiction. Any similarity to real persons, living or dead,
is coincidental and not intended by American Girl. References to real events,
people, or places are used fictitiously. Other names, characters, places, and
incidents are the products of imagination.

Cover image by Michael Dwornik and Juliana Kolesova
Cover photo of crowd reflection © Bob Adelman/Corbis
Author photo by Fran Baltzer Photo

Cataloging-in-Publication Data available from the Library of Congress

© 2016 American Girl. All rights reserved. Todos los derechos reservados. Tous droits réservés. All American Girl marks are trademarks of American Girl. Marcas registradas utilizadas bajo licencia. American Girl ainsi que les marques et designs y afférents appartiennent à American Girl. **MADE IN CHINA. HECHO EN CHINA. FABRIQUÉ EN CHINE.** Retain this address for future reference: American Girl, 8400 Fairway Place, Middleton, WI 53562, U.S.A. Importado y distribuido por A.G. México Retail, S. de R.L. de C.V., Miguel de Cervantes Saavedra No. 193 pisos 10 y 11, Col. Granada, Delegación Miguel Hidalgo, C.P. 11520 México, D.F. Conserver ces informations pour s'y référer en cas de besoin. American Girl Canada, 8400 Fairway Place, Middleton, WI 53562, U.S.A.

To everyone who hears the call of justice, and answers.

Beforever™

The adventurous characters you'll meet in the BeForever books will spark your curiosity about the past, inspire you to find your voice in the present, and excite you about your future. You'll make friends with these girls as you share their fun and their challenges. Like you, they are bright and brave, imaginative and energetic, creative and kind. Just as you are, they are discovering what really matters: Helping others. Being a true friend. Protecting the earth. Standing up for what's right. Read their stories, explore their worlds, join their adventures. Your friendship with them will BeForever.

♪ TABLE *of* CONTENTS ♪

1	Meet the Ellisons	1
2	Table Talk	10
3	Let Your Light Shine	23
4	Another Home	31
5	Dances and Dollars	42
6	Mother's Day Surprises	55
7	A Family Reunion	66
8	Signs and Songs	83
9	The Power Inside	92
10	What Feels Right	107
11	The Walk to Freedom	116
12	Fireworks	128
13	Practice	147
14	Never Give Up	159
15	One Sunday	173
16	Scary Stuff	180
17	Whispers	192
18	Voices Lifted	205
	Inside Melody's World	216

When Melody's story takes place, the terms "Negro," "colored," and "black" were all used to describe Americans of African descent. You'll see all of those words used in this book.

Today, "Negro" and "colored" can be offensive because they are associated with racial inequality. "African American" is a more contemporary term, but it wasn't commonly used until the late 1980s.

Meet the Ellisons

♪ CHAPTER 1 ♪

It was a perfect day in May, and Melody Ellison could hardly wait for her father to pull the car to a stop in front of her grandparents' house. Every Sunday, Melody and her family had dinner here after church. But today was different. Melody was almost bursting with news. She hopped out of the station wagon so quickly that she forgot to hold the door for her sister Lila, who was coming out behind her.

"Hey!" Lila shouted, but nine-year-old Melody was already halfway up the front walk. She only slowed to look at the purple petunias clustered near the steps. Then she skipped up to the front porch and peered into the big front windows. She could hear music coming from inside, and couldn't help tapping her shiny shoes. Music always made her want to *move*.

♪ No Ordinary Sound ♪

"What are you so hot after?" asked Dwayne, Melody's older brother. His long legs had brought him around the car and up behind her in only a few steps.

"I'm not hot," Melody answered, before she realized that Dwayne was joking. He only meant that she was excited, and she was. She couldn't hold her surprise in any longer.

"Miss Dorothy asked me to sing a solo for Youth Day," she said proudly. Youth Day was far away in October, but it was the biggest children's program at their church. Kids from all over the city came to sing, play music, recite poetry, and even perform in skits. Only a few kids got the chance to stand in front to sing solo parts, and they had to be very, very good.

Dwayne raised his eyebrows, and Melody watched his face nervously. It wasn't easy to impress him. Dwayne was eighteen, and he'd done his first solo when he was eight.

"Wow, congratulations!" he said. "You've gotta write Yvonne and tell her."

Melody grinned. Yvonne was their oldest sister, who was away at college. She was a good singer too. In fact, all the members of Melody's family were musical.

♪ Meet the Ellisons ♪

"I will," she promised. "As soon as we get home."

"Tell Yvonne what?" Lila joined them, trying to balance a plate with their mother's foil-wrapped triple-chocolate cake and push her eyeglasses up on her nose at the same time.

"Melody's going to be the star of the New Hope Baptist Church Youth Day," he said, grabbing the plate as it wobbled. "Just like I'm going to be the biggest Motown star since Smokey Robinson."

"I don't know," Lila sniffed matter-of-factly, and nodded toward Melody. "Dee-Dee might beat you to it." Lila was thirteen, and sometimes acted like she knew everything in the world.

"Not me." Melody shook her head. She liked to pretend she was a singing star at home, using her hairbrush as a microphone. But she didn't like to be in the spotlight. She felt safe from her spot in the children's choir when the congregation was full of the church family she'd known all her life. But she was nervous about standing alone on Youth Day, in front of a big crowd full of faces she didn't know.

Melody's parents crowded onto the porch. The delicious aroma of Big Momma's pot roast and gravy

♪ No Ordinary Sound ♪

wafted outside. "Boy, that sure smells good, doesn't it?" Melody's father whispered.

Melody's tummy answered with a gurgle, and she nodded.

Melody's mother laughed. "Will, you always did think my mother was the best cook in the world."

"Well, she is, Frances!" Mr. Ellison said, loosening his tie.

"Did anybody ring the doorbell?" Lila asked.

Melody shook her head and reached out to push the bell. Just then, Big Momma swung open the door.

Melody had always thought it was funny that they called her grandmother Big Momma, since she wasn't much taller than Melody. But the name was a sign of respect. Besides, when her grandmother sang, her voice was very big.

"Hello, my chicks!" Big Momma said. She greeted each of her grandchildren with a rose-scented squeeze.

"Big Momma, this is Detroit, Michigan. You left all your chickens back in Alabama, remember?" Dwayne said, ducking out of her arms.

Melody lingered a little longer, until Lila nudged her to get a turn. But when Lila strolled over to check

♪ Meet the Ellisons ♪

out the latest magazines on the coffee table, Big Momma folded her arms and gave Melody a stern look. "I believe you've got something to tell me," she said.

"Yes!" Melody exclaimed. "Miss Dorothy asked me to learn a solo over the summer for the Youth Day pro—" She stopped. Big Momma was smiling and nodding. Melody stared at her grandmother in wonder. "You already knew!" Melody said. "How?"

"Are you kidding?" Lila said from the sofa. "Big Momma and Miss Dorothy are best friends. They tell each other everything. They were in a gospel singing group together before we were even born."

Big Momma laughed. "Yes, Dorothy and I trained to be music teachers together back in Alabama, and we traveled around singing in churches. She says you're ready to carry a song on your own."

"Who is ready for what?" Melody's mother asked from the dining room.

"Melody's doing a Youth Day solo," Lila told her.

"Oh, that's wonderful, honey!" Mrs. Ellison clapped her hands and rushed to give Melody a hug.

"Thanks, Mommy," Melody said, suddenly feeling shy at all the attention.

♪ No Ordinary Sound ♪

"I believe our Melody is ready to sing out," Mr. Ellison said, as he placed extra chairs at the dining table. Melody heard the pride in his voice and wished she felt as confident as he did. She tugged at the end of her braid.

Big Momma put her arm around Melody's shoulders. "It's okay to be nervous, baby chick," she said, reading Melody's mind. "You have all summer to practice. I'll help."

"But what about your students?" Melody asked. Big Momma taught piano and voice lessons to kids and grown-ups, right in her living room.

"Don't worry, I'll find the time."

"Thanks, Big Momma." Melody felt her nerves flutter again. But she felt good knowing that her family believed so much in her. She skipped into the dining room, where Lila was setting the blue plates onto the yellow-checked tablecloth.

"Remember," Melody's mother said, handing Melody a stack of paper napkins. "We've been a musical family for generations."

"See? I *knew* I was born to be a big name in the music business!" Dwayne said. He did a quick

♪ Meet the Ellisons ♪

spinning dance move before he set a basket of rolls on the table.

Melody laughed as she carefully folded each napkin into a triangle and tucked one beside every plate.

"You're so silly!" Lila said to him, shaking her head.

"The thing about Youth Day is that I get to pick my own song," Melody told her brother. "But I don't know which one to sing."

"We could try some songs after dinner." Dwayne winked at Melody. She knew he took every chance he could to play Big Momma's beloved piano.

"*After* dinner means we need to *eat* dinner first, doesn't it?" Melody's father said.

"But we can't start without Poppa," Dwayne said.

Melody looked up from the napkins. Where was her grandfather, anyway, she wondered, turning to Big Momma.

Big Momma shrugged, but Melody saw a twinkle in her eyes. Before Melody could ask anything, she heard the back door of the house open and shut. Poppa's heavy footsteps crossed the floor.

"Hello!" his voice boomed. Poppa always talked loud. Melody's mother said it was because of his work around all the loud machines years ago at the auto factory. Melody liked the sound—it reminded her of drumbeats.

"Guess who I brought to dinner!" Poppa called from the kitchen.

Everyone turned in his direction. He opened the door wider, and there stood Yvonne with a huge smile on her face.

"Surprise!" she sang.

"Vonnie!" Melody ran around the table to give her big sister a hug.

"We didn't expect you till next week!" Mrs. Ellison said. Melody could tell that her mother was very happy. Yvonne had been gone since January.

"I took all my exams and I finished my last paper early, so I caught the bus," Yvonne explained. "Poppa picked me up at the Detroit terminal. Boy, that ride from Alabama takes forever!" She barely took a breath before dropping her bag and greeting everyone. "Wow, Dee-Dee. Did you get taller? Got any new sounds, Dwayne? Lila, are those new glasses? Dad, you're wearing the birthday shirt we gave you! Big Momma, that roast smells really good. And Mommy, I know you

♪ Meet the Ellisons ♪

made your triple-chocolate cake. Can we eat?"

Melody laughed. College hadn't changed Yvonne's habit of talking a mile a minute.

Big Momma brought the roast in and everyone took their places around the table, with Poppa at one end and Daddy at the other. And now the family was truly all together, the way their Sundays used to be.

"Dee-Dee, why don't you sing grace for us?" her father said.

"Yes, Daddy," Melody said. She felt comfortable singing in front of *this* crowd. She bowed her head and sang in a strong, clear voice:

> *By Thy hands must we be fed;*
> *Give us, Lord, our daily bread.*

Table Talk

♪ CHAPTER 2 ♪

o," Yvonne said, "what's the news? What have I been missing?" She glanced around the table.

"I'm doing double shifts at the factory again this week," Daddy told her.

Melody opened her mouth to speak, but Mommy beat her to it.

"There's a lot of talk about some of the city schools only having half days next year," she said.

Everyone looked up at that. "Really?" Yvonne asked.

Mommy nodded. "Can you believe that? School three or four hours a day? Children need as much time as they can get to learn. We teachers are against it, but the district says there may not be enough money for full days."

♪ Table Talk ♪

"Wish they'd shortened the days when I was in school!" Dwayne grunted.

"I have news . . ." Melody started to say. But Yvonne nodded in Dwayne's direction.

"What's up with you?" she asked him.

"Not much," Dwayne said, leaning over his almost empty plate.

Melody looked at him curiously. When he wasn't working at the factory, Dwayne was always busy singing with his friends or writing new music—and playing Big Momma's piano every chance he could get. Why would he tell Yvonne "not much"? She wanted to ask him, but she also wanted her turn.

Melody waved her fork in the air at her sister, trying not to see Mommy frowning at her poor table manners. "Vonnie, I was going to write you, but now I can tell you in person."

"Spill it, Dee-Dee!" Yvonne laughed.

"I'm going to sing my first solo!"

"In the Mother's Day program next week?" Yvonne asked.

"No, Miss Dorothy picked me for the Youth Day program. I have the whole summer to learn a song."

♪ No Ordinary Sound ♪

"That's great!" Yvonne said. "Now you can show that girl—what's her name? The one who always tries to boss the other singers around?"

"You mean Diane Harris?" Melody made a face. Diane was in the same fourth-grade class as Melody and took piano lessons from Big Momma. She had a nice voice, but she wasn't at all nice about that.

"I hear she's a solo hog," Dwayne mumbled with his mouth full.

"We can't be jealous of other people's gifts," Mommy said to Dwayne sternly. She turned to Melody. "Besides, didn't you just say that Miss Dorothy asked *you* to sing a solo?"

"Yes." Melody looked down, twiddling her fingers in her lap. "But I'm really not as good as Diane."

"Who says that?" Daddy asked.

Melody said out loud what she'd been thinking since Miss Dorothy's request. "Well, Diane has a big, grown-up voice, and I only have a girl voice." She looked at Dwayne, expecting him to remind her that she *was* only a girl. He didn't say anything.

"Everybody's got a right to shine, baby chick," Big Momma said. "Diane does and you do, too.

♪ Table Talk ♪

You've got a beautiful voice, and plenty of other gifts."

"What about that green thumb of yours?" Poppa reminded her.

Lila said, "I bet Diane can't name every car off the Ford line, the way you can!"

Melody smiled. It was true that she was good at all those things. And she liked being good at them, too. But Diane was so sure of herself when she sang! She could hear a song once and sing it without one mistake. Melody remembered music easily, but she had to practice and practice to get the words right.

"You're a hard worker, Melody. That's a gift, too," Mommy said, and then turned to Yvonne. "Speaking of hard work, how was your second year at Tuskegee?"

"Yes, Vonnie. Did you study all the time?" Melody asked. Mommy had gone to Tuskegee, and this year Dwayne had applied and been accepted. Melody knew that her parents hoped all their children would graduate from Tuskegee one day, too.

Yvonne shook her head so that her small earrings sparkled. "There's so much more to do at school besides studying," she said, reaching for more gravy.

♪ No Ordinary Sound ♪

"Like what?" Poppa asked, propping his elbows on the table. Melody held back a giggle when she saw Big Momma frown the same way Mommy had, but Poppa paid no attention.

"Well, last week before finals a bunch of us went out to help black people in the community register to vote," Yvonne said. "And do you know, a lady told me she was too afraid to sign up."

"Why was she afraid?" Melody interrupted.

"Because somebody threw a rock through her next-door neighbor's window after her neighbor voted," Yvonne explained, her eyes flashing with anger. "This is 1963! How can anybody get away with that?"

Melody looked from Yvonne to her father. "You always say not voting is like not being able to talk. Why wouldn't anybody want to talk?"

Daddy sighed. "It's not that she doesn't want to vote, Melody. There are a lot of unfair rules down South that keep our people from exercising their rights. Some white people will do anything, including scaring black people, to keep change from happening. They don't want to share jobs or neighborhoods or schools with us. Voting is like a man or woman's voice

♪ Table Talk ♪

speaking out to change those laws and rules."

"And it's not just about voting," Mommy said. "Remember what Rosa Parks did in Montgomery? She stood up for her rights."

"You mean she *sat down* for her rights," Melody said. Melody knew all about Mrs. Parks, who got arrested for simply sitting down on a city bus. She had paid her fare like everybody else, but because she was a Negro the bus driver told her she had to give her seat to a white person! *But that happened eight years ago,* Melody realized. *Why haven't things changed?*

"Aren't we just as good as anybody else?" Melody asked as she looked around the table. "The laws should be fair everywhere, for everybody, right?"

"That's not always the way life works," Poppa said.

"Why not?" Lila asked.

Poppa sat back and rubbed his silvery mustache. That always meant he was about to tell a story.

"Back in Alabama, there was a white farmer who owned the land next to ours. Palmer was his name. Decent fellow. We went into town the same day to sell our peanut crops. It wasn't a good growing year, but I'd lucked out with twice as many sacks of peanuts as

🎵 No Ordinary Sound 🎵

Palmer. Well, at the market they counted and weighed his sacks. Then they counted and weighed my sacks. Somehow Palmer got twice as much money as I got for selling half the crop I had. They never even checked the quality of what we had, either."

"What?" Lila blurted out.

"How?" Melody scooted to the edge of her chair.

"Wait, now." Poppa waved his grandchildren quiet. "I asked the man to weigh it again, but he refused. I complained. Even Palmer spoke up for me. But that man turned to me and said, 'Boy—'"

"He called you *boy*?" Dwayne interrupted, putting his fork down.

"'Boy,'" Poppa continued, "'this is all you're gonna get. And if you keep up this trouble, you won't have any farm to go back to!'"

Melody's mouth fell open. "What was he talking about? You did have a farm," she said, glancing at Big Momma.

"He meant we were in danger of losing our farm—our home—because your grandfather spoke out to a white man," Big Momma explained. She shook her head slowly. "As hard as we'd worked to buy that land,

♪ Table Talk ♪

as hard as it was for colored people to own anything in Alabama, we decided that day that we had to sell and move north."

Although Melody had heard many of her grandfather's stories about life in Alabama before, she'd never heard this one. And as she considered it, she realized that on their many trips down South, she'd never seen the old family farm. Maybe her grandparents didn't want to go back.

Melody sighed. Maybe the lady Yvonne mentioned didn't want to risk losing *her* home if she "spoke out" by voting. But Yvonne was right—it was hard to understand how that could happen in the United States of America in 1963!

Poppa was shaking his head. "It's a shame that colored people today still have to be afraid of standing up or speaking out for themselves."

"Negroes," Mommy corrected him.

"Black people," Yvonne said firmly.

"Well, what *are* we supposed to call ourselves?" Lila asked.

Melody thought about how her grandparents usually said "colored." They were older and from the

♪ No Ordinary Sound ♪

South, and Big Momma said that's what was proper when they were growing up. Mommy and Daddy mostly said "Negroes." But ever since she went to college, Yvonne was saying "black people." Melody noticed that Mommy and Daddy were saying it sometimes, too. She liked the way it went with "white people," like a matched set. But sometimes she wished they didn't need all these color words at all. Melody spoke up. "What about 'Americans'?" she said.

Yvonne still seemed upset. "That's right, Dee-Dee. We're Americans. We have the same rights as white Americans. There shouldn't be any separate water fountains or waiting rooms or public bathrooms. Black Americans deserve equal treatment and equal pay. And sometimes we have to remind people."

"How do we remind them?" Lila asked. Melody was wondering the same thing.

"By not shopping at stores that won't hire black workers," Yvonne explained. "By picketing in front of a restaurant that won't serve black people. By marching."

"You won't catch me protesting or picketing or marching in any street," Dwayne interrupted, working on his third helping of potatoes. "I'm gonna be onstage

♪ Table Talk ♪

or in the recording studio, making music and getting famous."

Mr. Ellison shook his head, and Melody knew there was going to be another argument, the way there always was when Dwayne talked about becoming a music star.

"Don't forget," Daddy said, "when you graduated high school early, we agreed that you'd work in the factory until the summer was over, and then go on to college. I couldn't go to college, and now I'm working double shifts at a factory so you can! You could *study* music in college!"

Mommy was nodding. Melody knew that her parents were disappointed whenever Dwayne talked about skipping college. She saw Dwayne stop eating to look down at his plate—not at his father—and she felt bad for her brother. Melody hated when they argued. So when her brother looked as if he might say something, Melody interrupted.

"Daddy," Melody said. "Dwayne can sing and write music already, and he can play the piano almost as good as Big Momma can. He's really talented. It's like Big Momma says—everybody's got a right to shine."

♪ No Ordinary Sound ♪

Daddy smiled at Melody. "I hope your brother is smart enough to appreciate it when you girls stick up for him," he said. "But with a college degree, your brother would have a whole lot of opportunities."

"Let's save this talk for later," Mommy said.

Melody blew out a relieved breath. She didn't want their great day to be ruined by a disagreement.

"I say everybody needs to cool down with some ice cream and cake," Big Momma said. She got up and headed for the kitchen.

Dwayne escaped to the living room. Yvonne stayed at the table, talking to their father and grandfather about her plans for a summer job. Melody gathered the salt and pepper shakers, which were shaped like two fat penguins, got up, and put them away.

A soft, slow tune was coming from Big Momma's piano. Dwayne was playing, making up a new song. Melody listened for him to sing some words, but there weren't any. Maybe he hadn't thought of them yet. She wandered to the archway between the rooms just as the phone beside the sofa rang.

"Children, answer that for me!" Big Momma called from the kitchen.

♪ Table Talk ♪

Melody started into the living room, but Dwayne had already grabbed the big black telephone receiver without noticing her.

"Hello!" Dwayne answered breathlessly. And then, instead of calling either of his grandparents or taking a message, he lowered his voice.

"Yeah?" he almost whispered. "Make it quick. I told you this is my grandfather's number. Okay. I'm working on the song now. I'll meet you later."

"Who is it?" Poppa asked from the table. Dwayne dropped the receiver into the cradle with a clatter.

"Are you getting calls from your girlfriends on my telephone?" Poppa laughed. So did Daddy and Yvonne.

"No, sir," Dwayne called quickly. His eyes met Melody's. He had a funny expression on his face. She'd heard him talking to girls on the phone before, and that wasn't how he'd sounded. Dwayne definitely had a secret.

"Was that about your singing group?" she asked.

Dwayne pulled her farther into the living room. "Yeah, but after that scrape with Dad, I'd rather not announce this, okay? That was Artie's brother. He just got hired as a musician at Motown, and he's gonna try

♪ No Ordinary Sound ♪

to get us an audition." Artie was Dwayne's buddy and a member of his singing group, The Detroiters.

"That's so exciting, Dwayne!" Melody exclaimed.

"Shhh," Dwayne insisted. "Can you keep it a secret?"

Melody pinched her finger and thumb together and slid them across her lips, as if she were closing a zipper. That was the signal she and her brother and sisters used with one another, meaning, "I won't tell anyone!"

Dwayne's shoulders relaxed, and he went back to the piano. Melody followed.

Dwayne held his hands dramatically over the piano keys. "How about you singing this for your Youth Day solo?" he said, beginning to play and sing something different—and lively. *"Grandpa Poppa had a farm . . ."*

Melody giggled, shaking her head at how he'd changed the words of the old kindergarten rhyme. From all around the house, her family joined in:

"E-i-e-i-ohhhh!"

Let Your Light Shine

♪ CHAPTER 3 ♪

The next morning, Melody and Lila left home together to walk to school. Lila's junior high was only two blocks away from Melody's elementary school. As usual, they had trouble untangling Bojangles, their small mixed terrier, from their legs when they got to the front door. Lila took Bo's red ball from the bag hanging on the coat tree and tossed it. And as usual, he fell for the trick and went scampering after the ball. The girls hurried out.

At the corner, they paused to wait for Melody's best friend, Sharon. Sharon lived three blocks up the street, and Melody always watched to see her front gate swing open as Sharon ran to meet them. Sharon always ran.

"Hey!" Sharon waved as her strong legs flew along the sidewalk.

Melody was eager to see if Sharon had remembered

♪ No Ordinary Sound ♪

that it was "Matching Monday," and had worn red hair ribbons as they'd planned. "You didn't forget!" Melody said.

"'Course not," Sharon said, turning her head so Melody could admire the crisply ironed satin ribbons that were tied in neat bows at the tops of her two pigtails.

"Nice." Melody nodded and checked quickly to see if her own red ribbons were still tied tightly. They were.

"So, are you super excited about Youth Day?" Sharon asked. They were both in the children's choir. "What are you going to sing?"

"I don't know yet," Melody answered.

"Does it have to be a church song?"

Melody hadn't considered that question. Both girls looked at Lila, who was walking and reading a book at the same time.

"Lila, Mommy told you to stop doing that," Melody reminded her sister.

"Yeah," Sharon chimed in. "Didn't you run right into a light post one time while you were reading?"

Lila glared at them. She slapped her book closed and promptly dropped it. Melody picked it up.

♪ Let Your Light Shine ♪

"Anyway," Melody continued, "did you hear Sharon? About the song?"

"Yes," Lila said. "And of course it has to be a church song, sillies. It's a program at the church!"

Melody hadn't said a word about Dwayne's secret to her sisters or even to Sharon. But the tune that he had been playing on Big Momma's piano snuck into Melody's head during her morning math class, and stayed there through her spelling quiz. At lunchtime, she tapped her milk carton to the rhythm while Sharon and a boy named Julius argued about the Detroit Tigers baseball team.

By the time she and Sharon lined up for dodgeball in gym that afternoon, Melody was humming her brother's nameless, wordless tune out loud. A high-pitched voice spoke behind her.

"What's *that* song?" It was Diane Harris.

Melody glanced at Sharon. They always thought it was interesting that Diane's speaking voice was high and screechy, but that when she opened her mouth to sing, such a smooth sound came out.

♪ No Ordinary Sound ♪

"Just music in my head," Melody said. She wouldn't give away anything about Dwayne's new creation.

"Well, I've never heard it before," Diane said, as if she'd heard all the music in the entire world. She blew a big bubble-gum bubble, and popped it.

Melody took a deep breath, thinking of what Big Momma had said about letting other people shine. "I guess you're one of the first, then," Melody said.

"Harris!" the gym teacher shouted. "Gum in the trash can! Ellison, you lead Team One."

Melody smiled and stepped forward. She wasn't very good at sports, so whenever she got a chance to make up a team, she tried to pick some kids who were good and some who weren't. Julius was chosen as captain of Team Two. He picked Sharon before Melody could. It was no surprise that Diane was the last to be picked. It wasn't that she was a bad player—she was just so bossy! She always seemed to think *she* was the team captain.

"Okay, Harris," the teacher called. "You're on Team One. Let's go!"

Diane waved Melody over. "I'll tell you how to position everybody," she said as the class trailed out to

♪ Let Your Light Shine ♪

the playground. "Our team is pretty weak except for me, so—"

Before Diane could finish, Melody thought of something Mommy always said when things didn't quite go the way she'd planned. "That's okay," Melody said cheerfully. "We'll make it work."

The game was fierce and fun. The score was tied just before the bell rang. Diane sent the ball flying in Team Two's direction. Julius dodged it. Sharon jumped up to catch it. All at once the ball was sailing back. Melody jumped up, but it bounced right off her fingers.

"I got it!" Diane yelled, running from the back of the field. She spiked the ball back. Then the bell sounded, and most of the kids ran for the school building.

"See, I should have been in front because I'm taller," Diane grumbled. "It was a lucky win."

"It's a win just the same, right?" Melody smiled at her as Sharon jogged up to them. Diane walked on by without saying anything.

"Right," Sharon whispered, before the girls went inside arm in arm.

♪ No Ordinary Sound ♪

After school, Melody said good-bye to Sharon at her corner. "See you at choir rehearsal!" she called as she raced ahead of Lila. Melody was hoping that Yvonne was home and that the three sisters could spend time together the way they used to before Yvonne went away to college. They ate cookies and combed one another's hair, and talked about anything that popped into their heads without Dwayne or their parents hearing. The "sister-thing" was what Yvonne called it.

"Why are you and Sharon always running?" Lila yelled after her. But Melody was already at the front door, pulling magazines and envelopes out of the mailbox.

"See? You had to wait for me anyway," Lila laughed, pulling out her heart-shaped key ring. Inside, Bo barked excitedly at the sound of their voices. Melody flipped through the mail in her hand. There was a small purple envelope in the bunch. She saw her own name written across the front in careful cursive handwriting.

"Oh! I got a letter from Val!" she said. Val was their

♪ Let Your Light Shine ♪

cousin who lived in Alabama. She was between Lila and Melody in age, and she was Melody's favorite playmate when they drove down to visit family every summer. Val and Melody had been pen pals since Melody was in second grade.

Lila looked interested. "What's she say this time?"

Melody ripped open the envelope as soon as she stepped inside and began reading out loud.

"*Dear Dee-Dee. How are you and—*"

"Skip that part," Lila said. She bent to pet Bo. He rolled onto his back and stuck his paws in the air.

"Okay. *You'll explode when you hear my news. We are moving to Detroit as soon as school is over!* What?" Melody screamed, forgetting all about the sister-thing. This news was even more surprising than Dwayne's secret.

Even Lila was surprised. "That's big!" she said. Bo sat up and barked in agreement.

"What's big?" Yvonne yawned, padding downstairs barefoot and still in pajamas.

Melody waved the letter in the air. "Val and her mom and dad are moving to Detroit!"

"That sure is news," Yvonne said. "I wonder what made Charles and Tish decide to move?"

♪ No Ordinary Sound ♪

"I don't know," Melody answered. "But I can't wait!"

"I think this calls for a celebration, don't you?" Yvonne asked.

"Yes!" Both Lila and Melody answered at once.

"Great." Yvonne rubbed her hands together. "Now, I think we need to start by raiding Dwayne's cookie stash."

Lila grinned. "They're hidden in the cupboard behind—"

"—the tuna fish!" Melody finished.

When Dwayne came home from his factory job an hour later, the house was full of loud singing coming from upstairs. There was an empty vanilla wafer box on the kitchen table.

"This little light of mine, I'm gonna let it shine!"

"Oh, man! Not the sister-thing again!" he yelled. But no one heard him over the laughter, which was even louder than the singing.

Another Home

♪ CHAPTER 4 ♪

That evening, after a quick dinner, Melody's mother drove the girls to choir rehearsal. Yvonne decided to tag along since their father was working a double shift and Dwayne was working an evening shift. Melody had been so busy getting her homework done that she hadn't had a chance to tell her mother about Val's move until they were all in the car.

"Mommy," Melody said from the backseat, "I got a letter from Val today. She said they're moving to Detroit, and they're coming as soon as school is over!"

Mommy looked at Melody in the rearview mirror. She didn't seem surprised.

"Yes, Big Momma told me a few weeks ago," Mommy said. "Until they find a house of their own, they'll be staying with Big Momma and Poppa."

♪ No Ordinary Sound ♪

Melody's grandparents lived just a few blocks away from the Ellisons. "That means I can walk over to see Val all the time," Melody announced. "We can do everything together!" *I couldn't have come up with a better plan myself,* she thought.

"Val has lived in Birmingham her whole life," Lila told Melody matter-of-factly. "Detroit sure is different. It's going to take her a while to get used to things."

Yvonne nodded. "I hope she'll like it here."

"Of course she will, Vonnie . . ." Melody said. But then she was quiet for a moment. Melody realized that she'd lived her whole life in the same house. It wouldn't be easy if she had to leave her neighborhood.

"Do you think Val is bringing her bike?" Lila asked, breaking the silence in the car.

"I don't know," Mommy answered. "All of their belongings will be coming on a moving truck later. The bike might take a while, so you girls will have to share some of your things with Val. You'll have to—"

"—make it work!" both Mommy and Melody said at the same time. Melody sounded exactly like Mommy, which made everyone laugh as they pulled up in front of New Hope Baptist Church.

♪ Another Home ♪

When Melody got out of the car, she heard the voices of the adult choir floating out of the open doors. She ran up the steps into the church and sat on the first pew inside the door. She closed her eyes and soaked in the sounds.

"This is my story, this is my song." A single soprano voice hit the notes and sang the words beautifully, clearly. The music echoed inside Melody's body. She opened her eyes and looked at the tall stained-glass windows. On Sunday mornings, they sparkled like jewels when the sunshine poured in.

Melody's sisters soon slid onto the bench, one on either side, and she was squeezed between them just like when she was small and Yvonne snuck her lemon drops to keep her from wiggling during the service. Melody smiled to herself at the memory. Now that she was older, she didn't wiggle during church. She listened to the pastor and to the music. She loved the Sundays when the children's choir sang and she stood in front, looking out at her family. Melody also loved the Sundays when she sat in the pews with her whole family. It was one of the few times they were all together. *And soon Val will be here, too!* she thought.

♪ No Ordinary Sound ♪

Melody listened to the soloist sing the last lines of the hymn.

Watching and waiting, looking above,
Filled with His goodness, lost in His love.

That's how Melody felt in church. There was goodness all around. When the song ended, it seemed that her heart beat a little bit differently.

Melody was still swaying to the tune inside her head when Miss Dorothy walked past them, shuffling her sheet music.

"Hey, there's Miss Dorothy. Let's go." Lila pulled Melody up. The adults filed out of the choir stand, some going home after their long workday. Some, who were the parents of the children, went to sit in the back of the church to watch and wait.

Kids started filling in the choir stand. Melody saw Sharon run in, and she watched Diane take her seat in the front row.

As everyone gathered, Miss Dorothy started playing the piano softly. She knew everything about music. Like Big Momma, Miss Dorothy knew just how to talk

♪ Another Home ♪

to a singer to help make her voice better. And like Big Momma, Miss Dorothy could read and play from sheet music, or she could hear a tune and then play it herself without any music at all.

Melody thought Miss Dorothy was pretty amazing. She wished she could have heard her and Big Momma sing together back in the day. That would have been amazing, too.

When all the children were in place, Miss Dorothy walked in front of the choir and stood with her hands clasped behind her back. That was the sign for everyone to stop talking.

"All right, choir," she said. "On Sunday we'll be honoring all the New Hope mothers. We want to do our very best, don't we?"

"Yes, Miss Dorothy!"

"Remember that this will be our last choir rehearsal for this school year," Miss Dorothy went on. "I know all of you will spend some time singing over the summer. When school begins in September, we'll begin practicing for Youth Day. Melody, our soloist—I want you to find a song to sing. Your grandmother and I will start working on it with you over the summer if you'd like."

♪ No Ordinary Sound ♪

"Yes, Miss Dorothy," Melody said happily.

Diane leaned over to the girl next to her and loudly whispered, "If *I* were doing a solo, I wouldn't need the whole summer to practice."

Melody felt her face burn with hot embarrassment. Yvonne, who was sitting in the back of the church, stood up and crossed her arms over her chest. Melody was afraid she might say something, but then Miss Dorothy cleared her throat. Yvonne sat down again.

"Remember, even when one of us does a solo, we all work together," Miss Dorothy said sternly. "We all support one another. That's very important in a choir. The chorus helps the soloist. The soloist helps the chorus. Let's *all* remember that." She clicked her baton on the edge of the piano. "Now, choir, rise!"

Everyone stood. After Miss Dorothy led the group in vocal warm-ups, she repositioned the microphone in front of Diane, who was doing a solo for Mother's Day.

Diane stood straight and tall. She didn't blink. She didn't seem nervous at all. Melody had to admit that when she thought of her own faraway solo, she thought about what could go wrong. When Diane sang by herself, she acted as if she expected that everything would

♪ Another Home ♪

go right. She had what Dwayne called "stage presence."

Miss Dorothy stood at her piano and began playing. She played and directed and sang, all at the same time. Melody had always found it fascinating that she could do everything at once.

Diane sang the first line of the song. *"Be not dismayed whate'er betide . . ."*

The other children hummed in the background while Miss Dorothy played the chords. Diane sang the rest of the verse, and then the chorus came in with the refrain.

> *God will take care of you,*
> *Through every day, o'er all the way;*
> *He will take care of you,*
> *God will take care of you.*

Miss Dorothy stopped playing. "Sopranos, I can't really hear you. Let's try that again," she called out.

Melody looked at Yvonne, who was watching her. Yvonne cupped her hand behind her ear and grinned. She was telling Melody to sing out. When the choir began again, Melody heard Lila clearly in the row

♪ No Ordinary Sound ♪

behind her, and Sharon beside her. Encouraged by their voices and by Yvonne's smile, Melody sang louder. Miss Dorothy nodded her approval.

"Well done," Miss Dorothy said. "Let's go on to 'His Eye Is on the Sparrow.'"

Miss Dorothy played the first chords. Diane began to sing again, and she did sound wonderful. Melody looked out and saw Mommy come in to sit down beside Yvonne. When it was time for the chorus, Melody sang out with all her heart.

> *I sing because I'm happy. I sing because I'm free.*
> *His eye is on the sparrow, and I know He watches me.*

Melody felt the entire choir's sound swell around her, and she was filled with a peaceful calm that made her feel happy and free.

After school the next day, Melody was sprawled on Big Momma's living room rug watching an old movie on TV. In it, a lady was coming home after a long trip and her friends gave her a "Welcome Back" party.

♪ Another Home ♪

Melody sat up, hugging her knees. It would be a great idea to have a party for Val! They could have cookies and punch, and she could make a big sign that said "Welcome." She could pick some flowers from her garden—pink ones, because that was Val's favorite color.

Melody didn't have any homework to do, so she could start on the sign right away. She got up to get the art supplies Big Momma kept in a shoebox. Big Momma called it the "just in case" box, just in case somebody wanted to create something beautiful.

Melody found the box in the dining room and set it on the table. Then she headed back into the living room to get the construction paper from its spot in the piano bench. Big Momma came downstairs and shut off the TV.

"Big Momma, I think we should have a welcome party for Val and her parents," Melody said excitedly. "I'm going to make a banner with all their names on it."

Big Momma smiled in approval. "That sounds like a fine idea," she said. "You go on and work quietly in the kitchen, though. It's time for my first afternoon lesson."

♪ No Ordinary Sound ♪

Melody gathered her supplies and went to the kitchen, closing the door behind her as the doorbell rang. She arranged her crayons on the table, spread her paper just so, and carefully began to outline the word "WELCOME" in big block letters. She could hear the low hum of Big Momma's voice, a few piano chords, and then a familiar child's voice.

It was Diane Harris! Melody stopped working to listen.

The metronome that Big Momma used to show her students how fast or how slow to play their music started to *tick, tick, tick*! Diane's fingers fumbled over the piano keys. "Try again," Big Momma said calmly.

The choppy playing started and stopped, and then started over very slowly.

"Go on, go on." Big Momma sounded encouraging. But suddenly the piano was silent.

"Mrs. Porter, I can't do it!" Diane said. "I'll never play the piano as well as I can sing."

What had happened to Diane's bossy gym voice, Melody wondered. *And her sure and steady choir voice?* She sounded just the way Melody felt about doing a solo—nervous.

♪ Another Home ♪

"Don't fret," Big Momma said to Diane. "This is new for you. Sometimes people are afraid of what they don't know."

Melody felt that Big Momma was speaking directly to her about the Youth Day solo.

Big Momma went on. "You have to take your time, and open your heart to learning. It may not be easy, but the things worth having usually don't come easily."

"Do you really think so?" Diane asked.

"I really do," Big Momma assured her. "You can shine with this instrument if you work hard enough."

In the kitchen, Melody smiled. *Maybe,* she thought, *Diane and I are more alike than we are different.* Melody picked up her crayon again, and drew a big yellow sun in the corner of her sign.

Dances and Dollars

♪ CHAPTER 5 ♪

On Thursday afternoon, Poppa picked Melody up from school so that she could help him in his flower shop. Poppa knew all about growing things. Melody knew that back in Alabama he had grown vegetables and fruit trees as well as peanuts on his farm, and he had an enormous flower garden. He'd taught Melody how to plan a garden and how to care for it through all the different seasons. When her flowers bloomed, Melody loved to pick a bouquet and arrange it so that all the blossoms looked their best. Putting different colors and shapes together reminded her of different voices blending together in the choir. Melody had learned so much that now Poppa let her work in the shop sorting his weekly flower shipment and getting ready for the big weekend orders.

♪ Dances and Dollars ♪

Melody settled back in the worn seat of his old work truck. It smelled like warm soil and flower petals. She inhaled deeply.

"How was school today?" Poppa asked, shifting gears.

Melody was distracted for a moment because she was watching people drive. Daddy said she was a true daughter of Detroit, the Motor City—the place where so many cars and trucks were built. Melody dreamed of driving her own car one day. She'd play the radio loud and sing along, maybe to one of Dwayne's hits . . .

"Melody?"

"Oh! Sorry, Poppa. School was okay."

"Just okay?" He gave her a curious look. "Hmm. Well, I have an idea that I think is more than okay."

Melody took her eyes off the sleek blue Thunderbird hardtop car passing by. "What is it?"

Poppa laughed. "*Now* I have your attention!" He slowed on 12th Street in front of his shop, Frank's Flowers, and pulled the truck around to the delivery entrance at the back. "How would you like to make a special arrangement for your mother and Big Momma for Mother's Day?"

♪ No Ordinary Sound ♪

"Yes!" Melody said, jumping out of the truck.

They stepped into the workroom, which was one of Melody's favorite places. The walls were lined with shelves that held vases of every shape and size, rolls of ribbon, and dozens of flowerpots and baskets. An old wooden worktable stretched along the length of the wall, and shears, floral tape, pins, and other supplies were arranged neatly on its surface. There was always music on the radio. This afternoon it was jazz. She recognized the saxophone sound because Daddy used to play one.

Melody dropped her book bag beside the door. There was a long cardboard box at one end of the table.

"Go on, look," Poppa said. Melody took a deep breath and carefully lifted the top off with both hands.

"Ohhh!" she gasped, smiling up at him. Inside the box wasn't candy, or toys, or anything else that would delight most nine-year-olds. The box was filled with flowers and feathery green ferns. "Red roses!" she said, taking a long sniff of their sweetness. Roses were Big Momma's favorite. "And yellow lilies, and pink freesia."

"Somebody knows her flowers," her grandfather said, taking a delicate china vase from the shelf.

♪ Dances and Dollars ♪

Melody looked up at him proudly. "Can I really make this one all by myself?"

He tilted his head to one side, and the sun from the windows made his silver beard shine. "Yes you can, Little One," Poppa said. "When you're done, we'll leave it here in the cooler so it stays fresh. I'll bring it to the house early Sunday morning, and I'll hide it so your grandmother doesn't see it until after church. Watch out for the thorns."

"I will!" Melody said. She opened a drawer and took out the girl-size gardening gloves that she kept at the store. She pulled on the gloves, climbed up on a stool, and carefully picked up one of the roses. She was so busy imagining just how she would mix the colors and flowers in the vase that she didn't notice Poppa leaving the workroom.

Melody hummed along with the music as she clipped the ends of the stems carefully, the way Poppa had shown her, so the flowers could "drink" more water when she put them into the vase.

She ignored the tinkling of the bell on the front door as customers came and went. But when the telephone rang, she heard a voice that wasn't Poppa's

♪ No Ordinary Sound ♪

say, "Hello. Frank's Flowers." It was Yvonne!

Melody put down her shears and peeked out front.

Poppa was talking to a customer in front of the huge cooler full of dozens of different types of flowers and greenery. Yvonne was standing behind the counter near the cash register. She was wearing her best pleated skirt and stockings, and her straightened hair was pulled back by a headband.

"What are you doing here?" Melody asked after Yvonne hung up the phone.

Yvonne didn't look happy. "I'm taking a break from my summer job hunt."

"Why?" Melody was trying to pay attention, but she noticed a pretty yellow flower in the cooler that she'd never seen before. It would be a perfect addition to her Mother's Day arrangement, she thought.

"I just applied for a job at the bank. The newspaper said they were hiring students for the summer, but no luck for me."

"Maybe the jobs are all full, and they don't need anybody else," Melody suggested.

"That's what the manager told me, but it wasn't true. He didn't even look at my application. A white girl

♪ Dances and Dollars ♪

about my age went into his office after me, and I heard him say they still had several summer positions open."

Melody jerked her head away from the cooler. "Is that the same bank where Mommy took me to open my savings account?"

Yvonne flushed angrily in answer. She looked as if she might cry.

Melody was outraged. "If they won't give my sister a job because she's black, then I'm going to take my money to a different bank."

Yvonne tried to smile. "Thanks, Dee-Dee."

"I'm serious," Melody said. The hurt on her sister's face made Melody think about something from a long time ago.

Once when Melody was only four and everyone else was already going to school, her grandparents had taken her south to see their cousins. It was very hot, and the lemonade in Big Momma's thermos was gone. Melody was still thirsty, so when Poppa stopped at a gas station in Alabama, Melody begged for a drink. There was a Coca-Cola machine, red and white and shiny. Poppa had given her a nickel so that she could buy an ice-cold soda pop. But when they got closer,

♪ No Ordinary Sound ♪

Big Momma said, "Stop, baby."

"I want a drink!" Little Melody had stomped her foot.

"I know," Big Momma said, "but we can't today. The machine is broken. Put your money in your pocket now."

Big Momma had taken Melody's hand to guide her away, and as Melody cried and followed, a little blonde girl about her size went to the machine. She stood on tiptoe and dropped a coin in. Then she reached in and pulled a frosty bottle out of the machine.

"It's not broken!" Melody had shouted. "It's not! I want a soda pop, too!" she'd cried, pulling against Big Momma's arm. Melody remembered crying for a long time, and none of Big Momma's other treats could make her feel better.

It wasn't until she was older and she could read that she understood. A few years later they were again driving south and stopped at a station, this time in Tennessee. Melody got out to stretch her legs, and she saw the same kind of soda machine. There was a sign above the machine that said "Whites Only." That's when Melody realized that the machine in

♪ Dances and Dollars ♪

Alabama must have had the same kind of sign.

When they got back to Detroit, Melody had asked Big Momma why she hadn't told her about the sign the first time.

"Because it hurt me too much," Big Momma said. "I didn't want it to hurt you, too."

Melody's memory faded as the bell on the door of the flower shop tinkled, but her determination to go to the bank the first chance she had did not.

Two teenage boys had wandered into the store, and the girls turned their attention to them. They seemed lost. Poppa was still busy, so Yvonne greeted them.

"You sell corsages?" one of them asked sheepishly.

Melody smiled. She knew that a corsage was the tiny flower arrangement that girls wore to dances and proms.

Yvonne looked very businesslike. "Yes," she said. "Are you looking for a corsage to pin on her dress, or for her to wear on her wrist?"

"I dunno," the boy said.

"How much do they cost?" the other boy asked.

"How much do you have?" Yvonne asked.

"One dollar!" they both said at the same time.

♪ No Ordinary Sound ♪

Yvonne rolled her eyes, and Melody tried not to laugh. One dollar wasn't enough money to buy a very fancy corsage. But she could tell that Yvonne had a plan. Poppa, finished with his customer, was watching.

"Well," Yvonne said, "we can give you a special prom deal. Two single carnations with two ribbons for one dollar! We'll even match the color of the ribbons to the young lady's dress."

Melody saw Poppa's eyebrows rise.

"For real?" The first boy was shocked.

"Tell your friends," Yvonne said. "I know there are three dances at different high schools next week. This special runs only till Wednesday."

"Cool! We'll spread the word! Do we pay now?" the second boy asked.

"Yes." Yvonne picked up a receipt book from the counter. Melody went over to her grandfather.

"Poppa, I think you should give Yvonne a job."

"I'm thinking the same thing, Little One," he said.

"Mommy!" Melody yelled, as soon as she and Yvonne got home. "Mommy!"

♪ Dances and Dollars ♪

The radio was playing a Smokey Robinson song when Melody burst into the kitchen. Her mother was snapping her fingers to the beat while she danced in front of the refrigerator. There was a stack of her students' math papers on the kitchen table and a pot of spaghetti sauce bubbling on the stove.

Mommy enjoyed music by dancing to it. Any other time Melody would have joined her, but not today.

"What in the world is it?" Mommy asked, putting a lid on the pot. She stopped dancing and turned down the sound on the radio.

"Yvonne didn't get a job, so I have to go to the bank!" Melody plopped into a chair.

"Explain," Mommy said, glancing at Yvonne. Yvonne only shrugged and tilted her head toward Melody.

"Yvonne tried to get a job at the bank, but they wouldn't hire her because she's black." Melody was angry again just thinking about the whole thing. "I want to protest by taking my money out. Will you take me to the bank tomorrow?"

"Yes," Mommy said, without asking any other questions.

♪ No Ordinary Sound ♪

The very next day after school, Melody held her mother's hand as they walked through the lobby of Detroit Bank. Melody had worn her best school jumper, and she carried her bank-account book. Melody looked around the large room. She and her mother were the only black people in sight, and she was the only child.

Melody and her mother stood in a short line, and for a few seconds Melody felt uncomfortable. Was everyone looking at her? Her cheeks were suddenly very warm, and her fingers felt sweaty as she curled them around her bankbook. *Can I do this?* Melody wondered. She had asked her mother in the car just what to say and how to say it, but now Melody was nervous. Then she saw a girl Yvonne's age working behind a desk. She was white. Did she get a job when Yvonne couldn't even apply? Melody took a deep breath and reminded herself that she was standing up for her sister—and for making things fair.

When it was her turn, Melody let go of Mommy's hand and stepped up to the counter, which came up to her shoulders. Melody made herself as tall as she could.

♪ Dances and Dollars ♪

The bank teller was an older white woman with red hair. "I would like to withdraw my money," Melody told her.

"And how much would you like to withdraw?"

"All of it."

The teller raised her eyebrows. "Are you sure?" she asked kindly.

"Yes," Melody said firmly. "My sister is really good with money and numbers, but this bank wouldn't let her apply for a summer job because she's black. That's not fair."

The teller looked confused for a moment. "Do you understand, dear, that if you withdraw everything you'll close your account?" She glanced over Melody's head in Mommy's direction.

Melody slid her bankbook across the counter. Her insides were quivering a little, but she looked straight at the teller. "Yes. I understand. This bank discriminates against black people. I don't want to keep my money here anymore."

It seemed like forever before the woman finally nodded and picked up Melody's bankbook. Melody watched the teller count out ten one-dollar bills and put

♪ No Ordinary Sound ♪

them into a small envelope. Melody noticed that the girl behind the desk was staring with her mouth open, as if she didn't believe a kid could do something this important. Melody turned away.

Her mother smiled and took her hand. "Good job," she said. "You know, your daddy says voting is a way to speak up for what we believe. Money has a voice, too. What we do with it says a lot about what we believe."

Melody blew out a breath of relief. "Thanks, Mommy."

"I'm proud of you, Melody," her mother said as they walked out side by side.

Mother's Day Surprises

♪ CHAPTER 6 ♪

Melody woke up early on Mother's Day. She rolled over and nudged Lila. "Get up! We've got to make breakfast for Mommy before church," she said. Lila groaned and rolled back over.

"Hurry," Melody told her. Melody expected to have to wake Yvonne, too. But when Melody looked over at her other sister's bed, it was empty. Yvonne was already up.

Melody hopped out of bed and ran across the hall to the bathroom. "Vonnie! Vonnie, we have to get breakfast," she whispered so as not to wake their mother.

Her sister nudged the bathroom door open with her foot as she finished tying a scarf over her head.

Melody raised an eyebrow. "Don't you usually take

that *off* in the morning?" Yvonne often wore the scarf to keep her hair from getting too tangled up while she slept.

Yvonne only nodded. "Let's get the Mother's Day surprises started," she whispered, waving Melody down the stairs.

In the kitchen, Melody opened the fridge and took out orange juice and eggs. Yvonne made coffee. Lila finally came down, dragging Dwayne by the arm.

"So early," he said sleepily. "Why can't Mom just have toast and orange juice?"

"Because," Melody said, "today's a special day to celebrate her. I'm going out to pick some flowers. Why don't you set up the tray?"

He groaned just as Lila had.

Melody stepped out the back door and went to the garden she had planted along the side of the driveway. Only a few flowers had bloomed so early in the season. She picked what was most beautiful and took the bunch back inside to arrange it in a teacup.

Dwayne had the tray ready. He had laid a fresh cloth towel over it, then a plate that matched the teacup, a paper napkin, and a fork. Melody placed the teacup

♪ Mother's Day Surprises ♪

of bright daffodils beside the plate, and then poured a glass of juice.

"Where's the coffee?" Melody asked.

"Coming," Lila answered.

Yvonne had already scrambled the eggs and made toast.

"She needs jam," Melody said.

"I'll get it." Lila went to the pantry and got an unopened jar of plum preserves that Big Momma had made last summer. "Are we ready?"

"Hey, did anybody remember to get a card?" Yvonne asked.

"I made one," Melody said. She ran to get it from its hiding place in the pantry, next to the box of Cheerios.

"Okay, everything is ready," Dwayne said. He picked up the tray, carefully carrying it up the stairs with his sisters following behind. At their parents' door, Melody raised her hand to knock.

"Hold it," Dwayne whispered.

"What?" Lila frowned.

"Let's not do the same old thing. Let's sing," Dwayne said.

"Ohhh! I like that!" Melody said. Dwayne bounced

♪ No Ordinary Sound ♪

his head as if he was listening to a beat. He quietly hummed a few notes. The girls hummed back. From inside their parents' room they heard Bo join in with a howl.

Dwayne laughed. "Of course we have the only dog in Detroit with perfect pitch," he said.

Melody knocked sharply on the door.

"Who is it?" Daddy said in his joking voice.

"It's me—I mean, it's us," Melody answered. "We're here with Mother's Day breakfast for Mommy."

"Come on," Daddy said.

Melody opened the door and they sang *"Happy Mother's Da-a-ay . . ."* together to Dwayne's new tune.

"That is wonderful!" Their mother clapped as Dwayne put the tray across her knees. "Thank you all." She eagerly looked at her breakfast. "Will!" she said. "They found plum preserves. I didn't know we had any left."

"Hey! I was hiding that for myself," Daddy said.

"I'll share," Mommy said. She broke off a corner of toast to feed to Bo.

While their mother ate, Melody, Dwayne, and Lila crowded onto the foot of the bed. "This certainly is an

♪ Mother's Day Surprises ♪

improvement over last year's Mother's Day breakfast," Daddy said, sneaking a bite of scrambled egg. "You delivered burnt pancakes."

Lila giggled. "That was Dwayne's fault."

"Oh, no it was *not*," Dwayne said. "That was Yvonne."

"Where *is* Yvonne?" Mommy asked.

Before anyone could answer, they heard water running in the bathroom. Melody looked at the clock on her parents' bedside table. "Lila! We have to get ready, too," she said, jumping off the bed. "Miss Dorothy asked us to be there early, so we can get one more practice in!"

An hour later, everyone was ready for church. Everyone except Yvonne. Melody tapped her foot and looked up the stairs anxiously, afraid they would be late. Both she and Lila had on the white blouses and navy blue skirts that the girls in the children's choir wore whenever they performed.

Dwayne came down wearing his dark suit and tie. Daddy called up the stairs. "Yvonne, this is not a beauty contest. This is church. We must go, or your sisters are going to be late."

♪ No Ordinary Sound ♪

"I'm coming!" Yvonne's voice floated downstairs.

Melody glanced at the living room clock and looked up the stairs again.

"Hurry up, Yvonne!" Melody said.

"On my way!"

Then came the biggest Mother's Day surprise. Yvonne walked slowly down the stairs. She wore a bright orange dress and heels. But as her entire body came into view, she was also wearing an Afro hairstyle. Her chin-length hair, which she usually straightened, was now a curly, crinkly globe standing out a few inches around her face.

Mommy gasped.

Dwayne chuckled.

"What did you do to your head?" Daddy asked in disbelief.

Melody looked at her mother and realized that for the first time ever, Mommy was speechless. No one they knew had ever worn an Afro. Melody and Lila and all their friends usually wore pigtails or braids so that their hair stayed neat, even when they ran around and played. Grown ladies like Mommy—and the Motown girl groups Melody admired—wore

♪ Mother's Day Surprises ♪

straightened hairstyles that were smooth and glossy and tidy. On special occasions, Melody got to wear her hair straightened, too.

"I'm going natural," Yvonne announced. "I'm honoring my African heritage. Happy Mother's Day, Mom. Do you like it?"

Mommy stared at Yvonne for a minute. "I—I don't really know how I feel yet," she said.

"I feel weird," Lila said.

Melody reached up to touch her sister's hair. It was tightly curled, soft, and springy. "It's nice," Melody said. "It's like a crown."

When they got into the station wagon, Dwayne complained that Yvonne's hair took up too much room. Daddy made him sit in the fold-down seat at the back.

As the Ellisons filed out of the car in front of the church, Melody heard whispers from the prim and proper ladies with straightened hair and fancy hats. "What sort of a hairdo is that?" one of them whispered to the others, not at all quietly. Melody knew that Yvonne heard them, too, but she just smiled. *She stands up for what she believes in*, Melody thought. *I'm so proud she's my big sister.*

♪ No Ordinary Sound ♪

The service was long, but Melody didn't mind. Pastor Daniels talked about how all people deserved respect, and how justice and fairness were ways of showing respect. Melody thought about her trip to the bank. Then the pastor talked about how important it was to respect, love, and obey your mother.

After he finished, Miss Dorothy went to the piano and raised both her hands. The children's choir stood up. As the music started, Melody looked out into the congregation and saw her mother in her usual seat right next to Big Momma. Both their hats were nodding in the air in time to the music. As Diane sang her solo, Melody kept her eyes on her mother and grandmother. When it was time for her to join in, she sang with love in every single note.

When the song ended, the congregation clapped and cheered. Pastor Daniels gave a single red or white rose to each of the mothers. Melody and Yvonne had tied ribbons to each flower at Poppa's shop yesterday.

As everyone sang the final song of the service together, Melody noticed three people coming into the

♪ Mother's Day Surprises ♪

church. *Who would show up now?* Melody wondered. Then her eyes grew wide. It was Charles and Tish and Val! Melody hadn't seen her cousin since last summer, but she knew it was her.

Val was wearing a frilly pink dress and pink socks with ruffles at the edges, and her hair was in a poufy ponytail tied up in a white bow. There was Cousin Charles, tall and skinny, with a mustache and a beard like Poppa, and Cousin Tish, as tall as Charles. She wore a hat with a huge feather that made her seem even taller.

Val looked at Melody and waved. Melody grinned. As soon as the song was over and Miss Dorothy gave the children permission to go, Melody pulled Sharon from her seat.

"My cousin's here. You have to meet her!" Melody said breathlessly. The two sped down the side aisle and zigzagged around chatting grown-ups to get to the back.

"Val!" Melody squealed, crushing Val's Sunday dress as she gave her an enormous hug.

"Dee-Dee!" Val knocked Melody off balance as she hugged back.

♪ No Ordinary Sound ♪

"You said you were coming when school was out," Melody said.

"I thought we were. But Mama and Daddy decided to start packing right after I wrote to tell you we were moving," Val explained. "We left yesterday. Daddy drove all night so that we could get here in time for church." Then she laughed. "I guess we didn't make it."

Melody linked arms with her cousin. "This is my best friend in Detroit, Sharon."

Sharon gave Val a shy smile. "Hi," she said.

"And Sharon, this is Val, my best friend from Alabama, and my best cousin, too."

Val stuck out a white-gloved hand to shake, and when Sharon grabbed it, the glove slipped off. The girls burst into giggles.

"Melody, I've gotta go—we're taking my grandma out to dinner. See you tomorrow! Remember, Matching Monday is blue!" Sharon vanished among the suits and dresses.

"What's Matching Monday?" Val asked. She took off her other glove and stuffed both of them into her little pink purse.

"Sharon and I wear the same color hair ribbons to

♪ Mother's Day Surprises ♪

school on Mondays. When we were in kindergarten, we pretended that we were twins," Melody explained.

"That's funny! You don't look anything alike!"

"It's our little joke." Melody smiled. "Hey—I've got an idea. You can be part of Matching Mondays, too."

After hellos and hugs outside the church, everyone headed for their cars to ride to Big Momma and Poppa's house.

Melody didn't want Val out of her sight for even a moment. "Daddy," she called out, "can Val and I ride back with Poppa?" Her father nodded.

"What a great surprise," Melody said, giving Val's hand a squeeze. "I'm so glad you're here!"

A Family Reunion

♪ CHAPTER 7 ♪

When Poppa pulled up to his house, Daddy, Dwayne, and Cousin Charles were already leaning against Charles's Ford Fairlane, talking and laughing. The mothers were walking slowly up the driveway, talking and laughing. Melody knew that the day was going to be full of talking and laughing.

"Look at you, man!" Charles thumped Dwayne on the back. "You weren't this tall last summer! Are you still singing?"

Melody saw Dwayne duck his head, but he answered, "Yeah, yeah I am."

"He's just playing with that music business in his spare time," Daddy said. "He's going to college in September."

Dwayne opened his mouth to say something, but

♪ A Family Reunion ♪

then closed it again. When Melody sighed, Val looked at her curiously. "What's that about?" she whispered.

Melody shook her head. "Tell you later. Look! Your mother and Big Momma have Yvonne cornered!"

Big Momma and Cousin Tish were standing on either side of Yvonne on the porch steps, studying her Afro while Mommy looked on.

"Oh!" Val whispered. "I wonder what Mama is saying." Cousin Tish had owned a hair salon in Birmingham. Melody loved the fact that she never knew what Tish's hair would look like when she saw her next. Each time it was a different style and color: curly and red, long and brown, short and black, or piled high and wavy like today. What would she think of Yvonne's crinkly crown?

"Let's hurry up so we can hear!" Melody said.

"Now, how did you get it to stand up?" Big Momma was asking.

"I have a special comb," Yvonne said.

"Some people don't like natural hair because it looks so different from what we're used to," Tish said. She looked at Yvonne thoughtfully. "I think that style suits your face. I'm going to open a salon here as soon

♪ No Ordinary Sound ♪

as I find a spot. I wonder if my future Detroit clients would like a style like that?"

"I'm not sure how many young women are as radical as our Yvonne," Mommy said, opening the front door.

"What does 'radical' mean?" Melody asked.

"It means somebody who's willing to raise her voice," Yvonne said.

"Willing to raise her hair, too!" Mommy said as she went inside.

Melody and Val followed, but they all bumped into a traffic jam just inside the living room. Everyone was looking up at the arch where Poppa had quickly hung Melody's colorful construction-paper signs all the way across, saying "Welcome Charles, Tish, and Val." Underneath, on a small round table, was the Mother's Day flower arrangement Melody had made at Poppa's shop.

"Oh!" Tish clapped. "Who made all this loveliness?"

"Melody did," Lila said, peering around for her sister.

"Melody?" Mommy called, and Melody made her way to the dining room with Val right behind.

♪ A Family Reunion ♪

"Thank you, honey!" Tish gave her a hug. "There's nothing like being around family."

"And there's nothing like Big Momma's fried chicken," Charles said, as Yvonne and Mommy brought plates and bowls of food from the kitchen.

"Come on, everyone," Big Momma called. "Let's eat."

There was so much talking and laughing that dinner went on and on. Everyone was so busy catching up on cousins and old friends that Big Momma served a second round of cake and ice cream.

"Say, Frances!" Charles said, scraping the last of the crumbs off his plate. "This reminds me of the first time you made a triple-chocolate cake. It was kind of lopsided, remember?"

"Lopsided?" Dwayne laughed. "Are you kidding?"

"No, he's not kidding," Mommy said. "And yes, I remember. I was a new wife, and I didn't bake very well."

"What your mother did was nothing to laugh at," Daddy said. "I had dreamed about chocolate when I was overseas during the war. I saw a cake like that in the window of a bakery in town the day I got back."

♪ No Ordinary Sound ♪

"Why didn't you just go into the bakery and buy it?" Melody asked.

Mommy poured more coffee for the grown-ups. "I tried," she said. "That bakery refused to serve Negroes. I was so angry that I decided to try to make the cake myself."

Daddy said, "There we were, fighting for freedom for the world, and we didn't have it when we got back home."

"But you two were Tuskegee Airmen!" Dwayne said. "I mean, you got a medal, Dad!"

"Yes. I was the most highly trained mechanic in my unit. I kept those planes in top flying condition. But when I left the service, I couldn't get a job in my hometown. I had to move all the way to Detroit, and even up here I had to start at the bottom doing the most backbreaking jobs at the auto factory."

Charles sighed. "Things sure haven't changed much. Here I am, moving to Detroit for the same reason."

"What do you mean?" Daddy asked.

"The black hospital where I worked closed down," Charles explained. "I tried to get a job at one of the

♪ A Family Reunion ♪

white hospitals, but no one would hire me. I'm a licensed pharmacist, but it seemed as if people only saw me as some black man they couldn't be bothered with."

Melody thought about what had happened to Yvonne at the bank. "That's wrong," she whispered to her sister. Yvonne looked at Melody and nodded. So did Mommy.

Charles's face was serious. "I got stopped by a cop when I was on my way to a job interview. I was wearing a suit and tie, not doing anything wrong, but the police still treated me like a criminal. When the hospital closed, I just felt it was time for us to get out of Birmingham."

"But if everybody like you and Tish leaves, who's going to stay and fight?" Yvonne asked.

"Girl, if you miss a day of work to participate in a march or a protest, you can lose your job," Charles said. "I have a family to support. I couldn't risk it."

"But things are changing," Yvonne insisted.

"Yes, but things are also getting tense," Charles said. He put his coffee cup down. "It was bad enough when white people threw food at peaceful protesters or pulled them off their seats at a lunch counter. But now the police are setting dogs and fire hoses on people!"

Tish tapped her bright red fingernails on the table. "Charles and I have been talking about this for months. There's a lot of good happening in the South, but some of it is getting dangerous. The police turned those hoses on children. *Children!*"

Melody knew what Tish was talking about. Everyone did. It had happened last week, and news of it was still on the TV every night. Melody had seen black schoolkids in Birmingham, singing and carrying signs. Then policemen chased them, and turned giant hoses on them. The blasts of water were so strong that they knocked the children to the ground.

Melody glanced at Val. Val looked down at her dish of ice cream.

"Those police in Birmingham were wrong," Big Momma said. She reached over and gently raised Val's chin with her hand. "And those children were very brave."

"I don't see why we have to fight fire with fire, as the old saying goes," Mommy said. "Dr. King speaks against hatred and fear. He believes we can change

♪ A Family Reunion ♪

hearts and laws without violence."

"He's coming to Detroit next month," Poppa said, "making a speech down at Cobo Hall."

Melody felt as if something big was happening right here at her grandparents' table. She wasn't quite sure what it was, but she had a feeling that some kind of change was in the air.

"I heard people at the flower shop talking about it," Yvonne said. "There's going to be a march. It's called the Walk to Freedom!"

"Yes, our union is marching," Daddy said. Melody saw her mother give her father an approving look. "We don't have the same sort of segregation as in the South," Daddy continued, "but we need more good jobs for black people here in Detroit."

"And better, less crowded schools for black children," Mommy added. "And fair housing laws."

"You make it sound like Detroit is a mess," Dwayne piped up. "Black people like Poppa have businesses—and Tish, you want to open a business, right? Well, you can! And don't forget that this is where the music starts. Hitsville, U.S.A. Motown." Dwayne started snapping his fingers and humming a tune. Everyone

♪ No Ordinary Sound ♪

around the table started laughing.

Daddy rolled his eyes at Dwayne, but he was smiling when he said, "I think we should all take part in the march as a family."

"Go, Daddy!" Yvonne clapped her hands.

"I don't know, Cousin," Charles said. "We're staying out of this marching business. I just want to get my family settled in, find a place to live. We're looking to get a fresh start here in Detroit."

There was silence for a moment. "I understand how you must feel," Mommy said gently, looking at Charles. Then she turned to Daddy. "I would like to hear what Dr. King has to say in person."

"That young man is a powerful preacher," Poppa said. "I'd like to hear him too."

Big Momma motioned to Lila. "Put the date on my kitchen calendar, Lila. When is it, Will?"

"June twenty-third," Daddy said. "Whoever's going will meet right here, so we can walk to freedom together."

After dinner, Melody and Val sat side by side on

♪ A Family Reunion ♪

Big Momma's sofa. "Are you tired after the long car ride from Birmingham?" Melody asked as Dwayne played his still-wordless tune. When Val didn't answer, Melody tilted her head sideways to look at her cousin. "What's wrong?"

Val shrugged, so Melody dragged her up and pulled her past Dwayne at the piano and out the front door. She sat down on the top step. Val hesitated a moment, then smoothed the skirt of her dress and sat down too.

"I'm happy to see you, and everybody," Val said quietly. "But everything happened so fast with our move. I couldn't really say good bye to my friends the way I wanted to." She sighed. "I just don't feel like I have any kind of home anymore. You wouldn't understand."

"Tell me what you mean," Melody said. She *wanted* to understand.

"Detroit isn't home," Val said. "Home's not home anymore either. I used to feel safe in Birmingham. Now there's always police, and people in the streets getting arrested. I knew one of those kids who got knocked down by the water hose. She said it was really scary."

♪ No Ordinary Sound ♪

"Wow," Melody said. She told Val what Pastor Daniels had said that morning about everybody deserving justice. "Those kids stood up for themselves. That's really brave."

"I know," Val said, looking at their reflections in the toes of her patent leather shoes. "But we're just kids."

"But we still count," Melody said. "This is our world, too!" She told Val what she'd done at the bank when her sister couldn't get a job there.

"That's brave, too," Val said. She looked at Melody and smiled slowly. "I think living in Detroit is going to be *real* interesting."

"It will be, I promise!" Melody said.

"I want to help Val feel at home in Detroit," Melody said the very next afternoon as she and Lila walked home from school. "Let's take her to the library today."

"Sure, that sounds like fun," said Lila. "Val might like the craft class, too."

Melody smiled. Lila loved to make things as much as she loved to read. At first, she made toys from branches or scraps of wood. Then she started taking

♪ A Family Reunion ♪

apart things around the house and trying to put them back together, like Dwayne's old record player. Now she was obsessed with the library's craft class.

The girls went home to drop off their book bags, change out of their school clothes, and have a snack. Lila also had to get the stack of library books she was returning. She had so many that Melody offered to help her carry them.

"Was this one any good?" Melody asked, holding up *The Kid's Book of Engineering*.

"Yes, it was," Lila said. "And that reminds me. Guess what happened this morning."

"What?"

"My teacher said she's nominated me for a science scholarship to a private high school."

"Wow!" Melody stopped and stared at her sister. "Wait till Mommy and Daddy find out!" Mommy always said that all of the Ellison kids were smart, but Melody thought Lila might be the smartest. She was good at math and science and reading. In fact, she was good in every subject.

"I don't know . . . it costs a lot of money," Lila muttered.

♪ No Ordinary Sound ♪

"Doesn't a scholarship mean you can go for free?" Melody asked, beginning to walk again.

"Maybe. The scholarship might not cover all the costs," Lila said. "And first I have to take a hard entrance exam to qualify for one."

"You can pass any test! You're a straight A student," Melody said. "Why are you worried?"

Lila looked at her. "For the same reason that you're worried about doing a solo for Youth Day even though you're a great singer."

Melody hadn't thought of it that way.

Big Momma was just finishing a music lesson with a student when Melody and Lila arrived. Val had been sitting at the kitchen table by herself, and she jumped up when Melody told her they were going to the library.

Big Momma smiled. "That's a good idea. You can get to know the neighborhood, Valerie. You girls go on, and be careful." Big Momma waved.

"Bye, Big Momma!" they sang together.

"Where is the library?" Val asked as they skipped down the porch steps.

"Not far," Melody told her. "Only nine blocks."

♪ A Family Reunion ♪

Val looked shocked. "My mama and daddy didn't let me walk that far by myself in Birmingham. Not with everything that was going on."

Melody nodded silently, thinking about yesterday's conversation. "Well, it won't take long to get to Duffield library," she said. "When school's out, Lila and I go a couple of times a week. We're both in the summer reading club. There are prizes and everything. There's lots of other stuff to do, too. There's a craft class, and a board-game club."

"So this is what you do all summer, when you're up here and not visiting us?" Val asked.

"Not *all* summer," Melody said. "We go swimming at the YWCA, and on weekends Mommy takes us across to Canada, and—"

"Canada?" Val repeated doubtfully.

"Yep. Canada is right across the river. We drive over the bridge and get there in no time at all," Lila said.

"There's so much stuff I don't know about this place." Val sounded interested.

"You can come with me to help Poppa at his flower shop," Melody suggested. "Or you can come and help me in my own garden," she added. "I could help you

♪ No Ordinary Sound ♪

plant a garden at your new house, if you want."

"Yes, I'd like that a lot," Val told her. "I think Mama would, too. We could plant loads and loads of pink flowers! What else?"

Melody wrinkled her nose as she thought. Of course there would be barbecues and maybe a baseball game or two—

"I can think of something," Lila said mysteriously. "And it's coming up."

"What?" Val asked, confused.

Melody knew what Lila was talking about. "Look across the street," she said as they turned onto busy Grand Boulevard. Melody pointed to a two-story house with a big white sign across the front windows.

"Hitsville U.S.A.," Val read aloud. "Oh my gosh! Is that what Dwayne was talking about yesterday? That's Motown?"

"Yes!" Melody and Lila said together.

Val's eyes became so wide that she almost looked like a cartoon character. Lila burst out laughing.

"This is their recording studio," Melody said. She thought of Dwayne's big secret—the audition he was waiting for. But she didn't say anything.

♪ A Family Reunion ♪

"Have you ever seen anybody famous?" Val seemed rooted to the sidewalk, but there wasn't anybody around.

"Well, not yet," Melody admitted.

"Come on," Lila waved them along. "Enough star-watching for today. Maybe we can catch sight of The Marvelettes over the summer!"

"The Marvelettes!" Melody and Val sighed together. Melody started humming the tune to their song "Please Mr. Postman," and Lila and Val hummed along.

Four blocks farther down they came to the large, low limestone building that was the Duffield branch of the Detroit Public Library. At the steps, Val stopped to stare. "The colored library is really big!" she exclaimed.

"Colored library?" Lila asked.

Val looked confused. "Isn't this where we're going? The colored library?"

"It's just a library," Melody said. "Anybody can go to any public library."

"You're in Detroit now," Lila reminded Val. "Not Birmingham."

"And we go in the front doors, just like this?" Val was wide-eyed again.

♪ No Ordinary Sound ♪

"That's right." Melody shifted her pile of books and skipped up the steps. "Have you ever read *The Secret Garden*?" she asked Val. "These kids find a hidden gate, and all kinds of stuff happens. It's one of my all-time favorite books."

Val shook her head. "I haven't read it, but I bet I'll like it."

"How do you know?" Lila asked.

"I'll like it because Dee-Dee likes it," Val said. "That's how friends are."

"Come on, cousin-friend," Melody said, opening the door. "I'll show you the children's section!"

Signs and Songs

♪ CHAPTER 8 ♪

It was finally June, and school was finally over. Melody had thought it would never end! She burst through the front door of her house on the last day and tossed her book bag into a corner.

"I'm done, I'm done!" She did a little dance right on the living room rug while Lila came in behind her.

"Don't forget to pick that up," Lila told her, before tromping up the stairs with her book bag thumping.

"I guess you're glad school is out," Yvonne said from the dining room.

Melody nodded. "Yes, but Sharon's going to New Orleans tomorrow for the whole summer. I'm glad Val's here already. I can't wait to call her!"

"You don't have to wait," Val said as she appeared from the kitchen.

♪ No Ordinary Sound ♪

"You're here!" Melody laughed, rushing over to give her cousin a hug. "It has been so hard to sit in school knowing that you're done already."

"It's been just as hard waiting for y'all to finish!" Val said, sitting down at the dining room table. "Daddy's started his new job, and Mama's looking for a place for her salon, so I could use some company."

"Yvonne, how come you're not at the flower shop?" Melody asked.

"Poppa gave me the afternoon off to work on a special project," Yvonne said.

Melody noticed that the table was covered with poster boards, paints, crayons, and glue. "What are you making?"

"Signs for the Walk to Freedom," Val said proudly. "Look at the one I just painted."

Melody read the big blue words out loud. *"Freedom Forever."* There were other slogans, too. *Justice for All! Fair Housing Now! Separate Is Not Equal!* "Wow. This is really cool," Melody said.

Yvonne nodded. "We're making as many as we can. I'll take them to the church. Someone there will pass them out on the Sunday of the march."

♪ Signs and Songs ♪

Lila came back down. She had changed out of her school clothes. "Oh, can I help?" she asked.

"Me, too?" Melody asked.

"Sure," Yvonne nodded. "But Melody, you'd better change out of your school clothes."

Melody hurried upstairs to put on a pair of shorts. When she came back, Dwayne was stomping through the back door, singing "Summertime." He stuck his head into the dining room.

Melody was surprised to see him. He was usually still at the factory at this time of day. She looked at the clock and then at Dwayne. When she opened her mouth to say something, Dwayne pulled his finger and thumb across his lips. *This has something to do with his secret*, Melody thought. She didn't say a word.

"What's up with all this?" Dwayne asked.

"Don't get too close," Yvonne warned. "You'll mess up our posters."

"They're for the freedom walk," Melody told him.

"I am not going on any freedom walk," he said. "I've got better things to do."

"Like what?" Lila asked suspiciously.

"Like none of your business," Dwayne answered.

♪ No Ordinary Sound ♪

"What could be more important than freedom?" Yvonne asked.

"Being lead singer of Dwayne and The Detroiters," he said.

Yvonne looked annoyed.

Lila said, "You'd better be thinking about college, too. You know what Daddy says."

"Plenty of people do just fine without a college degree!" he said. "Look at Tish!" He went into the kitchen.

Val stopped tracing the word "Justice" and pointed her pencil at Lila. "My mama says it's just as important for a colored person to run a business as it is to go to college."

Yvonne smiled. "That's because Tish is a successful business owner."

"Like Poppa, and the people who run the bakery," Melody added.

"And Berry Gordy at Motown. He's running a successful music business!" Dwayne called from the kitchen. A few minutes later, he came back into the dining room holding a saucer stacked with two peanut butter and jelly sandwiches. "Music is a *business*!"

♪ Signs and Songs ♪

"Bet you won't tell Daddy that," Lila said.

Dwayne rolled his eyes in her direction, and then nodded at Melody as he stood in the middle of the floor eating. "So how's *your* music coming?" he asked.

"My song?" Melody hadn't stopped thinking about her Youth Day solo. There were so many she liked. "I haven't picked one yet," she confessed.

Dwayne shoved the last corner of one of the sandwiches into his mouth and pulled Melody away from the table. "You love singing, don't you?"

"Yes," she said.

"And you want to do this solo, don't you?"

"Yes!" Melody answered right away.

"Here's the thing about that, Dee-Dee." Dwayne sat on the sofa so that he and Melody were eye to eye. He looked and sounded serious when he talked about music with Melody. "The songs you sing don't just have to be right for your voice, or for whatever audience you're singing for, okay? Your song has to *feel* right. The words have to mean something special to you. When they do, amazing things happen."

"Is that why all your songs are so good?" Melody asked.

♪ No Ordinary Sound ♪

Dwayne nodded. "I kind of think so."

Melody wondered if this was why Diane always sounded so good, too. Did the songs she sang *feel* right to her? Suddenly the tunes from dozens of songs popped into Melody's head: songs that made her happy, silly nursery rhymes that made her laugh, church songs, dancing songs, sad songs.

"Oh, I can see your music brain working hard!" Dwayne said, and Melody realized that her shoulders were moving to the music in her head. She stopped and laughed.

"See what I mean?" Dwayne smiled at her.

"Yes," Melody said. "But how will I know which one is right?"

"You'll know." Dwayne patted her shoulder. "You'll know when—"

Dwayne stopped talking when he heard their mother's key turn in the front door.

"Dwayne! Get off the sofa!" Melody whispered. "You're still in your work clothes."

He jumped and ran.

"I'm home!" Mommy called out the way she always did when she came in. "And I've brought company!"

♪ Signs and Songs ♪

"Hi, Mommy!" Melody rushed to give her mother a hug. She looked curiously at the older woman who followed Mommy in. Her hair was snow white and she carried a wooden cane, but her dark face had no wrinkles at all. The woman's sharp dark eyes twinkled as she looked back at Melody.

"This is Miss Esther Collins. She's just joined our church, and she's helping me on the finance committee. Miss Esther, this is my youngest, Melody. And those are my other two daughters, Yvonne and Lila, and Cousin Valerie."

"Hello, Miss Esther!" the girls said.

"Hello there," Miss Esther said in a high, quivery voice.

"Please sit down while I get those phone numbers for you," Mommy said, going upstairs.

Instead of sitting, Miss Esther headed to the dining room, clicking her cane across the floor. "You young people are always busy," she said. "What's this you're doing?"

"We're making posters for the Walk to Freedom," Melody told her.

"Oh, yes." Miss Esther nodded. "It's going to be

quite an event. That young Dr. King is speaking."

Yvonne looked up, impressed. "You know about it?"

Miss Esther nodded. "We've been fighting this fight for a long time, child. You're never too old or too young to stand up for justice."

Just then Mommy returned, carrying a sheet of yellow paper. At the same moment, the sound of a new Miracles hit came from the kitchen.

"What's that record?" Miss Esther asked. "Is that one of those Motown boys?"

"It's not a record," Melody said. "That's our brother, Dwayne!"

Miss Esther looked surprised. "My! He could be a professional singer."

Melody looked proud. "He sure could."

"After college," Mommy said gently, handing the yellow sheet of phone numbers to Miss Esther.

Miss Esther looked thoughtful. "Nothing takes the place of a good education," she said. "But each of us has our own path to follow."

It almost sounded to Melody as if Miss Esther knew Dwayne's secret.

"Let me walk you out," Mommy said brightly.

♪ Signs and Songs ♪

"Good-bye, all!" Miss Esther waved. "You take care of this wonderful family, Frances," she said.

When Mommy and Miss Esther stepped out of the house, Melody threw open the kitchen door. "Hey, Dwayne," she said. "Guess what?"

"What?" Dwayne popped his head out.

"Somebody just thought you were a record!"

"No joke?" He chuckled and walked through the dining room with his head held high in the air. "See?" he said to Yvonne over his shoulder as he passed. "I'm not walking to freedom. I'm *singing* my way up."

The Power Inside

♪ CHAPTER 9 ♪

A week later, Melody and Lila were in the kitchen eating bologna and cheese sandwiches and drinking ginger ale when they heard someone at the front door.

Lila stopped chewing. "Who in the world is that in the middle of the day?"

Melody put her cup down. "Maybe Yvonne came home early."

Before Lila could call out, the first notes of one of Dwayne's tunes came from their living room. Three male voices harmonized to the music.

"It's Dwayne and his group!" Lila whispered.

"Where's the music coming from? We don't have a piano," Melody whispered back.

Lila rolled her eyes. "Obviously they got a tape recorder from somewhere!" She got up and motioned

♪ The Power Inside ♪

for Melody to follow. The two stood at the kitchen door, listening.

The song was so lively that Melody started dancing to the beat. Then she bumped the butter knife that Lila had left on the counter, and it clattered to the floor. The music stopped.

"Oops!" Lila snickered.

In a second, Dwayne swung the kitchen door open. "Are you two snooping?"

"Sort of," Melody said.

Instead of getting upset, Dwayne shrugged. "So why don't you come on in? Be our audience."

Lila headed for the living room, but Melody held back and grabbed her brother's arm. "Shouldn't you be at work?" she asked. Melody was still keeping Dwayne's secret about the Motown audition. Now it seemed as if Dwayne was keeping a secret from her.

"I'll tell you later," he whispered. "I promise."

Melody followed him to the living room and plopped onto the couch beside Lila, who was talking to Artie and Phil. Dwayne, Artie, and Phil had been friends forever. Melody's earliest memories were of the boys showing her how to beat the bottom of a saucepan

♪ No Ordinary Sound ♪

with a wooden spoon like a drum, to keep up with their doo-wop beat. Big Momma had taught Dwayne piano, and he started making up his own music. For the last year, the three boys had been singing all over the city.

Dwayne seemed nervous as he huddled with the other guys. When he turned around he said, "Okay. This is a song I wrote for us. Check out our sound."

Artie, Phil, and Dwayne lined up with their backs to the sofa. Melody scooted forward, anxious for them to begin.

Dwayne started the tape recorder. They all spun around. *"Never thought I'd see the day that you made me feel this way,"* they sang together. *"Everything was sun, now everything is rain."*

Dwayne stepped forward. *"Never, ever dreamed you'd cause me this much pain."*

Melody smiled with pride. Big Momma said Dwayne's voice was a high tenor, like Smokey Robinson's. Melody thought Dwayne's singing was somehow even smokier.

At the last words, they all turned their backs to Melody and Lila again. The girls clapped and hooted

♪ The Power Inside ♪

and stomped their feet.

"Aw, come on!" Dwayne said happily, looking over his shoulder.

"We want a real critique," Phil said, smiling at Lila. Lila grinned back.

Melody noticed and leaned into her sister. "I thought you didn't like Phil," she whispered.

"He's turned kind of cute," Lila whispered back, adjusting her eyeglasses.

Melody shook her head. "What's the name of your group?" she asked the guys. "You need a catchy name."

"She's right," Lila said. "You're not still going by the name of 'Dwayne and The Detroiters,' are you?"

Dwayne looked sheepish. Artie pointed at Melody.

"Lil sis, you have a better idea?"

"Sure!" Melody thought for a moment. "How about The Three Ravens?" she suggested. "You could wear the same outfits, like The Temptations! Maybe black suits with matching purple shirts and ties—right, Lila?" Melody hopped up from her seat. "And those moves aren't cool enough. What if you spin one at a time—kind of bend and swirl around, like this?" Melody demonstrated. "When Dwayne is singing, you

♪ No Ordinary Sound ♪

guys can't stand still," she said. "The Motown guys really dance."

Phil and Artie were already nodding, trying some different steps.

"Yeah! Yeah!" Melody nodded. "What do you think, Dwayne?"

"I'm thinking I can't believe how good you are at this, Dee-Dee," Dwayne said. "I'm going to get us some Kool-Aid," he said to the other two Ravens. Then he motioned for Melody to follow him to the kitchen.

Dwayne took down the pitcher, and Melody got out two packets of the strawberry powder and a wooden spoon.

"Here's the thing," Dwayne said. "Dad thinks I'm still working day shifts, but I quit my job at the factory."

"So that's why you're always coming and going!"

Dwayne nodded. "I got a part-time gig as a janitor down at Cobo Hall," he said. "Now I have more time to write music and rehearse with the guys."

Melody frowned. "Daddy's going to be really mad! You promised him you'd work at that factory until college started."

Dwayne shook his head. "I'm not cut out for

♪ The Power Inside ♪

factory work, Dee-Dee. I got something good with Phil and Artie, and we have a chance to make it great." He turned on the water to fill the pitcher.

Melody looked down at the swirling red liquid. Dwayne seemed so sure that he was right! Just like Yvonne always did. Melody wished she had their kind of courage.

"Listen," he said, turning back to her. "It's not gonna be easy—I'm not fooling myself. But we can sell records, lots of them. And I believe that when people hear our sound, they won't care what color our skin is."

Melody hadn't known that was how Dwayne felt. "Maybe if you explain that to Daddy, he'll understand. I could tell him—"

"No!" Dwayne said quickly. "Promise you won't say anything to Dad. We're gonna knock 'em out at our audition. I just know it. Then I'll tell Mom and Dad."

Melody stirred the Kool-Aid slowly. "I'm not going to tell a lie, you know."

"I know," Dwayne said, putting a hand on her shoulder. "And I would never ask you to do that. Just don't volunteer any information, okay?"

"I guess."

♪ No Ordinary Sound ♪

"There's one more thing," he said.

"What?" Melody set the spoon on the counter, and noticed that it was the same kind Dwayne had given her to drum on a pan a very long time ago.

"I need a new suit for the audition. Would you go shopping with me, since you seem to know just what I should be wearing?"

Melody couldn't help but smile. "All right," she said. "All right to everything, especially you telling Daddy soon. But—"

"But what?"

"Once I pick a song for Youth Day, you help me, too."

"You got it! Whatever you need." Dwayne picked up the spoon to continue stirring.

On Saturday morning, Dwayne and Melody ate Cheerios together and then got ready to go shopping. Big Momma always said, "Look like you have money in your pocket when you go into a store," so Dwayne brushed his hair and put on a shirt with a collar. Melody wore a school skirt and borrowed Lila's

♪ The Power Inside ♪

shoulder purse. She took two of the crisp one-dollar bills that she had gotten when she closed her account at the bank and tucked them into the purse. Melody told Dwayne she had decided to buy herself something special to wear for her solo at Youth Day. She was excited that they both had something to shop for.

Dwayne whistled a tune but didn't say much as they walked. A few blocks from home, they turned onto 12th Street, which was lined with shoe shops, dress stores, delicatessens, ice cream parlors, and all sorts of other businesses. On a Saturday morning, the sidewalk was crowded with shoppers. At one of the corners, Melody headed for the bus stop, but Dwayne kept walking.

"Hey!" Melody called out, dodging a lady with two little kids. "Where are we going?"

"Fieldston's," Dwayne said over his shoulder.

"I thought we were going downtown, to Hudson's department store," Melody said.

Dwayne made a face at her, and for a minute he looked more like a boy and not an almost grown-up man. "I don't have Hudson's money, Dee-Dee."

"Oh," Melody said. "I forgot. You're only working

part-time." Then she added, "We'll make it work!"

Fieldston's Clothing was one of the older stores on 12th Street. Poppa had often told them how he had bought his first city suit there when he moved up from Alabama. When he opened his flower shop several years later, there were only a few businesses owned by black people in the neighborhood. Even though Mr. Fieldston was white, he'd given Poppa lots of good advice. Now Mr. Fieldston was long gone, and someone else ran the store.

A bell chimed as Dwayne held the door open for Melody. There were three clerks chatting at the front counter, but none of them said, "May I help you?" or even "Hello." They were all wearing blue jackets, and they were all white. As she and Dwayne began to look around, Melody noticed several other shoppers, but she and her brother were the only black customers.

"The men's suits are over here," Dwayne said, nodding to the left. "But you'll want to see what's over there," he said, motioning to the right.

Melody saw a display of women's jewelry, and she smiled. "I'll just look for a few minutes," she told Dwayne. "Then I'll come and help you."

♪ The Power Inside ♪

Melody hurried through the aisles crowded with clothing racks and display cases, her shoulder purse swinging. She stopped to admire some silky scarves. Melody wrapped one around her neck, turning to find a mirror so that she could see how she looked. She almost bumped into one of the clerks from the front of the store. "Excuse me," Melody said to the woman politely. The woman didn't say anything, but she watched as Melody took the scarf off and put it neatly back where she'd found it.

Melody wandered over to a glass case filled with necklaces. As she leaned closer, she saw the reflection of a man standing behind her. Thinking that he was looking too, she moved out of his way and on to a rack of barrettes. *Maybe I should get these instead of a headband,* she thought. She was about to take a pair from the rack when she changed her mind. She turned and saw the same man from the jewelry display. He looked at her suspiciously. Suddenly, Melody felt uncomfortable. She hurried over to Dwayne, no longer excited about shopping for herself.

Dwayne was holding up two black jackets. "How about one of these?" he asked.

♪ No Ordinary Sound ♪

"Oh! That's the one you need," Melody said, pointing to the one with the shiny gold buttons.

A young man came around the aisle carrying an armful of boxes. Dwayne held up the jacket with the shiny buttons. "Excuse me, what's the price on this?"

The man with the boxes gave Dwayne an annoyed look and brushed roughly past without answering. Dwayne shrugged and slipped the jacket on. Melody nodded her approval. It seemed to fit perfectly. Dwayne looked at the edge of the sleeve for a price tag, and then held his arm up high. "Can I get a price on this, please?"

"You can't afford it," a man said.

Melody turned to see the same man who'd stood behind her at the necklaces and the barrettes. Had he followed her?

"Take it off," the man said coldly.

"I have money," Dwayne said, frowning.

Melody looked toward the front counter. Mommy always said to ask nicely for a manager if you had trouble in a store.

The man shook his head, and Melody noticed that he was wearing the same blue jacket as all the other

♪ The Power Inside ♪

clerks. She suddenly suspected that he hadn't been standing behind her by mistake.

"I can guess what your kind really came in here for," he hissed.

"What do you mean?" Melody asked. "What's he talking about?" she whispered to Dwayne. Then she saw a look cross Dwayne's face—a look she'd never seen before. It was like anger and fear and something else all mixed together. Dwayne slowly took off the jacket and carefully hung it back on the rack, shaking his head.

"Wait," Melody said, tugging at her brother's arm. "You need a suit."

"Not at this price," Dwayne said quietly.

"I've had enough of your type," the clerk said. "Get out. And take your little shoplifting companion with you." His eyes flashed right at Melody.

"Shoplifting?" Melody's mouth dropped open. "That's not true," she protested. "We didn't steal anything," she said louder, her heart pounding. "We're just shopping like everybody else!"

"Dee-Dee, no." Dwayne didn't raise his voice. "Let's just go."

♪ No Ordinary Sound ♪

"You'd *better* go. Get out, before I call the cops!" the man shouted.

Melody realized with a sinking feeling that the man who was shouting was the manager. Dwayne was pulling her toward the door. She didn't want to stay, but she couldn't move. How could that man have accused her of doing something so horrible? As they left the store, Melody knew that Mommy had been wrong. That manager would never have helped them. He was the trouble.

Outside, Dwayne wouldn't look at Melody. He started walking so quickly that Melody had to almost run to keep up with him. She brushed away tears. Her insides were shaky, as if she'd just escaped something dangerous. Melody wanted to ask her brother if he was as upset as she was, and what he would do about his audition suit. "Dwayne?"

He spun around so quickly that she had to step back. His face was like a mask, as if he didn't feel anything at all.

"Should we go tell Poppa?" Melody asked.

Dwayne shook his head. "That won't help. Besides, this isn't the first time something like this has happened to me, and it won't be the last time."

♪ The Power Inside ♪

Melody stood very still. Would that happen to her again? Would she be accused of shoplifting when she was just shopping? Then Melody felt a prickle of fear for her brother. What if the store clerk had called the police? Who would the police have believed, Dwayne or the clerk?

Melody took a deep breath. "Yvonne says we have to change things. That's why we have to march! That's why we're walking with Dr. King next Sunday."

Dwayne put his hand on Melody's shoulder. "I don't think a march is going to change things for me. Don't you see now? I have to use my talent to become a famous singer if I want things to be different."

Would people really treat Dwayne fairly if he was famous? Melody wondered. "I understand that you want to be famous," she said. "And I believe in you, Dwayne . . ."

"But?"

"But what about everyone else? Shouldn't we try to change things for people who aren't ever going to be famous? People who are just ordinary, like me?"

Dwayne cracked a half-smile. "Now you sound like Yvonne. The answer is yeah, everybody has to work

♪ No Ordinary Sound ♪

to make things different. But we don't have to do it the same way. Everybody's got the power for change inside themselves. Music is mine."

Melody was shaken by what had happened in the store. But the idea that everybody had some great power inside made her feel more hopeful than she had just a few minutes ago.

"By the way, Dee-Dee," Dwayne said quietly, "you are not ordinary."

"I'm not?"

"Nothing close. I can't wait to see how you're gonna change the world, girl."

What Feels Right

♪ CHAPTER 10 ♪

Dwayne walked Melody back home without talking much, and then he left to meet his friend Artie. Melody went inside. Mommy was the only one home, and she was talking on the telephone in the kitchen. The house was unusually quiet as Melody changed her clothes. She couldn't get the shouting manager out of her head, so she decided to go work in her garden. Being around plants and flowers always made her feel calm.

Life is such a puzzle, she thought as she weeded her flower bed. *How can some people be so unkind? If we all have the power to change things, why don't we?* Dwayne had told her that she would change the world. How could she, when she was having so much trouble picking out one song to sing?

Melody was in the backyard getting water from

♪ No Ordinary Sound ♪

the hose when she heard a car pull into the driveway. Val suddenly appeared around the corner of the house. "Val!" Melody said. "What are you doing here?"

"Do you want to go for a ride? Daddy and Mama want to check out some houses. Your mama said you can come, too."

Melody thought a fun outing might be nice after the way her morning one had turned out. She slipped off her gloves, tossed them onto the back steps, and followed Val.

Mommy was standing in the driveway, leaning toward the open window of the burgundy four-door Ford Fairlane. She was talking to Tish. "Well, I want to hear every detail of the house hunt when you get back!" Mommy said as Melody and Val climbed into the backseat. Charles tooted his horn twice and pulled away.

Cousin Tish turned to the girls from the front seat. "Now, y'all sit back. We're just doin' a cruise by some houses we saw listed in the newspaper. It'll be fun."

Melody nodded and pressed her head back against the soft seat. Tish turned the radio on. The DJ on the local station was reporting news about all the details of

♪ What Feels Right ♪

the freedom walk coming up in a week.

"Have you decided what you're going to sing for Youth Day yet?" Val asked, scooting close to Melody.

"How's that coming, honey?" Tish asked. "You know, your mama's so proud."

"I'm still trying to find a song that feels right," Melody said.

"That's sort of what we're doing today with houses, isn't it, Daddy?" Val said. "We're trying to find one that feels right."

"That's right, Princess," Charles replied.

At that moment, the radio announcer started talking about the songs that people might hear during the freedom walk. He mentioned "Lift Every Voice and Sing." Melody had always liked the title, and now, as the song began to play, she realized that it said what she was feeling inside. At that moment, Melody knew it was exactly what she wanted to sing for Youth Day.

Tish suddenly turned the volume down. "Oh, Charles, look!" she said, pointing to a house that was for sale.

"Mama, that yard is tiny," Val complained. "We need room for Melody to help me plant lots of flowers!"

♪ No Ordinary Sound ♪

"Okay, baby." Tish said. "We'll keep that in mind. We want all of us to be happy with our new home."

"Now, I like the brick houses in this neighborhood," Charles said, swinging onto a street lined with shade trees.

Both Melody and Val crowded to the same side of the car to peer out the window. The houses were all set back from the street on perfectly green lawns. Melody counted the trees spaced along the sidewalk, and marveled at the flower beds decorating nearly every yard.

"This is really nice," Tish murmured.

"There's a 'For Sale' sign up the street, Mama!" Val shouted.

"Let's get out and take a look," Charles said, cruising to a stop at the curb.

The house was pretty—like something Melody had seen in a magazine. It was two stories tall, a little smaller than her own house, and made of speckled light and dark red brick. There was a big picture window on one side of the green front door. The narrow roof was peaked, as if the house was wearing a pointy hat.

"I've been hoping for an upstairs!" Val whispered to

♪ What Feels Right ♪

Melody. Melody smiled, remembering the fun she and her sisters and brother had sliding down the upstairs banister when her parents weren't looking.

Charles opened the car door for the girls, and Val squeezed Melody's hand tightly as they followed the adults along the walk and up the steps. Melody could tell that Val was excited.

"I'll take down the real estate agent's name and number from the sign," Tish said. She whipped out a pen and a small notebook from her purse. "Hmm. There's an open house tour next Sunday. You think we can make it after church, honey?"

"I don't see why not," Charles said.

Melody had hoped that Charles and Tish would change their minds and join the rest of the family at the freedom walk next week, but it didn't sound as if they would.

All four of them peered into the big front window. The house was empty, and they could see straight through to part of the kitchen.

"It's got a fireplace," Tish said, scribbling in her notebook. "I've always wanted a fireplace, Charles."

Val nudged Melody. "Let's see what the backyard

♪ No Ordinary Sound ♪

looks like!" she said. The girls raced around the house, but there was a high fence on the side and across the back. All they could see was the top of a skinny tree.

"I had a swing set back in Birmingham," Val sighed. "Daddy says I can have one here, too."

Melody was looking up at the house next door. "Hey! Somebody's looking at us," she said, stepping back from the fence between the yards. Melody smiled and waved, and Val joined her. The woman in the window did not wave back. Instead, she pulled the curtains closed.

"What was that about?" Val asked as they wandered back to the front yard.

"I don't know, but it was weird," Melody said.

Val's parents were standing at the curb, and Tish was taking pictures with a camera.

"This is what I'm looking for," Charles said. "A quiet neighborhood where a man can enjoy his home without any troubles."

"All right, y'all, this one is on my list," Tish said. "Let's keep going!" Her high heels clicked on the walk as she headed back to the car.

"It's on the *top* of my list," Charles said. He turned

♪ What Feels Right ♪

to the girls, who were lagging behind. "What do you think, Val?"

"I like it a lot, Daddy!"

"Melody," Cousin Charles asked, "is there sufficient flower-planting space for your liking?"

"Yes, sir," Melody answered. She and Val giggled as they climbed into the car. When Melody looked at the house next door, she saw the blinds in a downstairs window flutter.

Tish flipped the radio on just in time for them to hear a voice singing, *"My mama told me, you better shop around!"*

"Well, how do you like that!" she said with a laugh. "Even Smokey Robinson is giving us advice!"

Charles drove them around Detroit for another hour, and they saw dozens of other houses for sale. But everyone agreed that they liked the pointy-hat house the most.

"Let's head on home," Tish said. "I'll fix some lunch."

Charles nodded. "And I'll call the real estate agent."

♪ No Ordinary Sound ♪

When they arrived at Melody's grandparents' house, there was the sound of music coming from the open windows. Inside, Big Momma paused her piano playing to give everyone big hugs. "How was the house hunting?" she asked.

"We saw the nicest place!" Tish opened her purse, took out her notebook, and handed it to Charles.

"I'll make the call upstairs," he said. "Do you mind, Big Momma?"

"You go right ahead, honey," she said.

"Help me out with lunch, Valerie," Tish said, heading for the kitchen.

Val followed her mother, and Big Momma turned back to the piano. She started playing a tune softly, and that reminded Melody of the song from the car radio.

"Big Momma, could you play 'Lift Every Voice and Sing'?" Melody asked. She wasn't surprised when her grandmother stopped the song she had been playing and seamlessly started "Lift Every Voice." Big Momma didn't need any sheet music.

"Many people call this the Negro National Anthem," Big Momma said as she played. "A colored man, James Weldon Johnson, wrote the lyrics as a

♪ What Feels Right ♪

poem, and his brother wrote the music."

"What are the lyrics?" Melody asked. She had listened to the song many times, but now she wanted to hear all the words.

Big Momma stopped playing. "I have the music right here," she said. She stood and opened her piano bench and looked through several sheets of music. Then she handed Melody an old songbook.

"Lift every voice and sing, till earth and heaven ring." Melody read the first line and imagined being able to sing out, loud and strong, so the whole world could hear.

"Would you play it again, please?" Melody asked.

Big Momma sat down again. Melody propped the book on the piano and then stood close to Big Momma, reading the words silently as she followed the music. When the song ended, Melody felt the most wonderful feeling stirring inside her.

"Just in case you need to know," Big Momma whispered, "no one has ever sung this at a Youth Day concert before."

The Walk to Freedom

♪ CHAPTER 11 ♪

melody couldn't get the tune of "Lift Every Voice and Sing" out of her mind. She'd carried around the songbook Big Momma had given her all week. She'd memorized all three verses, and on the afternoon of the freedom walk, she was thinking hard about the words.

"Yvonne," Melody asked, "what does it mean to *ring with the harmonies of liberty*?" She could see her sister's face in the mirror over the dresser. Yvonne finished smoothing Melody's hair before she answered.

"Harmony is everybody joining together."

"You mean, playing nicely, like Mommy used to tell us?"

"Right. And liberty—"

"Means free. I know. Like the Pledge of Allegiance."

"That's a really important song you're learning,

♪ The Walk to Freedom ♪

Dee-Dee," Yvonne told her, adjusting Melody's headband.

"Why?"

"Well . . ." Yvonne wrinkled her face in thought. "It's about the future, really. I mean, most black Americans are relatives of people who were brought to this country in chains. Slavery went on for two hundred and fifty years. And even though last January was the one hundreth anniversary of the Emancipation Proclamation that outlawed slavery, black people today are still being oppressed."

Melody spun around from her chair. "Oppressed?"

"It means held back. You know, not allowed to shop where they want or get the jobs they want or live where they want. Not allowed to really be free."

Yvonne put Melody's brush down on the dresser and picked up the big, fork-like comb that she used for her Afro. "So, see?" she continued. "This song encourages us to remember how strong we were in the past, but also pushes us to keep being strong now, to keep fighting every day until—"

"—*until earth and heaven ring.*" Melody said. She was beginning to understand. "And that means never

♪ No Ordinary Sound ♪

giving up until everything is fair, doesn't it?"

Yvonne patted Melody on her shoulders and said, "Liberty and justice is for all, little sis. That's why kids in the South march, that's why I help folks register to vote, and that's why we're walking in Detroit today."

Melody thought back to how the man at Fieldston's had treated her and Dwayne so unfairly. Melody wanted the Walk to Freedom to keep things like that from happening in the future.

"Melody," Daddy called up the stairs. "It's time to go."

"What about you?" Melody asked Yvonne.

"I'm riding with friends," Yvonne explained. "I'll be walking with some other college students. You'd better hurry down."

Daddy drove Melody, Lila, and Mommy in the station wagon to pick up Poppa and Big Momma. As Melody watched her grandparents hurrying to the car, she realized that they were both frowning.

"What happened?" Mommy asked Big Momma when they had settled into the station wagon.

"Tish and Charles drove all the way out to that open house today—"

♪ The Walk to Freedom ♪

Melody chimed in from the fold-down seat. "The pointy-hat house, Big Momma? The brick one?"

"Yes. They got there, and the real estate agent told them the open house was cancelled."

Poppa made a "harrumph" sound.

"Where was the house located, exactly?" Mommy asked. When Big Momma told her, Mommy shook her head. Melody could see a flash of anger in Daddy's eyes through the rearview mirror.

Melody was confused. "What happened?" she asked.

"That neighborhood has been in the news lately," Poppa said. "Several home owners have done the same thing. I'll bet somebody doesn't want colored—black— neighbors. So if a black couple shows up, the agent cancels the appointment, or the owner decides not to sell to them."

"That's wrong!" Lila said.

"It *is* wrong," Poppa told her, "but it's not illegal. It should be against the law to keep colored folks from buying any home they can afford."

Melody thought about the woman she and Val had seen in the windows of the house next to the pointy-hat

♪ No Ordinary Sound ♪

house. Could that woman, who had been white, have told the real estate agent to keep Val's family away?

"Charles and Tish should come to the march," Melody said. "To protest."

"They never planned to walk," Poppa reminded them.

"That's a shame," Mommy said, "because one of the reasons for this walk is to call for fair housing laws."

Everyone was quiet. Melody stared out the window thinking about how disappointed Val and Tish and Charles must be. They had all been so excited about that house. Melody felt a little like a balloon whose air was leaking out.

As they drove along Woodward, Melody saw hundreds of people heading downtown on foot.

"This is like going to the Hudson's Thanksgiving Day parade," Lila said. "Look at the crowds!"

Melody perked up. She saw some people carrying flags and others waving signs that looked just like the ones she and Lila had helped make.

"This traffic is something awful," Poppa said. "Will, maybe we'd better park the car and start walking already." Daddy didn't argue. He pulled over at the

♪ The Walk to Freedom ♪

next empty spot near a curb.

"I see a group from New Bethel Baptist Church," Mommy said. "Reverend C. L. Franklin is pastor there. He helped organize the walk and bring Dr. King to speak." She stopped to tie a scarf over her hair and put on sunglasses.

"I hear a band," Lila said.

Melody strained to hear, but the music was too far away for her to recognize the tune. She looked up at the clear blue sky, and at the crowd gathering from all the side streets. This was different from a parade.

Daddy opened the back of the station wagon and pulled out two neatly lettered signs. One said "Down with Discrimination." The other read "Justice Now."

"That's the one I made," Melody said proudly.

Lila grabbed it. "I can hold it higher," she said.

Melody pouted, but she knew Lila was right. Daddy lifted the other sign high above everyone's heads.

"I believe there are thousands of folks out here," Mommy said as she took Melody's hand.

Poppa nodded. "More than they predicted on the radio."

Cobo Hall was the biggest auditorium in Detroit,

♪ No Ordinary Sound ♪

built right near the Detroit River. People flowed slowly toward Cobo as if they had become a river, and the river sang.

Melody listened. She knew the song, and she opened her mouth to join in, just as Big Momma did, too. Together they sang

> *We shall not,*
> *We shall not be moved.*
> *We shall not,*
> *We shall not be moved.*
> *Just like a tree that's standing by the water,*
> *We shall not be moved.*

Big Momma took Melody's other hand. Walking there, between her mother and her grandmother, raising her girl voice with theirs, Melody felt strangely light, as if she could fly if they let go of her hands. And all the other voices surrounding them were like hearts, beating together. *This is harmony*, Melody thought.

The sea of bodies slowed even more, and then stopped. Melody couldn't see Cobo Hall, but she knew they were still far away from the entrance.

♪ The Walk to Freedom ♪

Mommy let go of Melody and took out her camera to snap pictures. "This is even more remarkable than I expected," Mommy said.

"I wish Val were here," Melody said to Mommy. "And Dwayne." Dwayne had made good on his promise not to join them and had gone to Artie's after church.

"I know, sweetheart," Mommy said, taking Melody's hand again. "You'll have to listen hard. Then you can tell Val all about it."

"This is as close as we're going to get," Poppa said.

"At least we'll be able to hear the speeches," Daddy said. "They've got speakers set up."

The speakers crackled, and the singing faded. A man said something over the loudspeaker, and then someone else spoke. Melody's legs began to get tired, and she wondered when Dr. King would preach.

Then the roar of applause rose around them. Melody heard a different man's voice, a strong, clear, Southern voice. At last it was Dr. King! He talked about Abraham Lincoln, and the Emancipation Proclamation that freed Negroes from slavery. He talked about Birmingham, and how racial segregation was wrong.

♪ No Ordinary Sound ♪

Melody didn't understand everything Dr. King said, but she felt the excitement of the crowds around her as they shouted out "Yes!" at certain parts of his speech. People clapped and cheered so hard at other times that Dr. King had to pause. His words took on a rhythm, and he was almost chanting.

"I have a dream," he said. "With this faith I will go out with you and transform dark yesterdays into bright tomorrows . . ." Melody's insides began to shiver as she thought of the words to "Lift Every Voice":

> *Sing a song, full of the faith*
> *that the dark past has taught us*

All of her family's stories flashed through Melody's mind: Poppa leaving his farm, Mommy making the triple-chocolate cake because Daddy couldn't buy one, Yvonne being turned away at the bank, Dwayne being treated badly at Fieldston's.

> *Sing a song full of the hope*
> *that the present has brought us*

♪ The Walk to Freedom ♪

Poppa had moved to Detroit and opened his flower shop—where Yvonne now had a summer job. Now Mommy made the best cake ever, and Dwayne was determined to succeed in a music career so that he would be treated fairly. None of them had ever given up hope. Melody felt inspired.

Dr. King was chanting, "Free at last! Free at last!" The applause was like thunder in the sunshine.

On the walk back to the car, Melody made an announcement. "For Youth Day, I'm going to do 'Lift Every Voice and Sing.'"

"That's a big song for you, Little One!" Poppa said with a smile. She saw Mommy nodding her approval.

"Yes, it is," Melody said to him. "But when I hear it, I feel the way I did listening to Dr. King. That's how I want the audience to feel when I sing at Youth Day. Dwayne says when the words mean something special to a singer, amazing things happen."

Daddy looked at her with surprise as he unlocked the station wagon. "Dwayne said that, did he?"

"Isn't that the song that you've been humming in

♪ No Ordinary Sound ♪

your sleep?" Lila asked, climbing into the folding seat.

"I guess," Melody said, noticing that her grandmother hadn't said a word. "Do you think it's a good fit, Big Momma?" Melody whispered.

Big Momma gave Melody's hand a squeeze. "Your brother is right. And I believe my chick can do anything she sets her mind to."

Lila snapped her fingers. "Make it work, Dee-Dee. Make it work!"

Val was watching from the front window when they returned from the march. She threw open Big Momma's front door and ran out. "How was it? Did you carry my sign? Did you see Dr. King?"

"It was great! And no, and no!" Melody answered with enthusiasm. "Lila carried your sign, and we didn't get close enough to see Dr. King, but we heard him." Melody took a breath. "But are you okay? Poppa told us what happened with the house."

Val's shoulders drooped. "It makes me sad to think that it could have been our house. Mama was sad at first, too, but now she's mad."

♪ The Walk to Freedom ♪

Melody didn't want Val to give up her hopes of a swing set and an upstairs. She remembered something from the Walk to Freedom. "Dr. King said he has a dream that black people in Detroit will be able to buy the houses they want," Melody told her cousin.

"Really?" Val asked. "Dr. King said that?"

"Mm-hmm." Melody smiled, looping her arm through her cousin's. "Things are going to change. I just know it."

Fireworks

♪ CHAPTER 12 ♪

*M*elody was dreaming. She dreamed that she was on top of Cobo Hall, singing "Lift Every Voice and Sing" while the Detroit River rolled past like a mighty sea. And when she raised both her arms, she had wings.

She woke up, and for a few seconds, she thought she might still be dreaming. She smelled dinner instead of breakfast. Then she heard the low rumbling of men's voices outside, and sniffed the wisps of hickory smoke wafting through the open window. It was the Fourth of July. Daddy had the entire day off from work, and Melody knew he was up already, tending the barbecue. She squinted over at Lila and Yvonne, who were both still asleep, and then at the Mickey Mouse alarm clock. Mickey's hands pointed to six o'clock.

Melody hurried to get dressed, wondering what

♪ Fireworks ♪

time Val was coming over. She didn't stop to put on her shoes, and instead ran downstairs barefoot with Bo at her heels. She swung around the stair post at the end of the banister, saw a pink bundle curled up on the sofa, and almost tripped on the rug.

"Val!" Melody shouted, and Bo barked excitedly. "Shhh!" Melody frowned at him when she remembered how early it was.

Val sat up, blinking her sleepy eyes. Bo rushed over to her. "Hey, doggy." Val scratched between his ears and yawned at Melody. "My daddy came over to help your daddy, and I came along. How is your song coming?"

Melody had told Val that the Walk to Freedom had helped her pick her song for Youth Day. "I know all the words, but I have to start working on the music."

"My mama says 'Lift Every Voice and Sing' is beautiful, but it's not easy to sing." Val absentmindedly began to pat down her messy hair.

"Here, let me!" Melody said. She sat next to Val and parted her cousin's hair with her fingers, making two careful braids. "Big Momma says things worth having don't come easy."

♪ No Ordinary Sound ♪

"I wish she'd tell that to Mama and Daddy again," Val said. "Now they can't agree on where we're gonna live. I never knew it was so hard to buy a house."

"I know they'll make it work," Melody said.

Val pulled away to look at her and laugh. "You say that all the time!"

"That's because my mother does. Come on. Let's go see what the daddies are doing outside."

Melody, Val, and Bo sped through the dining room and burst into the kitchen. Melody didn't expect her mother to be up yet, so she was surprised to see Mommy wearing her red-white-and-blue-striped blouse and dancing to the radio.

"Happy Fourth of July, girls!" Mommy said. She was holding a bowl full of lemons that had been cut in half. "You're just in time to start the lemonade! Daddy put the big crock outside on the picnic table." She handed Val the bowl and Melody a juicer.

Melody looked at the mound of lemons. "Are there a lot of people coming over?"

Mommy spoke over her shoulder from the kitchen sink. "The family, Miss Esther from the church, a few of Yvonne's friends, and Dwayne's friends Phil and

♪ Fireworks ♪

Artie. You and Val can be a big help to me."

Melody crossed the cool linoleum of the kitchen, pushed the back door open, and held it for Val. Daddy heard it creak and waved his tongs. Melody smiled. No matter how late her father worked on the day before the Fourth of July, he was always standing at his grill as soon as the sun came up.

Cousin Charles was wearing the baggiest shorts that Melody had ever seen. She held back a giggle.

"Aren't Daddy's shorts the ugliest?" Val leaned her chin on Melody's shoulder.

"Yep," Melody laughed. The girls got to work, taking turns juicing the lemons.

Charles was busy setting up folding tables and chairs around the yard. "Dee-Dee, I heard you're going to sing today!"

"I kind of told Daddy you would," Val said.

Melody shook her head. "Not my Youth Day song, but we can still sing." Then she had an idea. "Let's put on a show!" Melody said to Val. "You and Lila and I could pretend to be The Vandellas or The Marvelettes."

"That's a great idea!" Val said.

"We've got one of Big Momma's old microphones

♪ No Ordinary Sound ♪

upstairs, and I bet Yvonne would help us dress up."

"Do you think Lila will sing?" Val asked doubtfully.

"Oh, I think so," Melody giggled. If Dwayne's friend Phil was going to be in the audience, she was pretty sure Lila would agree to be part of the act.

Mommy came out to help the girls finish the lemonade, and then gave them ears of corn to shuck. Afterward, Melody got her gardening gloves.

"I need to do some weeding," Melody said to Val. "Do you want to help?"

"You mean, dig in dirt?"

Melody laughed. "Sure. The flowers that make our neighborhood look nice grow in dirt. The tomatoes we're going to eat today grew in this dirt. I love growing things as much as I love to sing. Sometimes I sing to my plants, too."

"You do?" Val thought that was funny. "Sure, I'll help. But I've never weeded a garden before." Val borrowed a pair of Melody's gardening gloves, and the two of them knelt between the neat rows of cabbages and greens.

"This is kind of fun," Val said after they'd been pulling and singing. "I think I might like a garden of

♪ Fireworks ♪

my own—if we ever get our own place."

"You will," Melody assured her. "And I'll help you make it bloom."

"Hey, you girls have that garden looking like something from a magazine!" Charles called.

Val nodded. "Melody's a real gardener, Daddy!"

"Well the work goes much faster with four hands instead of two," Melody laughed.

When the vegetable garden and flower beds were weeded, Val cleaned up in the bathroom and Melody went to the bedroom she shared with her sisters.

Yvonne was already downstairs, but Lila was still in bed. She rolled over and groaned when Melody slammed a drawer.

"Are you awake, Lila?"

Lila opened one eye. "What time is it? Why are you making so much noise?"

"Sorry. It's nine o'clock. Would you put on a show with Val and me later, when everyone comes over? We'll be The Marvelettes!"

Lila closed her eyes again.

"Mommy says Phil will be here," Melody added.

Lila's eyes popped open and Melody skipped out

♪ No Ordinary Sound ♪

of their room. Val was waiting in the hall, grinning because she'd overheard the conversation.

"I think Lila will sing with us," Melody said. The girls giggled as they hurried down the steps.

Around two in the afternoon Poppa, Big Momma, and Tish arrived. Soon after, Yvonne's friends began to fill in the backyard. One of them was a young man from Ghana who was studying in Detroit. Melody was fascinated by his beautiful robes, which he said he wore "in honor of this Independence Day." Dwayne, Artie, and Phil cornered him near the back steps and asked him all about African music.

Melody and Val were playing jacks in the driveway when Melody looked up to see Miss Esther tapping her cane along the concrete. She was carrying a plate wrapped in wax paper.

Melody scrambled up. "I can take that for you, Miss Esther," Melody said, reaching for the plate. She wanted to peek at what was under the paper, but didn't.

♪ Fireworks ♪

"Tea cakes," Miss Esther told her.

Melody smiled. "Everybody's in the backyard," she said. "I'll walk you around."

"And I'll carry the tea cakes," Val said, taking the plate from Melody and heading up the driveway.

Miss Esther nodded, but instead of following Val, she stood looking at the Ellisons' yard. "I just want to take a minute to admire these lovely flower beds," Miss Esther said. "Your mother must spend a lot of time keeping them up."

"No, ma'am. I do it," Melody said proudly.

"*You* do? What an eye for color you have! I notice every time I drive by. You know, beautiful plants and flowers can change more than the look of a neighborhood. They can change the way a place feels, too."

"Do you have a garden?" Melody asked as she and Miss Esther strolled along the driveway.

"I used to," Miss Esther replied. "But I don't anymore." She stopped and pointed her cane along the side of the house. "Tell me about what you have planted here. And here!"

It took Melody and Miss Esther almost half an hour to make it to the backyard. They walked slowly

♪ No Ordinary Sound ♪

and talked about Melody's flowers and the garden Miss Esther used to have and how much they both liked to plant things and watch them grow.

"There's nothing better than seeing a tiny bud bloom into something beautiful," Miss Esther said as they joined the party. "You know that too, don't you, Melody?"

"Yes, ma'am," Melody agreed.

Melody's mother came over to greet Miss Esther and show her to a chair under the big shade tree. Val raced across the yard and grabbed Melody's arm. "I thought you'd never get back here."

"Miss Esther is one of the most interesting grown-ups I've ever met," Melody said. "We were talking about gardens. She knows as much about growing things as Poppa."

Val grinned. "I didn't think that was possible." Then she tugged Melody's arm. "Come on. Yvonne's going to help us get ready for our number."

As the girls headed toward the back door, Dwayne was pulling a bottle of Vernor's Ginger Ale out of a big tub full of ice. "Hey, Dee-Dee," he called. "You didn't ask me to join your group!"

♪ Fireworks ♪

Melody laughed. "It's just us *girls.* Do you want to be our stagehand?"

"Sure—whatever you need." He made a funny bow.

When Melody and Val got upstairs, Yvonne and one of her girlfriends were piling her bed with some of the dresses Yvonne had outgrown. Lila was fussing with the old microphone. "I hope this thing works," she muttered. "Somebody find me a screwdriver!"

Val sifted through the dresses on the bed. "I like this one!" she said, grabbing a blue dress. "And look at this, Dee-Dee! It's perfect for you!" Val held up a flowered dress with a bow at the waist.

Melody couldn't believe her eyes. "Can I really wear that one, Vonnie?" Yvonne hadn't worn the dress for years, but she hadn't ever let Lila or Melody wear it, either.

"For today," Yvonne answered. "Yes."

"Which Marvelettes song should we do?" Melody asked, holding the dress up in front of her. It was a little bit big, but they could pin it if they needed to.

"How about 'Please Mr. Postman'?" Yvonne suggested, sweeping Melody's hair up on top of her head. "You girls sing that all the time."

♪ No Ordinary Sound ♪

Val was tipping awkwardly in a pair of Yvonne's high heels. *"C'mon, deliver the letter, the sooner the better,"* she sang as Yvonne poked Melody's hair with bobby pins.

Once the older girls finished pinning and piling hair and buttoning and zipping dresses, Melody, Val, and Lila each twirled in front of the full-length mirror. Melody couldn't help grinning at what she saw. They weren't wearing matching dresses, but they still looked like Motown stars!

The girls hurried down to the kitchen, where they waited for Dwayne to hush the crowd in the backyard. "Ladies and gentlemen," Dwayne announced as the girls and their dresses floated onto the back stoop. "Introducing the Even More Marvelous Marvelettes!"

Val giggled at the name Dwayne had invented, and Lila made sure the microphone worked. Melody fidgeted with the bow on her dress, but she wasn't one bit nervous. Already the music was inside her head, and her feet began to move.

"Music!" Lila ordered.

Dwayne and his bandmates started doo-wopping the song, and Melody, Val, and Lila began singing.

♪ Fireworks ♪

Melody put her heart into having a good time. By the end of the song, she was dancing and waving her arms along with Val and Lila. Other people were dancing, too, including her parents, Charles and Tish, and even Poppa and Big Momma.

"Encore!" Dwayne yelled when they finished. "That means one more time!" They sang the song again, and everyone in the backyard joined in.

Finally breathless, Melody and Val collapsed on the steps. Tish handed each of them a cold bottle of Vernor's.

"That was so much fun," Val said.

"I am starved!" Lila gasped, biting into a hot dog. "You'd better get one. Dad says he's running out of charcoal."

Val shook her head, but Melody headed for the grill. Her father pressed a plump hot dog into a bun and handed it to Melody. "Nice job, daughter," he said, smiling. "I know you'll do the same on Youth Day."

"Thanks, Daddy."

He wiped sweat from his forehead and handed Charles his long grilling fork. "This crowd is still hungry. If you man the grill, I'll go for more charcoal."

♪ No Ordinary Sound ♪

"You got it," Charles agreed.

"I'm hot!" Val said when Melody returned to the back steps. "Let's go out front and see if there's a cooler breeze."

The girls were on the front porch, and Melody had just finished her hot dog, when Daddy returned. When he got out of the car, her father slammed the door so hard that both girls stared. "Is your brother still here?" he said in a low voice.

Melody nodded her head. "Yes, Daddy."

Her father didn't even get the charcoal out of the back of the wagon. He stomped past them and into the backyard.

"What happened?" Val asked.

"I think something bad," Melody said, the fun of the day fading. She heard Daddy yelling for Dwayne. The entire neighborhood could probably hear him yelling. The back door opened and closed, and Melody heard Dwayne and her parents in the living room.

Melody told Val, "I'll be back," and went inside.

"I just ran into Joe Walker at the store," Daddy was saying. "He says you're a part-time janitor at Cobo Hall. He says you work a few hours in the afternoons. I want

♪ Fireworks ♪

to know how you can be a day janitor at Cobo Hall when you're working a day shift at the factory."

Dwayne dropped his head for a beat. "I'm not working at the factory anymore, Dad."

"What?" Mommy said. She sounded shocked.

Dwayne sighed. "I quit the factory a while ago. I needed more time for writing and rehearsing, and—"

"Rehearsing!" Daddy said angrily. "Boy, what is wrong with you? You know how hard it is for a Negro to get his foot in the door at that factory? You could have a steady job every summer when you're home from school!"

"Dad, I don't want my foot in that door." Dwayne wasn't shouting. He was calm. "I don't want to work at the factory. I don't want to go to college. I want a music career!"

"Daddy, he's really good," Melody said.

Their father seemed not to hear. Mommy put a hand on Melody's shoulder.

"You promised us that you'd work at the factory and then go to college," Mommy said.

"I'm sorry, Dad. Mom. I can't keep that promise. I've got an audition at Motown next Thursday with my

♪ No Ordinary Sound ♪

band. This is my chance. I have to try."

Daddy narrowed his eyes as he stood almost nose to nose with Dwayne. They were the same height. They had the same chin. Melody held her breath. To her surprise, it wasn't her father who spoke first.

"I'll pack my stuff," Dwayne said.

Melody exchanged a worried glance with her mother.

"I didn't ask—" Daddy didn't finish.

Dwayne put one hand on his father's shoulder and looked directly at him. "I know you didn't, Dad. But if Mr. Gordy likes us, he'll send us on the road right away to see how we perform for real audiences. I'll go stay at Phil's." He held out his other hand for a handshake.

Daddy looked down at Dwayne's hand, then back at his face. In slow motion, he shook Dwayne's hand.

Dwayne looked at Mommy. "I can't be somebody I'm not," he said. "I'll make it work, Mom." Dwayne turned on his heel and bounded up the stairs.

Daddy looked at Mommy, and then at Melody. He seemed to notice her for the first time. "You say he's good?"

"Yes, Daddy," Melody whispered.

♪ Fireworks ♪

"Will, I don't go along with this notion of skipping college," Mommy said quietly. "But Melody's right. He's very, very good."

Daddy shook his head. "He'd better be. If he thinks factory work is hard, wait until he learns what that music business is like. I know some fellows who tried going down that road. It was too tough, and they couldn't make it."

Melody's parents went to the kitchen, talking and talking all the way outside. *Dwayne will make it work,* Melody told herself, trying not to cry. She sat on the bottom stair to make sure her brother didn't leave without saying good-bye. He didn't take long to come down.

"Melody, look. I didn't mean for things to happen like this."

Melody bit her lip. "Will you ever come home again?"

"If you're trying to tell me good-bye, forget it, sis," Dwayne said. "I'm gonna keep turning up, when you least expect me."

Melody looked down at her toes. "You won't be here to help me get ready for Youth Day."

♪ No Ordinary Sound ♪

"I'm sorry about that. You don't really need me, though. Big Momma has you covered. You listen to her. You'll be all right." He stood up. "I gotta go. Tell the sister-things I'll catch them later. And be good."

As soon as Dwayne had gone and closed the door behind him, the house felt different to Melody. She closed her eyes and listened. In the kitchen, the news was droning on her mother's radio. Outside, voices mingled with Bo's barking. Something had changed, though. Without Dwayne's humming or singing in the background to all those sounds, her family was off-key.

In a few minutes, Lila and Yvonne came in.

"What happened?" Lila asked.

"Dad looked really mad," Yvonne said. "So we didn't dare ask him anything."

Melody told them everything.

"Well, it *is* Independence Day," Lila said. "What better day for Dwayne to go out on his own? Right, Vonnie?"

"Face it," Yvonne said, "Dwayne is hardheaded. Sooner or later, he would have quit the factory. Dwayne lives and breathes music. I know Daddy wasn't happy, but how could he be surprised?"

♪ Fireworks ♪

Melody thought about the expressions on her parents' faces. They were surprised all right. And hurt.

Lila and Yvonne went back out, but Melody didn't feel like rejoining the party. She sat inside for a long time. By the time she went back outside, the sun had set. Miss Esther was gone, and her parents were talking to Yvonne and her friends. Her grandparents were sitting side by side under the tree in the deepening dark of dusk.

"If you're looking for Val and Lila, Charles took them to the fireworks," Poppa said. Big Momma motioned for Melody to come over to them. Melody sat on the grass near their knees.

"How are you feeling about your brother?" Big Momma asked.

"Kind of down," Melody said.

"Dwayne needs growing-into-a-man space," Poppa said. "He has to leave home to find it."

Big Momma said, "One day, you'll need growing-into-a-woman space, and you'll leave home too. It's what we all do."

Melody twisted her neck to look up. "Did you?"

Big Momma chuckled. "Yes, I did. Dorothy and I

went on the road as gospel singers, remember?"

"Oh, yes."

"It's time, chick."

Melody nearly choked as she swallowed a gulp of ginger ale. "Time for *me*?"

"Time for you to grow. Time to lift that beautiful instrument of yours. We'll start on Monday. Ten o'clock sharp."

Practice

♪ CHAPTER 13 ♪

n the Monday after the Fourth of July, Melody was at her grandparents' house at exactly 9:59 a.m.

"Valerie," Big Momma said, "I'm afraid you can't sit in on Melody's session. She needs to concentrate. Go on in the kitchen, darlin'."

Val faked a wide-eyed, fearful expression, then winked at Melody and scurried into the other room. Val's goofiness made Melody smile, even though she was actually nervous.

"Let's do a few warm-up exercises, all right?" Big Momma sat on the piano bench and began to play scales. Melody stood beside the piano with her back straight and her arms at her sides. She hummed to match the notes that Big Momma played. When Melody's voice was ready, they moved on to her Youth Day song.

♪ No Ordinary Sound ♪

Melody had sung only a few lines when they were interrupted by a furious knocking at the door. When Big Momma stopped playing and got up to answer it, Melody was surprised to see Diane Harris.

"Mrs. Porter! My mother got my lesson time mixed up, and she's on a double shift, and my dad dropped me off, and—" Diane's frantic explanation squeaked to a halt when she noticed Melody. The girls stared at each other for a moment.

"Mistakes happen, Diane," Big Momma said. "You'll have your lesson after Melody's. Come on in and pass right through to the kitchen. Melody's cousin Valerie is there, and you can sit with her. I need y'all to be as quiet as possible."

Big Momma sat back down at the piano as if nothing had happened. "Let's start at the beginning. Key?" Big Momma played a note, and Melody adjusted her voice by singing "Ahhh."

"Good. Here we go." She played.

Melody exhaled, thinking of the Walk to Freedom and how inspired she'd been after hearing Dr. King speak. She wanted people to feel the same way when

♪ **Practice** ♪

they heard her sing this song.

She sang the entire first verse, but she didn't always hit the right notes. It was hard to keep up with the tempo because of the way the music swooped up and down, especially in the middle. Melody anxiously watched her grandmother's face for a sign of how she was doing.

Big Momma stopped playing. "Again," she said. "From the beginning."

For half an hour, Melody sang. Big Momma stopped frequently to give Melody direction. Melody had to sing one line over and over again. Finally, Big Momma closed her music book.

"Good," she said. Melody's heart thumped. Big Momma hadn't said "Excellent!" or "Wonderful." Just "Good." Melody waited.

"We have to work on tempo. That's every singer's challenge with this song. Your lyrics aren't quite keeping pace with the music. And you have to make your voice sound bigger."

Melody nodded. "Lifting it, you mean. I'll work hard, I promise." She meant it.

Big Momma handed Melody a cassette tape. On the

♪ No Ordinary Sound ♪

case, written in Big Momma's scratchy handwriting, were the words: "For Melody's Practice."

"I made you this tape recording yesterday so you will have music to work with at home," Big Momma said. "You've given yourself a real challenge, my chick. And I know you'll conquer it. Now, enough. Wednesday, we'll do it again."

Melody twirled herself to the kitchen door, only remembering as she pushed it open that Diane was there.

"That was the Negro National Anthem," Diane said. "Are you singing that for Youth Day?" She looked surprised. "I never knew you could sound so good," she said, pushing her way past Melody and through the kitchen door.

Melody was speechless. *Did Diane just compliment my voice?* Melody looked at Val. "What did you say to her?"

Val laughed. "It wasn't anything I said. It was what you sang, Dee-Dee."

On Thursday evening, Melody and her sisters were

🎵 Practice 🎵

waiting anxiously to hear about Dwayne's audition. Mommy was still at a church meeting when the phone finally rang around nine o'clock. Melody jumped off the sofa, but Yvonne got to the phone first. Dwayne asked to speak to their father. Daddy had worked a full day's shift and was asleep already, but Yvonne went to wake him up.

Melody and Lila hurried up the stairs after her and huddled outside their parents' bedroom with Yvonne, listening.

"Say what?" Daddy said. He sounded sleepy.

"I'm not so sure it was a good idea to wake him up," Lila said, poking Yvonne with her elbow.

"Is he even going to remember talking?" Melody asked.

Yvonne put her finger to her lips. "Shh! Listen!"

"Yeah?" Daddy sounded a bit more awake. "No kidding? So what do they pay you for that? What? You would've done better on the assembly line. I'm going to sleep." There was a pause and then Daddy said, "You watch yourself out there. And call your mother." Daddy slammed the phone down. "All you sisters! Your brother is working for Motown. Good night!" In a very

♪ No Ordinary Sound ♪

few minutes, Daddy was snoring as loud as the car engines he helped build at the Ford factory.

"I can't believe it," Yvonne said. "Dwayne is making his dream come true."

"You think Daddy is still mad at him?" Melody asked.

Lila yawned. "He didn't sound like it." She took off her eyeglasses and cleaned them with the edge of her shirt.

Yvonne made a clucking sound at her. "You need to take a break from studying. You're going to wear your eyes out."

"I have one chance to get into this school," Lila said. "I'm not going to mess it up."

"Of course you won't." Yvonne stood up. "How about some cookies and milk to feed your big brain? We can celebrate for Dwayne. Then you can go to bed and wake up to a new day with your books."

Lila laughed, and Melody had to smile. As the girls headed to the kitchen, Melody found herself humming and singing in her head: *Facing the rising sun of our new day begun, let us march on till victory is won.*

♪ Practice ♪

Mommy got a short note from Dwayne soon after his call, telling her that The Three Ravens were touring with a few other groups. Melody got a postcard of New Orleans from him that only said, "Everything going real good. Thought I saw Sharon running by the stage. Ha, Ha! Dwayne."

Melody was glad that her brother was getting to perform, but home didn't quite feel like home without him. Other things were also changing. Mommy taught summer school four days a week, so she wasn't around to take Melody to the movies or to the soda fountain at Barthwell's. Yvonne spent most of her time either working at the flower shop or at meetings of the Student Walk to Freedom club she'd started. Lila was closed up in their room or at the library preparing for her test at the end of August. She was so snappy now that Melody only said "Hi" and "Bye" to her. Melody felt like the harmony her family had always shared was missing. She wondered how they could make it sound right again.

Melody was grateful that Val was close by, even

♪ No Ordinary Sound ♪

though it meant that her parents hadn't found their new house yet. Tish *had* found a space for her new salon, though, and she was busy getting ready to open.

One day at the end of July, Melody and Val were in Big Momma's kitchen arranging flowers in a vase. The sounds of a halting piano lesson came from the living room. "Diane?" Val asked.

Melody nodded. "She's getting better."

"A little," Val agreed, picking up a snapdragon. Her eyes brightened. "I love this shade of pink. Do you think Mama might let me have pink walls in my new bedroom?"

Melody imagined sleeping inside a cloud of bubble gum. She wasn't sure she'd like it, or that Val's mother would. "I don't know," she answered. "What do you think?"

"Mama would probably let me have pink hair before she would let me have pink walls." Val started to laugh, and covered her mouth.

Just then, the piano music stopped. Big Momma called to them from the front of the house: "Melody, you have company."

Melody and Val exchanged puzzled glances.

♪ Practice ♪

"Company?" Melody repeated.

Filled with curiosity, both girls hurried to push through the swinging door and cross the dining room.

"Miss Dorothy!" Melody said happily. Miss Dorothy was sitting on the sofa, and Diane looked on from the piano bench.

Big Momma introduced Val.

"Welcome to Detroit," Miss Dorothy said to Val. Then she turned to Melody. "I've heard that you have selected a song for Youth Day—quite a special song."

"How did you know?" Melody asked. She looked at her grandmother. They had agreed that Melody would tell Miss Dorothy about her song choice, but she hadn't done so yet.

Big Momma shook her head. She didn't know either.

"I did it," Diane said in her bossy, too-loud voice. "I told Miss Dorothy."

"You?" Melody stared at her hard. "Why?"

Diane squirmed uncomfortably for a moment. "I wanted Miss Dorothy to know how good you might be! I mean, I was surprised at how good you were. I mean—"

"Melody," Miss Dorothy said, "I'd like to hear

♪ No Ordinary Sound ♪

you sing. I know that you've been working with your grandmother, and I expect you're doing quite well."

Melody was a little bit irritated at Diane for saying something to Miss Dorothy, but she was also flattered that Diane had told their choir director that she was good. "All right," Melody agreed.

Diane and Val went to sit beside Miss Dorothy. Big Momma took Diane's place on the bench, and Melody stood beside the piano. She wasn't a bit nervous—after all, she'd been singing in this very same room beside this very same piano for as long as she could remember. And she'd been practicing "Lift Every Voice" at home every day. She was ready to sing.

> *Lift every voice and sing,*
> *Till earth and heaven ring,*
> *Ring with the harmonies of liberty.*

The words and their meaning flowed out of Melody with confidence.

When Melody finished, everyone clapped. "Oh, very nice!" Miss Dorothy said. "Diane was right. You do sing this song well." Miss Dorothy looked at Big

♪ Practice ♪

Momma. "You have a good teacher."

Big Momma laughed. "Girls, how about some lemonade? Dorothy, will you have a glass?"

"Thank you, but I must be going," Miss Dorothy answered. "Girls, I'll see you back at choir practice in September. Valerie, I hope you'll think about joining our group."

Val smiled. "I'll ask my mama!"

While Big Momma walked Miss Dorothy to the door, Diane followed Val and Melody to the kitchen. Melody took three glasses out of the cupboard and filled them with ice. Val poured the lemonade. The girls sat down at the table.

Diane looked at the ice cubes in her glass. "I'm sorry I told Miss Dorothy about your song," she finally blurted out. "My mother and I saw her at the grocery store yesterday, and I just sort of said something. I couldn't help it! I never would have picked such an important song." Diane paused and looked at Melody. "I would have picked something . . . safe."

Melody looked at Diane as if she was seeing her for the first time. "You're saying you would have been *scared* to try this song?"

♪ No Ordinary Sound ♪

Diane took a sip of her lemonade. "I only like to do what I'm good at. You're braver than I am."

"But you're always so confident," Melody said. "You're such a good singer! You're always singing solos at church."

"Why do you think Miss Dorothy picked you to do the Youth Day solo?" Diane asked. "It's because *you're* such a good singer!"

"Maybe it's possible that you're *both* good singers!" Val interrupted. There was a pause, and the three girls looked at one another. They burst out laughing.

"Okay," Diane said.

"You're right," Melody agreed.

Diane emptied her glass and stood up. "I have to go. I'll see you both next week?" she asked shyly.

"Yes!" Melody and Val answered together.

After Diane left, Val turned to Melody. "You were right," she said.

"About what?" Melody asked.

Val smiled. "About Diane. She *is* getting better."

Just then, Big Momma swung the kitchen door open. "How's my chick?" she asked.

"I feel—brave," Melody said.

Never Give Up

♪ CHAPTER 14 ♪

Hot August came, and Sharon came home with it. She called Melody, and it was so unusual to hear Yvonne yell "Dee-Dee! Sharon's on the phone!" that Melody almost didn't understand what her sister meant. Melody was in her room, practicing her song with the tape recording Big Momma had given her. Melody ran down to the kitchen, and Yvonne handed her the telephone receiver. "Sharon?" Melody asked in disbelief.

"Hi! Did you miss me? We got back last night. My mother said I could come over this afternoon. I brought you some praline candy and a postcard."

Melody laughed. "Aren't you supposed to mail those things?"

"What? Pralines? I couldn't find any stamps," Sharon joked. "Have you been doing anything fun?

♪ No Ordinary Sound ♪

Did you decide on your solo for Youth Day?"

"Yes, and I'll tell you all about it. Val's been helping me, but I'm glad you're back. Choir practice starts next week."

"I know. I can't wait to hear you!"

"And I can't wait to see you. I'll be at my grandparents' this afternoon. Come over to their house after lunch."

"Okay," Sharon said. "See you later."

Melody hung up. She'd forgotten to tell Sharon that she and Diane had sort of become friends. "Vonnie, do you think Sharon will be mad that Diane and I are singing friends now?"

Yvonne was opening a bottle of mustard, and Melody noticed that she was making sandwiches—lots of them. Everything was spread across the kitchen table. "What?" Yvonne asked, as if she had only been half listening.

"Never mind," Melody said. "Who are all these sandwiches for?"

"They're for the group taking the bus trip down to D.C.," Yvonne said. "We're leaving tonight, and everybody's bringing food to share. Want to help

♪ **Never Give Up** ♪

wrap the sandwiches in wax paper?"

Melody nodded. "Are you excited about the march?" Yvonne was going to another freedom march, but this one was in Washington, D.C.

"Yes, I am!" Yvonne's Afro crown was tied back by a scarf, so that it was more of an Afro puff at the back of her head. Her earrings dangled as she nodded. "Especially after what happened to Charles and Tish. Nobody has the right to tell you where you can and can't live! If we had open housing laws everywhere, that real estate guy couldn't have done what he did."

Melody sort of understood. "But how is marching in Washington going to help them get a house in Detroit?"

"Hopefully there will be thousands of people at the march. A crowd that big will force government officials to listen to black people and change the laws all over the country."

"Will it be bigger than the freedom walk?"

Yvonne smiled. "Maybe. I bet all the TV news programs will cover it. Dr. King will be speaking, too."

Melody remembered how moved she'd been at the freedom walk, and how Dr. King's speech had helped her begin to understand "Lift Every Voice and Sing."

Melody stacked a wax-paper-wrapped square on top of four others. "And then you're going back to school," she sighed. "I can't believe the summer's almost over."

"Time goes fast when you're doing important work," Yvonne said, setting the stacks of sandwiches in the refrigerator. She put her hand on Melody's shoulder. "I'm sorry I won't be here for Youth Day. I expect you to write and tell me everything, okay?"

"I guess."

"I'll send you a postcard from D.C., all right? Now, will you come with me to the flower shop? Poppa needs as many hands as he can get today."

Frank's Flowers was as busy as a beehive when Melody and Yvonne arrived. Tomorrow was the grand opening of Tish's hair salon, and Poppa was making a dozen arrangements for her shop. He also had to do flowers for a wedding and a church program, and the store was full of customers. Gospel music filled the shop.

♪ Never Give Up ♪

"Yvonne! You're late," Poppa said. "I need you to cover the phones and the cash register. Melody, go in back and help Val add greenery to the arrangements for Tish. And unroll that banner so I can check it before it goes out!"

Melody headed to the workroom. Val was sitting on a stool at the worktable, facing a row of small gold vases filled with daisies and red carnations. Lying on the table were bunches of ferns and pointy aspidistra leaves.

"I'm so glad you're here," Val said, shoving a bundle of spicy-smelling eucalyptus at Melody. "I don't know what to do with all these leaves!"

Melody smiled and climbed onto a stool. She tilted her head and turned one of the vases around to look at how the flowers were mixed together. Then she pulled a stem of eucalyptus, clipped it short, and eased it between two carnations.

"Wow," Val said. "Now it looks perfect. How do you do that?"

"I don't know." Melody shrugged happily. "Big Momma says everybody's got a way to shine. I guess arranging flowers is my light."

♪ No Ordinary Sound ♪

"You mean one of your lights. You've got plenty," Val said. Before Melody could argue, Val began to sing, *"This little light of mine."* She left Melody with the flowers and got down to unroll a long white banner across the floor.

"Look at this!" Val said, reading out loud: "Welcome to Tish's Touch of Beauty Hair Salon!"

Melody turned to see the large, glittery gold letters. *"Let it shine, let it shine, let it shiiiine!"* she sang.

"It's shiny, for sure," Poppa said as he came in to stand beside Val. "Are all the words spelled right?"

"Yes, sir," Val answered. "I know Mama will like it."

"Good," he said. "Let's box this all up and take it over there. She'll have time to get everything in place for tomorrow. You know how to take care of this, don't you, Little One?" he asked Melody.

"I know, Poppa!" She pulled two cardboard boxes and some old newspapers from underneath the worktable. Val watched as Melody put a couple of vases into the box and surrounded them with crushed newspaper so that they wouldn't bump into each other.

"Let me help," Val said, following Melody's lead. Soon they had both boxes neatly and safely filled.

♪ Never Give Up ♪

Poppa rolled the banner up, tied it with a length of string, and tucked it into one of the boxes.

"I'll load the truck, and you two can go with me," he told them before he took one of the boxes outside.

"I'm so excited to see the salon," Melody said as she followed Poppa with the other box.

"Just wait until Girls' Day," Val said. When Melody looked confused, Val explained. "Mama always says that salons are for grown-ups, but right before special days, like Easter and Christmas, girls can come and get fancy hairdos and nail polish and stuff. It's lots of fun!"

Melody had never had her hair done at a salon before. Either Mommy, Yvonne, or Big Momma shampooed her hair at home. Then she sat for a long time underneath the noisy bubble-shaped hair dryer. Finally, Mommy or Yvonne would comb her hair out and braid it up. The whole process took all of a Saturday afternoon, and wasn't much fun at all.

When she followed Poppa and Val into Tish's Touch of Beauty Salon, she saw that getting her hair done in the salon would be quite different. Along the counter, there were three high chairs with footrests, all red. On the other side of the salon were two deep black sinks,

♪ No Ordinary Sound ♪

and three big armchairs with hair dryers attached. Between the chairs were small tables piled with magazines, and mounted high on the back wall was a TV set. *It **would** be fun to get my hair done here,* Melody thought.

"Hey, what do y'all think?" Tish was cleaning the long mirror that stretched along one of the cheery yellow walls. She stopped and stood in the middle of the red-and-white-checked linoleum floor to wave her arms around.

"Looking good!" Poppa said, putting a box of flowers on the speckled red Formica counter.

"It'll look even better with the flowers. I like my place to be beautiful, so my customers start feeling beautiful when they walk in." Tish smiled proudly.

"This is so cool!" Melody said.

"These chairs go up and down!" Val explained, spinning one of the chairs with the footrest. Every time she pushed on a lever, the chair slowly cranked up.

"Be careful, baby," Tish said. "Why don't you girls put a vase on each of the tables for me?"

"And where do you want the banner?" Poppa asked.

"On the back wall," Tish said. "Let me get the stepladder."

♪ Never Give Up ♪

Melody and Val finished quickly and then sat in the comfy chairs near the front window to watch the banner hanging.

"It's a little crooked," Melody said, squinting. Poppa pulled his end up.

"Now it's too low on your end, Mama." Val motioned with her hands.

"My goodness!" Tish raised her arms higher. "Tell me this is it!"

"That's it!" the girls shouted, giggling.

Tish clasped her hands and stared up at the banner. "Thank you so much for your help and advice," she said to Poppa. "At least this salon has gone the way we wanted."

"Remember the old song that goes, 'Trouble don't last always'? You and Charles are going to be fine," Poppa said.

"Looks like things are going to move more slowly than we planned when we came up here," Tish said. "So we'll be with you a little longer, and Valerie will go to the same junior high as Lila."

Melody was excited about the news that Val would still be living a few blocks away. That meant they could walk to school together. She grinned at her cousin, who looked pleased, too.

"That's all right," Poppa said. "We don't give up in this family, do we, girls?"

"No, sir," Val and Melody said, shaking their heads. At the exact same time, they said, "We make it work!"

When they finished at the salon, Poppa took Melody and Val back home, where they all had lunch with Big Momma. Melody was anxiously peeking through Big Momma's lace curtains at the front window when Sharon exploded around the corner and hopped up the steps. Melody pulled the door open before her friend's first knock. "Welcome back!" she said happily.

"Hey!" Sharon dangled a white paper bag in front of Melody's nose. "Pralines," she said, and then held up a second bag in her other hand. "I got some for Val, too. So, what's this amazing song you're doing?"

Melody was surprised. "Amazing? Who said?"

Sharon shrugged and walked into the living room. "I just heard, that's all."

♪ Never Give Up ♪

Big Momma and Val were playing cards at the dining room table. "What did you hear?" Big Momma asked.

"Hello, Mrs. Porter. I was telling Melody that I heard the song she chose for Youth Day is amazing. My mother told me Diane's mother told her. But I still don't know what the song is."

"Diane's been helping me," Melody blurted out.

Sharon's eyes got wide. "Diane's been helping someone else work on a solo? Really?"

Melody didn't quite know how to explain to Sharon that she'd seen a different side of Diane—the Diane who struggled, even though she seemed confident. The Diane who was the same as they were.

"Diane knows how hard Melody's been working," Big Momma said, putting her cards down. "This hasn't been easy, but Melody isn't giving up. I think Diane respects that."

Sharon was silent for a moment, but then she grinned. "I guess a lot happened while I was gone this summer. So, what song are you going to sing?"

"Lift Every Voice and Sing," Melody said proudly.

"Melody didn't just learn the words," Val told

♪ No Ordinary Sound ♪

Sharon. "She learned what the words mean."

Sharon nodded. "I knew you would do something serious, Melody. Would you sing it now? I want to hear you."

Melody agreed, and Big Momma moved to the piano to play. As her grandmother began the introduction, Melody took a deep breath. She sang the song all the way through without any mistakes.

"Boy, you were *good*," Sharon said. "With our whole choir singing, and you leading? We're gonna turn Youth Day out!"

"Lila!" their mother called from the kitchen. "Have you got the television on?" Melody was already on the sofa with Val and her father. Daddy had stayed up after dinner on a work night especially to watch.

"Yes, Mom!" Lila was standing at the TV, turning channels.

"Stop there," Daddy said.

"Good evening," the announcer said. "Today, Wednesday, August 28, 1963, Washington, D.C. has seen what may be the largest gathering of peaceful

♪ Never Give Up ♪

civil rights marchers in the country's history."

Mommy hurried in and squeezed next to Melody, while Lila plopped down onto the rug. Everyone stared intently at the screen.

Melody could see a mass of people in front of a big white building with a row of columns along its front.

"Hey, that's the Lincoln Memorial!" Lila said.

The TV camera was way up high, as if it was in an airplane or something, so the people looked like thousands of tiny moving shapes.

"Oh, let's look for Yvonne," Val said, bouncing on the sofa.

"No way will we see her in that crowd," Daddy said.

The TV screen switched to a close-up of the marchers. The people were black, white, Asian, and other races, too. They were young and old. Then the screen showed Dr. Martin Luther King Jr., who was at the top of some high steps in front of them all. "I have a dream!" he was saying.

Melody's mouth dropped open. "He said that at the freedom walk!"

"Shhh!" Her mother patted her knee.

♪ No Ordinary Sound ♪

Melody listened, feeling trembly and strange inside. It was just as Yvonne had said. There weren't just a few families marching for fairness and justice, but so many people that a TV camera in an airplane couldn't get a picture of all of them at once!

"Will you look at that," Daddy said, smiling. "All kinds of people coming out for justice! This—this is history, girls. Our history."

Melody thought, *Surely someone will hear their voices this time.*

One Sunday

♪ CHAPTER 15 ♪

School began during the first week of September, and everyone settled into a new routine. Dwayne was still traveling with The Three Ravens, and Yvonne wouldn't be home from Tuskegee until Thanksgiving. Val walked to school with Melody, Lila, and Sharon every day. Lila had taken her school entrance test at the end of August. Even though she wouldn't know the results for a few weeks, she was much more relaxed and more fun now that the test was over.

Melody felt more and more confident about her Youth Day performance, too. Choir practice had begun again, and Miss Dorothy kept saying how pleased she was that the choir was working together. Now that Melody had gotten to know Diane better, Diane was being a lot nicer—both at school and in the choir.

♪ No Ordinary Sound ♪

On the third Sunday of September, Melody, Lila, and Val sang together in the children's choir. Afterward, Poppa and Big Momma stayed at church for a meeting, but everyone else headed to their house for dinner. The men were outside looking at Charles's new car, and Mommy and Tish were talking in the kitchen. Lila was upstairs reading. Melody and Val had set the table with the yellow-checked cloth for the family dinner, and then sat down in the living room with a jigsaw puzzle. The only sounds were the low buzz of their voices and the hum of the radio.

"It's too quiet around here," Melody said.

"I used to like the quiet," Val said, carefully fitting a strange-looking piece into the puzzle. "But now I like some noise."

"Oh, that's because you're getting used to all of Big Momma's students coming and going around here," Melody said. She tried to press a turtle-shaped piece down. It didn't fit.

"And Poppa whistling in the morning," Val added.

"Mm-hmm." Melody turned the turtle piece a different way and squinted at the puzzle-sky.

Val pointed with her puzzle piece. "And you and

♪ **One Sunday** ♪

Lila and even Sharon are always running in and out!"

Melody suddenly saw where her piece slid in perfectly. "I knew it!" she said, looking up. "I mean, I knew you really liked a noisy, big family as much as I do."

Val smiled shyly. "I guess I do," she said.

But the noise they heard next they'd never heard before. It came from the kitchen.

"Oh, no! Oh, my goodness!" Mommy cried out.

"Lord!" Cousin Tish moaned.

Melody jumped at the sound, knocking the puzzle off the coffee table and breaking it apart. Outside, her father was yelling, asking what was wrong. The back door opened and slammed, opened and slammed as the men came inside.

"What do you think is going on?" Val whispered.

Melody heard her mother crying. Something terrible must have happened.

Lila came running down the stairs. "What is it?" she asked. When she saw the girls' faces, she asked again. "What?"

Mommy pushed open the kitchen door. Her eyes were red, and her face was wet with tears. Cousin Tish

♪ No Ordinary Sound ♪

was right behind her, looking worried. She hurried past all of them to the phone. Daddy and Cousin Charles followed Mommy into the dining room.

Melody's stomach hurt. "Did something happen to Dwayne? Or Yvonne?"

"No, no." Mommy answered quickly. "But we heard terrible news on the radio from Alabama."

"What happened?" Lila asked.

"A church in Birmingham was bombed this morning," Mommy said.

Melody's tummy knot felt tighter. "Was it . . . was it the Russians?" she asked, confused. "Is it a war?" Mommy had said "bomb." Bombs were not by accident. At school they'd learned about countries like Russia making bombs and planning to use them against other countries, to prove they were strong.

"No, honey," Mommy said. "It's not that kind of war."

"Some people aren't happy about black people fighting for equal rights," Daddy explained. "They think bombing a church will scare us so much that we will stop marching and protesting and speaking up."

Charles looked at Tish. He was shaking his head.

♪ One Sunday ♪

"This is why we left Birmingham," he said.

Tish nodded. "There have been so many bombings."

Melody couldn't understand it. She knew that people disagreed all the time, even people in the same family, like Daddy and Dwayne. But a bomb!

"But what kind of people—I mean, how could anybody do that to a church?" Lila was still holding her open book. It was by Langston Hughes, and the title was *Laughing to Keep from Crying*.

"Did—did anybody . . ." Melody's throat felt tight. She couldn't get out the word that she wanted to say.

"I think lots of people must be hurt," her father said.

"Sunday school was in session." Her mother sank into one of the dining room chairs, as if she couldn't quite stand up anymore.

Melody walked slowly over to lean against her. Only a few hours ago she'd been in Sunday school herself.

Cousin Tish came to stand in the archway. She folded her arms around Val. "I can't get a soul on the phone," she said, her eyes wide with worry.

A car pulled into the driveway outside, and the sounds of Poppa and Big Momma filled the kitchen.

♪ No Ordinary Sound ♪

"Have mercy!" Big Momma came in with her church hat and her pocketbook in her hands. "Four little girls are gone! We heard on the radio in the car."

Val burst into tears, and Cousin Charles went over to her and Tish. Daddy rubbed Mommy's back.

"Gone? You mean—they died?" Melody pulled away from her mother. "At Sunday school?" Her knees felt suddenly shaky, and she sat down fast right on the floor, feeling as though she might throw up. She swallowed, and her tight throat hurt.

"This is insane!" Lila shouted, taking off her glasses to rub her eyes.

"It's evil." Daddy's voice shook in a way Melody had never heard before. When she looked up at him she saw that his eyes were red, and they flashed with anger.

"How can anyone have so much hatred that they'd harm children?" Cousin Tish whispered.

Melody balled her hands into fists, determined not to cry, determined to stop her insides from shaking. She couldn't stop either one. She wondered how old the four girls were. She wondered if their houses would be too quiet forever, because they weren't coming home.

In the kitchen, Poppa turned from one radio station

♪ One Sunday ♪

to another, but the news reports just kept saying the same thing over and over: "There's been a race bombing at the 16th Street Baptist Church in Birmingham, Alabama. The church is a meeting point for many civil rights activities. Four Negro girls were killed in the blast, and an unknown number were injured."

Charles switched on the TV, but it was too early for the news. Some sports show was on. Melody wished they would turn everything off. "Do we have to listen?" she asked.

"No, child, we don't," Big Momma said gently. She began to sing. Her voice was a contralto. It was rich and deep and now, sad.

> *There is a balm in Gilead,*
>   *to make the wounded whole.*
> *There is a balm in Gilead,*
>   *to heal the sin-sick soul.*

Melody knew the song. It was about healing. She closed her eyes, and then blinked them open, breathing hard. But she didn't sing.

Scary Stuff

♪ CHAPTER 16 ♪

Melody went home with her sister and parents in silence. Her head was spinning. Her stomach was spinning. Her throat felt as if it was throbbing open and closed. She had no more questions or words.

Lila went straight to the TV. "Oh, Daddy!" she called. "They're showing pictures of that church!"

Mommy went upstairs, and Daddy stood with Lila in front of the television. Melody didn't want to look. The telephone rang, and she hurried out of the room to answer it.

"Hello?" Melody sounded like she had a cold.

"Hello? Hello?" It was Dwayne!

Melody tried to clear her throat. "Dwayne, it's me! Are you—are you okay?"

"Yeah, yeah. We just played at Clark College in

♪ Scary Stuff ♪

Atlanta last night, and they put us up in the dorms. Man, the kids here are out of their minds over what happened in Birmingham. I can't believe it—a church on Sunday morning! That's some crazy, scary stuff. Listen, I just called to let Mom and Dad know I'm all right. My pay-phone money is gonna run out. Let me speak to Mom."

"Mommy, Dwayne is—" Melody tried to shout, but her voice was scratchy and faint.

"I've got it, Melody," Mommy called down. There was a click, and Mommy picked up the upstairs phone.

Melody hung up, relieved that her brother was all right. She passed Daddy and Lila, still watching the news.

"Going up so early, Melody?" Daddy asked without taking his eyes off the screen.

"Yes, Daddy," she said, hoping that he wouldn't notice her scratchy voice and tell Mommy to give her nasty medicine.

"All right, then."

Melody ran upstairs and curled up on her bed, staring at the poster from the Walk to Freedom. She stayed that way for a long time, long enough to hear the

♪ No Ordinary Sound ♪

water running as Lila brushed her teeth, and Lila's bed squeaking when she lay down on it. Long enough to hear her parents murmuring to each other after Daddy came slowly up the stairs.

Melody tried to go to sleep, but sleep wouldn't come. *What were those little girls doing when the explosion happened? Laughing? Praying? Singing? What were their names?* Finally she must have closed her eyes, because when she opened them it was daylight again. Monday morning. Melody blinked at the Mickey Mouse clock.

"You okay?" Lila asked softly. "You tossed and turned all night."

Melody opened her mouth to speak, but instead of the words "I don't know," a strange croaking sound came out.

Lila stopped buttoning her blouse. "What's the matter with you?" Melody tried to answer, but croaked again. She put a hand to her throat.

"I'm going to tell Mommy," Lila said, rushing into the hall.

Mommy came in, half dressed for work.

"What is it, baby? What is it?"

Melody shook her head, trying to say something.

♪ Scary Stuff ♪

"With all that singing you've been doing, you may have laryngitis," Mommy said, smoothing Melody's hair. "I want you to stay home from rehearsal tonight."

Melody opened her mouth to protest, but Mommy put her finger to Melody's lips.

"There's another practice on Thursday. Let's see how you are then. I'll call Miss Dorothy. In the meantime, I think you should stay with Big Momma today. She'll take good care of you."

The next thing Melody knew, she was riding to her grandparents,' still in her pajamas. Val met them at the door, already dressed. Mommy and Big Momma whispered in the kitchen before Mommy came to kiss Melody on the forehead and slip out.

"What happened?" Val looked worried. She was wearing a white ribbon on her ponytail, and Melody remembered—it was Matching Monday. "Mama said you can't go to school today."

"My throat," Melody whispered. She really wanted to talk to Val about yesterday. Was she still upset, too? Had she been able to sleep last night? But Melody didn't get a chance. Tish came out of the kitchen wearing her salon smock.

♪ No Ordinary Sound ♪

"Let's go, baby," Tish said to Val. "I have an early customer."

Val slung her book bag over her shoulder. "Mama is driving me to school," she told Melody. "She says she doesn't want me walking for a while. She'll give you a ride too, tomorrow."

Melody nodded as Val and her mother left. Then the house was totally quiet.

Big Momma had put soft pillows on the sofa in the living room.

"Have a little of this," Big Momma said, placing a mug of lemony-smelling tea on a flower-shaped coaster at one end of the coffee table. Melody sipped some and then eased back onto the pillows. Her throat hurt a little when the sweet liquid trickled down.

"You just rest," Big Momma said. "I'm cancelling my lessons for today, so you can stay right here." Big Momma went upstairs, and Melody could hear her speaking in low tones on the phone.

Melody tried to get comfortable. She rolled onto her side, facing the piano. The heavy old upright was as tall as Melody was, with flowers carved into its music stand. The keys were no longer black and white, but

♪ Scary Stuff ♪

had aged to a worn blackish-brown and tan. But Big Momma kept it tuned so that it played like it was new. Melody wondered if human voices could be tuned when they became worn.

"*Lift every voice and sing.*" She mouthed the words silently as she lay back on the sofa. Melody couldn't go on, even in her mind. What if she couldn't sing again? Youth Day was only a few weeks away. They were supposed to practice twice a week until then. She had to get better.

Charles stopped by during his lunch hour to bring Melody some special drops from the pharmacy for her throat.

"You just suck on these like candy," he said. "They'll melt in your mouth. Don't talk any more than you have to." Melody was glad she didn't have to say anything. She popped one of the rosy-colored lozenges into her mouth. It was warm and soothing and tasted like cherry.

For lunch, Big Momma gave her soup and brought her a brand-new book of paper dolls that she'd been

♪ No Ordinary Sound ♪

saving for a birthday. Melody ate the soup, but couldn't concentrate on cutting out the paper dolls neatly. She rolled another cherry drop around in her mouth as her thoughts kept going back to Birmingham.

What did the four little girls look like? Were they dark brown, with skinny legs, like Sharon, and did they run so fast that their hair came undone? Were they tall and golden like Val, with ponytails that bounced and swung from side to side when they talked and waved their hands? Did they have sisters and brothers? The thought that something awful like this could happen to Melody's brother or sisters—or her cousin Val—shook her.

Melody heard Val come in the front door. It seemed like she was home much earlier than usual.

"Melody! Can you talk yet?" Val dropped her book bag with a thump near the TV.

Melody discovered that she could whisper. "How'd you get here so fast?"

"Sharon's mother picked us up. I got your homework. School was so weird today! Nobody knew the girls in Alabama, but we were sad like we did."

Melody nodded and sat up straight. Suddenly she wanted to do something that would take her mind off

♪ Scary Stuff ♪

all the sadness. "Let's go out," she whispered.

Val made a face. "In your pajamas? You'd better put on some of my clothes." Melody smiled, and realized that she hadn't smiled at all since yesterday. She borrowed a pair of Val's shorts and a shirt.

"What do you want to do outside?" Val asked, changing out of her school clothes.

"Plant," Melody whispered. Poppa had bought dozens of tulip and daffodil bulbs from the Eastern Market downtown over the summer. He and Melody had planned to plant them during the fall, before the frost. She knew that the bulbs would burst out of the ground in spring and bloom—the first flowers of the season. Poppa always reminded her that every season brought change.

In the yard, Melody felt like a mime she'd seen on TV. She used her hands to go through the motions, showing Val what to do and how.

"I got it!" Val said, digging with her spade just the way Melody did.

Melody wished she could use her voice to explain that thinking of new flowers blooming made her feel that the world didn't have to be ugly and bad, but could also be good, and beautiful.

Val held one of the dusty brown bulbs up to look at it closely. "It's hard to believe these things will grow into something pretty someday," she said.

Melody only nodded. She couldn't help thinking again of the girls who wouldn't grow up at all.

By Thursday, Melody's speaking voice was almost back to normal. Mommy had kept her home from school all week, so Melody had to beg her to let her go to choir practice.

"Do you think you will be able to sing?" Mommy asked in the car after supper.

"I hope so," Melody said.

Mommy drove up in front of the church. "You girls go on in. I'm going to find a spot to park and meet you inside." Val and Lila got out. As Melody slid across the backseat to follow, Mommy turned to her. "Did you bring the throat lozenges Charles gave you?"

"Yes, Mommy. But I don't think I'll need them," Melody said. Mommy seemed satisfied. Melody got out and closed the door. Then she started toward the

♪ Scary Stuff ♪

wide stone steps leading up to the open doors.

The adult choir was clapping and singing, "*Oh, freedom! Oh, freedom! Oh, freedom over me.*"

Melody's steps slowed, and her heart beat faster. The voices were familiar. The song was familiar. Yet somehow each beat and each step went through her entire body. *Thump, thump.* She heard her own heartbeat loudly in her ears. At the top step she stopped.

"Hey!" Val's face popped around the door frame. "Why are you so slow?"

Melody couldn't answer, because she did not know.

The adults were finishing, and Miss Dorothy was coming toward her. "I'm glad you're here, but don't feel that you have to sing tonight," Miss Dorothy said.

Melody was mystified by the odd way she was feeling. Every one of her footsteps on the worn red carpet seemed to tingle. Her throat began to throb. Miss Dorothy was still talking, although she sounded farther and farther away.

"Melody?" Someone was calling her name. It was Mommy.

Melody blinked. Faces were crowded around her. She froze right in the middle of the center aisle.

♪ No Ordinary Sound ♪

"Melody!" Mommy shook her. Melody opened her mouth to answer. Nothing came out. Not a whisper, not a croak. Nothing. Suddenly Melody just had to get out. She wanted to be anywhere other than this church, any church! She jerked away from her mother and ran for the door.

"Dee-Dee!" Lila shouted.

"Melody!" Val called. "Come back!"

Melody ran outside, down the steps, and straight into Big Momma.

"Melody! Whatever is it?"

"It's her throat. She's lost her voice again!" Lila called from the door.

Big Momma took Melody's hand and started up the steps, but Melody shook her head hard, pulling away.

Her grandmother took one look at her and then called out to Lila. "You go on back inside," she said. "Tell your mother that I'm taking Melody home."

Big Momma raised Melody's chin with one of her strong hands, and looked hard into her eyes. Melody burst into tears.

"It's not only your throat that's hurting, is it? Something more is wrong," Big Momma said. "It's

♪ Scary Stuff ♪

your heart that's hurting for those four little girls in Birmingham."

Melody nodded, still breathing hard, still feeling her heartbeats thumping.

"And you don't feel very good about going into the church right now."

Melody nodded again.

"I know. Honey, don't be afraid of the building. This is God's house. Everyone here loves you." Big Momma wrapped her arms around Melody. "Baby chick, I know it's hard to understand. Life is so special, so precious—and anyone who would take a life just doesn't hold love in his heart. Maybe there's no understanding it. But we have to stand up to the wrong of it. We have to keep our hearts and voices strong in the face of such a wrong."

Melody swallowed hard. How ever could she be strong, when she felt so bad?

Whispers

♪ CHAPTER 17 ♪

Big Momma told only Mommy and Daddy that Melody was afraid of the church. Melody was embarrassed for anyone else to know, even Val. The idea that she might ruin Youth Day troubled Melody more than losing her voice did.

Instead of sending her to school on Friday, Mommy took Melody to the doctor. He looked into Melody's ears and looked down her throat and listened to her chest.

"I don't see anything that's really wrong," the doctor said. "There's no swelling in her throat. You say she's been rehearsing for a big singing performance?"

"Yes," Mommy said. She looked at Melody, but didn't say anything else to the doctor.

"She's not sick," the doctor insisted. He scratched his head. "Maybe it's stage fright," he said.

♪ Whispers ♪

Melody looked at her mother. He was getting close to the truth without giving her any way to fix things. She wanted to leave.

"She's been singing in front of audiences since she was three," Mommy said.

"Well, then," the doctor said. "We'll just have to wait for her voice to come back on its own."

Melody pointed at a pad on the examining room counter. The doctor handed it to her with a pen.

What if it doesn't come back? she wrote.

"Oh, it will," the doctor said. "Sooner or later."

"Is there anything we can do?" Mommy asked.

"I suggest warm drinks and whatever else soothes her throat."

Melody hung her head. She'd been drinking tea and hot lemonade till she thought she might float away. She'd swallowed spoonfuls of honey, as Miss Dorothy suggested. She'd sucked so many of Charles's lozenges that she wasn't sure she liked cherry-flavored anything anymore.

The doctor peered over his glasses at Melody. "This must be a very special performance," he said. "Or a mighty special song."

♪ No Ordinary Sound ♪

Yes! Melody wanted to say. *I want to lift my voice and sing, but I can't! Now I'm letting everybody down.*

"Thank you, doctor," Mommy said as Melody hopped from the table.

Mommy tried to cheer Melody up in the car by telling her they'd have a big pancake breakfast on Sunday morning. Melody knew that was because they wouldn't be going to church.

Melody looked out the passenger window at the Detroit streets, where people were walking and talking and living their lives. A memory flashed in her mind of the TV screen, and the quick glimpse that she'd seen of smoking bricks. Nobody would be going to the 16th Street Baptist Church on Sunday. Melody shivered.

Would she ever be able to *not* remember?

Bo greeted her with a gentle nuzzle at her ankles, and then followed her like a shadow. Melody picked him up for a comforting cuddle.

Melody was surprised that Daddy was not only home from work when they got there, but he was awake, waiting just for her. He smelled like cinnamon when he gave her a hug.

"What did the doctor say?" Daddy asked.

♪ Whispers ♪

"Wait for her voice to come back. Warm liquids," Mommy said.

Daddy smiled. "Well, how did I know that? I've got my all-time special Daddy cocoa with cinnamon sticks and whipped cream ready!"

Daddy only made cocoa when snow had fallen outside and everyone except Mommy had been out shoveling. Melody followed him to the kitchen, where she put Bo back on the floor. There was her favorite mug on the counter, waiting to be filled.

"You sit right there," Daddy said, tilting his head toward Melody's seat at the table. He poured the steaming cocoa into her mug without one spill. Melody leaned to sip around the puff of whipped cream and got a dollop on her nose, just as there was a knock on the back door. In came Poppa and Val.

Poppa was carrying a small basket of pink carnations, with sprigs of eucalyptus tucked at the edges. "How's our girl?" he asked, kissing the top of Melody's head. "Your cousin made this just for you."

Melody was beginning to feel uncomfortable with all the attention. She wasn't really sick. But she didn't feel well, either. Her voice was refusing to work. And

♪ No Ordinary Sound ♪

despite what Big Momma had told her, she just wasn't sure that their church was safe. Couldn't hateful people choose any church to blow up?

Val held something that looked like a folded sheet of construction paper. "Sharon asked me to give this to you. Your class made you a get-well card," she explained, sitting down.

Melody pushed her mug to the side and opened the card. There were the names of almost everybody in her class, including her teacher. Big block letters said "GET WELL SOON." Next to Sharon's and Diane's names were drawings of small musical notes. Val had signed her name in one corner.

"I know I'm not in the same class as you, but I wanted to sign it, too," she said.

Melody mouthed the words "Thank you." She was feeling very tired. Not being able to talk was hard. Trying not to feel was harder.

"We're going to go," Poppa said, nodding to Val.

Val didn't seem to want to leave, but she got up anyway. "I'll come by tomorrow," she said.

When they were gone, Daddy picked Melody up, the same way he used to when she was tiny, and

♪ Whispers ♪

carried her to bed. "You have a big heart for such a little person," he whispered to her. "You take your time finding your way."

Melody wasn't sure what Daddy meant, but she rested her head against his chest, calmed by the steady beat of his heart.

Everyone tried to help Melody get her voice back and get her spirits up. On Saturday morning, she woke to hear the phone ringing. Lila was already up and out. Mickey Mouse was pointing to ten. Melody couldn't believe she'd slept so late.

"Melody! Telephone, in my room!" Mommy called.

Melody frowned as she got up. Mommy knew she couldn't speak. Why would she make her come to the phone?

Mommy and Daddy's room smelled like Mommy's fancy perfume. Melody always liked looking at all the pictures tucked into the frame of their dresser mirror and at Daddy's colorful ties hanging on the closet door. Mommy patted their blue-striped bedspread, handed Melody the blue telephone, and then slipped

♪ No Ordinary Sound ♪

out of the room. Melody sat on the edge of the bed and put the receiver up to her ear.

"Dee-Dee, this is Vonnie. I know you can't talk. Just listen. I want you to know that the bombing in Birmingham won't stop us. Remember that lady who was afraid to vote? We went back this week, and she signed up. We've been singing 'Ain't Gonna Let Nobody Turn Me Around.' You know that one. Don't let anything turn *you* around. You've been working so hard on this song. The New Hope choir needs you. Don't be afraid to let your Dee-Dee light shine and shine and shine, you hear?"

Melody wanted so much to tell Yvonne that she *did* hear.

"Tap on the receiver if you get what I'm saying."

Melody tapped three times.

"Good!" Yvonne said. "I wish I could be there to hear you. You can do it! Love you. Bye!"

Melody sat for a minute after she hung up the phone. She was happy that her big sister hadn't forgotten her. If Yvonne believed in her, maybe she *could* go back to the church.

Mommy appeared. "Now, you get dressed, honey.

♪ Whispers ♪

We're going to the salon."

Melody held both palms out as if she was asking a question, which she was.

Mommy laughed. "Why? You'll see!"

Tish's Touch of Beauty Salon was having a Girls' Day. When Melody pushed the door open, she saw all the girls from the children's choir, including Lila.

"Surprise!" Tish said, spinning a chair around. At the sound of her greeting, most of the girls turned to wave at Melody. There was Diane underneath a dryer, reading an *Ebony* magazine. She wasn't quite tall enough for her head to reach the dryer, so she was sitting atop two city telephone books. Sharon was getting shampooed. Some of the girls were getting their hair set on giant rollers, and one was having her nails painted. Some of the mothers were laughing and talking in the customer chairs by the front window.

"This is your seat, right here," Tish said, tapping the chair. Melody climbed in and Tish pumped the chair up so that when she turned it, Melody saw herself in the long mirror.

"Now, what kind of hair do we want for Youth Day?" Tish asked.

♪ No Ordinary Sound ♪

Melody shrugged in the mirror. *Will I even be at Youth Day?* she wondered.

"Hmm. Not sure?" Tish looked at Mommy. "I think the soloist deserves something a little special, a little fancy," Tish said. Melody saw Mommy raising her eyebrows.

"Fancy it is!" Tish said to Melody. "If you like what I do today, I'll do the same for you before the program." Then, as The Temptations crooned over the speakers, Tish combed out Melody's braids. She took her over to a shampoo sink. Melody wasn't tall enough either, so she sat on one fat telephone book.

"Now, lean back," Tish said. Melody closed her eyes. Tish's shampoo was so relaxing that Melody almost went to sleep. Tish wrapped Melody's hair in a towel and took her to a dryer right between Val and Diane. Tish took the towel off and lowered the helmet of the hair dryer over Melody's head. When she turned it on, the noise of the dryer blocked out all other sounds. For once, it didn't matter that Melody couldn't talk.

After her hair was dry, Tish straightened it with a hot-comb, and curled the ends up. When she spun

♪ Whispers ♪

the chair around for Melody to see the finished look, Melody gasped.

"She's talking!" Sharon shouted.

Melody shook her head. She still couldn't talk. She'd gasped because she looked completely different, like a more grown-up Melody. When she leaned toward the mirror for a closer look, she saw that her old self was still there. She was the same, but different. She was changed.

"So, you approve, Melody?" Tish asked.

Melody nodded.

"What do you think, Frances?" Tish turned the chair again.

Mommy looked long and hard.

"I think our baby girl isn't such a baby anymore," she said.

On Monday morning, Melody still couldn't talk, but she went back to school. She felt as if she'd been away for more than a week. Everything looked different.

When they got home, Lila opened the mailbox. "You got mail," she said, handing Melody a long plain

♪ No Ordinary Sound ♪

envelope.

Melody didn't recognize the return address or the scratchy, cramped handwriting. She took the letter to her room and stretched across her bed to read it.

> *Dear Melody,*
>
> *I bet you're shocked to know that your brother can write a whole page! Are you jazzed about taking over Youth Day? I heard you were having throat problems, but I'm sure that's all over now and you can't wait to sing your solo.*
>
> *I am learning a whole lot about the music business, and not everything is roses like I first thought. We're just colored people on the road, like anybody else. Not even the big names can stay in the white hotels. Can you dig that? I mean, these guys have sold thousands of records, but they have to go in the back doors to perform in the top clubs! At the colleges, it's all right. But I thought talent would get more respect. Seems like our talent is colored first, and great second. I'm not*

♪ Whispers ♪

*quitting, though. I love seeing how the crowds enjoy my voice. I can't wait until I'm singing my **own** songs! I'm not letting any stupid laws or people with crazy ideas about us hold me back. I know I'm good! You're good, too . . . almost as good as me. Ha, Ha! Best luck on your big day.*

   Your one and only brother-man,
Dwayne

Melody rolled over on her back and read the letter again. Dwayne had been so sure that fairness would come along with fame! It sounded like it hadn't. At least not yet. She folded the letter carefully and slipped it under her pillow. Melody remembered her father saying something about the men he knew who had given up when the music business got hard. But Dwayne wasn't giving up. She decided she wouldn't give up, either.

Melody turned on the tape recorder to listen to her song again. She pictured Dwayne in front of the college crowds. When she opened her mouth to sing, the words came out!

♪ No Ordinary Sound ♪

Melody jumped up. She started the tape over, and she sang the entire first verse. Her voice was a bit squeaky, but she wasn't whispering.

"Dee-Dee!" Lila stepped in from the hall. "You're singing again! How?"

"Dwayne," Melody said.

"This means you can practice! This means Youth Day might not be a disaster! I'm going to tell Mommy."

"No." Melody took a deep breath. "I will."

Voices Lifted

♪ CHAPTER 18 ♪

elody called Val and then Sharon. She even called Diane. They were all thrilled to hear Melody's voice.

"Can you really sing?" Sharon asked when Mommy dropped Melody, Val, and Lila in front of the church for choir practice that night.

"I think so," Melody said. She was starting to feel nervous again.

"Well, let's find out," Sharon said, waving them toward the church.

At the steps, Melody froze. She couldn't make herself move. Her insides shook, and the awful fear of the fifteenth of September came back.

"I—I can't!" She looked at Val.

"Maybe if you just take one step at a time," Val suggested, taking Melody's hand.

♪ No Ordinary Sound ♪

"No. Don't make me." Melody pulled her hand away from her cousin's.

"I'll get Miss Dorothy," Lila said, sprinting up the steps.

Melody didn't care who they got—she could not, would not go in. If she did, she might be silenced again.

"What is it, exactly?" Val whispered. "Is it because you lost your voice in there?"

"It kind of looked like you ran into a force field from a cartoon," Sharon said. She and Val stared at Melody.

Melody wasn't sure what her friends would say if she told them the truth. She swallowed, half expecting her throat to close up again.

Mommy came around the corner from the parking lot at the same time Miss Dorothy came out of the church. They both hurried to where Melody stood at the bottom of the staircase.

"Melody, I'm happy you've recovered your voice. However . . ."

Melody sighed. "I know. You don't have to say it, Miss Dorothy. If I can't come into the church, I can't do the solo."

♪ Voices Lifted ♪

"Melody—" Val pulled at her. "Melody, don't give up!"

Miss Dorothy looked sad. "I'm afraid you're right, dear. If you can't do this, the choir will have to perform a song it already knows. And," she added, "I will have to choose a different soloist."

"We understand," her mother said. "Don't we, Melody?"

"Yes, Mommy."

Melody sat in the car while Lila and Val went into the church to rehearse. Melody needed time to think. She had to figure out what to do. Months ago, when Miss Dorothy had asked her to solo, she had been so proud! She had wanted to carry on her family's singing tradition. She had wanted to show Diane that she was good, in her own way. When she had finally picked her song, she had wanted to understand what Mr. Johnson was trying to tell the world with his words.

Then the church in Birmingham was bombed, and those girls died. Her voice had died with them, and now she was afraid of a place that had meant so much to her.

Melody remembered Yvonne's words: *Don't let anything turn you around.* When rehearsal was over

♪ No Ordinary Sound ♪

and everyone got into the car, Melody leaned over and whispered into her cousin's ear, "I need help."

Val's ponytail bobbed in the darkness. "What can I do?" she whispered back.

"Let's meet with Sharon and Diane after school tomorrow," Melody said.

"I can't go into the church because I'm scared," Melody said, looking around Big Momma's kitchen table. "I can't figure out how not to be."

Val passed out sugar cookies and napkins.

"But what are you scared of, in our church?" Sharon asked, munching a cookie.

Diane was frowning with her elbows on the table. "It's not anything in our church," she said, looking steadily at Melody. "It's what happened to the girls in church in Birmingham, right?"

"Right," Melody said. There, it was out. Nobody looked at her funny. Nobody said she was weird.

"That scared *everybody*, Melody. Even grown-ups," Val said.

"I still have bad dreams about it," Sharon said.

♪ Voices Lifted ♪

"You do?" Melody was surprised. "You never said so!" Melody had thought she was the only one who was having bad dreams.

"You never asked," Sharon said. "You never talked about that at all."

"Did you all talk about it?" Melody asked.

"Sure," Diane said. "At school. Last week, when you weren't there."

Val put her hand on Melody's arm. "But we're talking now," she said gently.

"I know you worked hard on that song," Diane said. "We've all worked hard, helping one another. We won't let you down, and you can't let us down."

Melody tugged at one of her braids. "But what if I lose my voice again? What if I think about the Birmingham girls and—"

"We'll all go inside together," Sharon said. "You don't have to be scared."

"*We're* four little girls," Val pointed out.

Melody nodded. She felt stronger, now that she wasn't hiding her fear. Maybe she could do this for the four girls who would never speak again. She could lift her voice and sing, just for them.

♪ No Ordinary Sound ♪

On the first Saturday of October, Melody stood in the midst of the excited young people gathering outside New Hope Baptist Church. Buses were pulled up to the curb, and cars were dropping people off. There were children's choirs in neat white shirts and dark skirts and pants; there were youth choirs wearing flashy robes and sashes. Churches from all over Detroit were represented.

"There you are!" Val elbowed her way into a space very near the steps.

"I'm nervous," Melody sighed. Their plan had worked for the last three practices. All the girls had met out front and walked into the church together. Today, that seemed impossible. The steps were crowded, and groups of people blocked the front doors. Melody felt a twinge of worry. Miss Dorothy had told them to be prompt, and now they had only five minutes before they'd be late.

"Let me through!" Lila said, pushing her way past two tall boys, pulling Sharon and Diane along with her. "My goodness! This crowd is huge! You all had better get in there now, if you're doing that

♪ Voices Lifted ♪

hand-holding thing." She gave Melody's headband one tug to straighten it, and disappeared.

"Wow!" Diane said. "This looks like the biggest Youth Day showing ever!"

"Mmmm." Melody took a deep breath. "Can we just go in?"

The girls clasped each other's hands tightly and spread out side by side on one step.

"Ready?" Sharon asked.

"Ready!" the others practically shouted, and started to march up the church steps. Halfway up, two older ladies cut into the group, separating Melody and Diane from the others. Melody felt her hand dangle free, but she kept going. In the vestibule, Diane was suddenly gone.

Melody was alone at the edge of the center aisle. Her heart fluttered, and she swallowed. Miss Dorothy was already up front when she glanced up and saw Melody. Melody stood still. People were surging around her. It was no use trying to find the other girls again—she had to get to the choir. She started walking. The organist was playing softly, and the sound echoed all around Melody as she moved.

♪ No Ordinary Sound ♪

I have to do this, she told herself. *For the girls who can't go to church.* Melody locked eyes with Miss Dorothy and kept stepping. Val appeared from somewhere when Melody was halfway up the aisle, grabbing her hand. Then Sharon took the one on the other side.

When they made it to the front, Melody was trembling. She took her seat in the first row. Diane rushed up, breathless. Lila leaned out to smile and give Melody an "okay" sign. Melody couldn't smile yet.

After Pastor Daniels welcomed everyone, Miss Dorothy stood with her baton. The choir rose and took their places across the front of the church.

Melody stepped forward as the introduction began. In a move she did not expect, her three friends stepped forward, too. Melody wanted to say something to thank them, but she couldn't. It was her time to sing.

> *Lift every voice and sing,*
> *Till earth and heaven ring,*
> *Ring with the harmonies of liberty;*
> *Let our rejoicing rise,*
> *High as the list'ning skies,*
> > *Let it resound loud as the rolling sea.*

♪ Voices Lifted ♪

Then the chorus joined her, and it sounded as if Miss Dorothy's piano and their voices were doing a kind of dance.

> *Sing a song full of the faith*
>   *that the dark past has taught us,*
> *Sing a song full of the hope*
>   *that the present has brought us;*
> *Facing the rising sun of our new day begun,*
> *Let us march on till victory is won.*

The four girls held tightly to each other's hands. The audience clapped, and cheered, and stomped. It was no ordinary sound. Melody was overwhelmed by it, and also by the truth of the words they'd just sung. She tried to scan the packed room for her parents, or for Val's parents, but she couldn't find them. Then she looked to the place where Big Momma had been sitting, but she wasn't there anymore.

Dwayne was. He was wearing a black suit and a purple shirt and tie. He was clapping and cheering.

Melody felt faith, and hope, and rejoicing all at once.

♪ No Ordinary Sound ♪

When there was a break in the program, Melody rushed out into the congregation and threw her arms around her brother. "Dwayne!" she cried. "You came!"

"I wouldn't miss this for the world, Dee-Dee. You were fantastic!"

Melody stood back to look into his eyes. "Really?"

Dwayne nodded and draped an arm around her shoulders. "No kidding, kid. I knew nothing could keep you quiet for long. I just want to ask you, now that you're famous and everything—"

"—Dwayne!"

"You think you might find time to work a little with me, maybe do some backup singing when I cut my first record in a few months?"

Melody stared at him, wide-eyed. "You mean it?"

"Of course! But let's keep it between you and me for now." Dwayne craned his neck as he searched the crowd for the rest of the family. "I see Big Momma's hat feathers," he said, taking Melody's hand. "Let's go."

Melody felt herself grinning as she followed her brother. She had regained her voice, and it had been the

♪ Voices Lifted ♪

hardest, scariest experience she'd ever had. Now she knew she would never stop speaking out for what was right. Melody Ellison would never, ever stop singing.

INSIDE Melody's World

The 1960s were an important decade for the civil rights movement in America—and Detroit was an important city. The automobile industry employed thousands of African Americans. Detroit's black community thrived, with its own cultural, economic, political, and religious establishments. Detroit was home to some of the country's first African American theater companies, publishing houses, radio stations, and history museums. In 1963, activists formed the Freedom Now Party, the first all-black political party in the United States.

When Melody's story takes place, Detroit had more independent black-owned businesses than any other city in the United States. The most well known was Motown Records, which was founded in 1959. The "Motown Sound" quickly became famous and influenced music and culture all over the world. People of all races listened to and loved the music that was born in Detroit.

While many African Americans had good lives in Detroit, they still experienced segregation and discrimination. There were no "White Only" signs on businesses, but African Americans could be refused service in stores, restaurants, and even hospitals. Black children went to separate schools, which often had fewer supplies than schools for white children. And as Melody's cousins discovered, some black people were not allowed to buy homes in neighborhoods that were mainly white. African Americans often had to pay more for housing, even though those homes and apartments were frequently in disrepair. This sort of discrimination existed all across America. The struggle for civil rights was not just a Southern issue.

Throughout the country, people spoke up about and fought for equal rights for black people. Activism was an important part of Detroit's culture. The city had the largest chapter of the National Association for the Advancement of Colored People, or NAACP. There was an NAACP Youth Council, and high school students and children as young as Melody were involved. Before the historic March on Washington, Detroit hosted the Walk to Freedom to support civil rights struggles in the South and to call attention to the inequalities that existed in the North. With a crowd of more than 125,000 people, it was the largest civil rights demonstration in America up to that point. Dr. Martin Luther King Jr. attended the event and debuted his now-famous "I have a dream" speech.

Although the civil rights movement had several key leaders, it existed because of the hundreds of thousands of ordinary citizens who played a role, however small. Children like Melody made a difference. They attended marches, participated in boycotts, and even spent time in jail. They lifted their voices in protest of inequality and in praise of social justice.

Read more of MELODY'S stories,
available from booksellers and at *americangirl.com*

♪ Classics ♪
Melody's classic series, now in two volumes:

Volume 1:
No Ordinary Sound
Melody can't wait to sing her first solo at church. She spends the summer practicing the perfect song—and helping her brother become a Motown singer. When an unimaginable tragedy leaves her silent, Melody has to find her voice.

Volume 2:
Never Stop Singing
Now that her brother is singing for Motown, Melody gets to visit a real recording studio. She also starts a children's block club. Melody is determined to help her neighborhood bloom—and make her community stronger.

♪ Journey in Time ♪
Travel back in time—and spend a few days with Melody!

Music in My Heart
Step into Melody's world of the 1960s! Volunteer with a civil rights group and meet Rosa Parks, sing backup in the Motown recording studio, or take a trip to Canada for the Emancipation Celebration. Choose your own path through this multiple-ending story.

♪ A Sneak Peek at ♪

Never Stop Singing

A Melody Classic

Volume 2

Melody's adventures continue in the second volume of her classic stories.

♪ Never Stop Singing ♪

rom the backseat of her grandfather's tan Ford Falcon, Melody read the big green sign at the side of the highway out loud: "Welcome to Alabama."

"We're going to pass Birmingham and go straight to the farm," Poppa told the girls. "I want to see it today, before nightfall."

Melody's knees were stiff from sitting in the car so long, but she could tell from her grandfather's voice that it wasn't a good idea to ask questions. She exchanged glances with Val, who gave her the zipped-lip sign.

The music on the radio was country-western, and Melody enjoyed listening to the way the lyrics and instruments sounded so different from the Motown music she listened to at home. Poppa often played country-western music while he worked in his flower shop, so Melody recognized many of the songs. She and Val sang along to the ones they knew, and they learned new ones as Poppa drove and drove.

When Poppa turned off the paved highway onto a dirt road, Melody thought they were almost at the farm. But Poppa drove for another hour to an out-of-

♪ Never Stop Singing ♪

the-way place, where he suddenly stopped the car. Melody's mother and grandfather got out and walked ahead into a field of slightly overgrown grass.

"This looks like nowhere," Val whispered, not getting out of the car right away.

Melody nodded and stretched, and then stumbled out to follow the adults.

Although she'd never been here before, there was something Melody liked—maybe it was the wildflowers dotting the field with shades of yellow and bright blue.

"It's hotter here than Birmingham!" Val said, pulling on a sun hat.

"Poppa?" Melody started after the adults. "When will we get to your old farm?" she asked, shading her eyes from the blazing sun.

Her grandfather didn't answer. He'd stopped to stare off at something Melody and Val couldn't see. Melody's mother turned to them.

"This is it," she said. "This is the farm."

Melody looked around in surprise. There was no orchard, there was no beautiful flower garden surrounded by a wooden fence Poppa had built himself.

♪ Never Stop Singing ♪

All she could see were a few old trees and a dusty path cutting through the grass. In fact, nothing here was the way her grandparents had described the farm they had loved but had left years ago to move to Detroit.

"Poppa?" Melody said softly, tugging on her grandfather's sleeve. "Where is it?"

Poppa tapped his chest, and when he spoke, his voice sounded hoarse. "In here," he said, patting his heart. Then he bent to scoop up a little of the dirt. "And here," he said, letting the dirt run through his fingers back to the ground.

"You're standing on it. Standing on the shoulders of all our people who came before."

Melody looked down at her dusty sandals, imagining her grandfather as a boy, and his parents, and maybe even their parents, walking on this same path. She looked up at Poppa, and tried to stand just a little bit taller than she had before.

About the Author

DENISE LEWIS PATRICK grew up in the town of Natchitoches, Louisiana. Lots of relatives lived nearby, so there was always someone watching out for her and always someone to play with. Every week, Denise and her brother went to the library, where she would read and dream in the children's room overlooking a wonderful river. She wrote and illustrated her first book when she was ten—she glued yellow cloth to cardboard for the cover and sewed the pages together on her mom's sewing machine. Today, Denise lives in New Jersey, but she loves returning to her hometown and taking her four sons to all the places she enjoyed as a child.

Advisory Board

*American Girl extends its deepest appreciation
to the advisory board that authenticated Melody's stories.*

Julian Bond
Chairman Emeritus, NAACP Board of Directors, and founding
member of Student Nonviolent Coordinating Committee (SNCC)

Rebecca de Schweinitz
Associate Professor of History, Brigham Young University,
and author of *If We Could Change the World: Young People and
America's Long Struggle for Racial Equality* (Chapel Hill:
University of North Carolina Press, 2009)

Gloria House
Director and Professor Emerita, African and African American
Studies, University of Michigan–Dearborn, and SNCC Field
Secretary, Lowndes County, Alabama, 1963–1965

Juanita Moore
President and CEO of Charles H. Wright Museum of
African American History, Detroit, and founding executive director
of the National Civil Rights Museum, Memphis, Tennessee

Thomas J. Sugrue
Professor of History, New York University, and author of
*Sweet Land of Liberty: The Forgotten Struggle for Civil Rights
in the North* (Random House, 2008)

JoAnn Watson
Native of Detroit, ordained minister, and former
executive director of the Detroit NAACP

Never Stop Singing

*A Melody Classic
Volume 2*

by Denise Lewis Patrick

★ AmericanGirl®

Published by American Girl Publishing

16 17 18 19 20 21 LEO 10 9 8 7 6 5 4 3 2 1

All American Girl marks, BeForever™, Melody™,
and Melody Ellison™ are trademarks of American Girl.

Grateful acknowledgment is made to the following for permission to quote previously published material: "Dream Boogie" and "Youth" from THE COLLECTED POEMS OF LANGSTON HUGHES by Langston Hughes, edited by Arnold Rampersad with David Roessel, Associate Editor, copyright © 1994 by the Estate of Langston Hughes. Used by permission of Alfred A. Knopf, an imprint of the Knopf Doubleday Publishing Group, a division of Penguin Random House LLC. All rights reserved. Any third-party use of this material, outside of this publication, is prohibited. Interested parties must apply directly to Penguin Random House LLC for permission.

This book is a work of fiction. Any similarity to real persons, living or dead, is coincidental and not intended by American Girl. References to real events, people, or places are used fictitiously. Other names, characters, places, and incidents are the products of imagination.

Cover image by Michael Dwornik and Juliana Kolesova
Author photo by Fran Baltzer Photo

Cataloging-in-Publication Data available from the Library of Congress

© 2016 American Girl. All rights reserved. Todos los derechos reservados. Tous droits réservés. All American Girl marks are trademarks of American Girl. Marcas registradas utilizadas bajo licencia. American Girl ainsi que les marques et designs y afférents appartiennent à American Girl. **MADE IN CHINA. HECHO EN CHINA. FABRIQUÉ EN CHINE.** Retain this address for future reference: American Girl, 8400 Fairway Place, Middleton, WI 53562, U.S.A. **Importado y distribuido por** A.G. México Retail, S. de R.L. de C.V., Miguel de Cervantes Saavedra No. 193 Pisos 10 y 11, Col. Granada, Delegación Miguel Hidalgo, C.P. 11520 México, D.F. Conserver ces informations pour s'y référer en cas de besoin. American Girl Canada, 8400 Fairway Place, Middleton, WI 53562, U.S.A. **Manufactured for and imported into the EU by:** Mattel Europa B.V., Gondel 1, 1186 MJ Amstelveen, Nederland.

*This book is dedicated in friendship to
Sharon Shavers Gayle
and in gratitude to the unforgettable
Mr. Horace Julian Bond*

Beforever

The adventurous characters you'll meet in the BeForever books will spark your curiosity about the past, inspire you to find your voice in the present, and excite you about your future. You'll make friends with these girls as you share their fun and their challenges. Like you, they are bright and brave, imaginative and energetic, creative and kind. Just as you are, they are discovering what really matters: Helping others. Being a true friend. Protecting the earth. Standing up for what's right. Read their stories, explore their worlds, join their adventures. Your friendship with them will BeForever.

♪ TABLE *of* CONTENTS ♪

1	Melody's Eve	1
2	Watch Night	14
3	Double-Digits Birthday	24
4	Challenges	39
5	The Block Club	45
6	Books and Banners	62
7	We March!	83
8	Wish List	95
9	Grandfathers and "Grandflowers"	102
10	Singing Together	116
11	Open Doors	136
12	More Letters	148
13	Important Work	160
14	Standing Tall	166
15	Civil Rights	179
16	Keep Going	189
17	A Playground and a Party	202
	Inside Melody's World	212

When Melody's story takes place, the terms "Negro," "colored," and "black" were all used to describe Americans of African descent. You'll see all of those words used in this book.

Today, "Negro" and "colored" can be offensive because they are associated with racial inequality. "African American" is a more contemporary term, but it wasn't commonly used until the late 1980s.

Melody's Eve

♪ CHAPTER 1 ♪

Melody Ellison stared for a moment at the bright new calendar in her hands before she put it up on the kitchen wall. The picture on the January page showed a tall evergreen tree, its thick branches frosted with snow.

"O Christmas tree, O Christmas tree, how lovely are your branches," Melody sang, even though Christmas had been over for a week. It was New Year's Eve, and tomorrow would be the first day of 1964, her tenth birthday!

Melody loved the idea that having a New Year's birthday meant that the whole world was having a birthday, too. Until now she'd been too young to stay awake past midnight, or to attend the special Watch Night service at their church. Now that she was turning ten, her parents had decided that she was old enough to do both.

♪ Never Stop Singing ♪

"Dee-Dee's almost double digits!" Her sister Lila playfully tugged at one of Melody's braids, then reached into the refrigerator and got out the eggs.

"That's right!" Melody said proudly. Lila was already thirteen, and Melody somehow felt as if she was finally catching up.

"Good morning, Melody," her mother said, joining the girls in the kitchen. "I see you're carrying on your calendar-changing tradition!" Bo, the family's black-and-white mixed terrier, ran in at her heels.

"Yes, I am, Mommy," Melody said, watching her mother tie on a colorful apron. "Are you about to make my birthday cake?" Her mother's triple-chocolate layer cakes were so good that Melody couldn't imagine celebrating anything special without one.

"We are." Mommy set ingredients on the table: butter, sugar, baking powder, cocoa. Bo must have guessed that something good was coming, because he began to bark. Melody bent down to pet him, and Bo flopped onto his side, waving one paw in the air.

Mommy took out the large mixing bowl and started sifting flour into it. "Lila, will you separate the eggs?"

"Sure. Five, right?"

♪ Melody's Eve ♪

Mommy nodded at Lila and smiled. "Why, I think soon you'll be able to make this cake on your own."

"It's more fun to bake with you," Lila said.

One of the things Melody loved most about her family was that they always worked together—to set the table, do chores around the house, or even solve one another's problems. Big Momma, Melody's grandmother, called it "harmony." She was a music teacher, and she said their family was good at putting their voices together to make one great sound. Melody knew that Big Momma didn't just mean singing. She meant they helped and supported one another in all sorts of ways.

"If I weren't going to help Poppa decorate the church hall for tonight, I'd help make the cake," Melody said, standing up.

"Hey! You can't help make your own birthday cake!" Lila said, cracking an egg against the side of a cup. Melody giggled as the egg almost slipped onto the floor. Bo scrambled up and began to bark again.

The soft swishing of the flour sifter stopped, and her mother looked at Melody. "My baby girl is going to be ten tomorrow!" she said. "Seems like it was just

♪ Never Stop Singing ♪

yesterday that you were born."

"Mommy, I'm not a baby anymore," Melody reminded her, skipping out to the living room. "I'm about to become double digits, remember?"

Melody glanced at the sunburst clock over the sofa. Her grandfather, Poppa, wouldn't be picking her up for another half hour. She turned the TV on and waited while it warmed up. When the picture appeared, Melody turned the knob through all the channels, looking for something fun to watch. It was morning and there was no school, so she was hoping for cartoons, or at least a music show. Instead, every station seemed to be running a program that looked back on the year's news. Melody didn't really want to be reminded. She reached for the knob to shut the TV off.

"Wait, Dee-Dee!" Melody's other sister Yvonne called out from the stairs. "Don't turn it off. I want to watch."

Yvonne was home from college for the holidays, and Melody was glad to have her back for a few weeks. Now, if only their brother Dwayne were here! This was the first Christmas he'd ever been away, and Melody really missed him. He and his singing group, The

♪ Melody's Eve ♪

Three Ravens, were traveling around the country singing for Motown, the famous record company. Dwayne was a talented musician, but Daddy didn't like his new career one bit. Dwayne was only eighteen, and Daddy and Mommy wanted him to go to college instead. *It's funny,* Melody thought. *Dwayne's job as a singer isn't bringing much harmony to our family.*

Melody sighed, and together with her sister watched a grainy replay of the new president, Lyndon B. Johnson, being sworn into office in November.

Yvonne shook her head. "I still can't believe somebody shot the president of the United States," she said, turning up the sound. They listened as the grim-faced newscaster told the whole story again: how President John F. Kennedy and the First Lady were in a motorcade in Dallas, Texas, on November 22. They were riding in the back of a Lincoln Continental convertible when a man with a gun fired at the car, killing the president and wounding the governor of Texas.

"The country remains in shock as our new president faces a grieving nation, problems overseas, and growing civil rights protests here at home," said the newscaster. Then he began to talk about the bombing

♪ Never Stop Singing ♪

of a Birmingham, Alabama, church in September that had killed four little girls. Melody turned away from the screen. Somebody who wanted to frighten black people away from fighting for equal rights had set off the bomb on a Sunday morning.

Although it had happened miles and miles away from Detroit, Melody had been frightened—so much so that she'd lost her voice right before the big Youth Day concert. For a long while she'd even been afraid to go inside her own church.

"I'll never forget that day," Yvonne said, interrupting Melody's memories.

Melody looked at her sister and remembered that Yvonne had been away at Tuskegee, her college, when it happened. Tuskegee was also in Alabama—only a few hours' drive from Birmingham.

"Vonnie," Melody suddenly asked, "were *you* scared?" She'd never really thought about that before. Yvonne had called to tell their parents that she was all right, but Melody had never considered that her brave big sister might have been frightened, too.

"Well, yes, at first," Yvonne said. "I had signed up to go to Birmingham that very next weekend. We were

♪ Melody's Eve ♪

going to sit in at a lunch counter to protest the fact that they refuse to serve black people. But after that Sunday I was thinking, *What if something awful happens to me and my friends? Maybe I won't go after all.* Then I remembered Mom telling me that I should always stand up to wrong. Bombing that church was wrong. Treating black people unfairly is wrong. So I decided that I had to go to Birmingham and support what I believe in, you know?"

Melody nodded. "Big Momma told me something like that, too! She said we should keep our hearts and voices strong when bad things happen. I tried really hard to be strong for the little girls in Birmingham. I *wanted* to be, only I wasn't sure I could."

Yvonne smiled and gave Melody a hug. "You didn't let fear turn you around, did you?" she said. "You went back to church to sing. You *were* strong."

"I guess . . ." Melody said slowly. Her family and friends had helped her find courage, and her voice, again. But there was another reason she had wanted to sing. "I didn't want to let the choir down," she said.

"That's because you weren't thinking only about yourself," Yvonne said, switching off the TV. "You

♪ Never Stop Singing ♪

were thinking about lots of other people, too. Hey, only a responsible person can do that, Dee-Dee."

Melody didn't say anything, but she felt herself smiling. Yvonne had made her feel a little less sad and a little more grown up.

Just then there was a hard knock on the front door. Yvonne answered it, and their grandparents came in, along with a blast of cold air.

"Well, Happy Melody's Eve, everybody!" Poppa's voice boomed. It was his joke to call the day before New Year's "Melody's Eve."

"Hello, my chicks!" Big Momma said, taking off her coat. As Melody hurried to hug them, she noticed the large wrapped box her grandfather had brought in and propped beside the door.

"Poppa, what's that?" Melody asked, peeking curiously at the mysterious package. But when she looked to her grandfather for an answer, he only shrugged.

Big Momma smiled. "Well," she said, "it's a day early, but we brought our birthday girl a little something."

"Ohhh!" Melody gasped at the surprise.

♪ Melody's Eve ♪

"Wow. That's a pretty big box for a *little* something," Yvonne said.

Melody picked up the box and carried it to the sofa. It wasn't heavy, but it wasn't exactly light, either. She shook it gently, hearing only a soft swish-swishing sound.

"Can I open it right now?" she asked.

"That was the idea, Little One," Poppa laughed. "Go right ahead!"

Melody didn't wait another second. She ripped off the wrapping paper, tugged the top off the box, and peeled back two layers of tissue paper to find a beautiful cream-colored dress with gold lace. It was folded neatly on top of a matching double-breasted coat with gold buttons. Melody looked up, wide-eyed.

"We thought you might like to dress up, since it's your first Watch Night and Melody's Eve all rolled into one," Poppa told her.

"Do you like them?" Big Momma asked.

Melody nodded. "I've never owned anything so fancy," she said. "Thank you!"

"Dee-Dee, try the coat on!" Yvonne said.

Melody eagerly slipped into the coat and felt warm

♪ Never Stop Singing ♪

all over. The cream-colored collar and cuffs were soft against her skin. She held her arms out and did a little twirl across the living room floor.

Big Momma clapped. "A perfect fit!"

"I could be a model in the *Ebony* magazine Fashion Fair," Melody said proudly.

"You can be anything you want to be," Yvonne said seriously.

Melody thought about their earlier conversation and smiled at her sister's compliment.

Poppa cleared his throat. "How about being my helper in getting the church decorated for tonight? Or did that fancy coat make you forget?" he teased.

"Oh, no, Poppa," Melody said quickly. "I'll be ready in just a minute." She carefully took off her new coat and started to fold it back into the box.

"Let me hang those up for you," Yvonne offered. "So they don't wrinkle."

Melody handed her sister the coat and the box and followed Poppa to the front door. She grabbed her old jacket from the hook and then turned back to her grandmother.

"I love my birthday present. Thank you!"

♪ Melody's Eve ♪

"I'm so glad," Big Momma told her. "You'll look beautiful. Now you two go and make our New Hope church beautiful for tonight, too."

"We will!" Melody said enthusiastically.

Poppa's truck was in the driveway. The words "Frank's Flowers" were on the passenger door. Poppa owned a flower shop on 12th Street, and he had taught Melody everything she knew about plants and gardening.

Melody climbed into the truck and peeked through the back window to see evergreen branches just like the ones on the kitchen calendar. "Oh, Poppa! The hall is going to smell so good!" Melody said. One of her favorite things about this time of year—besides her birthday—was the strong scent of evergreens.

"Yep. I have flowers, too," Poppa said. "Poinsettias and amaryllis. We'll make things look real nice for this evening. Are you excited about your first Watch Night service?"

Melody knew from her brother and sisters that Watch Night wouldn't exactly be a New Year's Eve party like the ones that were on TV. But there would be singing, and preaching by Pastor Daniels, with food

♪ Never Stop Singing ♪

and fellowship afterward in the church hall.

"I'm glad I can finally wait up with everybody else till midnight," she told him. "But why isn't it called 'Wait Night' instead of 'Watch Night'?"

"Well, Watch Night is a tradition for some colored folks, especially those of us with family in the South. It goes back a hundred years, when word got out ahead of time that President Abraham Lincoln planned to announce to the country that all slaves were free. The president was going to make the announcement on New Year's Day, 1863. So colored people, slave and free, sat up all night, keeping watch for freedom—Watch Night."

"But you can't *see* freedom," Melody said.

"Are you sure about that?" Poppa asked.

Melody wondered for a moment what freedom might look like. Would it look like the thousands of people who had marched in Washington, D.C., last August? Or maybe like Detroit's own Walk to Freedom in June? Melody and her family had joined thousands of others to hear Dr. Martin Luther King Jr. speak.

"Would freedom look like people of all races, doing things together?" she asked.

♪ Melody's Eve ♪

"Maybe," Poppa said, glancing at her. "Back in 1863, *that* kind of freedom was just a dream. But I think on that first Watch Night, they could see freedom coming. How many times have you tried to stay awake on Melody's Eve, because what's coming is so special? When you're expecting something big, something wonderful to happen, you can't rest. And when that Emancipation Proclamation did come, our people celebrated. We've been giving thanks ever since, during Watch Night."

"Wow," Melody murmured. She was thankful that she was finally going to stay up for Watch Night. And she was proud that her birthday was linked to such an important tradition.

Watch Night

♪ CHAPTER 2 ♪

At eleven-thirty that night, Melody walked into New Hope Baptist Church wearing her birthday dress and coat. She felt as if she sparkled as she settled into her seat between Lila and Yvonne. She had sat between her sisters ever since she was a tiny girl. Now, half an hour away from turning ten, Melody felt very grown up.

She inhaled the spicy smell of the pine branches she and Poppa had woven into a garland across the choir stand up front. As she watched for Poppa and Big Momma and her cousins to arrive, Melody glanced around at everything else that was so familiar: the beautiful stained-glass windows, the many faces she'd known forever. New Hope Baptist Church had always been her home away from home. There had been a time, right after the church bombing in Birmingham,

♪ Watch Night ♪

that being here had frightened her, but now New Hope made Melody feel safe again.

When her cousin Val and the rest of the family arrived, they all oohed and aahed over Melody's dress and coat. "It was so hard not to tell you about them," Val said after she'd talked Lila into letting her sit next to Melody.

"You knew about it?" Melody asked.

Val grinned. "Surprise!" she giggled. Val and her parents were staying with Poppa and Big Momma until they could find a house of their own. They'd moved to Detroit from Birmingham in May, and it was taking them a long time to buy a house.

Before Melody could ask Val anything else, Pastor Daniels stepped up to the pulpit.

"Good evening!" the preacher said. His voice was always loud and clear, and he never needed to use a microphone.

"Good evening!" everyone answered together.

Pastor Daniels peered out at the crowd over the tops of his glasses. "A week ago, many of us received gifts," he began. "Isn't that right?"

"Yes, sir!" a young voice answered from the back.

♪ Never Stop Singing ♪

A few people laughed, and Melody turned to look.

Pastor Daniels chuckled before he continued. "Well, New Hope church family, at midnight everyone here will receive another gift. When the New Year comes in, each of us will receive a new opportunity to make a difference in the world. That's a special gift. And I want each one of you to ask yourself: What will I do with *my* gift? What will *I* do to help justice, equality, and dignity grow in our community?"

Melody sat up a little straighter. She thought of the seeds she and Poppa planted in their gardens every spring and of the work it took to make those seeds grow and blossom. *Can a person really make justice, equality, and dignity grow, too?* she wondered. *How?*

Pastor Daniels kept speaking. "In honor of all those hopeful souls who first sat watch for their freedom so long ago, now is the time for every one of us to use this gift we receive tonight. I want each of you to pick one thing you can work on, just one thing you can change for the better, right here in our community."

Murmurs rippled through the congregation. Melody saw Lila scribbling notes on a corner of her program.

♪ Watch Night ♪

"I want you to give this idea some serious thought," Pastor Daniels said. "But don't take too long. When Reverend Dr. King visited with us here in Detroit last summer, he said, '*Now* is the time to lift our nation.' Now is the time, New Hope, for us to lift *our* nation. Now is the time for you"—he pointed one way—"and you"—he pointed the other way—"and you! To take action!"

Melody was sure he was looking directly at her. She held her breath.

"The new year, 1964, is a season of change. Change yourself. Change our community. Change our nation!"

Miss Dorothy, who directed Melody and her friends in the children's choir, began to play the piano. The adult choir rose and began to sing. Melody sang along, clapping in time with the rhythm.

> *We've come this far by faith,*
> *Leaning on the Lord,*
> *Trusting in His holy word,*
> *He's never failed me yet.*
> *Oh, oh, oh, can't turn around,*
> *We've come this far by faith.*

♪ Never Stop Singing ♪

At the conclusion of the song, to Melody's surprise and delight, the church bells sounded, drowning out the final piano notes. It was midnight! It was 1964!

"Happy New Year!" Pastor Daniels shouted.

"Happy Birthday, Melody!" Val shouted, too, squeezing Melody in a hug. But in the din of bells and cheers and applause, only Melody heard.

The Watch Night celebration continued downstairs in the church hall, where everyone greeted each other saying "Happy New Year!" Melody, Val, and Lila stood in line with Yvonne to get cookies, while the rest of the family found seats at one of the tables. Melody tried to spot her best friend, Sharon, in the crowd, but the room was packed.

"There's Diane," Val said.

Melody saw her friend Diane Harris helping her little sisters carry cups of punch. Across the hall Melody saw Miss Esther Collins sitting with a group of other elderly people. Miss Esther was a neighbor who loved gardening just as much as Melody did. She looked up and waved. Melody smiled and waved back.

♪ Watch Night ♪

Yvonne nudged Melody when the lady behind them commented on how pretty the amaryllis flowers were.

"Were they Poppa's idea, or yours?" Yvonne asked.

"Poppa's. But it was my idea to tie the gold ribbons around each pot," Melody said proudly.

Yvonne nodded. "They match your dress,"

"Hey, she's right," Val said.

Melody grinned and tried not to yawn. She didn't want anyone to think she was still too young to be at Watch Night.

With cookies stacked on napkins, Yvonne led them back to a table in the corner where everyone else was sitting. There weren't enough chairs, so Melody sat on Big Momma's lap. She hadn't done that in a while, and tonight something felt different—either Big Momma's lap was getting smaller, or Melody was getting bigger. *Well, I am double digits*, she thought.

"Everyone is talking about the decorations," Yvonne said, passing around the cookies. "And Pastor Daniels's Challenge to Change. I think this thing is going to be big!"

Daddy nodded at her. "'Challenge to Change.' I like that, Yvonne. You know, sometimes when people listen

♪ Never Stop Singing ♪

to the news, they think all the change in the way black people are treated only needs to happen down South. But there's plenty of change work to do here in the North, too."

"You're right about that, Will," Val's father, Charles, said.

"Yes," Val's mother, Tish, said, "like the fact that decent, hardworking people can't get a real estate agent to show them certain houses just because they're black!" Tish sounded angry. Although she owned her own hair salon and Charles had a good job as a pharmacist, they were having trouble buying a house.

"You two aren't the only ones facing that battle," Melody's mother said. "Come to our next Block Club meeting. Someone from the Fair Housing Practices Committee is coming to talk to us."

"Is that so?" Charles said.

"We'll be there," Tish said.

"Housing laws need to change," Melody's mother agreed. "But Pastor Daniels asked us to change ourselves, too. I think I might start tutoring after school again."

Yvonne nodded. "I'm going to take Pastor Daniels's

♪ Watch Night ♪

challenge with me when I go back to school. I'm not sure what I'll do on campus, but I know what I can do in the community—well, a community in Mississippi. There's talk about students going there this summer for a civil rights project. I want to go."

Melody's mother shifted in her seat. "What exactly would you all be doing?" she asked.

"A bunch of things. I heard there will be more voter registration, and volunteers will talk to black folks to remind them that they have a say in how this country works. I think they'll also be setting up community centers and schools. I might try working with kids." Yvonne was speaking fast, the way she did when she was excited about an idea.

"Teaching?" Melody asked. "Just like Mommy!" Melody looked at their mother, who looked pleased.

"I thought you were studying business," pointed out Lila, who liked to get all the facts straight.

Yvonne laughed. "I am, Lila. But let's just say that I want to make it my business to help teach black history. Schools are really poor down there. Lots of kids in black communities don't know about the contributions black Americans have made."

♪ Never Stop Singing ♪

"You mean, like Dr. King?" Melody asked.

"And many others," Big Momma said. "Harriet Tubman, Frederick Douglass, and Mrs. Rosa Parks."

"Yes, yes!" Yvonne was bouncing in her seat. "I think when you know about your history, and when you're proud of it, it makes you stronger."

"We sent you to college to learn," Melody's father said, looking steadily at Yvonne.

Daddy paused, and Melody saw Yvonne take a deep breath.

"Seems like you *are* learning," Daddy continued. "To follow your own mind, and make justice and equality grow."

Yvonne let out the breath she'd been holding and smiled. "Thanks, Dad."

"However," Daddy said, leaning forward so that his arms rested on the table, "I want you to be careful in Mississippi and to be safe."

Yvonne laughed. "I know, Dad." But when Daddy gave her a stern look, Yvonne said, "Yes, sir."

Melody smiled, hoping she could have just as much courage in her choice for change as her brave big sister.

"What about you chicks?" Big Momma said to

♪ Watch Night ♪

Melody and Val. "What are you going to do with your gift?"

"Us?" Val replied. "Did Pastor Daniels mean kids, too?"

"Of course he meant kids, too," Melody said excitedly.

"He certainly did," Big Momma said as the grown-ups around the table nodded and smiled.

Suddenly, Yvonne slipped her arm around Melody's shoulder. "Speaking of gifts, somebody should be thinking about her birthday gifts."

"That's right!" Lila slapped the table with her hand. "Dee-Dee is officially ten years old!"

"I am," Melody said, realizing that she'd just stayed awake past midnight for the first time ever. The New Year had begun, and it was her birthday. As she blinked away sleep, she thought about Pastor Daniels's challenge and wondered what great big idea would come her way.

Double-Digits Birthday

♪ CHAPTER 3 ♪

On the afternoon on New Year's Day, Melody sorted through the neat stack of records in the living room to find just the right music for her birthday celebration. As she flipped past names she'd heard on the radio or seen on TV, she imagined one day picking up a record with Dwayne's name on it. *Today would be absolutely perfect if only he were here, too,* she thought.

Melody was only halfway through the stack when the doorbell rang.

"*Happy Birthday to yooouuu!*" Sharon and Diane sang as Melody opened the door.

"Are we too early?" Sharon asked, peeling off her coat and hanging it on one of the hooks by the door. "My dad wanted to drop us off before his football game came on."

♪ Double-Digits Birthday ♪

"My daddy's upstairs right now listening to a game on the radio," Melody laughed. "And you're right on time."

"What're you doing?" Diane asked, hanging her jacket over Sharon's. She gave Melody a tube-shaped package tied with yarn at either end. It looked like a big piece of candy.

Melody put the package on the coffee table and motioned toward the record player. "I'm trying to find some music."

"Wouldn't it be great if your brother and his group could be here to sing?" Sharon asked.

"Yeah! A live concert would be so cool!" Diane said.

"It would," Melody nodded. "But The Three Ravens aren't in Detroit. They sang at a New Year's concert somewhere in Ohio last night."

"Too bad," Sharon said, sorting through the records lying on the sofa. "Hey! Here's Little Stevie Wonder's 'Fingertips.'" Melody put the record on the turntable and carefully moved the needle arm to its edge.

"*This* is birthday music!" Sharon hopped up, and the girls began to dance.

Sharon was right. The sounds of the harmonica and

♪ Never Stop Singing ♪

Stevie Wonder's 12-year-old voice made Melody want to move, laugh, celebrate, and sing. They danced their way across the floor and into the dining room.

Melody barely dodged the kitchen door as her mother opened it, carrying the triple-chocolate cake on a blue glass plate.

"Whoa, there, birthday girl!" Mrs. Ellison said, placing the cake safely in the center of the table. Melody stopped. Sharon and Diane froze.

"Sorry, Mommy!" Melody said, still bopping her head to the music.

"Sorry, Mrs. Ellison!" Diane chimed in.

"Me, too!" Sharon said.

Melody's mother gave them a hard look, but then smiled and shook her shoulders and bopped her head a few beats, too. Sharon burst out laughing.

Mrs. Ellison shrugged. "Who can keep still when it's Little Stevie Wonder?" she asked.

As if the music had stirred the entire house into movement, all at once Daddy, Yvonne, and Lila trooped downstairs. Then there was a knock at the front door, and at the same time the telephone rang and someone was coming into the kitchen from the back door.

♪ Double-Digits Birthday ♪

Mommy went into the kitchen to answer the phone as Yvonne answered the front door. In came Melody's grandparents and her cousins. In the blink of an eye, the dining room was filled with people. Melody didn't know which way to turn first.

"Happy Birthday, chick!" Big Momma was first to give Melody a hug.

"Big Ten!" Cousin Charles said. "Congratulations!"

"Happy Birthday, baby." Cousin Tish gave Melody a kiss. "Love that hairstyle!" she whispered, fluffing Melody's curled bangs. Val, peeking from behind her mother, rolled her eyes and grinned. When she stepped forward, Melody saw that she was holding a small box with a bow on it.

"This is for you," Val said. "Happy, Happy!"

"Gee! I forgot your present!" Sharon said, rushing to the hooks by the front door to dig into her coat pocket. She came back with a soft, tissue-paper-wrapped package. "Sorry, it got a little squished," she said.

Melody didn't care. She was so pleased to have all—nearly all—of her family and friends together on her special day that everything felt pretty wonderful.

"How about we get some candles for this cake and

♪ Never Stop Singing ♪

celebrate our birthday girl?" Melody's father rubbed his hands together and winked at her. He loved Mommy's triple-chocolate cake just as much as Melody did.

"Here we go!" Yvonne placed ten tiny blue candles atop the chocolate frosting in a circle, and another in the middle.

"To grow on," she laughed.

"Ready to sing, everybody?" Lila pulled Melody to stand right in front of her cake, and Daddy lit the candles.

"Where's Mommy?" Melody looked over her shoulder.

"Here!" Her mother stepped in from the kitchen, breathless.

"Happy Birthday to you. Happy Birthday to you. Happy Birthday, dear Melody. Happy birthday to you!"

Melody was beaming. She loved when her family sang together—it was almost like they had their own choir, the way all their voices blended and harmonized in just the right ways! She took a breath but didn't blow out the candles yet. In her family, there was one more verse of the birthday song to sing. Melody smiled and looked around at all their faces, waiting. Suddenly, a

♪ Double-Digits Birthday ♪

solo voice came from the kitchen. It was a high tenor, almost like Smokey Robinson's.

"How o-old are you? How o-old are you? My kid sister, Dee-Dee . . ."

"Dwayne!" Melody squealed, throwing open the kitchen door.

"How o-old are you?" Dwayne finished singing and gave her a bear hug. "Didn't I tell you when I left that I'd show up when you didn't expect it? Happy Birthday!"

Melody pulled Dwayne into the room.

"Well, I declare!" Tish laughed.

"When did you get here?" Lila asked.

Melody noticed that the only people who didn't seem surprised were her mother and father.

"Parents know how to keep secrets, too," Daddy said. "And it was a good one, wasn't it?"

"The best ever!" Melody agreed. Since Dwayne had started working for Motown, he was rarely at home. And when his singing group did come back to town, he spent more time at the studio and at his bandmate Phil's house than he did with the family. Their father wasn't very happy about that, but now they were

♪ Never Stop Singing ♪

both smiling, and Melody was glad her birthday had brought them together.

"Let's cut this cake. I'm starved!" Dwayne said. He turned to Melody and gave her a bow. "Birthday girls first, of course."

Melody sat on the floor between Diane and Val with her paper party plate balanced on her knees. Everyone was listening to her brother's stories about traveling around the country with the famous Motown singers. He was telling how he'd accidentally almost tripped one of The Supremes backstage when Val nudged Melody with an elbow.

"When are you going to open your presents?" she whispered, not very quietly.

Dwayne stopped mid-sentence. "Val, they call that a 'stage whisper,'" he laughed, "because the audience is supposed to hear it, too."

Val ducked her head in embarrassment. "Sorry, Dwayne!"

Charles shook his head. "I believe our Valerie likes watching other folks open presents as much as she

♪ Double-Digits Birthday ♪

likes opening presents herself!"

Val had already scrambled up to get Melody's gifts and cards, bringing them to her.

"Open mine first," Sharon said eagerly.

"No, wait." Dwayne went back into the kitchen and came out carrying a record album. "I didn't exactly have time to wrap it," he told his sister.

Melody looked carefully at the bright red cover, and the three young black women looking over their shoulders in the picture. Big orange letters announced the album's artists, Martha and The Vandellas. The album was called *Heat Wave*. That was the name of one of Melody's favorite songs.

Scrawled across the lower corner was a handwritten message. Melody read it out loud: *"Happy Birthday, Dee-Dee. Stay Cool. Martha."* Melody's mouth dropped open.

Sharon, Val, and Lila crowded around to see.

"Wow, Dwayne! Martha Reeves is one of the hottest stars at Motown right now," Yvonne said. "She's world famous!"

Melody looked at Dwayne. "You got Martha Reeves to autograph it for *me*?" she asked.

♪ Never Stop Singing ♪

Dwayne shrugged and nodded, but he looked pleased that Melody liked her gift.

"Do you really know her?" Sharon asked, starstruck.

"Sort of," he said. "I mean, we're at the studio at the same time . . . sometimes."

"Thank you, Dwayne," Melody said. "You're the best brother ever."

"That's something special," Big Momma said. As Melody passed the album to her grandmother, she saw her father squinting at it.

"How long before we see your face on something like this?" Daddy asked, looking over at Dwayne. Melody shot a look at her brother.

"Dad, I know I have a long way to go. I'm working real hard at it. I'm hoping to get into the studio to record my own music soon."

"I know you'll be just as famous as Martha Reeves one day," Melody said confidently. But Daddy just shook his head.

Melody picked up Sharon's gift. She didn't waste any time unwrapping carefully, the way her sisters did. She tore everything open. The tissue paper ripped

♪ Double-Digits Birthday ♪

away easily, and a length of shiny purple satin ribbon fell into Melody's lap.

"It's for Matching Mondays," Sharon said. "My mom says purple is really hard to find, but she got enough for both of us."

"I love it!" Melody said. Almost every Monday since she and Sharon had met in kindergarten they'd worn the same color hair ribbons to school. Melody carefully wound the ribbon into neat loops. "I got a purple plaid skirt for Christmas," she told Sharon. "This ribbon will go with it perfectly."

Melody was curious about the tube-shaped gift from Diane. When she pulled the paper off, she discovered a tin kaleidoscope. "Neat," she said, holding one end up to her eye and twisting the other end. A colorful burst of patterns shifted inside the tube. "Thanks, Diane."

Next was Val's small box. Inside was a bright new set of jacks and a tiny rubber ball to go with them. "I know you lost one of your other set," Val said.

"I did." Melody gave the ball a quick test bounce, and it flew right into Yvonne's Afro. "Oops!" Melody made a sheepish face. Yvonne simply pulled the ball

♪ Never Stop Singing ♪

out, patted her hair back into place, and smiled.

"No ball bouncing indoors!" Daddy said sternly, scooping the ball away from Yvonne. Then he reached to drop it back into its box, which Melody shut quickly. She moved on to her parents' gift, which was wrapped in Christmas paper. It was heavier than she expected. *What could it be?* she wondered.

"Be careful there," Daddy warned. Melody slipped one finger under the lid and popped it off. Inside, nested in crumpled newspapers, was a green transistor radio.

"Ohhh!" she sighed. "My very own radio. Now I can play the music stations I like whenever I want! Thank you, thank you!" Melody immediately turned the radio on and began turning the dial to tune in a station.

Dwayne snapped his fingers when music began to play. "Isn't this a dancing party?" He reached for Melody's hand and pulled her up from the floor. "Come on, Dee-Dee Double Digits. Let's dance!"

Melody followed Dwayne's smooth steps toward the dining room where the floor was clear. In seconds, Charles had gotten Tish up, Lila and Yvonne were

♪ Double-Digits Birthday ♪

moving to the beat, and Val and Sharon were doing a silly bird-like step.

"Are you back to stay? Did you write any new songs? When are you going to make your own record?" Melody asked Dwayne all at once.

"So many questions!" he laughed. "Am I on a quiz show?"

"No," Melody answered. "I missed you, that's all."

"In that case, we're in town for a few weeks to sing backup for some folks and work on a new song I wrote."

"How does it go?"

Dwayne sang:

> *Girl, it's time that I move,*
> *Time for movin' on up.*
> *Yeah, it's time for my move,*
> *Time to start changing my luck.*

"Oh, that sounds good," Melody said. "I like it."

"I do, too," Dwayne told her. "I think it could be a hit. When we get studio time, I want you to sing it with me. I'm not kidding!"

♪ Never Stop Singing ♪

"I know," Melody answered. "I'll do it." But right now she couldn't imagine anything better than this wonderful moment.

Dwayne took her by one hand and spun her around. She almost felt as if she were flying. Everyone was laughing. Her grandparents were clapping. She looked over her shoulder and saw her mother and father dancing, too. She closed her eyes to take a picture with her mind. She felt happy. She felt strong, as if she could do anything.

Later that evening, Melody lay across her bed holding her radio, but it wasn't on. She was listening to her brother and sisters arguing and then laughing down in the living room, the same way they always had. She was smiling when her parents stuck their heads into her room.

"The idea was that you would listen to the radio," her father teased, "not to your squabbling siblings."

"I know, Daddy," Melody laughed. She sat up as Mommy came into the room.

Her mother waved a package. "One more gift!"

♪ Double-Digits Birthday ♪

Melody could tell from the shape that it was a book. Even though her mother was a math teacher, she loved to read. And she always encouraged other people—especially her children—to love reading, too.

Mommy sat on the edge of her bed. Daddy leaned against the doorway. Melody untied the ribbon and peeled away the paper. "*The First Book of Rhythms*, by Langston Hughes," she read.

As long as she could remember, Melody had heard her father reading aloud poems written by the famous black author. He could even recite some Langston Hughes poems from memory. Sometimes, the poems sounded like music.

Melody flipped through her new book, suprised to see that it wasn't poetry. It was about finding rhythms in poetry and music and even nature. She couldn't wait to read it.

"I saw in the newspaper that Mr. Hughes is going to make an appearance at Hudson's department store in February," Mommy told her.

"Can we go?" Melody asked excitedly.

Mommy nodded.

Melody had started paging through the book again

♪ Never Stop Singing ♪

when a yawn snuck up on her. "I think Melody needs to listen to the rhythm of her sleep," Daddy laughed.

Melody set the book and the radio on the shelf behind her bed and crawled under the covers. Mommy tucked her in, and Daddy kissed her on the forehead. "'Night, my ten-year-old girl."

"'Night, Daddy," Melody murmured. "'Night, Mommy." Her parents went across the hall to their room, and their voices mingled with Lila's, Yvonne's, and Dwayne's. Melody fell asleep listening to the rhythm of her family.

Challenges

♪ CHAPTER 4 ♪

At the end of the first week back at school, Melody decided that doing long division and writing compositions weren't quite as interesting as Christmas, Watch Night, or her birthday. She was having trouble staying awake. Big Momma said her body was playing catch-up for all the sleep it had lost while Melody was having fun. On Friday afternoon, Melody blinked as Mrs. Butler rapped on the edge of her desk with a ruler and told the class that she had a special announcement.

"I know it's hard to get back to our schoolwork after having so much free time. But here's something we can all look forward to." She unrolled a poster and tacked it onto the bulletin board.

Melody recognized the face of Frederick Douglass from a book at her grandparents' house, and she

♪ Never Stop Singing ♪

remembered his amazing life story: He was born a slave but taught himself to read and write when he was only a boy. He later escaped from slavery, and grew up to travel free all over the world to speak against it. Melody's grandfather said Frederick Douglass's story had always given him the courage to fight for civil rights.

"Our entire school will be celebrating Negro History Week next month," Mrs. Butler said. "We'll have a big assembly, and every class will participate. You can recite a poem, act out a skit, sing, or even present artwork. Which class will do the best job?"

"We will!" Melody chanted with the rest of the class. Melody remembered what Yvonne had said about being proud of what black Americans have contributed to history, and suddenly she had an idea. She pumped her hand into the air.

"Can I make a banner?" she asked when Mrs. Butler called on her.

Mrs. Butler gave her an approving nod. Other kids were eagerly raising their hands. Mrs. Butler began to write their ideas on the chalkboard.

Diane Harris stood up. "Could I sing?" she asked.

♪ Challenges ♪

"That would be very nice, Diane," Mrs. Butler said.

Diane sat down, leaning across the aisle to Melody. "Will you sing with me?" she whispered.

Melody was flattered. Diane was one of the best singers in their children's choir at church, and she usually sang solos. "I—I guess so," Melody answered sheepishly. Unlike Dwayne, Melody didn't like the attention of standing alone in front of a crowd. She preferred to be one of many voices in a chorus. But singing with Diane at a school assembly would be fun.

"Can I help with your banner?" Sharon asked from her desk on Melody's other side. "My dad can get us a long roll of paper."

Melody nodded. Sharon was good at drawing. "I want to make a banner that includes the names of great people from black history," Melody said.

"We can have important events on it, too," Sharon suggested.

"Great idea," Melody smiled. She couldn't wait to write to Yvonne at college to tell her about the project.

After school, Melody and Sharon waited for Val to

walk the few blocks from her junior high so that they could all walk home together. Lila usually walked with her, but she was staying at school for a meeting of the science club.

"Have you guys thought any more about what Pastor Daniels said on Watch Night?" Melody asked as the girls trudged through the snow. Five inches had fallen while they were in school, and most of the sidewalks were still covered.

"Yeah," Sharon said. "I was thinking I could help out more around the house."

Melody laughed and shook her head. "That doesn't count! He talked about making things better in our *community*." She turned to Val. "Isn't that what he said?"

Val didn't answer. She was looking at her feet. At first, Melody thought it was because of the snow. Val had told them that it almost never snowed in Birmingham. In fact, Val had never needed a winter coat or mittens or boots before she'd moved to Detroit.

Melody tilted her head to see her cousin's face. Val's silence wasn't about the snow. "What's wrong?" Melody asked.

♪ Challenges ♪

"How can I make a difference in my community when I don't even have one yet?" Val asked, her voice shaking. It sounded like she was trying not to cry.

"Come on, don't say that," Sharon said. "You're a part of *our* community."

"How can I be?" Val said as the girls stopped at Sharon's corner. "We don't even have a house of our own."

Sharon gave Val's arm a reassuring squeeze, said good-bye, and ran the rest of the way home, her boots stomping through the snow.

"Does she always run?" Val asked, watching in amazement.

"Yep," Melody replied. "Ever since kindergarten." But she was thinking about what Val had said. When Val had moved to Detroit eight months earlier, Melody had wanted to help her feel at home. Melody still wanted to help.

"You've got to keep your hopes up," Melody told Val. "Think about the garden I'm going to help you plant at your new house. Think about your own room and painting it any color you want. Your daddy promised, remember?"

♪ Never Stop Singing ♪

Val sighed. "I remember. I just didn't think it would be this hard to find a house."

"Big Momma says, 'Things worth having . . .'"

"Don't come easily," Val finished. "I know."

Melody scooped up a pile of snow in her mitten-covered hands and packed it into a snowball. "Sharon's right," she said. "You don't have to have your own house to be part of the community. You still belong."

Val was silent as they walked the rest of the way to Big Momma and Poppa's house. Melody tossed the snowball from one hand to the other.

As they climbed the snowy steps to the front door, Val said, "I'm in the church choir with you already. I heard some kids talking about a drama club at my school. Maybe I could be part of that. I kind of like that stuff."

"Like plays and musicals?" Melody was excited for her cousin. "Go for it!"

Val smiled. "I think I will. And I'll keep hoping for my bubble-gum-pink bedroom, too."

Melody laughed. "Good," she said brightly, tossing her snowball into the front yard. "Now, don't you hope Big Momma has some of those oatmeal raisin cookies left?"

The Block Club

♪ CHAPTER 5 ♪

The following Friday evening, Melody and Lila helped their mother tidy up while Dwayne brought up folding chairs from the basement. The Ellisons were hosting a meeting of the Block Club.

Once a month, several families from the neighborhood got together. The kids played games while their parents talked about what was going on in Detroit and in their community.

"How many chairs do you need, Mom?" Dwayne asked, brushing dust off his pants.

"Four should be enough, with the dining room chairs," their mother said, plumping up the sofa cushions.

Melody stopped stacking Daddy's newspapers for a moment and looked at her brother, remembering last

♪ Never Stop Singing ♪

summer, when he had worked at the auto factory after graduating from high school. He'd come home from his shift dirty then, too. Now he was almost always neat and clean and had a fresh haircut. She giggled.

"What?" Dwayne smiled.

"Nothing. It's just so great that you're at home for a while," she said.

"Home?" Lila shook her dusting rag in Dwayne's direction. "He's never at home. He's always over at Motown, acting like singing is real work."

"Sure it is! We don't just sing. We have classes on how to dress up, how to talk if we get interviewed by reporters, even how to eat in a fancy restaurant. And . . ." Dwayne spun in one of the new moves that he'd learned. "We get dance lessons from a real choreographer."

Mommy was nodding her approval. "Mr. Berry Gordy must care a lot about how his performers behave," she said.

"Yes, he does," Dwayne said.

Lila shrugged and kept dusting.

Dwayne snapped his fingers in her direction. "If you feel like that, Lila, I guess you don't want an invite

♪ The Block Club ♪

to see Hitsville U.S.A. up close, and get a tour of the Motown studio, huh?"

Lila froze. "Wh-what?"

"I do! I do!" Melody shouted.

"So do I," Mommy said.

"I'll see what I can do," Dwayne answered. Melody thought he sounded very important.

Dwayne looked at his watch. "Speaking of the studio, I gotta run. The Three Ravens are doing backup for a new singer. Bye!"

Melody's mother had a funny look on her face as Dwayne pecked her on the cheek and rushed away. After he left, Mommy shook her head. "I do wish Dwayne were going to college," she said, almost to herself. "Still, he's turning into quite a young man."

"Does Daddy think so?" Lila asked.

Melody was wondering the same thing.

"Your father is proud of all of you," Mommy said firmly. "Let's get the sandwiches made. People will start showing up in less than an hour!"

They were all heading to the kitchen when the doorbell rang. "I'll get it," Melody said, wondering who was arriving so early.

♪ Never Stop Singing ♪

"Miss Esther!" Melody said when she opened the door. "Come in."

"I know I'm early for the meeting," Miss Esther said, tapping her way into the living room with her cane. "But I have something for you."

Melody took Miss Esther's coat and hat. The scent of gardenias from Miss Esther's perfume filled the air. It reminded Melody of summer. "Please sit down," Melody said, using her best company manners. But Miss Esther didn't really feel like company. She felt like family.

"I'm so sorry I missed your birthday celebration," Miss Esther said. She sat on the sofa with her big brown purse upright on her lap. "So tonight I came before the others to give you a belated gift." She opened the purse with a loud snap, and took out two small burlap pouches that were no larger than Melody's hands. One had a red drawstring cord, the other a green one.

"Thank you," Melody said, sitting down on the sofa. She peeked inside the red-corded pouch. "Seeds!" She smiled up at Miss Esther. "What kind are they?"

"Those are hollyhocks, and they're very special. They're called 'heirlooms.' They grow from seeds that

♪ The Block Club ♪

are collected from plants every year and passed on from generation to generation."

Melody's face lit up. Poppa had taught her about heirloom plants. He'd taken her many times to the botanical gardens at Belle Isle Park. He said some of the plants came from seeds that were a hundred years old. "My grandfather calls heirloom plants 'great-great-grandflowers,'" Melody said.

"Is that right?" Miss Esther laughed.

"Oh, I can't wait to plant these," Melody said.

"They'll grow almost as tall as you are," Miss Esther said. "I brought them up from my mother's garden in Alabama when I first came to Detroit as a young woman. I had a big, beautiful garden at my first home here in the city. Now I don't have the space—or the energy—for one."

Melody wanted to ask lots of questions, like where in Alabama Miss Esther came from, and what kind of garden she had, and what her other Detroit house had looked like. But before she could say anything, Miss Esther pointed to the other pouch.

"That's a type of bean. It's called Good Mother Stallard."

♪ Never Stop Singing ♪

Melody laughed. "That's a funny name for a bean! Is it an heirloom, too?" She poured a few of the seeds into her palm to look at them more closely.

"Yes, it is." Miss Esther sat back and smiled. "Did you know that planting is one of the traditions we keep from some of our African ancestors? Thousands of years ago they were growing beans—and okra and squash, and yams."

"Yams came from Africa?" Melody thought of the yams Big Momma baked at Thanksgiving. "No, ma'am. I didn't know," Melody said, admiring the pretty maroon-and-white beans. Was it her imagination that they seemed to tingle in her hand?

"Well, gardening is a very good thing to carry on. I knew I'd picked the right young person to hand these heirlooms down to. We can talk more about how and where to plant them another time, all right?"

"Yes, ma'am," Melody said, putting the seeds back in the pouch. Miss Esther's confidence in her made Melody feel special. It reminded her of the conversation with Yvonne on New Year's Eve when Yvonne had said that Melody was a responsible person.

Right then Melody's mother came out of the kitchen

♪ The Block Club ♪

holding a plate piled with triangle-shaped sandwiches. "Hello, Miss Esther! How are you this evening?"

"I am well, thank you, Frances," Miss Esther said. "Melody and I have been discussing gardening."

While her mother and Miss Esther chatted, Melody went upstairs to put the burlap pouches away in her dresser drawer. Across the hall, Melody heard her father getting up from his after-work nap. Downstairs the doorbell sounded, and she heard people's voices greeting one another as they came in. Melody grabbed her pack of Old Maid playing cards and headed down.

The living room was crowded with familiar faces, and Melody politely said hello to each adult. There was Sharon's mother, and Diane's parents, and the parents of Julius Sterling, a boy from school. Val's father and mother were there, too. They were standing right in front of the kitchen door talking with Julius's father, and they didn't notice Melody waiting to pass. They all wore serious expressions.

"I'm glad you came tonight," Mr. Sterling said to Charles and Tish.

Charles nodded. "You know, in Birmingham there were plenty of neighborhoods where Negroes weren't

♪ Never Stop Singing ♪

welcome to live. But I didn't think we'd find housing discrimination so bad in Detroit."

"That's one of the reasons we marched in the Walk to Freedom last summer," Mr. Sterling said. "Tonight's speaker is from the Greater Detroit Committee for Fair Housing Practices. That group works with black families wanting to buy homes in certain neighborhoods. They find white families who are willing to sell to them, no matter how their neighbors feel about it."

"We didn't move from Alabama to be told what Negroes can or can't do because of the color of their skin," Tish said. "That's not American!"

Charles nodded. "We love staying with my Uncle Frank and Aunt Geneva," he explained to Mr. Sterling. "But my wife and daughter have their hearts set on us being in our own home by spring, and I'm ready to do whatever it takes to make that happen!"

"I'll take you over to meet our speaker," Mr. Sterling said. When the grown-ups moved toward the living room, Melody was able to get into the kitchen. Val, Sharon, and Diane were sitting at the table, munching on popcorn.

Julius was there, too. "Hey, Melody!" he said.

♪ The Block Club ♪

Melody liked Julius a lot. He didn't seem to care whether he was around boys or girls. He told jokes and talked baseball just the same.

"Hi, everybody. Hey back, Julius." Melody said. She turned on the radio that her mother kept on the counter beside the refrigerator.

"This meeting is going to be boring," Diane said, folding her arms across her chest.

"Maybe not," Melody said, glancing at Val. Val raised her eyebrows, as if to ask, "What is it?" But Melody couldn't tell her. Big Momma always said families shouldn't discuss their private business in front of people who *weren't* family.

"Well, anyway, we don't have to be bored," Melody said. "I brought my Old Maid cards."

Sharon waved her bingo game in the air, but Julius plunked a box on the table.

"Dominoes." He looked around at all the girls. "Anybody know how to play?"

"I do," Sharon said.

"Me, too," Val said, nodding. "My daddy showed me."

Diane unfolded her arms and relaxed. "I do, too.

♪ Never Stop Singing ♪

My granddad taught me," she said. "I'll play!"

Melody shrugged and laughed. "I guess I'm the only one who doesn't know."

"That's okay. I'll show you," Julius said. "It's a lot of fun."

Melody sat down. Two games and one big bowl of popcorn later, everyone was having a good time, and Melody had put all the talk of fair housing out of her mind. As Diane was adding up the score, the adult voices in the other room got louder. The kids stopped their own conversation to listen. Melody got up from her chair and went to ease the door open a crack.

"I tell you, we need to do something about the new management at Fieldston's Clothing Store," someone said. "They're right here in a Negro community, but they act as if every Negro customer is there to steal something!"

"That's not right," Melody's father said. "Old Mr. Fieldston never would have stood for that when he was alive."

Melody thought about what had happened to her and Dwayne. Without thinking, she opened the door wide and barged into the living room.

♪ The Block Club ♪

"Fieldston's *does* discriminate against black people!" she said, walking into the middle of the circle of chairs.

All eyes turned toward Melody, including her parents' and Miss Esther's.

"And how do you know that?" Diane's mother asked, surprised.

As that day with Dwayne flashed in her memory, Melody got angry again. "I know because the manager accused me of shoplifting," she said.

"Say what?" Her father half rose from his chair. Mommy put a hand on his arm.

"When was this?" Mommy asked.

"It was last spring. I went to help Dwayne pick out a suit," Melody said. "Dwayne was just trying on a jacket, and the manager made him take it off. Then he started yelling and made us leave the store before we could buy anything. I don't think we should spend our money in a store that treats us like that."

Julius's father was nodding. "My butcher shop is just a few doors up from Fieldston's, and I hear the same story over and over. I think we ought to protest by boycotting Fieldston's."

"You mean not shop there at all?" Mrs. Harris said.

♪ Never Stop Singing ♪

"Yes," Melody's father answered. "And I say we picket in front of the store, too. We can hand out leaflets that explain how they treat black customers. They may not want to notice us, but they notice our money. And they'll notice when it's gone."

Melody's stomach felt trembly as she thought of the TV news reports of black and white people protesting against racial discrimination. Sometimes there were police, and the protesters got arrested.

"You're talking carrying signs?" Charles asked.

Miss Esther cleared her throat. "I don't see why not. We should speak up with our voices," she said, giving Melody an approving look. "And with our pocketbooks."

Miss Esther's comment made Melody realize that some of the other adults thought she should be quiet. But she couldn't. She turned to her mother. "Mommy, you told me that what we do with our money says a lot about what we believe."

"I did say that," her mother said. "Thank you for reminding me, Melody. I think we should consider Miss Esther's and Mr. Sterling's suggestions." She glanced around the room. "Melody, I think that

♪ The Block Club ♪

concludes your part of the meeting," she said gently.

There was a buzz of reaction as Melody left the room. The kitchen door was wide open, and all her friends were bunched there staring at her.

"Oh, my goodness!" Val dragged Melody into the kitchen. "I can't believe you went out there and interrupted the meeting."

Melody thought of Yvonne, who always told her to use her voice and speak up about fairness. She knew Yvonne would be pleased.

"Do you really think people will boycott Fieldston's?" Diane asked. "My mom shops there all the time."

"She won't be able to if there's a picket line in front of the store," Julius said.

"I saw picket lines in Birmingham," Val said. "People carried signs and marched in front of stores or restaurants that wouldn't serve black people."

All of a sudden, Melody made a decision. "I'm going to make a picket sign, and I'm going to carry it in the boycott. If my parents let me."

"Are you nuts?" Julius asked.

Melody just shook her head. "This is about being

♪ Never Stop Singing ♪

fair. Maybe a boycott will make Fieldston's change. Wouldn't that be better for everybody?"

"Mostly for our parents," Julius said.

"That's not true," Val said. "If our parents don't get treated fairly, we don't either. In Alabama a sign on a water fountain that says 'Whites Only' means grown-ups *and* kids. That's why kids have been standing up and marching for equal rights."

Diane nodded. "Maybe all of us kids should march."

"Yes," Melody said. "And maybe there are other things we could do around here to prove that kids can make things better, too."

After breakfast the next morning, Melody took Bo for a walk. Her brain was busy—she was thinking about the Fieldston's boycott and her Negro History Week banner. Bo tugged at his leash as they passed Sharon's house, but Melody didn't stop, because she knew that Sharon's family liked to sleep late on Saturdays. They did stop across the street from Miss Esther's bright yellow house. Bo barked and sniffed at

♪ The Block Club ♪

something underneath the snow.

Melody realized that they were standing outside the community playground. She hadn't played there in ages! Along the chain-link fence, Melody looked for the small sign she remembered, the one that read "Park closes at dusk." But she couldn't find it—a wild tangle of a hedge had grown up almost as tall as the fence. Melody frowned at how messy it looked.

The gate was open, so Melody and Bo went in. It was a Saturday morning and not very cold, but the playground was empty. Melody looked around. There had once been flower beds along the fence, but Melody couldn't remember seeing anything blooming in the park last summer. Now she could see clumps of dead weeds and uncut grass bunched in the snow.

She smiled at the jungle gym, remembering how Yvonne had helped her climb it when she was little. But now the bars were rusting. Melody turned to the swings, remembering Dwayne pushing her and Lila and singing a made-up song:

> *Dee-Dee and Lila flying so high,*
> *Two little sisters touching the sky!*

♪ Never Stop Singing ♪

Now, three of the four swings were missing, and the remaining one was dangling from a broken chain, the seat touching the ground. Some of the bricks were missing from the handball courts, and others were crumbling. The paint on the benches was peeling, and the dented trash can was tipped over. It didn't look like anyone was paying attention to the park.

Melody shook her head. No wonder no one was using it. "This used to be such a fun place to play," she said to Bo. "Somebody should do something."

Bo looked up at her and barked.

"Me?" Melody bent to tickle the spot between Bo's ears. "I don't know . . ." She took another slow walk around the paths, and as she did her brain got busy again. But this time, she was imagining the playground filled with kids having fun. She pictured a shiny new jungle gym, spiffy swings, and tons of beautiful flowers. There could be a vegetable garden, and even a stage for music shows.

Melody felt her heart pounding with excitement. The Fieldston's boycott was important, but fixing up the playground could be her own special way of making things better in her community. "This is it, Bo!"

♪ The Block Club ♪

Melody said. "This is *my* Challenge to Change."
    Melody tugged Bo's leash. "Come on," she said. Her big sister was just the person to help her figure out where to start. If she hurried, she'd have enough time to write Yvonne a letter before the mailman came. Melody started to run.

Books and Banners

♪ CHAPTER 6 ♪

hen dinner was over on Sunday afternoon, Melody and Val were sprawled on the living room rug, sketching ideas for picket signs for the Fieldston's protest. Big Momma was playing the piano softly behind the girls while the other grown-ups read the Sunday newspaper. Melody hadn't told anyone about her playground plan yet. She thought it would be better to wait and see if Yvonne thought it was a good idea, first.

"Listen to this," Poppa said, crinkling the newspaper pages to get everyone's attention. "It says here that Detroit is planning big doings when that Langston Hughes comes to town in three weeks!"

"Oh!" Melody hopped up. "We're going to see him at Hudson's department store. I hope he'll autograph the book I got for my birthday." She leaned against her

♪ Books and Banners ♪

grandfather's arm to look at the paper.

Tish nodded. "My clients at the salon have been talking about it. There will be fancy dinners and parties all weekend. On Saturday night there's a big gala dance in Mr. Hughes's honor. I heard the mayor might even give him the key to the city."

"How can a city have a key?" Val asked.

Charles looked at her over the top of the sports pages. "It's really a way to show respect."

Melody's mother nodded. "Sometimes it's not even a real key. The idea is to say to a person, 'You're welcome to visit us anytime. We consider you an honorary citizen of our city.'"

"It's all so exciting. I can't wait!" Melody clapped her hands. "I hope there's a parade, and maybe fireworks."

Melody's father smiled. "I don't think there will be fireworks in February, daughter. But this is a big deal to have our city honor Mr. Hughes—not only because he's a Negro, but because he's a great poet."

Big Momma stopped playing to point to the bookcase in the corner. "Look over there, Melody. We have a volume of his poems."

♪ Never Stop Singing ♪

Melody skipped across the room to the neatly arranged shelves. "Oh, here it is." She reached to take the book out, and her eyes dropped to the shelf below. *"The Pictorial History of the Negro in America,"* she read out loud, and suddenly she thought of the banner she and Sharon were making. "Big Momma, may I borrow this book?" she asked.

"Of course, chick!" Big Momma turned away from the piano keys to give Melody a curious look. "Do you need it for school?"

Melody held the book against her chest with both hands. "Kind of. See, the week after Mr. Hughes comes to town is—"

"Negro History Week!" Val shouted. "Our school is having an assembly, and my class is doing a skit." She smiled at Melody. Val had joined the drama club, and Melody could tell that she was enjoying it.

"So what is your class doing, Melody?" Mommy asked.

"Mrs. Butler let us each decide," Melody explained. "I'm singing a song with Diane, but I'm also making a banner with Sharon. We want to put important people and stuff on it, so everyone can learn black history."

♪ Books and Banners ♪

Poppa's newspaper rustled as he clapped while he still held it in his hands. "George Washington Carver!" he shouted. "He did great research with peanuts at Tuskegee, and his work was important to black *and* white farmers!"

"Mary McLeod Bethune, educator," Mommy said.

"Marian Anderson, opera singer!" Big Momma said.

Melody dropped the book on the coffee table and reached for her pencil. "Wait, wait!" she said. "I want to write these names down."

"Charles Drew," Charles called out. "And not because we have the same name!" Everyone laughed. "Seriously. He was a surgeon who figured out how to preserve blood for sick people who needed transfusions."

"Elijah J. McCoy," Daddy said quietly. "Trained as an engineer over a hundred years ago, but couldn't get a job doing that because of his skin color. He went to work on the railroad, and invented a device to help oil move through engines. Lived the last part of his life right here in Detroit."

"Well!" Poppa said, nodding his head. "I learn something every day."

♪ Never Stop Singing ♪

"History is full of strong Negro Americans," Big Momma said, starting to play another piece on the piano. "Many people have heard of leaders like Mrs. Rosa Parks and Dr. King. But there are many less well-known people who have done extraordinary things, too. Your banner is a good idea, chick."

Melody smiled as she started making a list.

By the middle of the week, Melody had two pages full of names and dates. Sharon came to her house after school on Thursday, and they unwound a roll of paper across the kitchen table. Sharon anchored one end with her book bag, and Melody set her radio at the other end and turned it on. She plopped her 64-color crayon box in the center.

Sharon pulled a folded paper from her pocket, and Melody could see Sharon's tiny handwriting scrawled all over its back and front.

Melody looked at her own notes. "I think we might have more names than we have room on the paper," she said.

"Wow," Sharon said, looking at Melody's list.

♪ Books and Banners ♪

"Maybe we have some of the same names."

"Let's check that out first," Melody said. She began reading the names on her list, and Sharon started crossing those names off her paper.

Lila popped into the kitchen and grabbed a banana from the fruit bowl. Melody was surprised that she'd taken a break from her books. Lila had passed her exams and won the science scholarship to a private high school. She wouldn't start until the fall, but instead of taking it easy, she seemed to spend even more time studying. Melody believed her sister actually *liked* homework.

"Your friend Diane just pulled up out front," Lila said, looking over Melody's shoulder. She started reading the names aloud. "Joe Louis, Jackie Robinson. No female athletes? What is wrong with you two? Althea Gibson, first black person—man or woman—to win a Grand Slam in tennis!" Lila peeled her banana and marched out of the kitchen.

Melody quickly scribbled down the information as Sharon shook her head. "How does she know that stuff? Does she even play tennis?"

"Nope," Melody answered, and the girls broke into

♪ Never Stop Singing ♪

giggles as the doorbell rang.

Melody got up to answer the door. When she and Diane came back to the kitchen, Diane was explaining that she had just come from her music lesson at Big Momma's.

"Guess what," Diane said, laying her sheet music right on top of the banner paper. "I found the perfect song for us to sing at the assembly."

"What is it?" Melody asked.

"It's a freedom song," Diane said. "'We Shall Overcome.'"

Sharon's face lit up. "What a good idea."

"That's perfect," Melody said, nodding. "Yvonne told me that her friends at college sing freedom songs when they protest against discrimination. They sing to encourage one another. Sometimes they even change the words and sing about the people or businesses they're protesting."

"Your grandma said that freedom songs are part of our past, and that they're an important part of the civil rights movement now," Diane explained. "It's a way to be connected to the people who came before us."

"Just like the people on our banner!" Melody said.

♪ Books and Banners ♪

"Oh," Diane said, looking at the paper under her sheet music. "Is that what this is? If it's as good as those signs in your dining room, everybody will be talking about it at the assembly."

Sharon frowned. "What signs?"

"The ones my dad is collecting for the Fieldston's boycott," Melody explained. She shook her head at Diane. "We didn't make those. But when Sharon and I are done, our banner will look great. Right, Sharon?"

"Right," Sharon said.

Langston Hughes Weekend was the second weekend in February. On the morning of the book signing, Melody was too excited to sit still. As Lila combed and braided her hair, Melody held her purple hair ribbons and listened to the news on her transistor radio about Mr. Hughes's arrival at the Detroit airport the day before.

"Wow, there was a motorcade of seven cars!" she said. "What's a motorcade?"

"A parade with cars but no floats or marching bands," Lila said. "Hold still, or your braids will be crooked!"

🎵 Never Stop Singing 🎵

Melody nodded, forgetting that she was moving. Lila sighed.

"You sisters almost ready?" Dwayne stood in their bedroom doorway, dangling car keys.

Lila dropped the comb she was using. "Don't tell me Mom is letting *you* get behind the wheel! I still can't believe you learned how to drive."

Both the girls had been stunned when Dwayne told them he'd gotten his driver's license. He'd always been too focused on his music to care about much else, including taking the driving test.

"I didn't know you were coming to the book signing, Dwayne," Melody said happily.

"A couple of other Motown singers are supposed to show up at the store, so I thought I would check it out."

"Hmm," Lila mumbled, finishing Melody's hair.

"I can't wait to get my book signed," Melody said. "Maybe I can start an autograph collection. I already have a signed record album. What do you think, Lila?"

"I think we'd better hurry up."

They piled into the car a few minutes later, and Mommy sat in the front passenger seat instead of behind the wheel. Dwayne turned out to be a good

♪ Books and Banners ♪

driver. He was almost as smooth at handling a car as Daddy or Poppa. Melody was fascinated by cars and driving. She often daydreamed about cruising along the highway, wearing sunglasses and driving her own car. Maybe it would be a convertible.

"Remember," Mommy said on the way to the store. "We're going to use our best manners today."

"Mommy, we're not little kids," Melody said.

When Dwayne pulled up near the Woodward Avenue entrance to Hudson's, their mother leaned to check her reflection in the rearview mirror before she opened the car door.

"I think Mom is starstruck!" Lila whispered.

Melody smiled, but she was distracted. She was studying the line that had formed along the front of the store. It was so long! Men, women, and children were standing in it, and it stretched almost to the corner. There were old people, young people, people of many races. Lots of them were carrying books just like Melody was.

Dwayne went to park the car, and Melody, Lila, and Mommy went to the end of the line.

Melody couldn't keep still. She clutched her copy of

♪ Never Stop Singing ♪

The First Book of Rhythms closer to her chest, crushing and wrinkling the collar of the crisply ironed blouse she wore underneath her coat. Since her birthday, Melody had read the entire book three times. Now she was going to meet the person who had written it!

After a few minutes, Melody said, "The line's not moving at all."

"Do you think we're going to get in?" Lila asked.

"I'm sure we'll be fine," Mommy said. "Be patient, girls."

Melody stepped out of the line to look for Dwayne. She was amazed at what she saw. The line was getting longer. Hudson's covered an entire block, and now the trail of people stretched around the corner!

Melody joined her mother and sister again. The line crept slowly, reminding Melody of the tortoises at the zoo. Gradually she and her mother and sister passed the last of the huge display windows and walked through the doors. Dwayne came up just in time.

"Sorry, I'm with them," he said to the surprised man he stepped in front of. "Wow, what a turnout! People are treating this man like a rock 'n' roll star, or something."

♪ Books and Banners ♪

"He *is* a star," Mommy said in her teacher-in-the-classroom voice. "Langston Hughes is a *literary* star."

"I know, Mom," Dwayne said. He began to quote from one of their father's favorite Langston Hughes poems. *Good morning, daddy! Ain't you heard the boogie-woogie rumble of a dream deferred?"*

Melody was very impressed. "You actually listened when Daddy read that poem?" she asked.

"He didn't read it," Dwayne said. "He knew it by heart. So I memorized it, too."

"Looks like Mr. Hughes is a recording star, too, Dwayne." Lila pointed to the big poster on a stand just outside the book department.

Welcome, Mr. Langston Hughes! Motown Presents: **Poets of the Revolution**, *the first-ever spoken-word recording and collaboration between poets Langston Hughes and Detroit's Margaret Danner! Coming soon from our very own Hitsville U.S.A.*

Dwayne snapped his fingers and began to look around. "So that's why Marvin Gaye and The Supremes are here. Langston Hughes is working with Motown. He's making a poetry album!"

"I've got to write that title down," Mommy said,

♪ Never Stop Singing ♪

rooting around in her purse for a pen and paper.

Melody was eager to hear what Langston Hughes's voice sounded like. She peeked around Lila to see if she could catch sight of the author. Way ahead Melody could see a round-faced man wearing black eyeglasses. He was sitting at a table piled with books. *That must be him!* Melody thought.

A woman beside the table announced that Mr. Hughes was going to read his poem "Youth." Then she adjusted a microphone, and he began to speak.

> *We have tomorrow*
> *Bright before us*
> *Like a flame.*

Melody closed her eyes to listen to the rhythm in the way his words flowed. That's what *The First Book of Rhythms* was all about, how everything—voices speaking, plants growing, the sun's rise and setting—everything had a pattern or rhythm. The poet's soft voice reminded Melody of a musical instrument, and his poem was a song.

♪ Books and Banners ♪

Yesterday
A night-gone thing,
A sun-down name.
And dawn-today
Broad arch above
The road we came.

We march!
Americans together,
We march!

Everyone waiting in line broke into applause. Melody looked up at Dwayne, who was clapping hard, too.

When she got to the front of the line, Melody felt shy. Her mother nudged her forward. Melody put her book on the table, unable to say anything. Mr. Hughes smiled and asked how she wanted it signed.

"To Melody Ellison," she said. "Please!" she added. While Mr. Hughes was writing, she tried to think of something else to say. "My daddy knows some of your poems by heart," she finally whispered. "He likes your writing and I do, too!"

♪ Never Stop Singing ♪

Mr. Hughes smiled again and thanked Melody, and then he handed her book back to her. Melody barely remembered to say "Thank you" herself before turning away.

"You were wonderful," her mother said, giving Melody a hug. "Wait until Daddy hears about this. He's so pleased that you love words as much as he does. This will make his day!"

Melody opened her book, and Lila leaned in to see the autographed page. Melody touched the neat script handwriting carefully, so she wouldn't smudge it. She could hardly believe that she had just met and spoken to a real, world-famous literary star.

As they stepped out of the book-signing line, Melody turned around, looking for Dwayne. Her brother was walking toward a man and a woman who had just come into the book department. Melody recognized the man in the suit and tie—that was the singer Marvin Gaye! And next to him was a slim young woman with wide eyes and a fancy hairdo. It was Diana Ross of The Supremes! She stopped talking to Marvin Gaye and looked in Dwayne's direction. She smiled and waved one of her white-gloved hands.

♪ Books and Banners ♪

"Girls, did you see that?" Mommy said. "That was one of The Supremes, waving at our Dwayne!"

"That was really neat," Melody said.

Even Lila agreed. "It sure was," she said.

When Dwayne joined his mother and sisters, he acted like it was no big deal that Diana Ross had waved at him. But Melody knew that he was trying hard not to break into a grin.

In the days after the book signing, Melody couldn't get Mr. Hughes's poem out of her head: *"We march! Americans together, we march!"* The words were like a drumbeat. Like feet on pavement. And as she and Sharon were putting the finishing touches on their banner the day before the assembly, those words also reminded Melody of people marching through time.

Sharon had just stretched the banner to its full length across the floor of Melody's living room and into the dining room. They had written the numbers for each year in different colors, starting with 1619, the year the first African slaves had been brought to Plymouth Colony. That year was brown, for the people and for the

♪ Never Stop Singing ♪

land they'd left. The banner listed people and places and events, right up to 1964: *Langston Hughes Weekend, Detroit, Michigan.*

"It looks great!" Sharon said.

But Melody shook her head. "Sharon, we have to change the banner."

"What? Do you see a spelling mistake?"

"No . . . I just think it would be perfect if it said, 'We March Through Negro History.'" Melody tried to explain about Mr. Hughes's poem and the marching in her head.

Sharon squinted at the paper and sighed. "Why did you have to come up with such a good idea *now*?" she moaned. "We don't have time to start all over."

"We don't have to," Melody said, picking up a curled tube of leftover paper lying underneath the edge of the sofa. "We could write the headline on this and tape it to the beginning of our time line."

"We could make it look like the title of a book, or something," Sharon said thoughtfully.

"And we can use all the colors for the letters," Melody said.

"Let's do it!"

♪ Books and Banners ♪

They worked quickly, finishing just as the telephone rang. Melody's mother answered it in the kitchen. A few minutes later, she came into the dining room.

"Sharon, that was your mother, asking you to head home. Are you two almost done?"

Melody and Sharon got up from their knees as Mommy looked at the banner. "It's beautiful, girls!" Mommy said as she walked along the banner, reading. "This is great work."

"Do you really think so, Mrs. Ellison?" Sharon asked.

"Sharon, if I were giving you a grade on this, it would be an A," Mommy said.

The next morning, Melody, Sharon, and Diane sat together with their class in the school auditorium at the start of second period. Melody and Sharon's banner was on display above the stage. When Mrs. Butler had seen it, she had been so impressed that she had decided to hang it in the auditorium so that everyone could see it.

"Man!" Sharon whispered. "Look at that!"

♪ Never Stop Singing ♪

"And the 'March' part looks like we planned it all along," Melody whispered back.

"Thanks to you," Sharon said.

"No, thanks to you!" Melody said. Mrs. Butler turned from the row in front of them with a warning look, so they stopped talking.

The younger kids went first. With the exception of a very loud little girl, all the first-grade classes sang together. A second-grader bravely got onstage by himself and read an essay about Crispus Attucks, the black man who was the first person to die at the start of the American Revolution, when the American colonies fought to gain their independence from Great Britain.

A third-grade class did a skit about Ida B. Wells Barnett, who had been a black journalist. Her newspaper equipment had been destroyed by people who were angry about the stories she wrote demanding justice and equality for black Americans.

It seemed to take forever until it was time for Melody and Diane to go up on the stage. Finally, Mrs. Butler introduced them. "Now, boys and girls, fourth-graders Melody Ellison and Diane Harris will perform a very special song."

♪ Books and Banners ♪

"Do it!" Sharon whispered, as they got up from their seats.

Melody stood at one side of the upright piano with her hands at her sides, facing the audience but with Diane in her side view. Diane sat gracefully on the piano seat and held her hands over the keys. Melody took several deep breaths as she watched Diane play the introduction. Then it was time to sing.

> *We shall overcome,*
> *We shall overcome,*
> *We shall overcome someday.*
> *Oh, deep in my heart, I do believe,*
> *We shall overcome someday.*

Melody wasn't nervous. Seeing Sharon in the audience helped her relax. Melody thought of the banner that was hanging above her and about the names of all the people who had come before her. She sang louder.

From the audience, Melody heard two familiar voices begin to sing along. There, in the back of the auditorium, were Big Momma and Miss Dorothy! They must have decided to come to watch the assembly.

♪ Never Stop Singing ♪

The two had been friends, singing together, for years. Now they were singing with Melody and Diane. Gradually, the rest of the audience joined in until the auditorium was filled with the sound of one great big choir.

> *We'll walk hand in hand,*
> *We'll walk hand in hand,*
> *We'll walk hand in hand, someday.*
> *Oh, deep in my heart, I do believe,*
> *We'll walk hand in hand someday.*

As Melody sang, she thought of all the people whose names were on the banner, and how many of them had overcome hardships and injustice to do great things. She thought of last autumn when she'd overcome her fear and sadness once she decided to sing for the four Birmingham girls. She had walked hand in hand with her closest friends, and overcome everything. Now, singing this freedom song, Melody felt free in a way she hadn't before.

We March!

♪ CHAPTER 7 ♪

When Melody got home from school, there was a letter from Yvonne in the mailbox. *Finally!* Melody thought. Yvonne usually wrote back right away, but Mommy had told Melody that Yvonne was especially busy at school.

> *February 11, 1964*
> *Dear Dee-Dee,*
>
> *I'm sorry it took me so long to write back to you. I had to finish a big project for my economics class, and I was helping plan some events for Negro History Week here on campus. But I haven't forgotten about your idea. I'm so proud of you for wanting to clean up the park. I loved going there and playing on the jungle gym with you and Lila*

♪ Never Stop Singing ♪

when you were little. Remember how you loved to go down the slide but were afraid to climb up the ladder? I helped you up the steps, and we sailed down the slide together. I think it's a great answer to the Challenge to Change.

It's a big job, but I bet the other kids in the neighborhood will work with you. It would be fun to do it together. Just ask them. Oh, and don't be afraid to ask for help from a grown-up. Remember what Pastor Daniels said: It's a season of change!

Let me know how things go,
Love, Vonnie

Melody folded the letter. Vonnie supported her idea, just as she'd hoped. She knew her sister was right about asking for help. After tomorrow's protest, Melody would do just that.

At ten o'clock the next morning, a group gathered in front of Julius's father's butcher shop. Even though

♪ We March! ♪

it was cold, almost fifty people had shown up to protest. Melody stood in a line with her mother while her father walked among the people, passing out leaflets and some of the signs that had been piling up at the Ellisons' house. Melody had made her own sign. It said, "Support Our Boycott!" She was ready to hold it up high and march.

The picketing was to begin at ten-thirty, and by then the line was even longer. Melody saw Diane and her parents, and Sharon with her mother. She saw kids from school, and one or two teachers. Lila was up ahead, standing with her friends. Melody wished that Val was there, but Val's parents had taken the morning off from work to go look at houses, and Val had gone with them.

"Don't worry if you get tired," Melody heard her father telling an older member of their church. "We've got people to relieve you. This protest will go on until the store closes today, but we'll be back every Saturday until this store changes the way they treat black customers!"

Julius's father appeared at the door of his shop, took off his apron, and handed it to someone inside. Then he

♪ Never Stop Singing ♪

took Julius by the hand and stepped to the front of the line. He bent to pick up a sign.

"Shop in Dignity!" he chanted, walking slowly along the sidewalk.

Melody got a good grip on her sign and began to pick up the chant. At the corner past Fieldston's, the line crossed the street and marched on the other side. People turned their signs so that anyone looking out of the Fieldston's window could read them.

Many of the protesters looked straight ahead when they walked past the Fieldston's window, but Melody couldn't. When she was in front of the store, she turned to stare. She found herself looking right at the same man—the manager—who'd yelled at her and Dwayne. For a second their eyes locked.

Do you recognize me? Melody wondered. Maybe he had falsely accused so many people that he didn't remember her. The man's face grew paler as he realized that the line was not ending. The chanting was not stopping. Other clerks moved to the display window. Some looked shocked. One woman looked angry. But they all stood frozen, almost like mannequins.

Melody kept her eyes on the window after she

♪ We March! ♪

passed the store. She saw a white man stop at the door. But Melody's father handed the man one of the leaflets. The man read it, and then backed away and left without crossing the picket line.

Black shoppers who passed on the street but were not part of the picket line seemed to have mixed reactions. A few gave them curious looks. Some hurried past, as if they didn't want to be a part of it. Melody thought of Val's father. She knew he supported equal rights, but Charles had said that in Alabama, being part of even a peaceful march or protest could cause a black man to lose his job—or get put in jail. Today there was no trouble, and not a policeman in sight.

Someone began to sing. Melody didn't recognize the voice, but she knew the song. It was the same one the crowd had sung during the Walk to Freedom when Dr. King had been in Detroit. Melody sang along.

> *We shall not,*
> *We shall not be moved.*

The chanting stopped and the singing grew louder.

♪ Never Stop Singing ♪

We shall not,
We shall not be moved.
Just like a tree that's standing by the water,
We shall not be moved.

But then the words changed. Melody hummed along, listening to the part she'd never heard before.

We're fighting for our children,
We shall not be moved.

Melody was at the corner. She looked at the line and guessed there were now at least a hundred people protesting. She saw a young man, wearing a hat pulled low, ease between two of the marchers. It was Dwayne!

Melody was surprised. Last year, Dwayne had refused to go with the family to the Walk to Freedom. He'd said that he didn't think marches could change anything and that becoming a rich and famous singer was what would make people treat him fairly. But Melody knew, from the letters he'd sent home while he was touring, that Dwayne had changed his mind. He had told her that even the Motown stars were treated

♪ We March! ♪

unfairly at some hotels and restaurants. *Seems like our talent is colored first, and great second,* he had written.

Now her brother spotted her. Their eyes met and held for a moment. Then Dwayne shook his head. Melody understood that he didn't want her to tell anyone he was there. Melody pinched her thumb and finger together and slid them across her lips as if she were closing a zipper. It was their "I won't tell" signal.

Dwayne tugged his hat lower, and Melody crossed the street. When she looked, Dwayne's part of the line had passed the windows, and he was gone.

Melody kept walking and singing. She sang as loud as she could, becoming part of the rhythm of voices. Melody realized that because of her own experience at Fieldston's, she was connected to people she would never know: the people from the past who had been treated unfairly, just as she and Dwayne had been, and people in the future. After all, if their boycott was a success, Fieldston's would change.

Melody was part of that change. She could see her father, lifting his sign into the air as he marched, chanting the same words that she chanted. She thought of the poem Mr. Langston Hughes had read at the book

♪ Never Stop Singing ♪

signing and about how her father had given her a love of poetry. Now she knew that both her parents had also given her a love for justice and equality and dignity.

And so, to the rhythm of the words in the air, Melody marched.

The next day at church, Melody's legs were tired from walking, and her arms were tired from holding up her protest sign. But her heart felt stronger because she had been part of something she believed in.

After the service, everyone seemed to be talking about the boycott. "It made the news on the radio," Val said to Melody. "What was it like?"

"There were so many more people there than I expected," Melody explained. "It felt good to be a part of it."

"I wish I'd been there," Val said.

"Me, too," Melody agreed. "Maybe you can come next week."

"I'll ask my parents. I think they'll let me."

Melody smiled. "Did you see any houses you liked?"

♪ We March! ♪

Val's face brightened. "I did. There was one with a pink bedroom! But it didn't have a fireplace. Mama and Daddy said we're going to keep looking."

Melody nodded as her cousin talked, but she was giving Val only half her attention. Some of her other friends were heading down to Sunday school. This was her chance to find out what they all thought about her answer to the Challenge to Change.

"Hi, everybody," she said, stopping them at the classroom door. "I have an idea, but I need help."

Sharon leaned in. "What kind of help?"

"What's the idea?" Diane asked.

"The last time you had an idea," Julius said, "you ended up talking in front of the whole Block Club."

Melody took a deep breath and let the words tumble out. "The playground in our neighborhood is a mess, and I want to make it nice again!"

"I didn't know there was a playground," Val said.

Julius nodded. "My dad taught me how to play handball there."

"Nobody goes there anymore," Sharon said. "Maybe we're just too old for jungle gyms!"

"Well, my little sisters aren't," Diane said. "I took

them there last summer, and most of the swings were gone. The one that's left is broken. My mom says it's dangerous."

"When we get our own house, my daddy says we can have a swing set in the backyard," Val said kindly. "You and your sisters can all come over to play."

What Val said made Melody realize something. Most people in their neighborhood had small backyards. A few had swing sets, but many had vegetable gardens instead, like her family did. She'd heard Poppa say that there just wasn't room for both.

"I think having a fun, safe playground is really important," Melody said. Everyone nodded in agreement.

"If we work together as a team, maybe we could fix it up ourselves," she continued. "We could clean it up, paint the benches, pull out the weeds, and plant flowers—"

"Get new swings," Diane added.

"And maybe do something about the handball courts," Julius said hopefully.

Melody was encouraged. Her friends were getting excited. So she told them the rest of her idea. "What if

♪ We March! ♪

we start our own club, a kids' block club?"

There was silence for a moment. Then Julius nodded. "Count me in."

"Great idea!" Sharon said.

Diane smiled and nodded her agreement.

"I'll join for now," Val said, "but don't you think we might have to ask permission, or something—President Melody?"

"P-Pres—" Melody stuttered and blinked. *President?* She'd never intended to be a leader, just part of the club. It would be like the choir here at church, where she was one voice among many. Being the president of something meant being a leader—like Miss Dorothy or Pastor Daniels. Melody wasn't so sure she could do that.

"Don't try to get out of it now," Julius laughed. "It was your idea."

"I—um—okay." Melody stammered. "Let's start by asking the grown-ups' Block Club."

Sunday school began, but Melody's mind was still on the playground. Her friends were excited, but they wanted her to lead. Was she ready for that? Melody thought of Yvonne. If only she were here to help.

♪ Never Stop Singing ♪

Help. Hadn't Yvonne told Melody to ask for help from a grown-up? Suddenly, Melody knew just the right person.

Wish List

♪ CHAPTER 8 ♪

That afternoon, when Melody took Bo for a walk, they went to Miss Esther's house. After she rang the bell, Melody turned around to look at Miss Esther's view of the park. It wasn't pretty.

When Miss Esther opened the door, she was happy to see Melody. "What a nice surprise!" she said. "Come in, come in."

"Is it okay for Bo to come in, too?" Melody asked. Miss Esther smiled down at Bo, who wagged his tail politely but did not bark.

"I think Bojangles is a well-behaved dog," she said.

"How did you know—"

"It *is* Bojangles, isn't it?" Miss Esther led them into a comfortable-looking living room. "He's named after the dancer, Bill 'Bojangles' Robinson, isn't he?"

♪ Never Stop Singing ♪

Melody nodded her head in wonder. "Yes! We put him on our black history banner. He tap-danced in the movies with Shirley Temple. Mommy says it was a big deal."

Miss Esther nodded. "It was, because he was a black man and she was a little white girl. Movie audiences had never seen that on the screen before. It was an historic moment."

"You know so much about so many things," Melody said. "That's why I came to talk to you."

"What's on your mind, Melody?" Miss Esther sat in a soft armchair near the front window. She gestured toward another chair, and Melody sat, too.

"Do you always sit at this window?" Melody asked.

"I like to see what's going on in the neighborhood."

"Do you like what you see? Over at the park, I mean."

Bo was sitting on the floor beside Melody's chair, looking from her to Miss Esther as if he were following the conversation.

Miss Esther sighed. "I can't say that I do like it, Melody. It's in such bad shape." She leaned forward. "Why do you ask?"

♪ Wish List ♪

"Well, I sort of have a plan for it."

"I'm so glad to hear it!" Miss Esther said.

Melody scooted to the edge of her chair. "I want to answer the New Year's Challenge to Change by cleaning up the playground and planting a garden. I talked to some of my friends, and they want to help, too. We want to start a Junior Block Club."

"That's a lot of work," Miss Esther said. "Some people might say it's too much for a group of young people like you."

"But it's not!" Melody insisted.

"If you take your idea to the Block Club, you'll need a plan in writing to explain what you hope to do."

"Oh," Melody said, sitting back in her chair. "I don't know how to do that." Suddenly she felt discouraged.

"Well," Miss Esther said, getting up from her chair, "perhaps I can help. Let's start by making a list of everything you'd like to do. I call that the 'wish list,' because sometimes the plan changes and you don't get to do everything you wish you could do."

And with that, Melody and Miss Esther began to work together.

♪ Never Stop Singing ♪

Two weeks later, on the first Friday in March, Melody and her parents walked to Julius's house after dinner for the monthly Block Club meeting. Everyone gathered in the finished basement, where the grown-ups sat on folding chairs around card tables and drank coffee out of paper cups. Melody, Val, Sharon, Diane, and Julius perched on an assortment of stools.

At seven o'clock, Mr. Sterling quieted the group and began the meeting.

"Welcome, folks! I want to start with a quick update about the progress of the Fieldston's boycott. Our actions have shown that we believe every store in our community should respect the people of the community. We had some newspaper reporters asking questions about the boycott last week, and I got a call from one of the TV stations. But we have to keep up the pressure and keep up our protests. We all know that change doesn't happen overnight."

There was applause from the kids and the grown-ups. When the group was quiet again, Mr. Sterling said, "Now, some of the children want to speak."

Melody took a piece of paper out of her pocket. It was the wish list Miss Esther had helped her write.

♪ Wish List ♪

"Hello," she said, looking around the room. Her father raised his chin and smiled. She saw Miss Esther on the far side of the large room.

"We—all of us up here—would like to ask permission to start a Junior Block Club. The reason, um, our purpose, is to fix up the playground and change that part of our community for everyone."

"What a good idea," Sharon's father said from his seat. "It's a disgrace how the city has let that playground deteriorate." Other parents murmured in agreement.

Diane's mother raised her hand. Melody felt funny giving a grown-up permission to speak. "Yes?" Melody said in her best leader voice.

"Block clubs are not a game," Mrs. Harris said.

"I believe our youngsters have shown great responsibility by their participation in the boycott," Miss Esther said. Her voice was kind but firm.

"Yes, you're right," Mrs. Harris quickly agreed. "I just wonder if the children have a plan."

"Yes, ma'am, we do," Melody said. As she read her wish list aloud, there were nods of approval.

"And we plan to keep an eye on it after we finish,

♪ Never Stop Singing ♪

so it doesn't end up like it is again," Diane added.

Miss Esther tapped her cane on the linoleum floor. "I move that we allow the formation of a Junior Block Club."

Melody's father raised his hand. "I second that motion."

"Good! Let's vote!" Mr. Sterling said. "Raise hands to vote yes to a Junior Block Club."

Melody was holding her breath. Every hand went up.

"The ayes have it! Congratulations, Junior Block Club," Mr. Sterling announced.

Melody turned to her friends. They all jumped off their stools and cheered. Julius started shaking all the girls' hands.

Mr. Sterling cleared his throat. "Now, you *do* need an adult adviser."

"I have already been asked, and accepted that position," Miss Esther said, with another tap of her cane.

"And Melody is our president!" Julius shouted. The adults laughed and clapped again.

Melody's father spoke up. "Well, Junior Block Club, do you think you can have this playground cleaned up

♪ Wish List ♪

and ready for our annual Block Club picnic?"

"The picnic is August first, right?" Julius asked.

"Yes," his father said.

"That's almost five months away," Sharon said, counting on her fingers. "That's a lot of time."

Melody didn't say anything. She knew that growing a garden could take a long time. But her friends were so excited, and they were all eager to help, so Melody nodded her head. "We'll make it work," she said.

Grandfathers and "Grandflowers"

♪ CHAPTER 9 ♪

melody and Val were in Big Momma's kitchen helping get Sunday dinner ready. On the ride from church, the girls had told Melody's grandparents all about the Junior Block Club and their plans for the park. Poppa and Big Momma were excited about the way Melody and Val and their friends were answering the Challenge to Change, and they had offered to help.

"Oh, good," Melody had said as the car pulled into the driveway. "Because we don't know how to do some of the stuff we want to."

Now Big Momma's kitchen smelled of baked chicken and homemade rolls. She put the girls to work opening jars of tomatoes and green beans that she and Melody's mother had canned last summer.

"Did you grow all this?" Val asked Melody, pouring

♪ Grandfathers and "Grandflowers" ♪

the green beans into a pan for Big Momma to heat.

"I sure did!" Melody said, plucking a tomato up with a fork. "Taste!"

Big Momma pretended not to see as Val gobbled down the tomato and smacked her lips. "Mmmm!" Val said.

The rest of the family trickled in as Melody set the table. When Dwayne arrived, Melody wanted to talk to him about the Fieldston's protest. But before she could say anything, he said, "What's this I hear about Melody becoming president of the Junior Block Club?"

"How did you find out?" Melody asked, setting the penguin-shaped salt and pepper shakers in the center of the table.

"I have my neighborhood connections," Dwayne said, winking. "So tell me, Dee-Dee, what are your plans?"

Melody winked back. "You wait and find out," she said.

After Poppa said grace and they all began to pass the food around, Melody and Val took turns explaining the park project. When they got to the list of things they didn't know how to fix, Melody frowned. "The

♪ Never Stop Singing ♪

handball courts are falling apart," she said. "They're made of brick. What should we do?"

"One of my piano students is a bricklayer's son," Big Momma said. "I could talk to him."

"Would you, Big Momma?" Melody asked eagerly. "And Poppa, would you help us decide which plants would grow best in the park?"

"I will," he said, passing the bowl of beans to Charles. "You'll need to draw up a plan of the space so we know how much room we have."

"What about the swings?" Val asked. "We want to get ones that aren't broken."

"I think that replacing the swings is the city's responsibility," Mommy replied. "You can ask the Parks Commissioner. How do you think you can find his name?" she asked in her teacher's voice.

Melody and Val looked at each other and shrugged.

Lila sighed. "The library," she whispered loudly to them. Then Lila looked at Dwayne. "That's a stage whisper, right?" she asked, which made everyone laugh.

Charles took a serving of green beans and looked across the table at Melody's mother. "Frances, this

♪ Grandfathers and "Grandflowers" ♪

reminds me of all the canning you and Aunt Geneva did when we were kids. The fruit trees!"

"Fruit trees?" Melody asked curiously.

"Oh, yes," her mother said. "Back on the farm we had fig trees, along with plum and peach trees."

"Yes!" Poppa said. "We had quite an orchard."

Big Momma laughed. "And it was quite a lot of work for me every summer, to can all of those fruits and vegetables."

"But they tasted so good," Charles said.

"What else did you grow, Poppa?" Melody asked.

"When I was a young man," Poppa said, "I tried to do it all. We grew a little bit of everything. I had pecan trees and peanuts. Greens of all kinds, beans, tomatoes, potatoes."

"That sounds like a grocery store," Dwayne laughed.

"Yes, it pretty much was," Big Momma said. "In those days, we grew everything we ate. We planted, we weeded, we picked. If we had an extra-large crop of something, we'd share with neighbors."

Melody's mother nodded. "Oh, there was nothing like walking in the shade of the plum trees and

♪ Never Stop Singing ♪

plucking off a few to eat right there on the spot!"

"I loved that place," Poppa said, his voice becoming thicker and quieter. "I planted a big flower garden and built a wooden fence arond it." Poppa looked down at his knife and fork for a few minutes, and then looked up again. Everyone had stopped eating to listen.

"See, I'd grown up on that farm. My daddy worked it for a white man. Daddy scrimped and he saved, and he scrimped and he saved. He worked hard. We worked hard with him. I knew how much he wanted to own that place, so I worked extra jobs to help. Together, we finally saved enough to be able to buy a little piece of that land." He looked toward Big Momma, who smiled and put her hand over his on the table.

"Back then it was almost impossible for a Negro to own property," she said. "Not long after they bought the land, Frank's father died. So Frank took over the farm. We had only just gotten married. His sister Beck and his brother Roy—that's Charles's daddy—had already left and moved to Birmingham. I was teaching music at a school during the week and giving piano lessons on the weekends. Your grandfather worked hard day and night to keep the farm going."

♪ Grandfathers and "Grandflowers" ♪

"That land was special to me," Poppa said. "It was more than just dirt and trees and plants. It was . . . my life. It had been my daddy's life, and my mama's life. Hardest thing I ever did was leave it. But—"

He looked around at Val and Melody and Lila and Dwayne. "I did it for all of you. I passed it on to all of you."

Lila shook her head. "How could you pass it on, Poppa? We've never even seen it."

"You have it in you," Poppa said to Lila. "It's the way your parents teach you and how you work hard." He turned to Dwayne. "It's what we share, like our love of poetry and music." Finally, Poppa looked at Melody. "It's me, teaching you about plants. How to make them grow tall and strong. How to make things beautiful. And you know what? One day you'll pass my farm on to the children you have."

Poppa tapped his chest. "It's here."

Everyone at the table was quiet. Melody saw Tish dabbing at her eyes with her paper napkin. Big Momma still had her hand over Poppa's. Mommy looked as if she was remembering something from long ago.

"You know what, Poppa?" Dwayne said. "I know

♪ Never Stop Singing ♪

what you mean. It was hard for me to leave home, too."

Lila kicked Melody under the table. For once, Dwayne was very serious.

"I miss all of this, sitting around talking and eating Mom's and Big Momma's great food together, hearing Dee-Dee ask a million questions, and Lila trying to answer all of them. I miss it a lot." He looked at his father. "I even miss you yelling at me about college."

Daddy started to say something, but Dwayne went on.

"But like Poppa said, all of you are here." He tapped his chest. "Right along with my music. So every time I write a song, or sing a song, I've got all the Ellisons and Porters right with me. Dad, I know you think I got into this business for all the wrong reasons, for flash and fame. You were kind of right. It's hard work. I know that you and your father, and Poppa and his daddy—y'all broke your backs working hard to give us something better. An easier life than you had. It's not easy being black, no matter what we choose to do, right? I still believe that music can change things, and I'm not afraid to work hard at something I want. I learned that from you, Dad."

♪ Grandfathers and "Grandflowers" ♪

Melody's father had the strangest expression she'd ever seen on his face. He looked confused and proud all at once. He stared at Dwayne, but neither one of them said a word. Melody didn't quite understand why her mother was smiling.

Melody finally broke the silence. "I'd like to see the farm," she said.

Her grandfather smiled. "And you will, Little One. I'll make sure of it." He turned toward Melody's mother.

"Let's drive down once school is out, Frances. I'll get someone to take care of the shop for a week, and we can stay with my sister."

"I'd love that, Daddy. We could go for Aunt Beck's Fourth of July picnic."

Melody was excited about the trip, but she couldn't help thinking of the playground project. She would be planting flowers in June. Melody was the president, so it was her job to make sure everything got done properly. She put her fork down. *Would a good leader choose not to go to see the farm?* she wondered.

"What's the date today?" Melody blurted out.

Lila rolled her eyes, but Val said, "March eighth."

♪ Never Stop Singing ♪

The Block Club picnic was August first. Even if she was gone for a week, there would be enough time, when she got back, to get everything done.

Melody relaxed. The farm meant a lot to her family, and she wasn't going to miss her chance to see it.

After dessert, Melody went to sit beside her grandfather, on the arm of his big leather recliner.

"Poppa, did you bring any of your seeds up here when you left Alabama?"

"Why, yes, and bulbs too. Those orange daylilies that you like come from roots I brought. You know I call those great-great-grand—"

"—flowers," Melody finished, giggling. "Miss Esther gave me some heirloom seeds that came from her mother's garden," she explained. "Hollyhocks. I think I'd like to plant some along the playground fence, so she can see them from her window. They might remind her of where she came from."

Poppa gave Melody a kiss on top of her head. "I like the sound of that. On Friday, let's skip your work day at the flower shop and go take a look at that playground."

♪ Grandfathers and "Grandflowers" ♪

"That would be great!" Melody cried. "I'll ask Miss Esther and the Junior Block Club to meet us there."

As soon as school was out on Friday, Melody, Val, Diane, Sharon, and Julius raced to the park. While they waited for Melody's grandfather, Melody gave each person a copy of the playground wish list. She had spent all week writing out copies of the one she had made with Miss Esther, and now her friends were studying the pages.

Julius looked up from his copy. "Vegetables?" he asked. "Who plants vegetables in a playground?"

"Melody does," Val said loyally.

Diane shook her head. "I haven't even heard of some of the flowers on this list," she said.

"Me either," Sharon shrugged. "But Melody's the expert."

"No, my grandfather's the expert," Melody said. "And Miss Esther. She suggested some of these plants."

Julius grinned. "As long as the playground stuff gets fixed, I don't care what we grow."

♪ Never Stop Singing ♪

"Here comes Miss Esther now," Sharon said.

The group turned to see Miss Esther crossing the street, her cane in one hand and a shoebox in the other.

Melody rushed to the curb. "Can I help you?" she asked, taking Miss Esther's elbow.

"Thank you, dear," Miss Esther said. "You may take this box. I thought you all might like a little snack after school."

Melody removed the lid. The box was lined with wax paper and filled with slices of banana bread. "Thank you!" she said, smiling.

When Poppa's truck rumbled to a stop in front of the park, the members of the Junior Block Club were all nibbling their second slices of bread. "Hello there," Poppa called. "I see you've started on the important business at hand."

Melody grinned and wiped the crumbs from her hands. "Hi, Poppa." She gave him a copy of the playground wish list.

"Let's do it, then," Julius said, pushing open the creaking, squeaking gate and waving everyone into the park.

They all took a slow walk along the paths, talking

♪ Grandfathers and "Grandflowers" ♪

about what needed to be done and checking the list to make sure everything was on it. Poppa and Miss Esther followed, asking questions.

They stopped at a jungle-like area near the jungle gym. "This is where we can plant flowers," Melody said, pointing to a stretch of snow-covered grass next to a tangle of overgrown bushes. "Something really colorful, so that when you're hanging upside down on the jungle gym, it looks like a rainbow!"

"My sisters will love that," Diane said.

"And more flowers there, and there . . ." Melody pointed with her pencil. She looked up at the sky and then spun around. "And since there's full sun over there, we could do vegetables. Right, Miss Esther?"

"You are right, Melody. Now you can draw all this up in your plan."

"Yes, ma'am," Melody said.

"Drawing?" Sharon asked.

Melody had an idea. "Sharon, you are a great artist. Would you draw a plan for our playground?"

Sharon smiled. "Of course I will."

They all moved on to the peeling benches. "You'll need special paint for outdoors," Miss Esther said.

♪ Never Stop Singing ♪

"What about these swings?" Poppa asked.

"I need to write to the Parks Commissioner about that," Melody said.

Poppa folded his arms. "Good. And do you have a budget?"

"Budget?" Julius asked.

"You mean, money?" Diane said, looking at Melody.

Melody's stomach dropped. *Of course we'll need money,* she thought. She'd planned out everything except that.

"I suspect that our Block Club can provide some funds from our budget," Miss Esther said. "I'll bring it up at the next meeting."

Melody was relieved. "Thank you, Miss Esther."

Poppa nodded. "Some local businesses may be willing to donate supplies, too," he added.

Melody brightened. "I can dig up some plants from my garden this spring," she said. "That will save us some money."

"Now you're thinking," Sharon said.

The next morning, Melody and Lila went to the

♪ Grandfathers and "Grandflowers" ♪

public library. "Are you going to write that letter to the Parks Commissioner today?" Lila asked as they walked. She struggled with her armload of library books, so Melody reached over to take three off the top.

"Yes, I am. Everybody says getting new swings is up to the city. If the Junior Block Club is going to work hard to clean up the playground, then it's only fair that we get some help. Kids are citizens, too!"

"That's exactly what you should say in your letter," Lila told her.

"Really?" Melody asked. "Lila, would you look my letter over when I'm done?"

"Of course," Lila smiled. "Call it my contribution to the Junior Block Club."

Singing Together

♪ CHAPTER 10 ♪

April came, and it was warm enough for the Junior Block Club to start the cleanup. Poppa had given Melody some old gardening gloves from his workroom, and she had been saving paper grocery bags for trash, dead plants, and twigs. The club members had recruited some other neighborhood kids to help, and Melody had told everyone to wear long pants and long sleeves to the work day.

At nine o'clock on the second Saturday of the month, Melody and Val were the first to arrive at the park. Soon, Sharon came running up the block. A few minutes later, Mrs. Harris pulled up and Diane got out of the car.

"Where's everybody else?" Diane asked.

"I don't know," Sharon said.

♪ Singing Together ♪

Melody was concerned. She pulled out her notebook. "Well, I have the names of nine people who agreed to come. I wonder where Julius is."

"Here I am!" He walked across the street carrying two rakes. "I'm ready! I borrowed these from my dad."

"Good idea," Melody said, realizing that she hadn't thought of bringing rakes. "So, where's everybody else?"

Julius looked around. "Larry and Clifton haven't shown up yet? They promised they'd come."

"Well, I guess we just have to get started," Melody said.

They went through the gate. The park looked pretty much the same as it had the last time they were there, except that the snow was gone. Melody put her box of supplies down on one of the benches. She realized that if everyone had shown up, she wouldn't have had enough gloves.

"Okay." Melody stood with her hands on her hips. "I say we each take a part of the park to work in. Let's call them zones. Julius, you take the handball zone. Sharon, how about you and Val in the swing zone? Diane, do you want to clear the flower beds with me?"

♪ Never Stop Singing ♪

"Nah, I'm not much of a gardener," Diane said. "Sharon, switch with me?"

Sharon shook her head. "No, thanks."

Melody looked at Diane. *Oh, dear,* she thought. *Is there a problem? Already?*

"I'll switch," Val said. "Melody and I have worked in the garden together."

"Deal." Diane nodded.

Thank goodness, Melody thought. Everyone went to their zones, and Melody used one of Julius's rakes to show Val how to carefully clear the layers of dead leaves without damaging anything growing underneath.

As Val got started, Melody took out her transistor radio and turned it on. "Everything goes faster with music," she said, pulling the antenna all the way up. But after a few minutes, the only station that came in clearly was a talk show that no one wanted to listen to.

"We could sing ourselves," Diane suggested. "Then you wouldn't have to run down the battery on your radio."

"Good idea," Melody said, turning back to what had once been a flower bed near the first set of benches.

♪ Singing Together ♪

"What are we going to sing?" Julius yelled.

"A work song," Sharon yelled back.

"Which one?" Melody asked without looking up. Val had uncovered a few tiny green shoots of something poking up among the weeds.

"I know," Diane said. *"If I had a hammer, I'd hammer in the morning . . ."*

Val burst out laughing. "We're not doing construction work!"

"Not yet," Julius said, picking up the song. *"I'd hammer in the evening, all over this **park**!"*

He'd changed the last word, and the rest of the kids giggled. Then they all joined in.

> *I'd hammer out danger,*
> *I'd hammer out a warning,*
> *I'd hammer out love between my brothers*
> *   and my sisters,*
> *All over this land!*

As the verse ended, Melody heard the gate creak and looked up. Miss Esther came in, wearing a gardening apron over her sweater and carrying a pair

♪ Never Stop Singing ♪

of pruning shears. Melody was relieved to see her.

"Hello, Junior Block Club," Miss Esther called out.

"Hello, Miss Esther!" the children all called back. It sounded as if they were still singing together.

Miss Esther laughed. "I came to see if you need help identifying which shrubs need pruning," she said.

Melody stood up and looked around. She knew a lot about flowers, but nothing about bushes or shrubs. "Yes, we do," she said.

While Val, Sharon, and Diane kept working, Julius joined Melody. Miss Esther showed them how to hold the shears and where to cut branches so that the plant wouldn't be damaged.

"This is cool stuff," Julius said. "I feel like I'm a farmer."

"I think you would be an *arborist*," Miss Esther told him. "That's someone who takes care of trees. And that is *cool*, as you say."

Julius looked pleased, and Melody smiled.

After an hour, Miss Esther had to leave to go to a church meeting. By that time, Sharon and Diane had quit working and had started climbing on the jungle gym. Everyone was hot from working—and

♪ Singing Together ♪

playing—so the group took a break. Everyone was thirsty, too, but no one had brought anything to drink.

"Are we done for the day?" Diane asked, plopping down on one of the worn benches.

"I'm hungry," Julius said. "Maybe I'll head home."

"I have to go, too," Sharon said. "My mom's taking me to buy new shoes. Sorry, Melody," she called as she took off running.

Melody sat down next to Diane and sighed. She was sweaty and dirty and thirsty, and the Junior Block Club hadn't gotten as much done as she'd hoped they would. That's when Melody saw her grandfather's truck.

"Well, there," Poppa said, strolling through the gate carrying a large paper bag. "You all look a bit wilted." He set the bag down on the bench and pulled out a thermos and a stack of paper cups. "How about some water?"

"Thanks, Mr. Porter," Diane and Julius said.

Val joined them, and they all drank the water Poppa poured. Melody hoped Diane and Julius would stay, but after a few minutes, they both left.

Val went back to raking. Melody set her cup down and began to clap the dirt off her gloves. "Boy, this

♪ Never Stop Singing ♪

didn't go the way I thought," she mumbled.

"How did you think things would go?" Poppa asked, sitting down beside her.

Melody shook her head. "I thought because I knew about gardening that I'd be a better leader. But I didn't check to make sure everyone would show up. I didn't remember to bring tools. I didn't even bring water!"

"You're learning to be a leader, Little One," Poppa told her. "And being a leader doesn't mean you have to do everything yourself. Julius remembered tools. Why don't you make him head of the tool committee?"

"Really?" Melody asked. "I could do that?"

"Yes. And you could ask someone to remind the block club members when there's a work day."

"Diane would love that," Val piped up. "She's good at being bossy."

"I guess," Melody said slowly. "But if other people do things, doesn't that mean I'm not a leader?"

"This is a big project, and you need many hands," Poppa said. "A good leader helps everyone see that they're a special part of the team. Leading takes patience, just like gardening. And you're right. You're a wonderful gardener. You know how to make things

♪ Singing Together ♪

take root and grow. As your club works together, it will become stronger."

Melody nodded. "You make it sound like the Junior Block Club might blossom one day, Poppa."

"Won't it?" he asked.

Melody smiled. She sure hoped so.

Talking to Poppa made Melody feel better. She went home and cleaned herself up, and then she sat down in the living room with her father's book of Langston Hughes poems. She was engrossed in the rhythm of the words when the phone rang.

Mommy called from the bathroom upstairs. "Melody, can you answer that, please?"

Melody picked up the phone. "Hello?"

"Hey, Dee-Dee? It's me, Dwayne."

"I know your voice on the phone, Dwayne," Melody said.

"Oh. Whatcha doing?"

"Reading," she said. "Why are you acting weird?"

"Maybe because I have a little job for you."

Melody put her book down, and all thoughts of

♪ Never Stop Singing ♪

poetry flew from her mind. Dwayne could only be talking about one thing.

"You want me to sing with you?" she asked.

"Well, sing *for* me. For us. Sing backup. Look, Mr. Gordy is finally giving The Three Ravens a chance in the studio to cut our own single." Melody heard the excitement in her brother's voice.

"Can Val come? And Sharon? And Lila? Just to watch?"

"Hey, it's not a stage show, all right? I'll find out. Anyway, Mom or Dad needs to bring you, and one of them has to sign something so that you can work in the studio. I'm gonna copy the lyrics and music and bring them home. Can you be at Motown at four o'clock tomorrow?"

"Tomorrow?!" Melody gasped. "First, it's Sunday. Second, I can't learn a new song by tomorrow! You want me to mess it up?"

Dwayne laughed. "You won't mess up. But I can only get into the studio when they tell me I can. Listen, you check with Mom, see if it's okay."

As soon as Dwayne clicked off, Melody ran upstairs shouting, "Mommy! Mommy!"

♪ Singing Together ♪

"Is the house on fire?" her father mumbled, opening their bedroom door. Melody rushed in.

"No, Daddy. Sorry. Dwayne just asked me to sing backup on his record! Can I? I can't do it without your permission. Please, please!"

Melody's mother opened the bathroom door across the hall. "How wonderful! Will, this would be a great opportunity for Melody. She could see the real work behind the flash."

"Don't try to get me on Dwayne's side, Frances," Melody's father answered. "I still believe a black man can have a better life, an easier life, with a college education. Not a record." Then Daddy looked at Melody. His face softened. "But for you? This sounds like a once-in-a-lifetime chance." He tugged Melody's pigtail. "You may go."

"Thank you, Daddy!" Melody cried. She turned to leave and then stopped and looked at her father again. "What do you think my singing name should be? On the record, I mean?"

Melody's father tilted his head to one side. "Let's see . . . How about Melody Ellison?"

"Daddy!"

♪ Never Stop Singing ♪

"That's the name I give you permission to use," he said.

Melody didn't say another word. She didn't want her father to change his mind.

Dwayne was as good as his word. That evening he came home with a copy of handwritten music and lyrics, a tape recorder and a tape, and the other two members of The Three Ravens. If Daddy hadn't gone bowling, Melody knew he would have been there, grilling Dwayne and his bandmates.

"Hey, lil sis," Artie said with a wave. His hair was different, and Melody had never before seen him wearing pants that weren't blue jeans. Phil seemed to be looking for something, and when footsteps sounded on the stairs, he jerked his head up. *He's hoping Lila's home,* Melody thought, grinning in his direction. *But she's not.* Phil grinned back at her and ducked his head.

Mommy came downstairs. "Hello, boys. This is so exciting! What an opportunity!"

"Thanks, Mom," Dwayne said.

"May I see the lyrics?"

♪ Singing Together ♪

"Sure, Mom." Dwayne handed the sheet to his mother. "It's called 'Move On Up.' It's a good song for Melody."

Melody stuck her chin over her mother's shoulder to look, too. It was the song Dwayne had sung to her on her birthday. Melody stepped back, feeling even more excited.

"This is very nice, Dwayne," Mommy finally said. "I like the positive message."

Dwayne ducked his head, and Melody could see that he looked pleased. "I really didn't think of it like that. It just came into my head, and I wrote it." He handed Melody the cassette tape. "Melody, listen to this and follow along in the music. You'll see where I want you to come in."

Dwayne flipped the tape recorder on, and everyone was absolutely still. Melody had to concentrate very hard to focus on the music instead of her heart, which was pounding with excitement.

At four the next afternoon, a carload of girls and one mom spilled out onto the sidewalk of Grand

♪ Never Stop Singing ♪

Boulevard. Motown's Hitsville U.S.A. studio looked like an ordinary house except for the big display window in front. It was full of posters advertising performances by various Motown artists. Dwayne met the group at the door looking very grown up and serious.

"Is Mr. Gordy here?" Mommy asked.

"He lives upstairs, and he'll probably come down later. Right now it's just us. I wanted to give you a tour before Phil and Artie and the studio musicians arrive."

Dwayne led them through a maze of rooms, explaining what went on in each of them. As Dwayne talked about the songwriters and the people who designed the album covers, Melody began to realize that there was more to making a record than just singing.

The group went down a hallway, up a few steps, and then down a few others, and into a large room whose walls were covered with something that looked like a bulletin board. "Here's the studio," Dwayne said proudly.

"What's that on the walls?" Sharon asked.

"Soundproofing," Dwayne answered. "That way, no car sounds or people's voices from outside can mess up

♪ Singing Together ♪

the recording. This isn't really a fancy setup," he said. "But the sound that comes out of here is more than fancy."

"He sounds like he knows what he's talking about," Melody said to Lila.

Lila nodded. "He sounds professional," she said.

There were drums and cymbals in one corner, and other instruments resting against the wall. At one end of the room was a huge piano.

"That's a *grand* piano," Mommy whispered.

Melody imagined that Dwayne must have great fun with such a nice piano, after so many years playing Big Momma's upright and the church piano.

"Can you play a little something for us, Dwayne?" Mommy asked.

Dwayne sat on the bench and positioned his hands over the keys. Melody slid onto the seat beside him.

"Seems like a classic piano should be singing classical tunes," he said, and he began to play music that Melody had only heard on the radio at Big Momma's house.

"Hey, that's Chopin," Lila said. "When did you—"

Dwayne laughed. "When did *you*?" he shot back.

♪ Never Stop Singing ♪

"Who's Chopin?" Melody asked, looking from Dwayne to Lila.

"Frédéric Chopin. He was a composer in the 1800s," Lila explained.

At that moment, Dwayne switched to a fast Motown-sounding tune. Melody moved her shoulders to the music as Dwayne sang.

> *Let me tell you about this girl*
> *With a smile I know.*
> *She's as happy as the crowd*
> *At a carnival show.*

Dwayne nudged Melody and grinned. *"That's why she's my very special Melody,"* he sang.

"Are you singing about *me*?" Melody asked. She looked at Sharon and Val, who were clapping along.

"Well, isn't that a surprise?" Mommy said.

Melody gave her brother a hug. "What's my song called?"

"'Special Melody,' of course," Dwayne said. He nodded to Lila. "Don't worry. I'm working on songs for you and Vonnie, too."

♪ Singing Together ♪

Lila smiled, and Melody knew she was impressed.

Val pointed at a small window that looked down on the room. "What's that?" she asked. "Who's up there?"

"That's the control room," he said. "Those are the sound engineers, and they hear everything." Dwayne got up and crossed the room, motioning Melody to follow. "See these X's back here on the floor? This is where you'll stand. This microphone will be yours. Phil and Artie will be over here. I'll be at the piano."

"How come Melody's so far from the piano?" Lila asked suspiciously.

Dwayne smiled. "Those folks who work up in that control room know their business. Trust me, you'll hear Dee-Dee. And us and the instruments, too. It's what they call mixing the sound."

Just then, Artie and Phil came into the studio. Phil stopped and said hello to Lila. Then he turned to Dwayne. "I know we only planned for lil sis to do backup, but how about if the others hang out with us and dance? That will give us a great vibe."

Sharon's and Val's eyes grew wide. Lila smiled.

Dwayne thought for a moment. "Yeah. Okay." He said, nodded. "Let's try it."

♪ Never Stop Singing ♪

A soft-spoken lady appeared from somewhere. "Dwayne, may I take your guests upstairs now? The musicians are just about ready to start."

"Thank you," Dwayne said. "My mom is the only one going up to the booth."

"You girls do what Dwayne says," Mommy instructed. Then she blew Melody a kiss before following the lady out.

Sharon, who had been very quiet the whole time, turned to Melody. "This is amazing. You are gonna be so great!"

"Thanks," Melody said, grinning. She was nervous, but she was excited, too.

Dwayne put his hand on Melody's shoulder and guided her to the X he'd pointed out earlier. "So, we're just gonna do this like we're hanging around in our backyard, got that?"

"Got it," Melody said.

The studio began to fill with the other musicians, who talked and laughed as they picked up their instruments. They didn't pay much attention to Melody or the other girls. Most of them were much older than Dwayne. But when Dwayne sat down at the piano,

♪ Singing Together ♪

Melody could tell that he became the leader. He wasn't bossy or rude. When he spoke, his voice was a man's voice, and the others listened.

"Fellas, I have some family in the studio today. And we've changed this up a little bit from last time since our backup singer is here." He motioned toward Melody.

All the musicians turned to her with interest. Because of what Dwayne had said, the musicians thought of her as a real musician, too—not just a kid. Melody stood a little taller.

A voice filled the studio over a loudspeaker. It was coming from the control room. "Dwayne, Mr. Gordy wants to know if you're going to go right in, or riff a little first," the voice said.

"Riff, Mr. Gordy."

Berry Gordy is in there, Melody thought. *He's listening!*

Dwayne looked at Melody over the piano. "How're you feeling? Good?"

She nodded, and he began a jazzy tune, making it up as he went. Improvising, Big Momma called it. Melody felt herself moving to the rhythm.

♪ Never Stop Singing ♪

"One. Two. One, two, three, four," Dwayne counted, and he was into the song. Melody closed her eyes, and when it was time, she sang. And sang. At the end of the second verse, Melody suddenly didn't hear Artie or Phil behind her, only Dwayne's piano. As he picked up the tempo of the music, Melody blinked her eyes open.

"Move on up," he sang, nodding at her.

"Move on up," Melody repeated, feeling happiness bubble up inside. She knew just what Dwayne was "calling," and it was her job to "respond" by singing whatever he sang in harmony. She'd heard the adult choir at church sing this way, and it always excited the congregation.

"Yeah, I'm movin'! I'm movin'!" Dwayne's fingers flew on the keys as he smiled at her.

"Yeah, I'm movin'! I'm movin'!" Melody sang back.

Dwayne threw one of his hands into the air while still playing smoothly with the other.

Artie's and Phil's voices came back in, singing, *"It's time to moooovvve."*

Melody saw Sharon and Val and Lila dancing, and she grinned so wide that her face hurt. Dwayne hit

♪ Singing Together ♪

the final notes, and then everything was still. After a moment, all the musicians cheered.

"That was something, Dwayne!"

"Hey, great. What a bunch of raw talent!"

"Man, that is going to be a hit!"

Melody danced toward her brother, still feeling the music. "Was I okay?" she asked.

"Not okay," he said.

Melody stopped dancing, but Dwayne pulled her into a bear hug. "You were perfect, Dee-Dee. And you made our record perfect, too."

Melody spun around. The musicians and Lila and her friends were clapping. She glanced up at the window of the sound booth and saw her mother clapping and waving. The other people in the booth looked pleased.

As she looked around, she wondered how many wonderful, talented singers had stood in this very place, on that same X. Melody didn't think she'd ever be a professional singer, and she would never be famous. But she loved singing, and she knew that she'd helped Dwayne get a little closer to his dream. She was overjoyed at that.

Open Doors

♪ CHAPTER 11 ♪

On the following Saturday, Melody arrived at the playground pulling her old red wagon. In it was a thermos of water, some paper cups, a box of graham crackers, and a bag of apples. At the gate, she met Julius and a couple of his friends. They were carrying armloads of gardening tools. She smiled as Julius gave her a thumbs-up sign.

"Hi, Melody!" Diane greeted her just inside the park. "Today we have two third-graders, five fourth-graders, and two sixth-graders, not including Val, Sharon, or Julius. I called everyone yesterday to remind them. And I took attendance today."

"Thanks, Diane," Melody said. "You made sure we have plenty of hands for our work day." Melody rolled the wagon near one of the benches. Her grandfather had been right, again. Once she asked her friends to

♪ Open Doors ♪

do the things they were good at, they were even more interested in working on the work days. Now Melody could concentrate on the garden plan.

"Good morning, everybody!" Melody called out.

"'Morning, Melody!" everyone shouted back. But no one stopped working.

Melody walked around the paths, noticing where tiny new plants were breaking through the earth in the spring sun. She pulled out her pad and pencil to make notes, humming Dwayne's new song as she went. Soon, everyone else had picked up the tune and was humming along with her, without even knowing the words.

As Melody passed her, Val whispered, "Good job getting publicity for Dwayne's record!"

Melody grinned. "Wait until they hear the real thing!"

"Dwayne still doesn't know when he's going to have the record," Melody told Val a few days later. "He said Mr. Gordy doesn't release anything that's not perfect. They're still mixing the sound."

Melody was spending the night with Val at Poppa

♪ Never Stop Singing ♪

and Big Momma's because of a school holiday. Melody's grandparents were having their evening coffee in the kitchen, and Val and Melody were putting a jigsaw puzzle together while they watched TV.

"I know, I know. I just want to be the first person to hear it," Val said.

Melody laughed. "You'll probably be about the hundredth, after all the people at Motown listen to it, and then Mommy, and then Daddy, and Big Momma and Poppa and your parents and Yvonne and all her friends . . ."

"You're so silly sometimes," Val said. "Only not when you're talking about the playground. Did you get an answer to your letter yet?" she added.

Melody shook her head. "It seems like it's taking a long time. It's hard to wait."

"I know what you mean," Val said, fitting a piece into the puzzle. "I guess a challenge isn't a challenge if it's easy."

"I guess. We need to keep working anyway. The weather's getting warmer, and Poppa said we'll be able to dig up some daylilies from my yard to transplant into the park. And I was thinking—"

♪ Open Doors ♪

Melody stopped talking because there was a commotion in the kitchen. Val's parents had come in the back door. "This is it, Charles!" Val's mother cried.

"We haven't even seen it, Tish," Val's father replied. "We can't make an offer yet."

"Well, our new real estate agent set up a showing for tomorrow morning."

Val raised her eyebrows and then raised her self. "Let's find out what's going on," she said.

Val's parents were standing by the table. There was an open folder in front of Tish, and Melody saw a page full of numbers.

"We may finally be getting somewhere with this real estate agent who works with the Fair Housing Committee," Tish was saying to Poppa and Big Momma. "The people selling this house are white, but the agent said they're willing to sell to any buyer who has the money regardless of race."

Big Momma nodded. "You should be able to buy any house you can afford anywhere you choose. That's what Dr. King said last year when he was here in Detroit. That's what the law should say, too."

"Mama?" Val asked eagerly. "Is this it? Is this the

♪ Never Stop Singing ♪

house we've been waiting for?"

"I hope so, baby," Tish answered "I've seen pictures, and I think it's perfect." She looked at Val's father. "I think we should offer to buy it."

"And I think we should look at it first," Charles replied.

"We will," Tish answered. "First thing in the morning."

Val's face lit up. "Can Melody and I go?" she asked. "We don't have school tomorrow."

"I don't see why not," Tish replied.

It took Melody and Val a long time to fall asleep that night. They kept whispering about the bubble-gum-pink bedroom Val wanted. "I hope this is it," Val said before finally dozing off.

In the morning, Val was wide awake when Melody opened her eyes. "I can't wait anymore! Let's go!"

The girls got dressed and hurried downstairs. Tish was in the kitchen dressed in a blue suit and high heels, her hair pulled back in a smooth ponytail. Charles was wearing a suit and tie and looked nervous.

♪ Open Doors ♪

Big Momma poured the girls bowls of cereal, and they sat at the table while the grown-ups drank their coffee. Val ate quickly, without saying a word. "Let's go!" she said, standing up the moment she was finished. Everyone laughed.

Melody and Val and her parents drove quite a distance through different neighborhoods that Melody had never seen. She noticed that the farther away they got from her grandparents' house, the larger the houses and yards were. There were big shade trees everywhere.

"There's lots of room for my swing set in these yards," Val murmured.

"Yes, there is," Melody said. She thought again about the small yards in her own neighborhood. This was why the park project was so important. Lots of kids needed a place to play.

"Look, there it is," Tish said, pointing. "It's two stories, just like we want, and it has a fireplace."

Charles parked and they got out. The house looked welcoming. It had a front porch and a big bay window.

"There's our real estate agent," Charles said, nodding at the white woman by the front door.

♪ Never Stop Singing ♪

Melody didn't find the empty rooms very interesting, but when they got to the backyard, she got excited. It was huge. There were two shade trees at the back, but there was plenty of room for flowers and vegetables, and lots of sunshine.

"What do you think?" Charles stood behind the girls at the back door.

"Swing set!" Val shouted.

"Garden!" Melody said.

Charles called over his shoulder to Tish and the real estate agent. "It's time to buy ourselves a house!"

Val's parents took the girls to Melody's house and then went to the agent's office to "write an offer." Neither Melody nor Val knew what that meant, but they were both glad they didn't have to go along.

The girls went to the kitchen for a snack, and there on the table was a long white envelope addressed to Melody. It had a seal with the words "City of Detroit" in the corner.

"I bet it's an answer from the Parks Commissioner!" Val said. "Finally! Open it!"

♪ Open Doors ♪

"We're going to get our swings!" Melody said with excitement. She read the letter to Val.

> *April 17, 1964*
> *Dear Miss Ellison,*
>   *We regret to inform you that due to budget constraints, the Parks Department will not be able to replace the swings in your neighborhood park. Thank you for being a concerned citizen.*

Melody stopped reading. She couldn't believe it. "They said no."

"What's a constraint?" Val asked.

"I'm not sure," Melody said. "But it can't be good." She was angry. "They thank me for being a concerned citizen, but they won't help? That's not fair."

Val shook her head. "What are we going to do now?"

"Meet with the Junior Block Club," Melody said. "Right away."

♪ Never Stop Singing ♪

Melody called an emergency meeting that afternoon, and everyone gathered at Miss Esther's house. Melody read the letter out loud.

"This is so unfair," Sharon said.

Diane nodded. "It's wrong. Do you think the Parks Department said no because the park is in a black neighborhood?"

The kids looked at one another. "That doesn't make any sense," Melody said. She turned to Miss Esther, who hadn't said anything yet. "Is that why?"

"That's an important question," Miss Esther said thoughtfully. "Sometimes Negro neighborhoods don't get the same services as other neighborhoods. Trash isn't picked up as often, and potholes don't get repaired as quickly. One of the reasons we have a Block Club is to ask these sorts of questions. We have to call attention to things that aren't right and then figure out how to fix them."

The group was quiet, and Melody could see that everyone was as disappointed as she was.

"So how do we fix this?" Julius finally asked. "This is our big Challenge project and we can't even do it."

"That's not entirely true," Miss Esther said gently.

♪ Open Doors ♪

"You can't do everything you want all at once, but you have already accomplished quite a bit."

Melody remembered something Miss Esther had said earlier. "Miss Esther's right," Melody told the Junior Block Club. "New swings were on our wish list, but we didn't get them. That doesn't mean we give up. It means we change our plan."

"Okay," said Julius. "What's the new plan?"

"There's still a bunch of stuff to clean up," Diane said.

"We haven't painted the benches yet," Val added.

"And we have a lot of planting to do," Melody said.

Miss Esther nodded. "Even if the swings can't be used, the structure doesn't have to be an eyesore," she said. "You could plant around it."

Melody liked that idea. "Yes—we could plant something that would climb up, like morning glories! Let's keep working," Melody said. "How many can meet after school tomorrow?"

Everyone raised their hands, including Miss Esther.

"Good," Melody said, feeling hopeful again.

♪ Never Stop Singing ♪

After school the next day, Melody and her friends hurried home to change their clothes. On her way to the park, Melody stopped at her grandparents' house to get Val, and the two of them headed to the playground.

When they turned the corner, Melody saw everyone from yesterday's meeting standing outside the gate. *What are they waiting for?* she wondered.

When Sharon started to run toward her, Melody knew that something was wrong.

"What is it?" Melody said when Sharon got to her side.

"Come and see." Sharon pulled her to the park entrance. The gate was closed, and on it was a big fat padlock.

Melody gasped. "What happened?" she asked.

"Read that," Julius said angrily, pointing to a sign posted on the gate.

"Closed by the Parks Department," Melody read. "What does that mean? Closed for today? For the weekend?"

"I don't know," Julius said, "but it stinks."

Miss Esther was making her way across the street. "Hello, children," she called wearily. "I saw a truck

♪ Open Doors ♪

from the city pull up this morning. The inspector walked all around the park, and he looked at the broken swing. I believe he thought it was dangerous. That's when he put a lock on the gate."

"But why would he close the whole park?" Melody asked. "The swing's been like that forever! Didn't he see all the work we've done?"

Diane nodded. "They could have just taken that swing away, and let us keep everything else."

Melody was disappointed, but she was also angry. There was no other playground close enough to walk to in their neighborhood.

"Now what?" Julius asked.

Melody had no idea.

More Letters

♪ CHAPTER 12 ♪

melody could hardly pay attention in school the next day. All she could think about was the lock on the gate. Miss Esther had suggested that the Junior Block Club write several letters to the Parks Commissioner. "The more letters he gets, the more likely he is to listen," Miss Esther had told them. Everyone had agreed to write, but Melody hadn't started her letter yet. It didn't seem as though the city was going to help a bunch of kids, after all.

When Melody got home, she'd gotten a letter of her own, from Yvonne. Melody took it up to her room, flipped on her radio, and listened to The Supremes while she read.

> *April 18, 1964*
> *Dear Melody,*

♪ More Letters ♪

I had my interview for the Summer Project in Mississippi. It went well, and I really hope I get accepted. Now that I know more about the program, I've decided I want to volunteer with the Freedom Schools. It will be a lot of work—especially since I've never taught before. (Unless you count the fact that I taught Lila everything she knows about hair. Ha ha.)

But you know what? You've inspired me. You took on the playground project even though you've never done anything like it before. You're my role model, Dee-Dee. Pretty soon everybody's going to be talking about the park and all the work you and your friends have done.

Keep me posted on all your progress,
Love, Vonnie

Melody couldn't believe it. Yvonne thought *she* was a role model? Her brave, smart, strong big sister was inspired by what Melody was doing? For a moment, Melody was flattered. Then she sighed. Yvonne didn't

♪ Never Stop Singing ♪

know that the Junior Block Club was locked out of the park. What would Yvonne say if she knew about that "progress"?

The song on the radio ended, and a woman's voice filled Melody's room. "This is Martha Jean the Queen." Melody loved her smooth voice. Martha Jean Steinberg was one of the most popular DJs in Detroit. Any song she played became a hit, and anything she discussed on her show was what grown-ups all over the city talked about. Melody imagined the Queen one day introducing Dwayne's music. Everyone in Detroit would be singing his song.

Wait a minute, Melody thought. She reread Yvonne's letter. *"Pretty soon everybody's going to be talking about the park and all the work you and your friends have done."* If more people knew that the city had closed the park, maybe they would write to the commissioner, too.

Melody needed help letting others know about the problem. She got a clean piece of paper and a pencil. "Dear Miss Steinberg," she began.

A week passed, and the lock was still on the park

♪ More Letters ♪

gate. Melody was worried that every day they spent not working on the playground meant they were getting further and further away from having the park done in time for the picnic. They hadn't done any planting yet, and Melody was afraid that the garden wouldn't be ready.

Melody dragged around the house after school one day, feeling very out of sorts. She finally decided to go to the backyard to start turning over the soil in her own flower beds. Working in the dirt always helped her feel calm and peaceful. She'd just put on her gloves and taken out her small rake when her mother drove up.

"Is the park still locked?" Mommy asked, her keys jangling as she took her school things out of the car.

Melody nodded her head. "Is this my fault?" she asked her mother. "I'm the one who told the Parks Department about the broken swing."

"The lock on the park gate is not your fault," Mommy said, setting her books on the back step and sitting down. "Even a good leader can't make everything go right. You had a wonderful idea; you got people to trust you and work with you. No way is that a failure, and no way is what happened your fault."

♪ Never Stop Singing ♪

"Thanks, Mommy," Melody said. "I just miss working in the park."

"Well, since you've got some time on your hands, you can help Val move into her new room."

Melody's eyes were wide. "Her what? Did they finally buy a house?" she shouted.

Mommy nodded. "I stopped at your grandparents' on my way home, and Charles and Tish just found out. It's official. They bought a house!"

Melody had never experienced a moving day before, and on a bright Saturday in May, when she stood looking out of the picture window of Val's new living room, she felt as if she was at a circus.

"Look!" Val cried, waving wildly at the man who was getting out of the moving van. The huge truck that had pulled up in front of the neatly mowed yard was the biggest Melody had ever seen. She counted eighteen wheels.

"Mama! They're here. They're here!" Val shouted. Melody knew that her cousin was excited to see her things again. Most of her family's belongings had been

♪ More Letters ♪

in storage in Alabama for more than a year.

Tish, Big Momma, and Mommy had been busy cleaning and hanging curtains, but now they all trooped out to the front porch. Charles and Daddy were by Charles's car, unloading boxes of the belongings the family had had at Big Momma's.

"You girls stay right there, out of the way," Charles told them. He went over to the moving truck. The girls watched the moving men open the back door, put up a ramp, and then begin to unload. Off came boxes and beds and chairs.

"Where's *my* stuff?" Val said anxiously.

"All the boxes look the same," Melody said. And then a bicycle was rolled out.

"Oh!" Val ran down the steps, with Melody right behind. Before the grown-ups could say anything, Val had grabbed her bike and wobbled up the driveway toward the backyard. "The tire's flat!" she called, but Melody could tell that Val was still excited.

Melody stood aside to let the men carry a blue-and-gold-striped sofa in, followed by a blue-and-white kitchen table. Next came a pink chair with a fluffy cushion. Melody smiled to see furniture in both Val's

♪ Never Stop Singing ♪

and Tish's favorite colors. Melody watched the men come back out and then carry a series of boxes in, heading up the stairs. These boxes were all labeled "Valerie's Room."

The movers carried a twin bedframe and mattress upstairs, and Val's and Melody's fathers followed. A few minutes later, they came back outside. "Princess," Charles said. "You and Melody can start unpacking now!"

Val and Melody practically flew into the house and up the steps. In the bedroom, Val's bed had been put together, but the mattress was bare. The fluffy pink chair was in the middle of the floor, and an empty bookcase and a chest of drawers stood against one wall.

Melody didn't think cleaning her own room was fun. But unpacking Val's boxes was like unwrapping birthday gifts. By the time Tish called them to lunch, Val's clothes were put away, her books were on the shelves, and she and Melody had made the bed and arranged a row of stuffed animals across it.

"It's our first meal in our new home," Tish said as the girls arrived downstairs. As they sat down in the dining room, the doorbell rang.

♪ More Letters ♪

"Our first guest!" Tish said, hurrying to answer.

"What does that make us?" Daddy asked.

Charles laughed. "You're the family help!" he said. Melody could see that Charles was very happy.

"Congratulations!" Big Momma said. Poppa was behind her, carrying a huge dracaena plant.

"Thank you, Aunt Geneva, Uncle Frank," Charles said.

"Come in," Tish said. "Sit down. Have something to eat." She was beaming.

"I have a present, too!" Melody piped up. She pushed away from the table to find her mother's bag in the living room, and returned with a package that she'd wrapped and tied with pink ribbon.

"Is this a calendar for my new kitchen?" Tish asked as she opened the gift.

"Yes. I marked the week that Val and I are going to Alabama with Poppa and Mommy," Melody said. "And I marked today's date—May 16—too. I think it should be a family holiday." Everyone laughed, and Val took the pink ribbon to tie in her hair.

"Wait!" Melody's father said. "Our housewarming gift is in the kitchen." He left the table with everyone

♪ Never Stop Singing ♪

watching curiously. Soon they heard the crackle and static of a radio being turned on and tuned.

"Thank you, Will!" Tish said. "Now, come on back here and eat."

Everyone talked at once, and everyone was talking about the house. Charles told them that one neighbor had actually come by to say hello.

"It may take time to get to know everyone," Tish said. "But we love our new home."

There was a commercial on the radio, and when it was over, Martha Jean the Queen came on the air. "Welcome, Greater Detroit area!" she said.

Tish stopped talking and turned toward the kitchen. "Oh, I love the Queen's program! She plays the best music, and she brings up such interesting topics. We listen to her all the time in the salon."

"Turn up the sound, Charles," Big Momma said.

Martha Jean's voice got louder. "Let's give our support to a group of children from New Hope Baptist Church who banded together to do something special for their community. They asked the Parks Department for new swings. Not only did they get turned down, but they got locked out of their playground! It's

♪ More Letters ♪

a shame that the city and our wonderful mayor can't help these children who have worked *so* hard to improve their neighborhood. Call in if you agree."

Everyone turned to look at Melody and Val.

"That's us!" Val said. "How did she know?"

Melody grinned. "I wrote another letter. But this time I sent it to someone who would talk about our park."

"Melody to the rescue," Melody's mother said.

On the last Thursday in May, Melody received another long white envelope with the city seal in the corner. She tore it open and let out a shriek of joy. Melody called Sharon, Val, Diane, and Julius and asked them to meet her at the park right away.

When Melody got to the park, everyone else was there. "Melody, look!" Julius shouted. "The lock's gone!"

"I know," Melody said. "Listen, everybody."

May 26, 1964
Dear Miss Ellison,

♪ Never Stop Singing ♪

As a result of the many telephone calls and letters we have received about your local park, our inspectors have reviewed the conditions there. After removing the broken swing, we have determined that the park is safe for recreation. Thank you for being a good citizen.

"Let's get back to work!" Melody said, waving the letter in the air. She looked over at the yellow house. Miss Esther stood in the front window, smiling and waving.

After the lock came off the gate, the Junior Block Club sprang into action. That Saturday, a group of dads replaced the missing bricks in the walls of the handball courts with the help of Julius, Diane, and Sharon. While that was happening, Val, Melody, and Miss Esther planted more flowers. Poppa came and helped start the vegetable garden.

Things were looking good. On the next work day, Julius's older brother brought cans of paint and

♪ More Letters ♪

brushes. By then, some moms and kids were coming in to see everything, so Melody made big signs with leftover butcher paper that said: WET PAINT. Then it rained, so they had to do it all over again.

Whenever Melody went to the park to work, she took her transistor radio with her. And it was *always* tuned to Martha Jean the Queen's show.

Important Work

♪ CHAPTER 13 ♪

School ended in the middle of June, and Melody's mother announced to the family that they'd have a "Whatever You Want to Eat" dinner. Lila made bologna and cheese sandwiches with the crusts cut off from the bread. Melody and her mother baked cupcakes, which Melody was allowed to eat *before* she had anything else. Her father picked up hamburgers from his favorite restaurant.

"Well," Mommy said, "we've reached the end of another school year."

"And what a year!" Daddy said, piling French fries onto his plate. "Lila got a science scholarship. Melody took on a playground project. And Yvonne is going to be a teacher this summer."

Yvonne had called home to tell them she'd been accepted to the Mississippi Summer Program. Instead

♪ Important Work ♪

of coming home when her college classes were finished, she'd stayed in Alabama. Now Yvonne was in Ohio for training.

"Everyone kept their grades up, too," Mommy added. "I'm proud of all you girls."

"Well, Lila got straight A's," Melody said. "As usual."

"And you did a lot of work at the park," Lila said, swiping one of Melody's cupcakes.

Melody slapped her sister's hand playfully. "You mean you went to check it out?"

"Of course I did. If the Ellison name is on something, it has to be good!"

Melody made a face. "The Ellison name—"

"—is on the latest Motown record!" Dwayne banged in through the kitchen door waving a small black disc. "Here it is, for your ears only."

"It's out!" Mommy cried.

"Let's hear it right now!" Lila shouted.

Melody jumped up from her chair. "How does it sound?" She raced Dwayne to the record player. He slipped the record out of its paper sleeve, but he held it above Melody's head.

♪ Never Stop Singing ♪

"By the way, Dee-Dee," Dwayne said, "are you having any special entertainment for your playground opening? You know, like live music?"

Melody pretended she didn't know what he was talking about. "Live music? Oh, we don't have a budget for that," she teased. "But if you want to perform for free, we could work something out."

Even Daddy laughed at that.

"Listen to you, Miss President!" Dwayne said.

"I want to listen to *you*," Melody replied, grabbing at Dwayne's record. He handed it to her and let her place it on the turntable. She started the record player, and everyone listened.

> *Girl, it's time that I move,*
> *Time for movin' on up.*
> *Move on up!*
> *Yeah, it's time for my move,*
> *Time to start changing my luck.*
> *Move on up!*

When the song was over, Daddy pushed back his chair, got up, and shook Dwayne's hand. "I'm proud of

♪ Important Work ♪

you, son," he said, his voice full of emotion. "You did what you set out to do. Keep on doing it."

A week before their trip to Alabama, Melody's father was watching television in the living room while Melody and her mother sat at the dining room table talking about what they needed to pack. "That reminds me, Will," Mommy said during a commerical. "Would you bring the suitcases up from the basement?"

"Will do!" Daddy answered, and Melody laughed at his favorite joke. "I'll go down after the news."

The commercial ended and a silver-haired newscaster looked up from his desk. "In national news today, the search continues for three young civil rights workers who are missing in Mississippi."

"What?" Daddy said.

"Mississippi?" Melody repeated. "That's where Yvonne is going," she said in a small voice.

Mommy got up and went into the living room. Melody followed.

"According to CORE, the Congress for Racial Equality, James Chaney, 21, Andrew Goodman, 20,

♪ Never Stop Singing ♪

and Michael Schwerner, 24, were investigating the burning of a Negro church in the area. CORE members say the men were arrested on June twenty-first without cause, held in jail for several hours, and then released. The trio has not been seen or heard from since."

Melody felt the same knot in her tummy that she'd felt when she heard about the four little girls who had died in the church bombing in Birmingham.

"Oh, my goodness," Mommy said.

"Do you think they're all right?" Melody asked.

Mommy shook her head. "I don't know, Melody."

Melody tried to make sense of what she'd just heard. It frightened her to think that civil rights workers could just disappear. Then Melody had a horrible thought. "Do you think *Vonnie* is all right?" she asked.

"I pray she is safe," Mommy said. But she looked very concerned.

"There's one way to find out," Daddy said, getting up. "Where's her phone number, Frances?"

"By the phone, on the yellow paper," Mommy answered. She and Melody followed him to the kitchen.

Daddy picked up the phone and dialed. "Hello?" he said. "Yes, this is Will Ellison, Yvonne Ellison's father.

♪ Important Work ♪

I'd like to speak to her, please."

Melody stood beside her mother, waiting to hear that Yvonne was okay. The seconds seemed to tick by slowly. Daddy tapped impatiently on the telephone receiver. Melody could tell that he was nervous, too.

"Yvonne!" Daddy finally said. He looked at Melody and smiled. Mommy sighed.

"How's everything going?" Daddy asked. He began to nod. "We just heard about that on the news."

Melody turned to her mother. "Do you want Vonnie to come home?" she asked.

Mommy shook her head. "Even if I did, Melody, Yvonne is a strong person, and she makes her own choices now. The work she's decided to do is very important, but the struggle for justice isn't easy. Your sister is becoming a grown-up."

Mommy pulled Melody into a hug. "Mothers and fathers always hope that their children will be safe and make good choices, no matter how old they are. We hope that for all of you."

Melody's tummy settled down. Yvonne was brave and strong and smart, and Melody knew she would make good choices.

Standing Tall

♪ CHAPTER 14 ♪

e're going to pass Birmingham and go straight to the farm," Poppa told the girls. "I want to see it before nightfall."

Melody was stiff from sitting in the car for so long. The trip had taken almost twelve hours. They had left Detroit long before sunrise so that they could get to Alabama in the daylight.

Poppa turned off the paved highway and onto a dirt road. They drove for another hour. Melody was surprised when Poppa slowed down next to an empty field, turned onto a rutted path, and stopped the car. Without saying a word, he and Melody's mother got out.

Val looked at Melody, confused. "This looks like nowhere," she said, not moving.

Melody nodded, but she stumbled out to stretch.

♪ Standing Tall ♪

Although she'd never been here before, there was something that felt familiar to Melody. Maybe it was the wildflowers dotting the field with shades of yellow and bright blue. They reminded her of the flowers in her own yard as well as the garden at the park. *I hope Sharon and Diane remember to water everything,* Melody thought.

"It's hotter here than it is in Birmingham!" Val said, climbing out of the car and pulling on a sun hat.

"Poppa?" Melody called. "When will we get to your old farm?"

Her grandfather didn't answer. He'd stopped to stare off at something Melody and Val couldn't see.

Melody's mother turned to them. "This is it," she said.

Melody looked around in surprise. There was no orchard. There was no beautiful flower garden surrounded by the wooden fence Poppa had built. In fact, nothing here was the way her grandparents had described. All Melody could see were a few old trees and a dusty path cutting through the grass.

Melody walked over to her grandfather and tugged on his sleeve. "Is it gone?"

♪ Never Stop Singing ♪

Poppa shook his head. "No. It's here," he said, as he tapped his heart. Then he bent to scoop up a handful of dirt. "And here," he said, letting the dirt run through his fingers. "You're standing on it. Standing on the shoulders of all our people who came before."

Melody looked down at her dusty sandals, imagining her grandfather as a boy, and his parents, and maybe even their parents, walking on this same path. She looked up at Poppa, and tried to stand just a little bit taller than she had before.

Melody's mother and grandfather began to walk, and the girls followed in the late afternoon heat. The road curved, and Poppa pointed. Mommy took off her sunglasses and shaded her eyes. In the distance was an old building, and beyond it another field.

"Is that your house?" Melody asked her mother.

"No," her mother said. "Aunt Beck told us that a tree fell on the house during a storm about ten years ago. The house was too damaged to repair, so what was left was torn down."

"That's awful," Melody said, frowning.

"It was," her mother said. "But I still have great memories."

♪ Standing Tall ♪

Melody thought of the good times she'd shared with Yvonne and Dwayne and Lila in their home. She knew she wouldn't forget any of that, even if their house was gone.

"So what's that building, then?" Val asked.

"I think it's the old barn," Mommy said.

"That's just what it is," Poppa said in a firm voice. He started walking toward it.

They all followed the rough road. The wildflowers ended, and there was a rickety wood and wire fence on either side of the path.

"Remember coming along here in the wagon, Frances?" Poppa asked.

"You pulled Mommy in a wagon?" Melody asked.

Melody's mother laughed. "Our horse, Sugarfoot, pulled the wagon, sweetie. I sat in back with bushel baskets of peas and sacks of peanuts."

"That was before we got the truck," Poppa explained as he strode along. "Doesn't look like anyone's farmed the land in a long while. I guess the fellow I sold to ended up selling, too. It's a shame." Poppa shook his head. "This was such rich land."

The road ended in a gravel clearing, and the barn

♪ Never Stop Singing ♪

sat in the middle of it. The girls stopped and watched Poppa try the door. It didn't budge. He walked the length of the front, peering into two dusty windows.

"It looks sad," Val whispered. Melody agreed.

"Everything is different," Mommy said. "I can't even tell where the house was." Then Melody's mother did something strange. She walked to a corner of the barn, closed her eyes, and marched into the tall grass.

"Is she *counting*?" Val asked.

Melody watched her mother's mouth move. "Yes, she is!"

"Daddy!" Melody's mother called. "The house was over here!" Poppa and the girls hurried to the edge of the grass where Mommy stood.

"You're right, Frances. Good detective work!"

"So that must be the stump of the tree that fell," her mother said. She pointed away from the barn toward a dark mound overgrown with weeds. "It must have been that old oak, Daddy—the one you hung my swing on!"

Melody had never seen Mommy like this. For the first time, she thought of her mother as Frances Porter, a girl who'd flown in the air on her swing, canned

♪ Standing Tall ♪

fruits and vegetables, and ridden behind a horse named Sugarfoot.

"This way, girls!" Poppa called, heading past the barn. Despite the heat, he walked quickly.

Melody, Val, and Mommy hurried to follow Poppa. When they rounded the barn, Melody saw a broad grin stretch across Poppa's face, making his silver mustache twitch.

"Well, I'll be!" Melody's mother said. "The pecan trees!"

"There's some farm left, after all," Poppa said.

"Did you plant them all?" Melody asked.

"My father and I did," he said. He smiled at Melody. "Just like you and I plant tomatoes every year."

Melody smiled, too. "Tradition," she whispered.

They all walked a long way through tall grass to reach the trees. Their trunks were fat, gnarled, and gray, but their branches stretched up and spread wide across the sky.

"My pecan trees," Poppa said, touching one of the trunks.

"Melody," her mother said. "You and Val go over and stand with Poppa so I can get a picture."

♪ Never Stop Singing ♪

The grass tickled Melody's legs as she ran toward her grandfather. He put one arm around Melody's shoulders and another around Val's. Just before Mommy snapped the photo, Melody reached out to rub her hand against the pecan tree.

It was nightfall by the time they drove back into Birmingham, to the little green house where Poppa's sister, Aunt Beck, lived. They'd just gotten out of the car when Aunt Beck threw open her screen door. Her long silver braid was wound neatly around her head, and her eyeglasses were perched on her nose.

"I declare, Frank! What took you so long? I've had supper waiting for these babies"—she paused to squeeze Melody and Val in one tight hug—"for hours!" she continued. "Where have you been?"

Melody laughed at the idea of her grandfather having a big sister. When Poppa mumbled his answer, he sounded just like Dwayne talking to Yvonne.

"Hello, Aunt Beck," Mommy said. "Let's go in and leave the mosquitoes outside."

"You're right, Frances. Come in. I'll heat up supper."

♪ Standing Tall ♪

Melody and Val both loved visiting Aunt Beck, and her living room was one reason why. Every table and shelf was covered with knickknacks. There were china figurines, tiny dolls, picture frames, and small glass candy dishes filled with an assortment of sweets.

What Melody liked best was that Aunt Beck was not the type of adult who didn't allow kids to look at her special things. Aunt Beck happily let Melody and Val pick up anything they liked, and she had a story to tell about each object.

"Oh, girls!" Aunt Beck said. "My grandson Jimmy just sent me a doll all the way from Japan. Wait until you see it!"

Poppa rolled his eyes as he attempted to carry the suitcases through the room without knocking anything over.

"Look at this candy dish shaped like a house!" Val said.

Melody smiled at the fact that houses were still on Val's mind.

"Look at all this stuff," Melody said, pointing at a table in the corner. "Everything has an American flag on it." She was impressed by the ceramic bald eagle

♪ Never Stop Singing ♪

carrying a flag in its beak.

"Well, the Fourth of July is only five days away," Val said. "We'll see our other cousins, and go to the fireworks."

"And eat peach ice cream," Melody said. She opened the top of a flag-shaped tin box.

"Candy?" Val asked.

"Chocolate kisses," Melody answered.

"Mmmm . . . it's good to be back in Birmingham," Val mumbled through a mouthful of chocolate.

Melody liked the fact that members of the same family celebrated holidays differently. Back in Detroit, Daddy would be up early on the Fourth of July to start the barbecue. Here at Aunt Beck's, her son Clifford brought over barbecue in the afternoon. In the morning, Aunt Beck peeled peaches and made the custard for her homemade ice cream.

Melody woke up early to help. But when she got to the kitchen, ready to work, Aunt Beck insisted she have breakfast. "You go over there and get yourself a cinnamon bun."

♪ Standing Tall ♪

Melody did, and then sat at the kitchen table. Aunt Beck was humming a tune that Melody thought she recognized.

"I know that song from school. It's 'America the Beautiful,' isn't it?" Melody started to sing, and so did Aunt Beck.

> *And crown thy good with brotherhood*
> *From sea to shining sea.*

"I think that's the most important part of the song, isn't it?" Aunt Beck said to Melody. "That brotherhood part. That's what we've all got to figure out."

Melody nodded, her mouth full of warm cinnamon bun. She and Aunt Beck talked about Yvonne and the Mississippi Summer Project. When Mommy came in looking for coffee, Melody was telling Aunt Beck about the Challenge to Change.

"Now that President Johnson has signed the Civil Rights Act, I expect we'll see even more changes," Aunt Beck said to Melody. "Good morning, Frances."

"Good morning," Mommy yawned. "Yes, it's wonderful to have a law saying that we're all equal,

♪ Never Stop Singing ♪

and have equal rights. That's what we've been marching for and protesting about all this time."

"That's right," Poppa said, coming into the kitchen.

"Now we just have to get everybody to obey the law," Aunt Beck said.

Melody began to understand what her great-aunt meant—America the Beautiful, brotherhood, civil rights. They did all go together.

After Val woke up and had breakfast, she and Melody got to help Aunt Beck make custard. Melody had never broken so many eggs before. Mommy used the extra peaches to make a cobbler. In the afternoon, Aunt Beck's son Clifford, his wife, Katie, and their children and grandchildren arrived. The house was full.

"This can't be little Melody!" Clifford said in a booming voice that sounded very much like Poppa's. "And Val? How come you grew so fast up there in Detroit?"

Melody didn't get many chances to spend time with little kids, and neither did Val—so they had great fun playing tag and peek-a-boo with their much younger cousins. At dusk, Clifford announced that it was time

♪ Standing Tall ♪

to go find spots to see the fireworks. Aunt Beck stayed home, but everyone else piled into cars.

Melody stood next to Val, speechless over the beauty of the fireworks in the sky over a giant statue called Vulcan. She and Val argued all the way back over which city's celebration was better—Birmingham's or Detroit's.

"Hey, you live in Detroit now," Melody reminded Val. "So you have to be loyal!"

Clifford, a lawyer, looked at the girls in his rearview mirror. "I say Val can claim dual citizenship."

"What's that?" Melody asked.

"It means she can be a citizen of two places at the same time," Clifford told her. Melody folded her arms and pretended to be upset, while Val laughed.

When Clifford pulled into the driveway, Melody's mother said, "Now why does Aunt Beck have every light on in the house?"

Before anyone could say anything else, Aunt Beck swung the front door open. Her braid hung against her back. She looked worried.

"Frances, Will has been calling and calling!"

"He has?" Melody's mother hurried out of the car

♪ Never Stop Singing ♪

and up the porch steps. "What's wrong?"

"It's Yvonne," Aunt Beck said. "She's been arrested in Mississippi."

Civil Rights

♪ CHAPTER 15 ♪

Melody rushed into the house after Mommy. Val, Poppa, and Clifford followed. "You girls stay here," Poppa ordered before hurrying into the kitchen.

Melody and Val sat down in the living room. The TV was on, and somewhere a radio news program was blaring. All the sounds made everything more confusing.

Melody strained to hear what was happening in the kitchen. Her mother must have called home, because Melody heard Mommy say, "Will! Aunt Beck just told me. Have you heard from her? Not since when?"

Melody felt her lip tremble. She couldn't sit still and hurried into the kitchen. Val followed.

Mommy was on the phone, listening to Daddy. Melody crossed the room and tugged on her shirt.

♪ Never Stop Singing ♪

"What's he saying?" she insisted. But Mommy just motioned for her to be quiet.

"Come on, baby," Aunt Beck said, trying to steer Melody and Val out. But Mommy hung up, and Melody turned to face her.

"What happened?" Clifford asked.

"Yvonne called home yesterday to say she'd been arrested for disturbing the peace. Will hasn't heard from her since, and he can't get any answers from the police station in someplace called Meridian."

"What do you want to do?" Poppa asked.

"Go find her!" Melody's mother said. Melody heard determination in her mother's voice, but also fear.

"I want to come with you," Melody said. Her heart was pounding, and her throat felt tight. All she could think of were the civil rights workers who had disappeared. Yvonne was a civil rights worker.

"Let me help," Clifford said. "I'll drive. You don't need to be in Mississippi with a Michigan license plate on your car, Uncle Frank. Some people over there look for any reason to cause trouble for black people."

"All right, all right," Mommy said, grabbing her purse. "We need to go." She turned to Melody and

♪ Civil Rights ♪

squeezed her hand. "You'll have to stay here with Aunt Beck."

Then they were gone.

"Are you okay?" Val asked gently.

Melody only nodded. Her throat hurt, and she didn't feel like talking. Aunt Beck tried to convince her to sleep, but Melody couldn't. She was too worried. When both Aunt Beck and Val finally went to bed, Melody stayed up. She sat on the edge of the sofa in the living room, staring at the Fourth of July decorations on the coffee table.

She had so many thoughts crammed into her brain at once that she had a headache. *Is Yvonne okay? Is she missing, like those three civil rights workers who disappeared a few weeks ago?* Melody thought of Aunt Beck sounding so pleased that the Civil Rights Act was now a law. But what good was a law if it couldn't keep people safe?

Melody leaned back against the sofa. She tried to focus on the pecan trees at Poppa's old farm, standing strong and tall during a bad storm.

♪ Never Stop Singing ♪

Melody dreamed that her sisters were calling to her across a field of tall grass. "Melody? Melody!"

She opened her eyes to sunlight streaming through Aunt Beck's living room windows. Melody had fallen asleep on the sofa, and now Yvonne was sitting next to her, calling her name.

"Vonnie!" Melody blinked to make sure her sister was real. Yvonne looked tired. Her Afro was tied back with a scarf, and her left wrist was in a cast.

Melody carefully threw her arms around Yvonne. "Are you okay?" she asked, squeezing her sister tightly.

"I'm all right," Yvonne said, squeezing back. "I got banged up a little, that's all. I'll tell you everything, I promise. But right now, I need to sleep."

Yvonne slept well into the afternoon. After church, Clifford's college-age daughter Anne took Melody and Val to visit Val's old neighborhood. Even though Melody was anxious to talk to Yvonne, it was fun to meet some of Val's old friends and see her cousin so happy.

On their way back to Aunt Beck's, Val turned to

♪ Civil Rights ♪

Melody. "I think I understand why Poppa misses his farm," she said quietly. "He misses all the good times he had there with his family and his friends. That's what I miss too."

"Mm-hmm," Melody answered. "Now you have a new home and new friends in Detroit, but you won't ever forget the good times and friends you had here in Birmingham, will you?"

"I won't. Not ever."

At Aunt Beck's, Yvonne was awake and dinner was ready. "You just sit right down here, baby," Aunt Beck said to Yvonne, pulling out a chair at the kitchen table. Clifford and Anne joined Melody and Val while Poppa said grace.

"Thanks, Mom," Yvonne said as Mommy placed a plate of food in front of her. "Thank you all."

Melody noticed that her sister was quieter than usual. She picked up her fork with her right hand, and because she was left-handed, she had trouble using it.

"Can I help?" Melody asked quietly.

Yvonne nodded. "Gee, thanks, Dee-Dee."

Anne said what Melody was thinking. "All right. I want to hear it from you. What happened?"

♪ Never Stop Singing ♪

"Well," Yvonne began, watching Melody cut her meat into pieces. "It's not all that complicated. We had our training and orientation in Oxford, Ohio. That's where I learned to work with elementary school kids, helping improve their reading skills. We also got instructions to be calm when we got arrested."

Melody noticed that Yvonne said "when," not "if."

Yvonne continued. "When we got to Mississippi—to Meridian—we went out to invite parents to send their kids to our Freedom School. There were four of us in the car, two white college students and me, going along this tiny unpaved road where the black people in this community lived. The other person with us was a black high school boy who lived in the area."

"That was good," Aunt Beck said. "You were with somebody the people knew."

"Yes, exactly," Yvonne said. "So we were on the front porch of a house, and this family, the teenagers and parents, were really interested in talking to us. They were asking all kinds of questions. That's when the sheriff's car pulled up along the road. No siren, no flashing lights. I don't even know why he was there."

"Was that scary?" Melody asked.

♪ Civil Rights ♪

Yvonne took a deep breath. "Yes. But all of us knew what would happen. That part was in our training, too. The sheriff came up and told us that we were disturbing the peace. The man who owned the house was brave enough to tell the sheriff that he *wanted* to talk to us. But the sheriff repeated that we were disturbing the peace and said we were under arrest."

Anne shook her head. "That's just nuts. That's worse than getting turned away at a hotel or restaurant. Those people have a right to talk to whomever they want. And so do you."

"Yes, but the law enforcement in Mississippi is not interested in giving any black people any kind of civil rights," Clifford said.

Yvonne nodded. "The sheriff dragged us off the porch. As he was pulling me, I tripped on the steps. He kept pulling me anyway, and I fell and broke my wrist. He still took us to jail."

"That's horrible!" Val said.

Yvonne turned to Mommy. "I did get my one phone call. That's when I . . . that's when I called home and Lila answered. I told her to tell you and Dad that I was okay. I know that those three freedom workers are still

♪ Never Stop Singing ♪

missing, and I knew that everyone would be worried about me." Yvonne stopped because her voice got shaky. Melody put her hand on her sister's.

Yvonne smiled at Melody, and then she took a deep breath. She looked defiant. "I knew my rights, but I didn't know if I would get out of jail. I didn't know if I would ever come home. But now I know that I am not going to stop fighting for freedom."

"I want you to keep fighting," Mommy said. "But I want you to take care of yourself, too. You need to take a break and get yourself together."

Yvonne shook her head. "No, Mom. I want to go back."

Mommy put her fork down. "Yvonne, I don't know if—"

Melody interrupted. "Mommy, didn't you say that Yvonne was old enough to make her own choices?"

Everyone was quiet, and Mommy gave Melody a long look. Mommy sighed. "I did say that."

"I'll be as careful as I can," Yvonne said, "but we all know the fight isn't over. President Johnson just signed the Civil Rights Act, but this fight is not on paper."

Aunt Beck cleared her throat. "Yvonne, why don't

♪ Civil Rights ♪

you stay here for a few days to rest up? Then Clifford can take you back to Mississippi."

"Thanks, Aunt Beck. I'll stay if Mommy agrees to let me go back to Mississippi."

"Frances," Clifford said to Mommy, "if it makes you feel any better, I have friends in Meridian who can keep an eye on her."

Mommy nodded. "It does. But let me talk to Will about it tonight. For now, let's enjoy being with one another. All right?"

"That sounds fine," Aunt Beck said. "Now, I've got peach cobbler just waiting to get eaten up!"

Yvonne leaned toward Melody. "Thanks," she whispered.

"You're welcome," Melody whispered back.

"Girls," Mommy said. "Those were stage whispers."

For the next few days, Melody didn't leave Yvonne's side. She helped Yvonne do anything she couldn't do because of her cast. Yvonne rested a lot, but she and Melody talked a lot, too. Melody told her all about the trip to the Motown studio and how amazing it had

♪ Never Stop Singing ♪

been to see Dwayne as a real musician. She described Poppa's farm and how she had pictured Mommy as a girl growing up there. Yvonne asked Melody lots of questions about her park project, and she was impressed that Melody had thought to write a letter to Martha Jean the Queen. "That's makin' it work, Dee-Dee," she'd said.

Daddy had agreed that Yvonne could go back to Meridian on the condition that she call home every few days. So early on Thursday morning, everyone left Birmingham at the same time. Melody walked Yvonne to Clifford's car.

"I know this has been scary for you," Yvonne said, gesturing to the cast on her wrist, "but I'm glad we got a chance to see each other."

"Me, too," Melody said. "I'm glad you're okay."

"I am okay. And I'm not doing this alone. Neither are you, Dee-Dee," Yvonne said gently. "Remember. You came up with a great plan for the park, and you found great kids to work with. Trust them."

"Okay," Melody promised as Yvonne got in the car.

"And don't forget to send me pictures of that playground!" Yvonne yelled as Clifford pulled away.

Keep Going

♪ CHAPTER 16 ♪

When they got back to Detroit that night, Poppa drove them all to his house, where Big Momma had a meal waiting. Val's parents were there, and Daddy and Lila had come over for supper, too. Even Dwayne joined them. Everyone wanted to hear about the trip.

"So, Frances," Charles said, sitting down at the dining room table, "what happened with Yvonne?"

"I kind of want to know the answer to that question, too," Dwayne said, looking at his mother. "Is she safe down there?"

"I admit, I've been worried about Yvonne ever since I heard the news reports about those three young men who went missing," Big Momma said, folding her hands together.

Tish shook her head. "I just don't think we could

♪ Never Stop Singing ♪

ever allow Valerie to do something like what Yvonne is doing."

"Wait a minute," Daddy said. "We all care about our children, and we care about the world they grow up in, don't we?"

Charles nodded. "That's true, Will."

Tish nodded, too. She started to say something else, but Mommy put both her hands in the air.

"Listen, everyone. We have a freedom fighter. Her name is Yvonne Marie Ellison. She has decided to go where we will not go—" Mommy looked at Melody. "Or cannot yet go, to lift her voice and use her gifts to try to make the world better for all of us. Every day there are black people and white people putting themselves in harm's way to change the world." Mommy's voice was shaking. "And I am so very, very proud of my Yvonne!"

Daddy got up, walked around the table, and put his arm around Mommy's shoulders. "Ditto," was all he said.

"Wow. Mom and Dad have got Yvonne's back." Dwayne whispered to Lila. Lila nodded.

Melody was so very, very proud of all of them.

♪ Keep Going ♪

Melody was up early the next morning, and she dressed quickly so that she could go check on the playground. She was anxious to see how everything looked after her time away.

Bo was excited that Melody was home, and he ran around her in circles in the kitchen. She clipped his leash onto his collar and said, "Okay. You can come with me."

Outside, Bo barked and pulled at the leash. He knew exactly where he was going. As they rounded the corner by the park, Melody's heart beat fast. She saw the tall stems of the hollyhocks and daylilies standing at attention. The morning sun had already opened many of the lilies' orange flowers, and the hollyhocks looked like bright red ruffles.

As she swung the park gate open, Melody did a double take. It didn't creak! Someone had oiled the hinges.

To her surprise, Diane and Sharon were already at work in the vegetable patch.

"Hi!" Melody called out.

♪ Never Stop Singing ♪

"Melody!" Sharon stood up to run over, but then she took a look at her dirty shorts and shirt, and simply laughed.

"Hey, Melody." Diane pushed back the sun hat she was wearing. Behind her was a tall bamboo tepee with green-bean vines carefully wound around each slender stick.

"Nice beans," Melody said.

Diane grinned. "I've kind of started to like gardening," she said. "Look! The beans have *flowers* on them!" She pointed to the tiny white blossoms.

"Yes, they do," Melody said. "We—I mean, you—will have green beans soon. That's great!"

"Take a look around and check things out," Sharon said. "We've been working really hard."

Melody was pleased to see that the flower beds had been weeded and watered. The red geraniums were perky, and the tiny impatiens looked like mounds of orange, pink, and white popcorn. She glanced at the morning glory vines climbing up the swing supports. It was still disappointing not to have swings, but the trumpet-shaped flowers would be cheerful when they bloomed.

♪ Keep Going ♪

"It's looking good, huh?"

Melody turned to see Julius and his friend Larry. Julius was wearing gardening gloves. "Welcome back," he said. "Larry and I just stopped by to do a little weeding."

Melody tilted her head to see that Larry was carrying a ball.

"Well, we want to break in the handball courts before the opening," Julius said with a shrug.

Melody laughed. "It looks great. I can't wait for the picnic, so everyone can see what we've done."

"Three weeks and counting!" Julius said, heading off with Larry.

Melody wrote down a few things in her notebook. There were some bare spots in the flower border in back, and she wanted to get some plants to fill them in. And the hopscotch grids hadn't been painted on the paths yet. Other than that, all they had to do was keep weeding, pinch back the dead blooms so the plants continued to flower, and make sure everything was watered.

"Not bad, Bo," she said as they turned to leave. "Not bad at all!"

♪ Never Stop Singing ♪

Val's garden hadn't fared so well. When Val called in a panic, Mommy agreed to drive Melody to Val's house. Val met Melody on the front porch.

"You have to help," she said, taking Melody's hand and dragging her through the house. "It's a disaster!"

"It can't be that bad," Melody said. But when Val pulled her out the back door, all Melody could say was, "Oh."

"See?" Val almost squealed.

The pink impatiens that the girls had planted in neat borders around the trees were wilting. The pots of purple petunias they'd set along the back steps looked shriveled. The tomatoes in the vegetable bed on the sunny side of the yard had several yellowing leaves.

"I don't understand what happened," Val said.

"Not enough water," Melody replied. "Where's your hose?"

"Over here," Val said, leading Melody to the side of the house, where a green garden hose was neatly coiled. "But it's so heavy. Besides, I thought it would rain."

♪ Keep Going ♪

Melody made a face. "You mean, you were waiting for rain? You didn't even water things before we left?"

Val stood still. "That wasn't right?"

Melody shook her head.

"But I never see you watering with a hose," Val said.

Melody unwound the hose. "That's because I do it early in the morning, before it gets too hot, or late in the afternoon, after the sun goes down."

"I'm a bad gardener," Val said.

"Nope." Melody handed her the hose. "Just a new one. You'll learn. Let's give them a good drink now."

"So my tomatoes still have a chance?"

"Of course they do," Melody said with a smile, turning on the faucet.

In church the Sunday before the picnic, Pastor Daniels made an announcement. "Some of our fine young people have answered the New Year's challenge with good works."

He made the five of them stand up in front of the congregation. "I asked them to use their gifts to make justice, equality, and dignity grow," Pastor

♪ Never Stop Singing ♪

Daniels went on. "They did so by making an entire *garden* grow! Well done, Junior Block Club." Everyone applauded, and Melody and her friends beamed.

On Monday evening, Melody went over plans with Mr. Sterling, who was on the picnic planning committee. Every year, the club got permission from the city to close off a block to traffic. Neighbors set up tables and grills and brought food to share. Sometimes there was music, and this year the Junior Block Club was in charge of that. Sharon had drawn several posters promoting The Three Ravens, and Poppa and Mr. Sterling put them in their shops.

Tuesday started out bright and sunny as Melody headed over to the park with Bo and a wagon full of marigolds that Poppa had given her to fill in the bare spots. Sharon was there to paint the hopscotch grids, and Diane was checking the vegetables. They all sang and hummed while they worked.

By the time Melody headed home, it had gotten cloudy. "Looks like rain, Bo," she said, scooping him up into the wagon and running. "Let's move fast." Bo barked as the wagon bumped along the sidewalk. They made it home just as the rain began to pelt down.

♪ Keep Going ♪

Mommy was reading when Melody came in. "How's the garden?" she asked, sipping her coffee.

"Perfect," Melody said, wiping her wet sneakers on the doormat. "And the rain is just what all the plants need to look great this weekend."

Melody didn't know that the rain would turn into a storm.

Lila stomped in soaking wet, and later their father came home from work the same way. It was cozy inside. Daddy went to bed early, as usual, but Mommy stayed up with Melody and Lila and played board games. They listened to Dwayne's record over and over and tried to ignore the thunder.

But the fun didn't keep Melody from worrying about the weather. It rained through the night and all the next day. The wind blew and the rain pounded, and the windows of the house rattled. On the second night there was lightning.

By Thursday morning the storm had passed. When Melody turned on her radio, the weatherman was saying that there might have been a tornado.

"A tornado? In Detroit?" Lila mumbled sleepily. "What is he talking about?"

♪ Never Stop Singing ♪

Melody hopped out of bed and went to the window. "Well, I see a huge branch down in the yard behind ours, and the lawn chairs are all over the place. I hope the playground is okay," she said, getting dressed quickly.

Melody hurried downstairs to find her mother and grandfather sitting at the kitchen table.

"Where are you off to?" Mommy asked.

"I want to make sure everything at the garden and playground is all right," Melody said. "May I?"

"Why don't I go with you," Poppa said, putting on his cap. "I noticed quite a few big branches down on my way over here."

"Thanks, Poppa."

A few minutes later, Melody was tiptoeing around puddles on the sidewalk and holding her breath as she went in through the silent gate.

"Oh, no!" she cried.

An enormous branch from one of the trees along the edge of the playground had split and fallen. It blocked two of the three handball courts. "I'll find someone to help move that," Poppa said.

But that was just one part of the playground. The

♪ Keep Going ♪

rest was littered with twigs and leaves. Most of the geraniums had lost their clusters of red petals, and the bare stems were bent low. The morning glory vines had blown completely off the swing supports and were trailing on the ground. The green-bean tepees in the vegetable garden had toppled over. The hopscotch grids had disappeared in the storm.

"Poppa, it's ruined!" Melody moaned. "We can't possibly fix all this before the picnic! What will we do?"

Poppa patted Melody's shoulder. "Nature fixes itself, Little One. You clean up as best you can, and then you wait. Wait for sun, wait for the strong roots of these plants to keep growing down under the earth. They're anchored, remember? And as long as those roots remain strong, they will continue to grow."

Melody was discouraged. "We were all done, Poppa," she sighed.

"A garden is never finished," Poppa said gently. "Gardens—and good works—keep going, but they both need tending. Keep tending the garden. Keep contributing to your community. Keep going."

♪

♪ Never Stop Singing ♪

Melody went home to think. Yvonne had told her to trust the people she was working with. So she called Diane and told her about the park. "I need help," Melody said.

"We need hands!" Diane said. "Let me call around. I'll call you back." She clicked off.

Melody called Val, Sharon, and Julius, and they all said the same thing: "I'll be right over."

A short time later, Melody and the other four original members of the Junior Block Club stood and looked at the mess.

"Man!" Julius whistled. "It sure looks like a tornado hit! Look at that branch on the handball court!" He started toward it.

"Wait," Melody said. "You mean it's on the new brick wall?"

Julius scrambled through the leaves. "Yeah! Knocked out some of the bricks, too."

Melody shook her head. "My grandfather is going to move the branch, but there's no way we can get the bricks fixed by Saturday."

"People can still play on the courts, if we clear them out," Julius said.

♪ Keep Going ♪

Melody sighed. "Let's clean up the paths first."

"How can I help?" a voice behind them asked.

"Miss Esther!" Melody rushed to hug her. "Thank you for coming!"

"I'm here to work," Miss Esther said. "Where do you want me to start?"

Melody was about to answer when she saw a group of people appear at the gate. There were at least twenty kids from school and around the neighborhood. Some of them had rakes and brooms, and others carried garbage bags.

"What's going on?" Val asked.

"More hands," Diane said. "I asked a few people to help."

"Wow," Sharon whispered.

Melody smiled. "Okay," she said. "Let's keep going."

A Playground and a Party

♪ CHAPTER 17 ♪

melody could hardly believe it, but on Saturday, the playground was ready for a party. So many people had shown up to help on Thursday that all the branches and debris had been cleared from the paths. Most of the flowers had bounced back after a full Friday of sun. The morning glory vines hadn't survived the storm, so Melody and Miss Esther had trimmed them back. When Sharon had painted the fresh set of hopscotch grids on the path, she had surprised Melody by painting images of morning glories along the edges.

As she got dressed that morning, Melody looked at the wish list that she and Miss Esther had made as well as the plan for the playground that Sharon had drawn. Both pieces of paper were taped to the wall above Melody's bed. The real playground didn't look exactly

♪ A Playground and a Party ♪

like the drawing, and there were things on the wish list that were still just wishes. But since Poppa had said that a garden is never finished, Melody decided that a playground never is, either.

The Junior Block Club was meeting at the park at one o'clock to blow up the balloons that Poppa supplied for the party every year. At five minutes to one, Melody gathered her bags and called upstairs. "I'm going."

"We'll be there soon," Mommy called back down. "I've just got to pack up the food."

It was a perfect day to be outside. As soon as Melody got to the end of her block, she could see where the street had been blocked off. Neighbors were setting up card tables and lawn chairs in the road and putting coolers in the shade.

When she got to the park, Julius was standing at the gate, wearing a new striped T-shirt.

"Hey," he said, taking one of the bags from Melody.

"Hey, Julius." Melody grinned. "Thanks."

A minute later, Sharon came running from one direction while Diane arrived from the other. Val showed up with her mom. "We brought string for the balloons," Val called.

♪ Never Stop Singing ♪

The group headed into the park, and Melody was happy to see that the playground was already busy. Some girls were playing jacks near the morning glory hopscotch paths, and a father was helping his little boy on the jungle gym. Kids were zipping down the slide and then running back to the ladder to take another turn.

Dwayne and his bandmates were setting up a mini stage next to the handball courts. There were big speakers and a couple of microphones. Artie was fiddling with wires and a large tape recorder, and Phil was standing to one side talking to Lila. Melody walked over to her sister.

"I didn't know you'd be here already," Melody said.

"Well, um," Lila stammered, "I thought you might need some help with the balloons."

Melody grinned. "Sure. C'mon over," she teased before turning to Dwayne.

"What do you think of the setup?" Dwayne asked. "We recorded the instrumentals last night, but we'll be singing live today."

"This is great," she said. "I'm really glad you're here."

♪ A Playground and a Party ♪

"You didn't think I'd miss this, did you?" Dwayne tugged at Melody's braid. She grinned and hurried back to her friends. Sharon and Julius were blowing up the balloons. Tish was cutting lengths of string from a spool, and Val and Diane were tying them to the balloons.

Melody took a big bunch of balloons to the front of the park and was tying them to the gate when Miss Esther made her way across the street. "Hello there, Melody," she called. "I see everything is in fine bloom, thanks to you!"

"Thanks to all of us," Melody said.

The park and the street in front of it began to fill, and soon it seemed as though the whole neighborhood was outside. Poppa and Big Momma and all the parents of the Junior Block Club members arrived at the playground at the same time.

"I think they planned this," Sharon said.

"We did," her mother answered. "We want to take a picture of you five. We're so proud of all you've done."

At that moment, Dwayne spoke into a microphone. "Hello, neighbors," he said. "How about a hand for the Junior Block Club that worked so hard to clean up our

♪ Never Stop Singing ♪

park!" When the kids were all up onstage, Dwayne introduced them each by name. The crowd hooted and cheered, and all the moms took out cameras.

"Over here," Mommy said.

"Look this way," Diane's mother called.

"I thought you said *a* picture," Sharon sighed.

"Hey, who is that?" Julius asked, pointing.

Melody saw a glamorous-looking lady step through the park gate, nodding and waving to the crowd.

"Who *is* that?" Melody asked.

"I know!" Diane said. "It's Martha Jean the Queen, from WCHB radio."

Melody couldn't believe it. Lots of people had contacted the Parks Department about their playground because they'd heard about it on Martha Jean's radio show. And all the phone calls and letters were what had prompted the Parks Department to take off the padlock. But Melody had never expected Miss Martha Jean to come to the park's grand opening. How did she even know about it?

"Look!" Melody whispered. Martha Jean was heading straight for the stage.

"Ladies and gentlemen," Dwayne said into the

♪ A Playground and a Party ♪

microphone. "It looks like we have a special guest. Miss Martha Jean Steinberg, the Queen of Detroit radio!"

Everyone applauded. Miss Martha Jean smiled for Tish's flashing camera before she strode across the stage in her high heels to stand next to Dwayne.

"Melody Ellison?" Miss Martha Jean called out.

Melody's eyes grew wide. Dwayne motioned her over to the microphone. "Yes, ma'am?" Melody said, standing between her brother and Miss Martha Jean.

"So you're the young lady who wrote me about the playground project! Well, Melody, I came here today in person to congratulate you on your persistence, your dedication to your community, and . . ." she glanced around, "your hard work!" The crowd clapped again.

"Th-Thank you," Melody said.

"And I have some words from our mayor, the Honorable Jerome Cavanagh."

"The mayor?"

Martha Jean nodded. "I have a proclamation to read." She held up what looked like a picture frame with a letter under the glass. "Miss Ellison," the Queen's radio voice rang out. "On behalf of the City

♪ Never Stop Singing ♪

of Detroit, we thank you and the Junior Block Club for your service to the community, and hereby officially re-open the Junior Block Club Children's Park and Playground!"

Melody was stunned. The park had been named for the Junior Block Club! And the mayor knew her name! Melody heard the audience clapping as the other Junior Block Club members and their parents hooted and stomped.

"Thank you, Miss Queen," Melody said. "I mean, Miss The Queen . . . I mean . . ." She blinked and focused on the faces of her family.

Martha Jean patted her shoulder and laughed. "I think we should thank Melody for changing this park and playground into a beautiful place for all of us, and for being responsible enough to see it through!"

Now everyone began to cheer. Melody felt overwhelmed, but there was something important that she needed to say. She leaned into the microphone.

"Thank you," Melody said. She waited for the crowd to quiet. "But I didn't do this all myself. The playground changes only got done because lots of people made suggestions and gave advice." Melody

♪ A Playground and a Party ♪

looked at Poppa and Miss Esther, who were standing with Melody's parents. "And lots of people did the work." Melody waved the rest of the Junior Block Club over to stand by her. "There were also lots of neighborhood kids who helped, so thank you to them, too."

Everyone cheered again, and Tish took more pictures.

"Well, there's one more thing, Miss Ellison," Martha Jean said. "Since we got so many calls and pledges of support at the station, I would like to present to the Junior Block Club this check for seventy-five dollars, to cover some of the cost of getting new swings for your playground. Congratulations, and please continue your good work, all of you!"

Melody was so full of feelings that she couldn't respond with words, so she hugged Miss Martha Jean to thank her. Then she took the check and filed off the stage with the rest of her friends.

Martha Jean stayed at the microphone and introduced Dwayne's group. "And now, our neighborhood Motown stars, The Three Ravens, will perform a song that's destined to be a hit."

♪ Never Stop Singing ♪

The Queen suddenly stopped talking, and Melody turned back toward the stage to see why.

Dwayne had taken the microphone. "I'd like to ask my sister to come back up here," he said, motioning to Melody.

Melody's eyes met Dwayne's. "Me?" she mouthed.

Dwayne nodded. Then the music began and the audience went wild.

Melody stood still for a moment, smiling. Then she walked back to the stage along the hopscotch path, past some of the daylilies, past her parents' and grandparents' proud faces.

She thought about how hard Dwayne had worked to make his record, how hard Lila always studied, and about the hard work Yvonne and so many others were doing to help justice and equality grow.

As she took a spot onstage beside her brother, Melody realized that her little idea of fixing up the playground had grown into something bigger and more beautiful than she'd ever imagined. She began to bounce happily to the music, raising her voice to sing with Dwayne. Melody knew the lyrics by heart, but today, they meant something different to her.

♪ A Playground and a Party ♪

It's time for me to shine,
Make the jump to the big time.
Hit the road at a run,
Dance and jump and have some fun.
You know what that's gotta mean?
Girl, it's time that I move,
Time for movin' on up.

Melody knew in her heart that she would always remember this song, this place, and this day.

INSIDE Melody's World

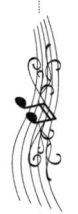

When Melody answered Pastor Daniels's call to make things better in her community, she formed a Junior Block Club and helped create a beautiful park. What Melody did in her neighborhood was exactly what civil rights activists were doing across the country: taking action. One example was the Mississippi Summer Project. In the South, African Americans were not allowed to vote, so they had no say in their local government. It was dangerous for black people to try to change things. They could get arrested, fired from their jobs, thrown out of their homes, or even killed. Civil rights organizations wanted to help, so they came together for what became known as Freedom Summer.

The goal of Freedom Summer was to support black people as they exercised their rights and to help them overcome the fear of violence. Hundreds of college students from the North—both black and white—went to Mississippi. They helped adults register to vote, and they set up schools and community centers for kids. Melody's sister Yvonne volunteered as one of the teachers. She went door to door inviting children of all ages to Freedom School. Black residents welcomed the college students. One woman was happy to discover that the white students "were just like anyone else."

Classes took place on front porches, under trees, and in church basements. Like Yvonne, most of the teachers

had never taught before. But they were eager to help the kids learn how to read, write, and do math. They led classes in black history, the civil rights movement, and leadership skills. At night, there were classes for adults.

Melody was proud of her sister for joining Freedom Summer. But she was worried about her, too. Volunteers were harassed, arrested, and even attacked. Three of the workers, James Chaney, Michael Schwerner, and Andrew Goodman, disappeared on June 21. Their bodies were found on August 4. Although several members of the Ku Klux Klan, a violent hate group, were responsible for killing the three activists, only one man was found guilty of murder. It took over 40 years to convict him.

As Freedom Summer began, an important bill was signed into law. On July 2, 1964, the Civil Rights Act made segregation in public places illegal in every part of the country. Restaurants, movie theaters, parks, hotels, and stores could no longer refuse to serve black people or make them sit in separate sections or use separate entrances. Although the law was passed, change did not happen overnight. It took months, and even years, before some public places provided black people with equal service.

The civil rights movement is not over. Americans have made great progress by ending legal segregation, but many people still face discrimination because of the color of their skin. People of all races and ages continue to take action to make justice, equality, and dignity grow.

Read more of MELODY'S stories,
available from booksellers and at *americangirl.com*

♪ *Classics* ♪
Melody's classic series, now in two volumes:

Volume 1:
No Ordinary Sound
Melody can't wait to sing her first solo at church. She spends the summer practicing the perfect song—and helping her brother become a Motown singer. When an unimaginable tragedy leaves her silent, Melody has to find her voice.

Volume 2:
Never Stop Singing
Now that her brother is singing for Motown, Melody gets to visit a real recording studio. She also starts a children's Block Club. Melody is determined to help her neighborhood bloom—and make her community stronger.

♪ *Journey in Time* ♪
Travel back in time—and spend a few days with Melody!

Music in My Heart
Step into Melody's world of the 1960s! Volunteer with a civil rights group, join a demonstration, or use your voice to sing backup for a Motown musician! Choose your own path through this multiple-ending story.

♪ A Sneak Peek at ♪

Music in My Heart

My Journey with Melody

Meet Melody and take a journey back in time in a book that lets *you* decide what happens.

♪ Music in My Heart ♪

It's funny how one song can change *everything*.

I'm sitting at the piano on Saturday afternoon, playing my recital piece again. The *tick, tick, tick* of the metronome keeps my fingers moving, but my mind wanders. *One more piano recital*, I remind myself. *Then on to guitar!* Our fifth-grade class will learn guitar at school this fall. I can picture it now . . . my best friend, Anika, and me jamming together. Bye-bye, classical music. Hello, pop!

The metronome grows louder. Then I realize that the sound is actually my piano teacher, clapping her hands to get my attention. "Stop, stop, stop . . ." Ms. Stricker scolds. She's frowning. Anika and I don't call her "Ms. Strict" for nothing!

My hands drop to my lap. "Did I make a mistake?" I ask.

"No," she says. "You're playing the notes perfectly. But there's no *passion* in the piece—your heart's not in it."

She sounds like my dad, who is always telling me to "find my passion." He's a politician, so he's really passionate about helping people and making a

♪ Music in My Heart ♪

difference in our community. *But what's my passion?* I wonder. I'm not so sure it's piano. Sometimes when I read music, it flows straight from my eyes to my fingertips. It must skip my brain, because I can think about something else while I'm playing. *Maybe it skips my heart, too,* I think sadly. "Sorry," I say to Ms. Stricker, trying not to stare at the mole above her left eyebrow. If I blur my eyes, it looks like a quarter note without the stem.

Ms. Stricker sighs. She checks the clock on top of the piano. "I think," she says, "it's time for a different song."

A different song? The recital is only two weeks away! As Ms. Stricker rummages around in her cabinet, I hum the melody of my new favorite song, "Lemonade Days." I can't hit the high notes like Zoey Gatz does in her music video, but Anika can. I wish Ms. Stricker would let me play *that* song!

Instead, she hands me an old, stained piece of music with dog-eared corners. The title is "Lift Every Voice and Sing." "Try this one," she says.

As my fingers find the notes, the music takes shape. It sounds like the gospel songs my grandma

♪ Music in My Heart ♪

and I used to sing at her church. As I play the slow, soulful song, I feel a pang of sadness. Grammy died a few months ago. I can almost hear her singing the first line: *"Lift every voice and sing, till earth and heaven ring."*

When I reach the second verse, something happens. That single voice in my head swells, joined by other voices. I glance up from the keys, expecting to see a room full of people. There's no one there.

I can't hear the metronome anymore. I don't hear the phone ring either. When Ms. Stricker says she'll be right back—that she has to take a call—I keep playing. It's as if I can't stop.

"Let us march on till victory is won," the imaginary choir sings. And my fingers march on, too, across the keys. My heart speeds up, urging me toward the end of the song.

As I play the final note, I feel a breeze. The sheet music flutters, and the room darkens, as if someone pulled a curtain. I see nothing except the blue numbers on the digital clock, blinking 1:26, 1:26, 1:26. Then it all fades away.

♪ Music in My Heart ♪

I rub my eyes. The sheet music is still in front of me, but everything else has changed. There's a clock on the piano, but it's round and squat, with two bells on top. And this isn't Ms. Stricker's piano at all! Hers is made of shiny mahogany, almost red. This piano is lighter and covered with a fine layer of dust.

There's a bulletin board hanging above the piano. My eyes are drawn to a familiar face—a black man—staring out from a poster. "Walk to Freedom with Dr. Martin Luther King Jr.," the poster reads. I squint to read the print at the bottom: "Detroit, Michigan. Sunday, June 23, 1963."

"Wow!" says a girl's voice from behind me.

I whirl around. She's standing in the doorway: a girl about my age wearing a sleeveless green-and-blue-checked dress that pops against her golden brown skin. The dress is short and flares out at the hem. It reminds me of the dress my grandma is wearing in a photo of her as a teenager.

"That was *amazing*," the girl says.

What is she talking about? I wonder, turning back to the poster. "The, um, Walk to Freedom, you mean?" I stammer.

♪ Music in My Heart ♪

She laughs. "No, silly—your piano playing!" she says. "But the Walk to Freedom here in Detroit last summer was pretty amazing, too. My family and I marched in it."

Last summer? The poster says that the Walk to Freedom happened in June of 1963. I do the math. That was more than fifty years ago.

Then I notice the room around me. It's filled with fold-up tables and chairs, like a meeting hall. On the table closest to me, I see an old typewriter. My mom has one in her office, but just for decoration. It's too hard to press down on those raised keys. There's a black telephone on the table, too, with a long, twisted cord. My grandma had one like that in her apartment.

Everything in this room seems old-fashioned, like a scene from a black-and-white movie. A question swirls through my mind. *Is this my craziest daydream ever, or did I just play my way back in time?*

"I'm Melody," says the girl in the doorway, "I *love* the song you just played. So does my grandma. She's here at church. If I go get her, will you play it again?"

♪ Music in My Heart ♪

Her brown eyes smile at me from beneath her turquoise headband. She's real. This can't be a daydream!

"Please?" she asks.

When I nod, the girl spins on her heel. I hear her footsteps clattering up a set of stairs.

I try to remember the last time anyone seemed so happy to hear me play piano. Definitely not Ms. Strict at lessons this afternoon! But there *is* something special about the song I just finished. My fingers stroke the keys again, softly at first. But after the first verse, I barely need to read the music. I sail through it, hearing the voices rise up around me.

> *Sing a song full of the faith*
> *that the dark past has taught us,*
> *Sing a song full of the hope*
> *that the present has brought us.*

I close my eyes and let the music fill me up. As the last notes fade away, I hear a *tick, tick, tick*. I open my eyes and see the silver bar of Ms. Stricker's metronome. It swings from side to side, as if gesturing toward the clock on the piano—the clock with blue

♪ Music in My Heart ♪

numbers that still read 1:26.

When Ms. Stricker steps into the room, I jump. Then I see the expression on her face. She's actually smiling.

"That was beautiful," she says—for the first time ever. I've heard her say "perfect," but never "beautiful."

Pride swells in my chest, followed by excitement. I did it again! I played this magical song and somehow traveled through time. Then I think of Melody, that mysterious girl I left behind. My fingers itch to play the song again and get back to her in that basement room.

"Your mom will be here in a couple of minutes," Ms. Stricker says. "Take the music home with you, my dear. Polish it up and make it yours."

I place the music carefully in my book bag. This song already feels like mine, more than anything else I've ever played. *Wait for me, Melody,* I think, trying to send a message across time. *I'll be back soon!*

About the Author

DENISE LEWIS PATRICK grew up in the town of Natchitoches, Louisiana. Lots of relatives lived nearby, so there was always someone watching out for her and always someone to play with. Every week, Denise and her brother went to the library, where she would read and dream in the children's room overlooking a wonderful river. She wrote and illustrated her first book when she was ten—she glued yellow cloth to cardboard for the cover and sewed the pages together on her mom's sewing machine. Today, Denise lives in New Jersey, but she loves returning to her hometown and taking her four sons to all the places she enjoyed as a child.

Advisory Board

*American Girl extends its deepest appreciation
to the advisory board that authenticated Melody's stories.*

Julian Bond
Chairman Emeritus, NAACP Board of Directors, and founding member of Student Nonviolent Coordinating Committee (SNCC)

Rebecca de Schweinitz
Associate Professor of History, Brigham Young University, and author of *If We Could Change the World: Young People and America's Long Struggle for Racial Equality* (Chapel Hill: University of North Carolina Press, 2009)

Gloria House
Director and Professor Emerita, African and African American Studies, University of Michigan–Dearborn, and SNCC Field Secretary, Lowndes County, Alabama, 1963-1965

Juanita Moore
President and CEO of Charles H. Wright Museum of African American History, Detroit, and founding executive director of the National Civil Rights Museum, Memphis, Tennessee

Thomas J. Sugrue
Professor of History, New York University, and author of *Sweet Land of Liberty: The Forgotten Struggle for Civil Rights in the North* (Random House, 2008)

JoAnn Watson
Native of Detroit, ordained minister, and former executive director of the Detroit NAACP